# WRATH
## OF THE
# DAMNED

More dark fantasy from Ella Fields

Deadly Divine Duet
*Nectar of the Wicked*
*Wrath of the Damned*

Royals Duet
*A King So Cold*
*The Stray Prince*

Fated Fae Duet
*The Savage and the Swan*
*The Wolf and the Wildflower*

*Kingdom of Villains*

# WRATH
## OF THE
# DAMNED

### ELLA FIELDS

HODDERSCAPE

First published in Great Britain in 2024 by Hodderscape
An imprint of Hodder & Stoughton
An Hachette UK company

1

Edited by Jenny Sims, Editing4Indies
Cover designed by Sarah Hansen, Okay Creations

A CIP catalogue record for this title is available from the British Library

Paperback ISBN 978 1 399 73185 0
ebook ISBN 978 1 399 73187 4

Typeset in Bembo by Hewer Text UK Ltd, Edinburgh
Printed and bound by in Great Britain by Clays Ltd, Elcograf S.p.A.

Hodder & Stoughton policy is to use papers that are natural, renewable
and recyclable products and made from wood grown in sustainable
forests. The logging and manufacturing processes are expected to
conform to the environmental regulations of the country of origin.

Hodder & Stoughton Ltd
Carmelite House
50 Victoria Embankment
London EC4Y 0DZ

www.hodderscape.co.uk

For the souls forged from the darkness that broke them.

# 1

**Tullia**

His warning burrowed inside me to thread into my weary bones.

*I've a wife to punish.*

My knees quaked. As did my heart when I finally drew a rattling breath. My eyes swam over the thicker growth at Florian's jaw to his throat. A throat I'd once kissed—adored with my lips and tongue and teeth.

Desperate hunger pulsed.

My mouth dried, the need to feed nearly erasing all rationality.

The tickle of the blade broke through the cloud. Reality returned as the steel left my skin to lift some of my blood-caked hair.

Florian's voice dropped, deepened as he lowered my soiled white-blonde locks. "I see meeting the beloved father went well."

The knife in my own hand was thin and far too light. My arm still shook as I raised it to that lovely throat. But before I could warn him not to touch me, for all the good it would do, his nostrils flared.

The sack he'd brought with him hit the floor with an odd thud.

"What has he done to you?" When I didn't answer, he barked, "Gane."

I flinched from the volume. From the dark force of his gaze, which refused to leave my face though I had yet to meet those blue eyes. I knew once I did, with him standing so close I was overwhelmed by his scent, I would be done for.

The goblin hurried back from wherever he'd been hiding, presumably in the kitchenette.

I gazed at Florian's clenched jaw, awaiting this punishment. My breathing shortened. Skies, I half hoped he'd just kill me so the torment of my injuries would be no more.

The blanket slipped down my shoulder, exposing it as the raised knife wavered from the increasing tremors in my limbs. The tip grazed his skin. He didn't seem to notice.

"I smell iron." The rough words were almost a question.

My arm fell, the weapon I was too weak to hold let alone use completely ignored. Finally, I surrendered and let my eyes climb to his.

But Florian stared down at my unveiled shoulder.

I supposed his murderous intent hadn't allowed room for assessing what I'd been up to since escaping his would-be assassins.

Until now.

The winter king took one step back. His features creased as his brows lowered with his eyes over my half-hidden body. "You're naked."

As soon as those murmured words left his mouth, his blade met the floor with a startling clatter. The lone ruby in the hilt caught the final rays of daylight floating through the tall rectangular windows of Crustle's mostly ignored library.

"Butterfly," he said, low and rasped. "Why the *fuck* are you naked?"

I blinked down at his dagger, swaying slightly. My mouth opened. Closed. Opened again. Even if I'd wanted to, I couldn't have answered him.

"Gane," he said, his gaze pressing harder upon me. "Get a cloak or coat from the apartment."

I glanced at the goblin who stood a few feet behind Florian. His spectacles bounced with his vehement nod. "Right away, sire."

Confused, I watched as he hurried to the door I'd fallen

through. He'd closed it since my arrival, and he did so again after crawling onto the landing of the stairwell beyond to do as Hellebore's king had commanded.

It was then I saw it.

A head.

Fellan's head had rolled from the sack near Florian's boots. Eyes darkened with hatred were now forever frozen with fear. A glimpse of long brown hair revealed another head inside.

Two more heads, I knew.

I clutched the blanket tighter, unwilling to believe it. Not expecting to have the ability to be sickened after all that'd transpired. A coppery taste corroded over my tongue. Bile climbed my throat.

I pushed it down and looked at Florian. "Why are you so familiar with Gane?"

He was so still, I failed to see his chest rise while I frowned at him, waiting. His jaw appeared to tick in tandem with each slow beat of my heart. His eyes remained clasped to my exposed shoulder.

When he finally spoke, he did so too softly and through his teeth. "Turn around, Tullia."

My laughter was breathy and sour. "I won't take orders from you again." Still holding the knife, I lifted it. "I'd rather you kill me than face more torment and lies." I was proud that, despite my struggle to stay standing, my voice was steady. Softer than I'd have liked, but steady nonetheless.

Florian didn't smirk or so much as blink. I would've assumed he hadn't heard me at all until his gaze met mine.

He studied my eyes as if they'd changed, as if trying to read every bloodstained memory I'd carry forever if I somehow survived him.

Then he moved to my side.

I stepped back, unable to trap a cry when I trod on a fallen

3

book.

Blistering pain shot up my back. I curled at the waist, tripping on more rotting books as I tried in vain to get away from yet another monster.

But the monster crouched before me.

I froze, hunched over and breathing between gnashed teeth like the wounded animal I was. Unbalanced and dizzied, the knife was easily taken from my fingers. It was tossed aside with a clang that made me tense.

My muscles spasmed, and I swallowed a whimper.

Florian noticed. His lips pressed together before he clipped, "Sit." When I merely continued to glare, his jaw loosened. "Tullia, sit down."

The gentler cadence had my knees lowering to the wood floor before my brain could order my heart to stay out of this. "I'm not your pet, Florian," I said, close to pleading. "Just leave me alone."

"I cannot do that."

My eyes snapped to his, tears blurring my vision.

Carefully, he shifted bloodstained strands from my cheek and tucked them behind my ear.

It took all the remaining strength I had to keep from recoiling and curling closer. "What do you want?" I croaked. "If you wish to finally kill me, then here's your chance. I'm hardly in a position to fight."

Foolish words to say, but all I wanted was to crumple to the floor and sink into oblivion. I needed the pain to end—all of it to just end.

Florian's fingers stilled, then fell. His features seemed to pale.

Gane returned, the small door creaking closed and his footsteps approaching from behind. "She needs a healer, sire. Desperately."

Florian took the cloak from him, his gaze never leaving mine. He draped the rippling violet velvet that was once Rolina's around

4

me, the blanket long stuck to the wounds on my back.

"A witch might even be able to remove it if we hurry."

There was no removing any of what had happened. The eerie calm to Florian's tense energy and his voice said he knew it. "That will be all, Gane."

I recognized that calm. It was the type that warned the beast beneath his skin was about to climb free to tear limbs from frozen bodies.

Florian stood, taking my hand with him.

But I couldn't do it. Not because of who he was and what he'd done and all he might yet do, but because the thought of moving an inch had lodged a spear of fear into my heart.

Realizing, Florian bent low and warned, "This will hurt, but we must go."

Before I could protest, I was seized. I groaned, my teeth sinking into the neckline of his silken shirt when he lifted me from the library floor.

He held me beneath my rear, and I clutched his shoulders as he said, "Hold on."

"She's been marked, sire. He brutalized his own . . ." The goblin cleared his throat, as if given a look I couldn't see from the king. "What else can I do?"

My eyes closed. My teeth tore through Florian's shirt as the world grew dark and snow flurries danced. There was no escaping him now, and I hadn't enough fight left within me to even care that I hadn't tried.

Florian murmured with that same menace he'd carried earlier, "Your orders remain the same."

The journey into the rifts threatened to fracture every bleating bone. Florian's hold tightened, a hand moving to the back of my head. We materialized with a jolt that made me moan and bite his shirt so hard, my teeth pierced his skin.

The taste of him was an explosion. A remedy I never wanted

to need.

I swallowed him down without hesitation, then immediately sucked more of his essence into my mouth. Disgusted with myself, I tried to stop after swallowing again. This male had intended to murder me. It was entirely possible he still would.

But he gently pushed my head. "Drink, butterfly."

And so I did, even as my eyes fluttered open and I absorbed Florian's bedchamber. Dying flames in the hearth and the drapes covering the balcony doors both comforted and alarmed.

"Majesty?"

Olin.

My legs clamped around Florian's waist as he lowered to his bed, and I braced for the pain to intensify. It didn't. With the hand at my rear, he lifted me slightly, then set me down over his lap as I continued to feed.

My frenzied sucking slowed when he ran his fingers over my head and ordered gruffly, "Have Fume fetch Darva."

There was a pause before Olin spoke. "You mean to have her come here?"

Florian must have dealt the steward a glare that said he did not wish to repeat himself. Olin muttered, "I'll send for the general right away," and then the doors closed with his exit.

A storm trapped within stone.

The male holding me broiled with tension and emanated a fury I didn't dare cease drinking to touch at. His insistence that I feed from him, and his careful embrace, sent my clouded thoughts into chaos.

If he did mean to kill me, perhaps he wanted me in better health to use me some more first. Perhaps he was merely furious that his pet had been tampered with. Sullied. Irreversibly branded.

No good to him now.

I didn't know. All I knew was the cooling of the blood in my veins as I drank him down with lazy greed. All I felt was the tightness leaving my limbs and a spreading warmth that dulled some of the misery I'd feared might never end.

Exhaustion dragged and lured.

I fought it, wanting more of this magic and hoping it would fix everything—all the while knowing it wouldn't. As fear for my fate increased the tempo of my heart, I pushed against the heaviness of my eyelids.

Sensing it, this king who'd planned to destroy me stroked my hair. "You're safe," he vowed with a softness that sliced at my chest. "Sleep."

It would be a mistake to believe anything he said, and I'd made far too many of those already.

What I believed didn't matter. Caged within the arms of a king with frost for a heart, I was given the sole option he gave everyone.

Complete surrender.


Consciousness came in waves of blood-numbed fire and tepid relief.

Florian hadn't moved from the side of his bed.

With the exception of caressing my matted hair, he'd remained unmoving. Murmured words of encouragement greeted me whenever I returned to the world with my tongue immediately lapping at the mess I'd made of his neck.

I woke for what I feared might be the final time, ready to sink my teeth into Florian's flesh, when hideous and breath-robbing pain swept across my raw back. Attempting to turn to snarl at the presence behind me, I faltered at hearing the feminine voice.

It was gentle but strong, like the morning call of a bird. "We just need to remove the blanket."

I clung to the sound, ignoring Florian's tighter hold and his gruff request to settle.

"Don't," I said, scratchy. "Don't touch me."

7

Her voice again. "The fabric is stuck to your wounds, Your Majesty."

I pushed away from Florian's chest, feeling stronger yet still so unbearably broken. "Don't call me that." My head spun and spun. The fire burning in the hearth was a blur I tried to focus on until my vision cleared.

Florian's shoulders were stiff beneath my braced hands. My arms shook when I pushed to gain leverage to leave his lap.

He tensed even more, and the heat of the female's nearness at my back retreated. "Tullia." Gently, he seized my arms when I again tried to leave. "Look at me."

The room began to twirl. Panic hitched my heartbeat.

My voice was strained, unfamiliar to my own ears. "Release me." My chest heaved. "Let go." Breath wouldn't come, rendering my order desperate and wheezed. "Let me go, Florian."

His hands dropped to the bed.

But I didn't move.

I collected new breath while staring at him. My blurred vision made his blue gaze appear watery. I closed my eyes and willed my breathing to calm. I willed this endless nightmare to disappear. To leave me the fuck alone.

It wouldn't. It couldn't because it wasn't over.

Clarity nudged. Just enough for me to understand that whoever this stranger was, she was here to help me.

Florian confirmed as much. "Darva is a witch, butterfly, and a trusted healer. She means you no harm."

"I know, but . . ." My head shook. "It hurts too much."

Florian exhaled, the heavy sound trembling his frame beneath me. I opened my eyes to find his had closed. I stared at his long and near-black lashes, and the tight press of his lips. When he finally looked at me, his hand shifted over the bed as if he wished to touch me.

He didn't. He swallowed thickly. "She doesn't intend to hurt you, but in order to help you, it's unavoidable."

I searched his eyes, my bloodstained lips between my teeth.

After a moment, I acquiesced with a nod.

"Feed again," he urged, his gaze narrowed. Within that gaze lurked a sea of darkness veiling emotions I could only guess at. Fury and anxiety seemed to be the most telling, as his need to speak, to perhaps pepper me with questions, continuously parted and sealed his lips.

I wouldn't fall into the trap those eyes had ensnared me in before, but there was no denying his genuine desire to help me. And although I had no idea how this witch would do that when I didn't believe anything could, I still pulled Florian's ruined shirt aside and lowered my head to his neck.

As I felt him nod once, I braced.

No amount of bracing or feeding mattered.

Florian's arms came around me, tight and more unbreakable than any gilded cage or iron chains, as the blanket was ripped away in one quick and skin-stealing tug.

I screamed as agony lanced across my back in an unending torrent of flames.

Panted breaths left me in sobs.

Words were whispered into my ear. Words I'd never expected to hear. Not from him. "I'm sorry."

I had a feeling he wasn't merely referring to the witch's ministrations, yet those words did nothing to soothe me. Nothing could as the witch doused my back with a liquid that singed and sizzled before she smeared it over the ruined skin.

Florian's hold endured my writhing.

"There's no removing it," she said when her touch mercifully left my body, her tone gentle but matter of fact. "Not without risking her life."

"Don't," I gritted. I wouldn't survive the mere thought of what that might entail. "Just leave it."

Florian and the witch said nothing for long moments. The

9

pain soon dulled to a restless warmth I'd never felt before.

"The numbing is taking effect," the witch eventually said. "But looking at this . . . I don't think it's enough. I think it's best she not feel it at all."

Florian nodded again. The sound of pouring and mixing followed. A minute later, his hold loosened. "Drink," he said.

He did not mean his blood, but a concoction that spread a milky aroma throughout the room. I pushed up from his chest and looked with bleary eyes to the small thimble of fluid.

"If you wish to keep your abilities, we must remove the iron before it settles too deep," he explained. I stared at the steam rising from the concoction as he added, "You're better off sleeping for the extraction."

"No." Terror forced the words free. "I need to know . . ." I stopped, unable to voice it properly. Not wanting to try.

The crackling flames snapped in the silence.

"You want to be aware of what is happening to you," Florian surmised, and when I didn't answer, I noted the tiny tremble of the liquid in his hand. "Darva will tend only to your wounds. No one will enter these rooms." The whisper was rough. "And I'll remain until she is done."

I continued to stare at the drink, tempted. One sip and I would be taken away from all of this. But it wouldn't keep me from returning to skies only knew what.

"Time is of the essence, Majesty," Darva said, "if we are to remove most of the iron."

As unimpressive as my abilities seemed to some, they had saved me numerous times now. I didn't want them hindered or, worse, lost for good. Regardless, a life—whatever life awaited me—lived with iron forever trapped within my skin . . .

I snatched and tossed the liquid straight down my throat, barely tasting the acidic milk.

Florian took the thimble from me. Carefully, he rose and set me upon the bed. "Lie down, sweet creature."

I was beyond caring that the witch would see me naked. Too many people had, including this confusing and malicious king. Gingerly, I stretched out across the familiar gray bedding and let my heavy head drop to the pillow.

My eyes closed before the sleeping draught took hold, the comfort of familiarity and his scent a dangerous trap.

Steps sounded. The bedding whispered and the mattress dipped as Florian's iced energy invaded. I opened my eyes to find him lying next to me.

My limbs grew warm. My racing heart slowed. My swollen eyes became weighted with each blink as I studied the increased amount of facial hair over that goddess-carved jaw and the tautness of those luscious lips.

My eyes met deep-ocean blue when he brushed my hair from my face. His hand retreated to fold over mine upon the bed between us. "Close your eyes, butterfly."

The rasped words and the heat of his reassuring touch jarred.

Before I could pull my hand free, everything went dark.

# 2

**Florian**

The fire raged, then blew out in a spray of ash across the floor as I stormed into the study.

Tullia's screams and sobs were all I could hear. An altered soul within those once-glowing dark eyes all I could fucking see. And her body . . .

With a roared curse, I swiped the pile of documents I'd neglected from my desk. They fluttered throughout the room upon the iced breeze I'd brought with me while I paced.

For days that had seemed to never end, I'd interrogated and tortured. I'd tried to discover how the fuck my wife had managed to slip free of my grasp.

There'd been no easily provided answers.

The guards I'd captured spun tale after careful tale about Tullia's daring escape from their escort to reach her father.

An escape that was utter bullshit because how could someone share all of what we had and then suddenly decide to flee? After spending her entire life without the ability to materialize unless she'd felt threatened?

I'd begged to fucking differ.

The tracks leading across the mountain rather than down it, and the disturbed foliage coupled with drops of Tullia's blood upon the dirt road were discovered by me and my most trusted. That, and Henron's report of a carriage horse being too spooked to remain in his stall, had prompted me to question the guards further.

The defiance in Fellan's eyes, the clipped words he'd used regarding my mate, were enough to confirm they'd indeed done something to her. Something that had made her so terrified, she'd materialized in order to escape them during what should have been a trip to the city.

But we'd trained our warriors too well.

Not one of them surrendered the truth during days and nights of torture that typically never failed to make even the most stoic fold. I hadn't needed their confessions—hadn't even needed them alive to learn the truth.

I'd merely wanted them to bleed.

For every day she was gone, something was taken from them.

It ceased only when I'd received confirmation of Tullia's whereabouts. When I'd received word that Molkan was preparing a ball to present his long-lost daughter to his insufferable court. I knew he'd hurt Tullia in ways I couldn't save her from, but I'd foolishly thought he'd give her back before that happened.

That he'd use her as leverage to stop me, and he would give her back.

He hadn't. He'd known.

Somehow, he'd fucking known that the only way to finally succeed in hurting me was to hurt her.

Fume arrived and waited in the chair while I paced—while I struggled to remember why I shouldn't just materialize to Baneberry and kill every asshole within that putrid palace. The wards were a problem not even an entire coven of witches could break, but I failed to care.

I was ready to climb that wall and take my chances.

I shouldn't have made the request for Tullia's return. It was so moronically out of character that it *must* have been what gave me away. And I shouldn't have made it more obvious by giving our warriors orders to march. I should have dug up my fucking patience from beneath the mountains of fear and desperation and formed a better plan.

I shouldn't have made it known she was my wife—Hellebore's queen. Not while he had her.

"Talk," I clipped, unable to stand still but impatient to learn what had been discovered.

Fume had something. He knew better than to disturb me this past week unless he had to—and he knew better than to drag me from my rooms now that Tullia had returned.

"One of our own has a contact who was at the ball. The contact sold the information to him for safety and three pouches of coin."

Frustrated, I stopped and growled, "Say it."

"The ball was hastily planned." His bright eyes stared beyond my desk to the fireplace. "But it was well attended. Tullia was asleep when he saw her." He cleared his throat. "He said she was in a tall cage upon a dais. When she woke, and he and his wife saw what was unfolding, they thought it wise to leave."

My entire body froze.

Ice crusted each breath and curled over my clenched fingers.

"Tullia was naked and tormented," Fume said, infuriatingly matter of fact. "That is all he knows."

"Tormented?" I repeated, loathing the direction my mind traveled.

Fume nodded once. "Some attempted to touch her through the bars. Most laughed and hurled food and insults."

My eyes closed, though there was no controlling it.

My father's overused words haunted yet again. *To remain in the dark archives of the heart is to ignite grave consequence. If you cannot find the balance, then you must feel nothing at all.*

I'd never been able to do as he had.

Remembering the shell of a male he'd become in the years before he'd ended his life, I didn't want to. Rage was better than nothing. Rage kept the blood flowing and the soul hungering.

Nothing gave purpose quite like revenge.

Frost climbed the windows beyond the desk.

The scratching creak of ice over glass echoed in the silence as I didn't so much as try to keep winter from prevailing. There was little point. After discovering my changeling's blood upon that dirt road, it had swept across the land days ago in blizzards.

I opened my eyes. "And that is all he witnessed."

"That is all," Fume confirmed.

Before I could snatch the lapels of his coat and demand he tell me more—demand he bring me this attendee so I could personally wring every detail of this sordid ball from his body—sickness roiled and stole my breath.

*Let me go, Florian.*

Not much was capable of turning my blood colder than it perpetually was. Nothing fucking shocked me anymore.

*Don't touch me.*

I pinched the bridge of my nose and leaned against my desk.

"How is she?" Fume asked with restraint. "The staff are talking, murmurs about a brand—"

"Then go shut them up," I bit between my teeth.

He rose from the chair, and I straightened from the desk to head back upstairs, unsure how I was supposed to handle this. Not entirely sure I had the strength to keep from handling this the only way I knew how—by spilling blood.

By destroying every rodent who'd so much as blinked at my wife.

And Molkan . . .

"I want that palace reduced to nothing but rocks. I want his remains unrecognizable and the stain of his existence eradicated from this entire fucking continent. I want . . ." My shoulders heaved with a violent exhale, my thoughts unraveling into blood and smoke and fury as I struggled to inhale.

I'd thought I'd known what it was to be angry. I'd thought I'd known what it was to have my heart robbed from me forever-more. After all, that had been the reason for all of this. For every single thing I'd done for twenty years.

I'd thought wrong.

My inhale seared as I seethed, "I want every fucking soul who attended that ball—"

Fume interrupted. "Flor, we'll reconvene with a proper strategy—"

I held up a hand when my spine locked.

The energy within the room quaked then stilled with a trace of bergamot. "Oh good, you're here." Shole materialized into the study. "Wasn't about to risk your stormy wrath by appearing in your chambers."

He stalked to the armchairs and took the vacant one beside Fume, who slowly lowered into his own again.

Shole reclined and crossed his legs, stating without a shred of caution, "Heard she's back." A quick appraisal of me, and he smacked his lips together. "Right." He rubbed his near-bald head and sighed. "I have news about that."

Fume spoke before I could unleash my aching fists upon the mercenary's face. "So share it already."

"Well . . ." Shole clasped his hands over his stomach. "Your changeling was branded, as you now know, then escorted beyond the palace gates and forced to walk naked over the bridge into the city."

I couldn't speak.

Didn't fucking breathe.

Shole went on. "My sources aren't yet sure how all of this came about, as there are rumors that Tullia spent some days within the palace unharmed and even roaming the grounds with her incredibly loving father." He lifted his shoulders. "I suspect things changed when you revealed your secret little marriage to Molkan by requesting the return of your wife."

Regret pummeled me anew.

Shole ensured I felt every blow. "The mobilization of our military probably didn't help, though something tells me that could very well be the reason she was released at all."

Fume cursed. He was one of the slim few who'd known about the marriage, and he wisely said nothing.

"Molkan's reaction to such news almost confirms that Tullia failed to mention that you weren't merely her cold and cunning captor." Shole made a sound of contemplation. "Therefore, given the traitor mark, perhaps she also failed to tell Father dearest much of anything from her time here at the manor."

"She knew nothing," I said, the words barely audible.

He scratched his cheek. "Be that as it may, there is still intel to be gleaned from your day to day routines. Staff, interests, meals . . ." He set his hand in his lap again. "You get the gist. My other source, who I must admit"—he let out a rough laugh—"is not always trustworthy, claims whoever escorted our tortured queen to the gates did not lock her shackles."

Leaving her free to remove them and materialize to the middle lands.

"Again," Shole said. "He's not my best source, but according to my *other* source, Tullia did indeed disappear mere minutes after stepping off that palace bridge."

Fume frowned. "They could have simply been negligent in restraining her properly after branding her."

I licked my teeth behind my closed lips, then clenched them.

Shole snorted. "Ever the comedian, you are."

"It's worth considering," Fume argued.

"Molkan is many things, but careless in the minimal actions he has taken after years of us tormenting him?" Shole huffed. "I think fucking not."

"Then why release her at all?" Fume questioned, his gaze upon the carpet beneath his mud-spattered boots. "For once, he had the upper hand, regardless of our advancing forces."

Silence descended.

I looked at the maps along the wall. The places we'd targeted and the wax decoys of those we planned to target next.

*Had* planned to target next.

The gale outside screamed louder. I rubbed my temples. "For the same reason he didn't kill her when she was a babe."

Fume shook his head. "Goddess-fearing idiot."

"He's murdered before," Shole said dryly.

As the memory of that swept forward to meet with the present, I gazed longingly toward the door. "Saving his soul doesn't count." Especially when he'd claimed my sister was sent from the pits of Nowhere solely to damn him. "Anything more?" I asked with no intention of waiting for a response.

There were none.

I had to leave. To lay eyes on her before what I'd been informed tore into my mind and chest with claws sharp enough to create another colossal mistake. Mistakes were for the weak and the desperate and the vulnerable.

Since Tullia's arrival in Folkyn, I'd lost count of how many times I'd been all three.

A cry, faint yet felt within the marrow of my quaking bones, broke through the study's privacy spell.

Fume cursed as I left the warriors in the rapidly chilling room and hurried into the hall.

"Still asleep." Olin met me upon the stairs. "I took a peek as soon as I heard the first whimpers."

"The first?" I looked up the second flight of stairs to the open doors of my rooms, tempted to snarl at him for not alerting me sooner. He'd been on his way to do just that, so I bit the inside of my cheek until I tasted copper.

Olin's forced smile eased his tight features only a fraction. "Just a bad dream, it seems."

I blinked.

The burn in my chest threatened to spread as I continued up the stairs.

# 3

## Tullia

Darkness unfolded into ribbons of growing light over the surface of water.

As the light drew close enough to touch, my eyes opened.

My eyelids were heavy, gritty, and the room slow to swim into focus. Daytime slashed across the room between the gaps in the closed drapes covering the balcony. A weight was pressed against my legs.

I peered down the bed to find white fur and staring dark eyes. Snow.

The wolf lifted her head and yawned. For what might have been the first time in days, I smiled. Some of the weight in my chest dissolved as the beast who'd grown even more in my absence shifted closer to my extended hand.

She sniffed it, perhaps curious about where I'd been. Then she nudged it with her wet nose until I petted her snout.

Safe. For now, I was safe.

But never for too long.

The reason for both slept upon the chaise. What looked to be an ice sculpture melted in Florian's hand. A dagger lay in his lap. One leg stretched over the chair, the other bent at the knee with his booted foot firmly upon the floor.

His neck was tilted at an uncomfortable angle, exposing the bruising from my teeth and mouth. A fresh silk shirt adorned his frame. Judging by his appearance and the half-melted ice, he hadn't intended to fall asleep.

The sculpture had melted too much to know what he'd made.

I forced my eyes from his heart-pinching form.

A small woven basket of medicinal supplies sat upon the drawers. Other than that, everything seemed unchanged. I looked back at Snow and realized I was wrong. Too much had changed.

Blood.

It marked the bedding in so many patches, it almost resembled an intentional pattern. My body appeared to have been cleansed, but blood still remained beneath my nails. Still crusted strands of my hair.

As though the sight of it erased whatever magic the witch had used on me, the ache in my torso flared into a bubbling throb.

Snow nudged my hand, as if sensing it. I stroked her head reassuringly. "So big now," I whispered.

The volume of my voice didn't matter.

Florian woke with a curse and immediately straightened. He blinked wide, then settled as a rough exhale shook his broad shoulders. He scraped his fingers through his hair and surveyed me from my head to my covered toes. My back remained exposed to the fire, the stained bedding scrunched before my breasts.

His eyes met mine. His lips parted, then closed. He said nothing. He just stared at me.

I stared back.

And as each passing second warmed the frosted air, I lost the strength to endure it—the foreign darkness that had overtaken those eyes. The way it softened his sharp features.

Rolling over to face the fire was out of the question when the throbbing intensified with every breath. Instead, I gave my attention to Snow. "You should've left me in the middle lands." Though my voice was brittle, the emotion rang clear.

"I know."

For some stupid reason, those words hurt more than discovering his deceptions. Hurt more than discovering we were not engaged but married.

21

Husband.

This male who'd lied to me, who'd manipulated me to wreak more of his beloved vengeance, and who'd sought to eradicate any future I'd envisioned was my husband. But that wasn't all he was.

He was also my goddess-gifted mate.

"Mythayla might just be crueler than you," I murmured dryly as I traced Snow's ears.

Olin's familiar tapping sounded before Florian responded. Though I knew, even if given the chance, he wouldn't have.

This king refused to acknowledge that empty space within his chest that once contained a beating heart.

Florian rose and dragged a hand through his hair again, shaking the sculpture's remains from the other. Ice fell to the floor in clinks to melt into tiny puddles.

"I know I should've let you be," he said as he reached the doors. His back faced me, stiff and his shirt uncharacteristically crumpled. "But although I do find myself regretting numerous things, I cannot regret that I didn't."

He was gone before I could demand he tell me what that meant.

I didn't need to know, and I didn't need to remember that he once said he held no capacity for remorse. I just needed to heal.

Then, regardless of what plans he now had for me, I would leave him and Folkyn behind.

Florian returned within the hour.

The click of the latching doors opened my eyes, but I hadn't been sleeping. Now that whatever the witch had given me had faded, I was reluctant to. Too afraid to return to the nightmares of the previous days.

He placed a tray containing fruit, bread, and a carafe of water upon the nightstand.

Pouring me a glass, he stated, "Darva left remedies. Bath salts that aid in healing, and a lotion to soothe." He set the water down and stalked into the bathing room before I could tell him I didn't wish for either.

I couldn't imagine anything touching my battered body as I attempted to reach for the glass and winced.

As the giant bathing pool filled, Florian returned, wiping his damp hands on his shirt. His hair was still free and unkempt. His gaze hardened with his jaw when he looked from me to the tray of food and water.

He cursed, as if inwardly admonishing himself.

Stunned, I watched with too much fascination as his features momentarily rearranged into clear annoyance before returning to indifference. Yet he was no longer as indifferent as I'd once believed. His facade had cracked.

Not daring to touch on why, I said, "I'm fine," when he offered the glass of water.

He didn't move, and neither did I.

The first hint of a smirk lit his dark blue gaze. He set the glass down, and before I could read his intent, he carefully seized me under the arms. "Put your elbow beneath you," he said, and I did so instinctively.

He waited while I breathed through the bite of pain between my teeth, then handed me the water. I took it, swallowing every drop and refusing to meet his pleased eyes.

Seeming to want to irritate me further, he crooned, "Good, butterfly." He poured me another glass, which I begrudgingly yet greedily drank, and then he placed it on the tray. "Time to get you clean."

"That will never happen," I muttered without thinking.

Florian turned to stone beside the bed. His desire to demand I explain what I'd meant by that singed like the threat of a new wound.

I wouldn't tell him. Not merely because of all he'd done, but because I just . . .

I couldn't.

There was little point in telling anyone when word of it would soon spread. If it hadn't already.

I pushed up higher on my elbow. I'd rather bathe in the medicinal salts than endure another interrogation of any kind ever again. But sweat immediately dotted my nape and forehead as every inch of my body protested the movement.

Snow leaped from the bed a second before Florian removed the bedding. She sat by the doors as the air blistered with the type of cold the fire in the hearth couldn't battle. "I can do it," I said, feebly as Florian gently slipped his arm beneath my legs.

"Put your arms around my neck."

Without looking at him, I said, "I'd rather not."

"I think you're lying."

"I think you'd just like to think that."

His jaw firmed once more, ice hardening his features. But he bent low, and I knew arguing was futile. I couldn't deny that washing the remnants of what my father had put me through was also far too appealing to resist.

So I placed my arms around his neck.

I knew it would hurt. What I wasn't prepared for was how much worse it would feel—being in his arms now that the terror and adrenaline was gone and all that remained was us.

Now that all that remained was a different type of torment that no witch could heal.

His steps to the bathing room seemed careful. Then he warned, "Better to just get it over with," before doing exactly that.

I was set upon the stone step within the bathing pool, my back clear of the rim and the water rising to lick at my wounded flesh. A breath hissed between my teeth, my legs trembling. My arms felt embarrassingly weak when I attempted to cover my breasts, though I wasn't sure why I bothered.

He'd seen them before. He'd seen all of me before.

Many people had now seen all of me.

Regret and sorrow and shame crawled into my chest to increase my heartbeat.

The sound of clothing hitting the stone floor interrupted my spiral. Florian stepped into the pool at the other end, wearing nothing. The sight was nearly enough to distract me from the frothing salts washing over my back. Nearly.

I swallowed and averted my gaze.

Pointless.

He walked straight to me. The pool was still filling, the water barely covering his cock. He wasn't erect.

Foolishly, I couldn't keep from wondering if that were because he knew. Even as the rational part of my mind tried to remind me that he had no good reason to be aroused since I was in no state to fuck. I was in pain and covered in remnants of blood and vomit.

"Look at me," Florian said.

The familiar words sank into my heart and tugged. A command my eyes didn't wish to disobey.

He stood right before my knees while I shook and gritted my teeth against the sting of the healing salts. He studied my eyes, my mouth, and when his gaze dropped lower, it paused upon the mark at my throat. The forming scar left by his guards.

Guards who were now dead.

He looked away with a clearing of his throat. "May I clean you?"

"Would it matter if I said no?"

His gaze snapped to mine, displeasure furrowing his dark brows. "You may do so yourself, of course, though it will pain me to watch you struggle."

"Right." I forced a laugh that lacked humor. My teeth chattered. "Wouldn't want to keep you from more pressing tasks of maiming and plotting to ruin more lives."

Something flashed across his face, brief and slackening his lips.

I couldn't decide what it was, and as regret I shouldn't feel took hold, I decided I didn't want to know. "Fine," I said, thick and unable to meet his eyes. "You may."

Though he continued to stare at me, I stared at the window stretching the length of the bathing pool. With each passing second, I became more tense. I felt more shame, and I hated it. I hated him, and I had every reason beneath the skies to.

But I didn't hate him enough.

I certainly didn't fear him as much as I should have, especially given all I'd endured.

Perhaps I no longer had it in me. The ability to care. The room to fear much of anything when everything already hurt beyond words—within and without.

Apathy couldn't stop my body from warming and ignoring the pain when Florian took the brush from the basket behind me and began to scrub the blood from beneath my nails. He did so diligently and gently, his eyes focused and his silence burning.

He then reached over me to return the brush. He sank back into the water with a cloth, comb, and a small tin cup. They were set beside us at the edge of the pool. "Are you able to turn around?"

I sensed his desire to help me as I turned, his hands hovering.

But he waited, then carefully gathered my long hair. "Tilt your head back for me."

I did, and he scooped water into the cup. He lifted the heavy strands, ensuring he'd thoroughly wet my hair before reaching for a bar of soap.

His fingers were too talented, rubbing my scalp with an expertise that relaxed and eased some of the lingering tension. Ever the calculated king, he chose then to interrogate me. "You don't wish to talk."

"What is there to say?"

"Too much, perhaps," he said, almost tauntingly.

It was true, but it didn't matter. I had all the truth I'd ever need and all the answers I'd foolishly craved. All I desired now was a quiet life away from what I'd found, and to escape him before he made that impossible.

Alas, I was once again stuck with this male who was more enemy than mate. So I decided to humor him and my own curiosity. "Who is Darva?"

"No one I am permitted to discuss."

*Of course*, I thought snidely.

At my scoff, he explained, "Not because I have anything more to hide, but because it is by her own request that no one knows how to find her."

"But you found her."

"Fume did," he corrected. Then a touch more firmly, he added, "He is the only one in this court who knows how to reach her. It must remain that way."

The witch had done me a great service, and it seemed it had been a risk for her to do so. I could surrender that much. "Okay."

Florian said nothing else as he rinsed the soap from my hair. I didn't dare look at the water, which was probably filthy.

I didn't wish to speak. Certainly not to him. But I was here being tended to for a reason. I still breathed for a reason, and I couldn't allow myself to believe it was merely because the goddess had forced the mating bond upon us.

"You want to know what Molkan's plans are," I said, a whisper as drowsiness overcame. "How many guards stand watch in those towers and roam the grounds—"

"I don't need to know, Tullia. Nor do I care."

"Liar," I said, but it was weak. I was so fucking weak. "You want me to talk."

It would have been wise to keep my mouth shut. To keep him from getting what he needed from me before I was healed enough to escape him.

"I do." He combed my hair, careful not to touch the ruined skin of my back. "But you misunderstand what I wish to talk about." My chest clenched when he added with a quiet murmur, "Perhaps intentionally."

There was no use in avoiding the truth that haunted. No good reason to suppress the desire to hear it from him. I had to. I needed his reaction. I needed to know what to expect while I was yet again at his mercy.

Including how much time I might have before someone attempted to snuff my existence or harmed me again.

"You will kill me, Florian," I whispered. "You were supposed to kill me."

His fingers stilled but only momentarily. "I've just cleaned blood and goddess knows what else from your hair, sweet creature. Is that how a male treats someone he wishes to kill?"

I ignored the increased patter in my chest. "Yes, actually. A predator who enjoys grooming their food before eating it."

He chuckled, and the low and unexpected sound sliced through the storm inside me. "I fully intend to eat you." His mouth dropped to the edge of my shoulder, brushing my skin with his words. "When you decide you will have me."

*Return to your wretched husband. Not even he will have you now.*

I closed my eyes against the burn of tears and the rising heat. I couldn't afford to care if he spoke true, even if I felt it. Even if I stupidly wanted to believe it. "I want to know, Florian."

I needed to know.

He ceased detangling my hair. A moment later, my chin was clasped.

He turned my head and waited until I dragged my gaze from his mouth to his eyes. "The moment I laid eyes on you was the moment I knew I could never end your life."

My heart thrashed.

"So you *did* plan to." I hadn't doubted it since learning of it—yet I'd wanted to. Even now, I so desperately wanted to.

"I was always supposed to kill you, butterfly." His dark lashes dipped, his thumb glossing my lower lip. "But now, I will bring you the remains of anyone who tries."

I waited for the alarm. For that deep wound caused by his betrayals to rip open and bleed anew. I waited and stared, absorbing the earnest conviction punctuated by his unwavering gaze, but nothing happened.

His fingers left as I turned without thought. My wounds bleated. He scowled when I winced and gazed up at him. "The severed heads."

"A gift." His face was untouched by the water, but his expression was clean—startlingly open and almost hopeful. "Though I understand that you do not care a thing for those right now."

He was right.

He was also wrong.

The demise of Zayla, Fellan, and the driver should have evoked guilt. Instead, I felt relieved and a tad irritated. Angered that I hadn't witnessed the same fear they'd bestowed upon me before their lives were taken.

I pushed the violent thought away when Florian left the bathing pool and wrapped a towel around his taut waist.

Shamelessly, I watched water slide down his broad back as he retrieved two more towels and exited the chamber. He returned seconds later and offered his hand.

Muscle and bone protested as I took it and rose to my feet. My arms curled around his neck when he collected me behind the knees. His forearm supported my rear, and his hand the back of my head.

A towel was spread over the stone before the fire. He lowered me to it, then folded another around my chest and shoulders.

Gingerly, I held it there and stared at the flames. "Why didn't he just kill me?"

Florian's departing steps halted. "For the same reason he loathes bloodfeeders." The silence trailing his response held the emotion his words had lacked.

It confirmed my belief. Molkan hadn't killed me for the very same reason he had killed his mate—his addiction—to protect his soul from being claimed by the pits of Nowhere.

Offspring were a blessing gifted by the goddess of creation.

And I'd now learned that being considered as such did not guarantee any form of love.

After tending to the bathing pool, Florian placed the food tray in front of me. "It's likely too soon for the lotion. Your skin is still too raw."

A relief, as I couldn't fathom having something else touch it.

"Eat," he said. "Or would you like me to feed you?"

Though his tone had been teasing, I knew he had no qualms about having me entirely at his mercy in every conceivable way.

"I'm not hungry."

He stood by the door to the balcony, his gaze warmer than the fire. I continued watching the flames with heavy eyelids.

"Some more water, then," he murmured.

I shook my head, and he exhaled roughly. Another knock broke the growing tension, this one different from Olin's tapping.

Florian crouched beside me, his fingers reaching for my cheek. I closed my eyes as they made contact. His knuckles skimmed, then he shifted my wet hair to my shoulder. "Try to eat something. I'll return shortly."

"There's no need," I rasped, even as my chest tightened.

"I disagree, my lovely liar," the king whispered.

He rose, still wearing only a towel, and exited his rooms.

It was strange to both loathe and crave his presence, and to both loathe and crave being alone.

Unable to tear my eyes from the fire, and afraid of how much it would hurt to return to bed, I didn't move until condensation speckled the carafe upon the tray of untouched food. I trapped a groan behind my teeth as I climbed onto my hands and knees to crawl to the bed.

Florian returned scant minutes after I'd managed to pull myself onto it.

Though my eyes were closed, he knew I was awake. He said nothing, and I listened as he lowered to the chaise. The warmth of his attention was unfaltering. A comfort that shouldn't be.

He didn't leave.

He watched as sleep came and went in fitful bursts of blue eyes and spring skies and blood dripping upon the toes of boots.

# 4

## Tullia

Days blurred together in a collection of differing pains.

If the cause had merely been my wounds, then maybe it would have been easier to bear.

Dreams were no longer dreams but nightmares. Always nightmares. They followed me into the waking hours, and those few hours were spent revisiting them.

Revisiting everything.

Distance didn't matter. A different realm couldn't stop Molkan from reaching me. The torture was a constant I'd come to expect with silent terror.

As were the king's visits to his rooms.

If he slept, it was not in his bed—of which I hadn't the energy nor inclination to leave for the rooms he'd once given me. The times I had caught him sleeping had been upon the chaise and with the black hilted dagger in his grasp or never far from it.

Morning light squeezed through the gaps in the drapes.

The king remained in shadow upon the chaise, awake and sipping tea as he read a document. His towering form was bent forward, the parchment between his knees and his forearms leaning on his thighs.

For the first time since I'd returned to the manor, his hair was tidied and tied at his nape. It allowed too much view of his perfect profile, that jaw he rocked ever so slightly while he frowned at something he'd read.

"Tea?" Florian asked without removing his gaze from the parchment.

I pushed up onto my elbows. Movement was easier yet everything was still too tender. Still sore and far too fragile. I loathed it. Maybe when the aching ceased, the nightmares and stalking memories might follow suit.

"No, thank you," I said, a little breathless as I reached for the glass of water.

It was always filled. Something fresh to eat always sat beside it, though I'd eaten little.

I was tempted to ask what he was reading. I assumed it was kingly business, and I couldn't allow myself to do that. To forget who he was and what he might do if I let my guard down as low as it once had been.

Freeing my limbs from the bedding, I quickly swung my legs to the side of the bed. My teeth clenched as I then pushed to my feet.

Florian did not offer to help. Not after I'd told him not to in the days following his capture of me. He did watch, though, as I traipsed to the bathing room.

He always fucking watched.

I closed the door, knowing it would make him bristle.

After relieving myself and splashing water onto my face, I braced my hands against the wash basin to catch my breath. To remind myself that I was okay, and that the silver gilded mirror housing my reflection was just a glimpse of who I was right now.

Not permanent.

My eyes rose from the scar at my throat to the smaller one on my cheek from a ring-bedecked hand that had reached through that cage to hit me.

My finger shook as I pressed the tiny spot of raised skin.

Laughter echoed like a faraway chime on the wind. A stalking song gaining volume.

My breath came faster, harder. My lungs tightened, the ginormous bathing room now suddenly far too small, too enclosed—

The door opened.

Florian leaned against the wooden frame. His features were calm, still, but his throat dipped harshly when he swallowed. He studied my reflection, and I wondered if he saw the same thing I did. Wondered if he could see the point in keeping something too tampered with to tame.

"Come outside with me, butterfly." It wasn't a request. Rather, a soft command.

Fresh air. Open space.

He knew I needed it. Could sense it, perhaps.

Fear stopped my hands from relinquishing their unyielding grip on the basin. Fear of more prying and probing eyes. Fear of more unknown and unexpected foes lying in wait.

Fear of forgetting that no one in these damned lands could be trusted.

My grip on the porcelain tightened, my fingers protesting. I didn't speak, wasn't sure I could, as I tore my eyes from his reflection in the mirror and stared down at the remaining beads of water.

Finally, I shook my head, assuming he would leave.

He didn't.

His nearing iced heat spread along my back, a blanket and a noose. He stopped there and reached around me. As he ran the water, his arm brushed my hip. It became even harder to breathe. He was too close. He was too much.

He was the reason I'd been torn into pieces I could only hope time might fix.

But I couldn't hope. Hope had hurt me the most. Perhaps more than the creatures who'd robbed me of my ability to believe in it.

Gently, my fingers were pried from the edge of the wash basin. I jolted, and he hushed me. "Here," he whispered, gathering my hands. Still standing behind me, he held them beneath the water. "Feel it."

"Cold," I said, stupidly and without meaning to.

Florian hummed, the sleeves of his shirt soaking wet. He didn't seem to mind. He turned my hands, allowing the water to trickle over each palm.

Gradually, my heartbeat slowed. As did my breathing.

He pressed his mouth to my bare shoulder. I dared another peek into the mirror to find his eyes had closed, even as his thumbs stroked my wet hands beneath the water. His scent was headier, the earthy notes stronger.

If regret had a fragrance, then perhaps he wore it.

Yet I couldn't believe he was capable when he'd shown no empathy or remorse during the time I'd known him.

"What do you intend to do with me, Florian?" I couldn't understand him, and trying to hadn't served me well thus far.

It never would, I knew, as his eyes opened to meet mine in the mirror. "Whatever you allow."

Only when all I could feel was him, all I could see were those midnight eyes, and all I could hear were those words, did he seem to force himself to leave.

When I returned to the bedchamber, Florian was walking out. "I know clothing may still be uncomfortable, but I suggest covering up," he said, rolling his wet sleeves. "You have a visitor who's been pestering me for days to see you."

The doors closed before I could tell him I didn't want a visitor.

But he knew I didn't.

Irritated and uneasy, I climbed back onto the king's bed and under the bedding.

There was no use in wondering who wished to see me. I hadn't thought anyone would. So when Gane was granted entry by Florian a few minutes later, I almost sat up in shock.

The king said to the goblin, "Remember what I told you."

Gane bowed, and after eyeing me for a moment, Florian stepped out and closed the doors.

Out of all the questions I had, I found myself asking first, "What did he tell you?"

Seemingly stupefied by his surroundings, Crustle's town librarian gripped the suspenders crinkling his plaid shirt. He turned this way and that, absorbing the lavish bedchamber with large almond eyes.

I supposed he would be stunned.

He stood in the private chambers of a king.

Finally, he shook his head and shuffled closer to the bed. His hairy features creased with what looked a lot like concern as he gave me a quick inspection. "Flea, my skies. I cannot begin to express how—"

"What did he tell you?" I asked again.

Gane scowled. It eased when he studied my face. "Not to stay long nor cause you any upset."

I huffed, but as I looked upon the creature who'd been my only friend, my annoyance ebbed. Apathy returned as I began to realize this was not a visit at all. "He's sent you to spy for him again, hasn't he?"

He tugged at his suspenders, indignant. "His Majesty has asked me no such thing."

"Did His Majesty even need to?" I said, tempted to look away from his dark eyes and to the ceiling.

"Flea." Gane sighed and clasped his gnarled hands before him. "The king is simply concerned. As am I. What you've been through—"

"How long?" I asked, tired of dancing around unearthed truths.

He knew what I meant, so he said nothing.

"Did you ever truly care?" I knew the question was redundant. I knew I was lashing out. Gane cared, though the possibility that I'd been entirely alone in the middle lands for all those years without knowing . . .

It held the power to erase the last patch of color the darkness of this world had yet to touch.

"Don't be absurd, Flea." His voice roughened. "That you would even ask me such a horrid thing only makes the king's grave concern understandable."

"The king you've served for years, all the while feigning eviction from Folkyn." I paused intentionally, then added, "That king?"

Gane appeared poised to grumble or growl at me as if I were a youngling making a mess of his library again. His nose twitched, and he resituated his spectacles. "I was given permission to leave."

"As long as you remained loyal to your king."

"Smoldering skies, Flea." He stomped his foot.

I almost laughed.

The sight of it seemed to settle his frustration. His thinned lips wriggled, jostling his reddened cheeks. "I'm not permitted to talk of the agreement between the king and myself, but I can promise you that I meant it when I warned you not to come here."

"All the better for Florian to scoop me into his plans when he so chose if I stayed right where I was."

"I can want you safe while also seeing to the duties I've been tasked with."

As it eternally was with faeries—the endless double meanings and deception.

I squeezed the pillow beneath my head. "Why did you come here?"

He frowned, as if that were a stupid question. "I wanted to see for myself that you're okay. You terrified me. What Molkan did to you—" He stopped when my eyes closed. "Apologies, Flea."

"It's fine," I lied. "I'm just . . ." I swallowed. "Tired."

"Then I will take my leave."

I kept my eyes shut and didn't protest.

Gane didn't move. "The answers you seek can only be found with the king." His tone softened. "Just know that I have never wanted to hide anything from you, and I've never been wholly aware of his intentions."

I listened to his shuffled journey to the doors, the scent of the library and cheese and ink trailing him.

Melancholy and nostalgia plucked at my heart. Tears burned when I opened my eyes and turned to stare up at the chandelier. "I'm sorry, Gane."

He stopped. "What in the skies for?"

*Everything*, I didn't say. For although I held so much insurmountable regret, there was also so much I could never regret. No matter how wrong.

Should something happen to me, I didn't want him believing I harbored any unkind feelings toward him after letting my emotions get the better of me.

"For talking to you so terribly."

He scoffed. "You still haven't met any other goblins, then."

I bit my lips to keep from smiling but looked over at him. The soft smile that lit his wet eyes dulled some of the sharp remains in my chest. "Save me some tea and cheese for when I return?"

He chuckled heartily and clasped the door handles. "We'll see." On his way out, he muttered dryly, "Don't count on the king letting you roam very far again, Flea."

Reaching hands, stinging slaps, and the scent of my own searing flesh chased me from sleep.

I woke with a scream to blue eyes. Florian loomed over me, my face in his hands. Breath expanded my lungs too fast, my chest rising and rising and close to bursting.

"Slowly," he said. "Exhale."

I did. It wasn't enough. The room twirled around me, his eyes the only stillness to be found.

"Feel," he said, his thumb brushing my cheek. His other hand smoothed my sweaty hair from my forehead.

I stared into his eyes.

Blue. Deep, depthless, distracting blue.

He was on his knees beside the bed, and as my vision cleared, I noted the fine lines at the corners of his eyes. He smiled, stroking my forehead, but his lips were tight, as was his jaw. Regardless, the sight of it distracted even more.

My breathing evened.

Then I remembered Gane's visit. Remembered all this creature had done to destroy the life I'd only just begun to live. I grasped his hands and removed them from my face. Though it was still tender, I turned onto my back to glare at the candles in the chandelier.

"I cannot force you to talk to me," Florian said, now standing. "But I would like you to."

"And I would like to live a life of my own choosing," I croaked. "Twenty years, and it hasn't happened yet."

His steps away from the bed became paced. That cruel cold returned to his voice. "Am I holding you captive, butterfly?"

I swallowed, the sound loud in my ears. "I will leave, Florian," I vowed, and turned to look at him. "I have to, and you have to let me."

"Do I?" He raised a brow, slowly striding back to the bed. "And then what?" He seemed to taunt with a familiar glint in his eyes. "What happens then, daring creature?"

I didn't know.

I had no idea what would happen, and he knew it. So I said nothing.

Again, he lowered beside the bed. I nearly flinched when he reached out to tuck my hair behind my ear. He traced the arch, then my jawline, his eyes trailing and aglow in the moon-brushed dark.

His voice was almost a whisper. "Run and hide from me if you must, butterfly." He leaned close to press his lips to the corner of my mouth, his eyes brightening and piercing mine. "Make my cock even harder than you already do."

I turned away, disgusted. Mostly with myself, as my body forgot every single one of his atrocious deeds in an instant.

His husked chuckle haunted as he left me to seethe in self-loathing.

# 5

## Florian

Sleep tormented, yet she needed it.

Although most of it had been scraped from her skin and drawn from her flesh, remnants of iron remained, slowing the healing process.

It was an uncanny type of torture, watching her suffer and sweat and moan in fear and horror. Watching and knowing I couldn't make it stop. Tonics would only do so much for so long.

Avoidance was futile.

She had to revisit her nightmares over and over again. To heal in all ways, Darva had warned when I'd requested another meeting to help Tullia. Though I knew, it still fucking flayed me.

She had to face it, or it would consume her. Destroy her.

So I sat guard. I carved Lilitha's favorite ice sculptures while ruminating over all the ways in which I would decimate Molkan Baneberry.

Playtime was over.

Everything he valued, everything that ego of his held dear, would die a painful death with him.

Tullia's breathing changed, but I didn't look at her. I gave her the illusion of privacy as she opened those big dark eyes and immediately checked that I was here.

For the past six days, she'd done so.

I hadn't any desire to let her know I was aware. Mostly because I feared she'd stop, and I liked it. No, I fucking loved it. That I was the one thing she sought as soon as she opened her eyes.

41

She could tell herself it was because I was another threat, and she'd learned that those lurked everywhere. Deep down, she knew it was more than that.

As usual, she didn't talk. My mate studied me, then the ice sculpture in my hands.

If she did speak, it was usually a barb to provoke or a flat response to my requests for her to eat, drink, and talk to me.

Out of everything, that ruined me the most.

The creature I'd tricked and stolen had once been filled with wonder, hope, and questions. An endless awe that should have irked me to no end. Instead, it ignited a desire to look at the world the way she did. In a way that made me see things I hadn't in a long time, and like I never had before.

In a way that made me itch to have her ask me everything under the fucking skies.

He'd taken that from her. Molkan.

A crime that felt worse than even those he'd committed to bring us all here.

My father had taught me the torturous art of patience. In all things, meticulous care and determination would deliver us what we desired.

My patience in this quest for vengeance, every careful strategy and perfect plan, had delivered me something unforeseen. Something no amount of revenge could replace. Something unbearably priceless.

A weakness, Fume had warned. I'd disagreed, though perhaps he'd been right.

For my patience had now run perilously dry.

I stood and gently set the rose sculpture on the tray upon the nightstand. The dagger, too, as I did whenever I left my rooms.

Tullia's gaze stalked me to the doors, as it did whenever she was awake.

★　　★　　★

Shole waited in the rotting corpse of a tavern.

"You have ten minutes," I said by way of greeting.

Cobwebs climbed the wooden shelves behind the counters, the dust-covered glass bottles, and the wineglasses smudged from time and neglect.

The male who'd earned a reputation as death's closest companion and every high-ranking creature's best friend and worst nightmare didn't care. He helped himself to the same bottle of whiskey he drank from when we needed to meet in privacy. "Generous of you, your coldness."

Outside the city, near the village outskirts of Morning Frost Valley, the tavern stood in the middle of a fire-ruined collection of buildings.

Travelers and unfaithful spouses had been the only ones to frequent the two-story layover. So I'd purchased it a decade ago from the bartender turned farmer who'd washed his hands of it.

"You never fail to disgust me."

"Some things are destined to taste great forevermore," Shole drawled and took another swig. He wiped his mouth with his tunic sleeve, then capped the bottle. "The last of the units will return to their posts by tomorrow's end."

I took the rickety stool halfway down the counter from his.

"Though if you ask me . . ." He turned to face me. "It seems a dreadful waste of resources and their energy to reel them all back in, only to inevitably send them journeying back to Baneberry."

"There will be no war." Words I never thought I'd say, let alone be at peace with thinking. Alas, I would find another way to take everything from Molkan.

A way that did not involve being without my wife for weeks on end until it was all said and done. I wouldn't risk her, and I wouldn't let our military see to our plans without me.

Shole made an odd expression, as if waiting for the punchline of a joke. Then he snorted. "Very funny."

"I've yet to make it known." I looked him dead in the eye. "So do keep your mouth shut."

He knocked his knuckles on the countertop. "We were so damned close. Our queen was right there . . ." He whistled and stared up at the ceiling.

"And now she's thankfully fucking not." My tone suggested he speak no more of it, and I gave him a moment to digest.

A moment was all he needed. "The goblin have any news?"

"None." Much to my irritation, Gane hadn't gleaned anything from Tullia about what had happened in that wretched palace.

I believed he'd spoken true. Not only because I'd learned his tells during the years he'd been reporting to me but also because I trusted that he cared a great deal for my reluctant wife. He would betray her if he felt it would help her—so that I could help her.

Except Tullia didn't want my help. She only wanted the freedom to leave me.

If she truly wanted that, then perhaps I would consider giving it to her. One day. Maybe. Right now, with Molkan's perceived slice of victory hanging over our heads, she was safest with me.

A fact she knew, no matter how much she loathed me.

If it weren't for her distrust, the newfound fear of this world she'd once desperately wanted to belong in, I was certain she would've already tried to flee.

I couldn't fathom returning to the manor to discover she was gone again. The mere memory of finding nothing but her scent and panicked wolf rendered me sick anew.

Before I could materialize back to my rooms to make sure she was still there, Shole spoke. "There's been more talk of what happened in the city before she materialized to the middle lands."

I waited.

"Supposedly, Molkan gave an impressive speech as he exiled her from the palace," he said. "Carried across the water from a guard tower. Something about informing his citizens that Tullia was a traitor sent to deceive him on your behalf."

My teeth gnashed. "Wouldn't surprise me if he actually believed that."

Shole rubbed at the near-silver bristle over his jaw.

There was more, of course, and such hesitation was vastly unlike him. The merc enjoyed talking almost as much as he enjoyed ridding people of their innards.

"Your inability to make words leave your mouth in a timely manner is starting to grate," I gritted, beyond agitated by the thought of Tullia naked and terrified and dripping blood in the city streets.

I stared down at the liquor stains in the wooden counter, fixed my eyes to each of them to keep from pummeling the information out of him so I could leave.

His chuckle was brief and followed by a sigh. "That unreliable source had more to say, but about the speech given during the ball. He claimed hearing rumors of Molkan telling all in attendance that Tullia was sent there to spy."

I glared, as he'd already said as much.

Shole tensed. "And under the guise of wedding one of their own."

The stool clattered to the floor as I stood, rage instantly blistering my blood. Shutters over the windows creaked with the howl of the wind outside.

Shole raised his hands. "Look, I had every intention of sharing this, but it was not the time, and I wanted to be sure. Since I've now heard similar stories, I called this meeting. I also believed you might have calmed down." He eyed me pointedly. "Seems I was mistaken."

I advanced. "You were mistaken in not telling me in the first fucking place."

His stool screeched over the rotting wood floor when he rose.

I shoved him, snarling, "*Who?*" My fingers curled as he stumbled back, and I reminded myself that I'd known this miscreant since I was a maturing prick sneaking into the city for fun after dark.

Besides, I couldn't kill him. I needed him.

He brushed his steel gray tunic. "No idea, Flor. I'll find out." His lips twitched. "But I'll take my sweet fucking time if we get into a brawl, and you know it."

Indeed, the asshole had never cared who I was. If I pissed him off, he'd piss me off even worse.

I stepped back, then I paced.

The anger wouldn't abate. My boot collided with a cobweb-covered chair beneath a table. It broke against the wall and met the floor in pieces.

"It could be another one of Molkan's lies. As for what else happened within Baneberry Palace, I can keep hunting," Shole said. "But no one will know better than your mate, Florian."

He was one of few who knew of the mating bond.

Those near us when we were in close proximity could sense it, and those within my estate had made oaths of secrecy before being allowed to breathe near my home. Although it didn't matter now that Molkan had made numerous foolish moves, I still thought it best not to further upset my creature by having word spread.

"Keep hunting." I continued to pace.

"With a little patience, she—"

"She won't talk to me." The words exploded with a ragged exhale. My fingers dragged through my hair, ripping it free of the tie at my nape. The strip of leather hit the floor. I left it there. "She loathes me."

"Sure," Shole said dryly. "That is absolutely why she looks at you like she's never seen a male before." He helped himself to more whiskey, snorting before he sipped. "Big doe-eyes and all."

My chest tightened.

"If you want my spectacular opinion, and we both know that you do." He swigged. "She likely loathes that she needs to hate you, yet she doesn't. In time, she will heal and speak of it." He belched. "But you already know this, and you're impatient." His gaze tracked my steps for silent seconds. He deduced, "You blame yourself."

I stopped at the boarded window. Through a hole made by a fist, I stared at the snow piling around the remains of a building across the debris-crusted street. "Her wounds are a result of my failures."

So many small failures where she was concerned that, in the end, had created an insurmountable mistake.

The merc huffed, setting down the bottle with a thud. "And you believe she blames you, too." Not a question.

Tullia did blame me, and rightfully so.

"If I'd just left her in the middle lands, then she would know none of this." She would never know the horror that now stalked her.

She would never know *me*.

An unbearable thought, yet it warred within me every time I watched her flail and whimper in her sleep. I could never regret taking her. Knowing her. Making her mine. Even if it meant deceiving her time and again.

But I would forever regret all that had befallen her because of my relentless pursuits.

Somewhere between meeting her in the pleasure house and tending to the heat, something had changed. Now, that change pounded within my chest with a strength that grew each day.

I could no longer ignore it, and it couldn't be undone.

The only option was surrender.

Of course, I'd been too stubborn. Too distracted by the battle within to notice the awaiting threats who'd almost taken Tullia from me. Too far gone to realize how easily she could slip through my fingers and into Molkan's grasp.

"Sorry to be the bearer of bad news." Shole's tone made it clear he wasn't sorry at all. "But I'm afraid you cannot claim victory over this, your coldness. One way or another, she would have made it to Folkyn, and Molkan would've sunk his poison into her."

My eyes closed.

He might have been right, but I didn't care to discuss it any further. I'd been away from the manor long enough. "Time's up."

Shole snorted again as darkness wreathed and began to snatch dust motes from the stale room. "All these years dedicated to enacting vengeance so as not to miss any minute detail, yet you've not an ounce of patience where this wife of yours is concerned."

Truer words had never been spoken.

# 6

## Tullia

Snow covered the empty paddocks and piled thick over the balcony.

Frost clung to the door I stood before with a blanket loosely clutched to my chest, drawn to the golden afternoon hues. My breath fogged the glass as I absorbed the winter-drowned estate.

Before I'd left with the guards who'd tried to kill me, Kreed had said winter was thawing. I'd even seen as much for myself. So although captivated by the beauty, I couldn't help but wonder what had changed.

All the while, a knowing nudge prodded at my gut.

Everything appeared exactly as it had been when I'd first arrived in Hellebore, yet nothing was remotely the same. The world had dulled. Gray encompassed all that had once shined so bright—that once glowed with promise.

I didn't want to stay.

And I had no desire to move.

The doors opened. Florian's heightened scent mingled with something foreign. Something musty. And liquor.

My tone was both flat and snide. "Been visiting more pleasure houses?"

He entered his dressing chamber without a falter in his stride. A rustle followed as he discarded his coat. "An abandoned tavern, actually."

Surprised he'd told me where he'd been, I almost turned to look at him. I traced the dagger I'd made from the fog of my breath on the glass instead. "Dare I ask what an almighty king might be doing in such a place?"

Ignoring my snark, he answered instantly. "Meeting with Shole." He added firmly, "The tavern is to be kept in strict confidence. Only he and one of my generals know I own and use the space."

Shocked again, my finger paused.

Vaguely, I recalled the male he spoke of. Silver hair and not much of it. Bulky and intimidating as he'd stared at me with ice-blue eyes in the foyer before the Frost Festival.

"And now me." I exhaled over the glass and drew the rose Florian was fond of carving from ice. "Why?"

Perhaps he'd lied. It would not be the first time he'd hidden the truth within elaborate reasonings and explanations.

"You asked," he said far too simply, his voice closer now.

My spine steeled—from his response and his nearness. "Liar."

Florian huffed, the sound stirring my hair as he stood behind me. "Will you loathe me further if I admit to also longing for some honesty from you?"

"Certainly." Though the word lacked scorn, lacked truth. If anything, it was a comfort. He was after an exchange, which meant he might have been genuine in sharing his whereabouts after all. I dug a little deeper to test. "Who is this Shole to you?"

Careful fingers swept over the hair at my back. He shifted it to my shoulders to inspect the healing monstrosity of dark ink. His hands hovered above the raised and tender flesh of the brand. Gooseflesh erupted, as if the wounded skin sought his touch.

With that cold calm, he murmured, "A friend."

I shivered, despite not wanting to. "One does not need to meet in secret with someone who is merely a friend."

"He's also a skilled warrior and assassin with deep connections." He hummed. "It scabs nicely."

My nose crinkled at that. "Nicely," I said with a rasped laugh. Before Florian could say another word about the snake I'd forever carry with me upon my back, I cleared my throat. "Your friend is a hunter for you, then."

"How astute you've grown, butterfly."

"No." I flattened my palm over the glass and spread my fingers, ruining the scribbles I'd made. "The stupid was merely beaten out of me until my eyes opened properly."

The air became frigid.

So much so, I nearly turned into him, in search of warmth. I clasped the blanket over my chest as his energy—his displeasure—became a frost biting into my skin.

He set his hands upon my shoulders. Lethally quiet, he asked, "He beat you?"

I shrugged his touch away and walked to the other glass door, pushing the drapes wide.

Florian took the hint and didn't follow. I expected he'd leave to tend to his winter-ravaged kingdom and hideous plans. I half-hoped he would. Not only so he'd cease causing me turmoil I was no longer equipped to handle, but because I was also beginning to desire more than escape from Folkyn.

I wanted his plans enacted. I wanted relief. I wanted a new type of freedom. One I knew would only be found with the news of Molkan Baneberry's demise.

I needed the father who'd destroyed every dream I'd ever had to pay for what he'd done.

Florian seemed to have different desires.

"Tullia." An aggression that could have been mistaken for anguish deepened his voice. "You think I don't see you weep and quiver in your sleep?"

Stunned, I released the drapes I'd been holding too tightly, but

51

I didn't dare look at him. Looking at him unveiled a weakness I could never quite outrun where he was concerned.

"Tell me what happened," he demanded, seemed to plead. "If not me, then tell someone. I can send for Gane—"

"Why?" I surrendered and turned to face him. "So you can use what I divulge to him against me?"

Something unreadable struck the perfection of his features. Something that paled them, his mouth slack and his brows furrowed.

I stepped closer, drawn to whatever it was I'd done and the way it had turned his entire body to stone, save for the rapid beat of his rotten heart.

I gave in to temptation and allowed myself just a touch. I placed my hand over his cheek.

His eyes closed. His throat bobbed.

"Stop asking." His eyes flashed open, sparking and searching as I rose to my toes to whisper to his jaw, "You cannot fool me again, Majesty. I won't let you."

"Fool you?" he asked, a brow raised.

He'd tricked me in so many ways, he needed no explanation. But I didn't mind sharing the one that hurt the most. "You seduced me," I said. "You made me think you cared because you enjoyed fucking me."

His lips curled with his snarled words. "*Fucking* you?"

"Yes, Florian," I hissed. "*Fucking* me."

"How wonderfully filthy your vocabulary is becoming." Darkness, eerie and splintering, saturated his eyes. He loomed over me like a cloud of thunder ready to roar. "Is that all it was, butterfly?" His teeth dragged across his lower lip. "Just me *fucking* you?"

My blood heated, causing me to retreat. "You know damned well that's all it was because you orchestrated it, *husband*."

"There's only so much a mere male can orchestrate, Tullia." Venom coated every word that left his mouth. "And wanting you was never part of my wicked plans, so cease giving me so much credit."

The sharp stall of my heart made my stomach dip. "Your lies might be tempting, but they're all I can see." I raised my hand when his eyes brightened. "Don't you dare."

He ignored me.

"Then are your eyes open at all?" He backed me against the door to the balcony and pressed his hands to the glass on either side of my head. His own tilted, gaze searching mine. "I don't think they are, *wife*."

I glowered at him, confused and cornered and reminding myself that he wouldn't hurt me. He never had.

At least, he never physically had.

"If they were, you'd see that I care far more than I ever wanted to." He laughed, but it held no humor. "You'd see that I feared for you. I've tortured and killed for you. I went insane with desperation to get you back, and I couldn't, Tullia. I couldn't reach you." His chest heaved. "Every time I came close to sleep, it was stunted by terror." He swallowed thickly. "By thoughts of what he might be doing to you, and you . . ."

Shocked breathless, I flattened my hands on the glass behind me.

"You believe . . ." His head lowered to my shoulder as his hands slid down the door. "You *choose* to believe I have another hidden agenda for you. Perhaps you need to believe that, and therefore, perhaps I should let you, but fuck . . ."

I couldn't have spoken even if I'd tried.

Sensing the rise in tension, Snow whined and rose from where she'd been sleeping on the bed.

Florian groaned. He licked his teeth as he stepped back and released another scathing laugh. "*Fuck*."

Helpless all over again, all I could do was watch as he left his rooms.

★   ★   ★

Night came with no return of the king.

Between nightmares of blood-spattered boots and chains that wouldn't uncoil from my body, glimpses of dreams visited. Dreams of lips and teeth. Dreams of bursts of laughter so deep and rare, and promising touches I'd known better than to trust.

A reprieve. One that failed to win the fight against the dark.

I woke sweat-misted with dawn. Snow and Florian were nowhere to be seen, but their scents were fresh. He'd returned while I was asleep, which was further proven by the ice-crafted dagger, still frozen as if freshly carved, upon the breakfast tray on the nightstand.

I studied it as I shook and sipped straight from the carafe, needing the cold. Needing to douse the dry heat still scorching my throat.

Setting it down, I swiped my mouth, then plucked some grapes from the bowl of fruit. I stared at them in my palm until they ceased quivering, and I thought of oats and Kreed. I thought of the twins, Olin, and the entire estate waiting to pick at my tender flesh.

Olin, perhaps, I thought with a slice of humor as I chewed a grape.

No matter which way I looked at the memories, I failed to find evidence of Kreed loathing anyone besides Molkan. Although I wanted to see the cook, I wasn't sure I could.

But I couldn't remain tucked away in these rooms, despite how grand and unfittingly comforting they may be. My wounds were healing well enough that I seldom felt sharp pain unless I was careless with my actions.

Being careless with my actions led me to receive them in the first place.

It was not fear of aggravating them that kept me prisoner.

It was just fear.

The more fruit I selected from the bowl, the more that pit within me burned with the multitude of ugly feelings I was struggling to keep leashed. The longer I stayed in these rooms, the longer they would fester, I knew.

So, rather than stay in bed, I stood and marched to the door that gave passage to the rooms I'd once been so excited to call my own.

Before fear won, I opened the door.

The dark and narrow hall forced me to pause as I was swept back to a dungeon with a soiled cot and no light save for the gold eyes staring at me with suspicion through iron bars.

Drawing in a breath, I counted to three.

Then I ran.

I hit the door to my rooms so hard, my back screamed as I frantically grasped for the handle and pushed the wood open.

My lungs expanded, breath exploding when I stepped into the bedchamber.

The bed was made. The books I'd been reading still perched upon the nightstand. The drapes were half-drawn, just as I'd once preferred.

Everything was exactly as I'd left it. I wasn't sure why I expected change when I'd only been in Baneberry a mere handful of days. Barely even a week.

Stories always portrayed it best—how life could change, hearts could break, and the world could crumble into unrecognizable pieces with the making of one decision. But that wasn't supposed to be real. It wasn't supposed to be like this.

None of this had been anything like what I'd dreamed of one day finding.

My eyes closed over an onslaught of tears. Opening them, I swiped furiously at my face and stormed across the room to the dressing chamber. The door was open, as I'd left it. Darkness drenched the small space.

I didn't need to light the sconce to know where they all were.

Plucking a cotton nightgown from the hanger, I slipped it on. The soft mauve material wasn't constricting. It also wasn't going to be warm enough. So I seized a cloak of dark blue velvet and slung it over my shoulders while stepping into a pair of boots I'd left by the armchair.

I might have been dressed for the first time in days, but I wasn't anywhere near presentable. My hair was wild. I hadn't combed it since bathing in Florian's absence yesterday. I didn't care. I walked out into the hall and to the stairs.

The typical quiet bustle filled the manor.

Thankfully, I didn't encounter anyone as I gripped the stone railing and descended the stairs. I had no idea where I was going, nor if I could find the courage to go far, but when I reached the landing to the second floor, I stopped.

Through the floor-to-ceiling panes of glass, the bright glow of winter lured.

The courtyard in the middle of the manor had been freshly shoveled, yet snow was already heaping upon the ground, hedges, and bench seats.

I continued down the stairs and veered right, heading past the dining and drawing rooms toward the tall door made of wood and glass. It wasn't locked. Stepping out into the winter chill, I nearly flinched from the harsh glare of snow and the cloud dusted blue above.

I chose the bench seat in the far left corner of the courtyard and turned my face toward the sky.

Cold.

It kissed my cheeks and filled my lungs. I was tempted to remove my cloak to better feel it.

A ripple of black across the courtyard lowered my gaze.

Florian leaned against the stone that tunneled between rooms to the rear gardens, a blue rose in his hand. The wind whistled through the archway behind him, stirring strands free from his bound hair to whisper over his harsh jawline.

And the way he studied me, seeming almost thoughtful with his mouth curved ever so slightly . . .

Maybe he did care, after all.

Maybe that was why I still breathed and why it mattered to him if I didn't.

Maybe the bond between mates, the lust and the inescapable longing, was to blame. Regardless of the reasons, and that I struggled to believe he'd ever once spoken true, guilt lingered from all he'd said the previous day.

I tried to squash it. "Thought I'd venture outside as you suggested."

"I can see that."

Peering down at my hands in my lap, I said, "Tell me about Gane."

He would deny me, certainly. He would leave and give me the privacy I craved even as I hungered for his presence.

The crunch of his booted steps sounded. But to my surprise, he crossed the courtyard to sit beside me on the bench.

He didn't leave much room, his knees opening and one knocking my own. Intentionally, of course. I refrained from moving, knowing he would only find it amusing. And that amusement would make me itch to stare at his beautiful face.

Florian offered me the rose. Our fingers brushed as I took it, and I studied the frost clinging to the dark petals.

"Gane was sent to Crustle by his own request."

That much I'd already known. I said, "He told me that after his wife died, he wished to leave."

Though I didn't look at him, I could feel his gaze upon my hands as I touched a thorn on the stem.

"He attempted to steal from me, knowing he would fail and wishing to be caught. Rather than merely exile him, I gave him one of the bloodstones Lilitha and I once used, found him work in the middle land's town library, and told him to report on anything of interest."

"Bloodstones?" I asked, looking over at him.

"They send an alert." His gaze remained on the rose in my hands. "Lilitha's was fashioned into a necklace. Mine a quill. They belonged to my parents. My father gave them to us after my mother died. They came in great use when Lilitha grew and found endless ways to worry me."

I recalled the necklace I'd found in Florian's nightstand drawers, and the jeweled quill Gane had never let me touch within a cupboard in his kitchenette. He'd seldom let me touch his belongings, so I'd never thought anything of it. "How do they work?"

Florian lifted his pointer finger to his canines and bit it. It came away with a tempting bead of blood upon the pad. He stole my hand and opened my fingers. "You press your blood to the stone and not only will they both glow . . ." Captivated by the gloss of his blood over the lines in my palm, I nearly forgot what we were talking about. "An odd sensation is felt by the owner of the stone's twin. A vibration of sorts that disturbs the energy around you."

Blinking free of the trance, I reclaimed my hand and gazed back at the rose. "So he told you I was a changeling."

"He did."

I didn't want to put voice to it, and I didn't have to. It was a truth I'd suspected before Gane's visit to Florian's chambers. I still did, if only to let him know I was aware. "You were watching me. You've watched me for years."

"No," he said.

I scowled at him. "You're lying."

"I'm not." His lips twitched when my glower intensified. "Disappointed, sweet creature?"

Snorting, I looked away. "Not in the slightest, *husband*."

An amused exhale preceded his admission. "You were not the only young and pure-blooded faerie in Crustle, so I could not safely assume a thing until you'd grown and I saw you. But I had Gane keep an eye on you."

As his blood dried to my palm, I mulled over that and the memories. "The padlock," I said, recalling the way it had unlocked at my touch all those years ago, allowing me access to the library when I couldn't escape the apartment building.

Florian hummed. "Gane's idea. Though he'd suspected you were a changeling, he was never certain until you eventually told him."

I couldn't remember when that would have been, but Rolina had frightened me so much as a youngling that I knew I'd been careful. I'd kept it to myself for a long time. "Then you did end up watching me."

"The first time I laid eyes on you was in the pleasure house," he said. "After your ordeal with the Wild Hunt, I knew you were of mature age, and that if you were his daughter, then I would need to act before Molkan also heard news of your endeavors."

That didn't make any of it better.

I'd been marked, destined for disaster when I'd been too young to even know much about Folkyn, and I'd never known.

Even if I had, I likely wouldn't have avoided any of this.

Molkan would have been just as he was—a liar, another manipulative male, and a thief of souls. Florian would have still used me to humiliate him.

And Gane's loyalty would have been to Florian.

"A pleasure house that you own," I said, laughing quietly as it dawned on me. "Rolina didn't have any debts, did she?"

"None that I care to be aware of," he confirmed.

Unbelievable yet so wildly conceivable at the same time. Out of all the things I wished to know, I couldn't resist asking next, "Why do you own a pleasure house?"

"You now own it, too." Huffing at my stunned silence, he then said, "It was my grandfather's. He visited it often, and my father chose to keep it when he passed for the extra coin and intel the establishment provides."

"And you kept it for the latter."

"Of course," he said, smug despite my hostile tone. "Such information has proven to be both useful and vastly entertaining."

Biting the inside of my cheek, I withheld a smile.

Nothing more was said for a chilled minute. Swallowing all he'd confessed shouldn't have been easy. Maybe I needed time for the shock and disgust to arrive. Maybe I'd expected it. Maybe I was simply grateful to gain a drop of honesty in this world of treachery.

"He cares for you," Florian eventually said. "Gane. I saw it whenever I asked of you, and he'd try to evade confirming who you might be. Some might even say that for a goblin, he came to care for you far too quickly."

Tears blurred the rose I twirled between my fingers. I gave that no response.

He said quietly, "I know I have given you ample reason not to trust me. After everything, I know it's unlikely that you trust anyone, or that you're willing to even try right now."

I ignored the urge to refute that—to say that I was nothing like him—when he was right.

Gently, he clasped my chin, forcing my eyes to his. "But that will change, butterfly. In time, I will earn your trust."

Looking at him, it was impossible not to believe him. The earnest timbre roughening his voice and the determination darkening his eyes. I swallowed, my throat and chest unbearably tight. "You don't need me to trust you in order to finish seeking your beloved revenge, Majesty."

Addressing him as such made him smirk. He stroked my lower lip, eyes exploring my every feature as his own lips parted with a soft breath. "What I seek is not the same as it once was."

My gaze lowered to his chest. To the exposed skin untouched by the cold and revealed by the usual ignored buttons of his shirt. "Nothing is, husband." Then I dropped the rose and stood, collecting my nightgown to cross the snow-covered stone.

Before I reached the door, Florian said, "Careful, wife." I looked over my shoulder as his eyes lifted from the hands clenched between his knees. He gave them to me, a hint of that familiar mischief within. "Or I might believe you enjoy calling me that."

I bristled and walked on with steps that were too heavy, barely feeling the tender skin at my back when he chuckled.

That afternoon, I craved the cold once more.

The courtyard was empty. I had to wonder if it often was as Snow trotted through the arched tunnel to the grounds on the other side.

With the exception of the crimson ivy falling from the rooftop of the manor, the hedges of roses, and the white and crystal decor of winter, there was nothing much to see. It was crisp and quiet, which made it perfect.

But I wasn't alone for long.

The door opened. It closed before he spoke. "Heard a whisper that I might find you out here."

Kreed.

A smile, so real it felt strange, reshaped my face. But it drooped as my eyes swept over his worn boots, trousers, and the tunic covered by his stained apron.

The cook's dark gaze was damp, his own smile close-lipped and concerned, and his jaw rigid.

I averted my eyes when they filled.

He stood there for crawling moments, then finally took a seat beside me on the bench. He asked me nothing. He just sat with his knees spread and his hands rubbing his thick thighs.

The sound of them grazing the material of his black trousers drew my gaze.

I tried, though I could think of nothing to say. Nothing that didn't seem ridiculous. I eventually settled on asking, "How are the troublesome twins?"

Kreed huffed, his hands stilling. "Still annoyed that Florian stole the wolf they sought to keep in your absence."

That surprised me, but not so much that I let it show. "Good then," I determined, a slight rasp to my voice.

"Good, Princess," Kreed confirmed.

"Tullia," I said after a moment, without the heart to enforce it and hoping he would know that I'd meant it. "Only Tullia."

"Fine." He feigned a sigh. "Apparently you're a queen, anyway."

I almost laughed, but as my throat thickened and my eyes grew more wet, I sniffed instead. Willing the tears to leave, I continued to stare down at the cook's hair-dusted hands.

Maybe he noticed, and that was why he moved one to the small gap between us. He turned it over, palm facing the sky.

Finally, I looked at him, only to find him gazing up at the clouds as snow began to fall. His eyes closed, white dotting his upturned face and sticking to his lashes.

I looked up too, and placed my hand over his. His fingers immediately slid through mine and squeezed. I squeezed back, even as something unlocked inside me and the threat of tears became an unstoppable avalanche.

They slid down my cheeks and jaw to tickle my neck. As they came faster, I sucked in a breath that hitched.

Kreed cursed and pulled me into his side, unaware or perhaps forgetting about my branded back. I didn't mind. I didn't have the capacity to care about the tight flare of pain. Not as my shoulders quaked and Kreed pressed my head to his chest, my shaking body gathered against his.

He said nothing. There was nothing to say when the sobs refused to cease and the anguish burned worse than any blade taken to my flesh.

He just held me as snow fell and my heart finished breaking.

# 7

---

## Florian

I'd taken to leaving the door of my study open.

So when I heard it, I was instantly out of the room and up the stairs.

Upon the landing to the second floor, I turned to the glass giving view of the courtyard. There, tucked in the corner as she'd been earlier, Tullia's white-blonde hair shone a shade darker than the snow falling atop her head.

It fell faster when I noticed she wasn't alone.

Kreed held her close as she grieved in a way I'd been anticipating.

Now that it was happening, I couldn't say that I was pleased.

My fingers ached from their tight grip on the stone railing. Ice crusted and spread from beneath my palms. I removed them, my teeth meeting as I tried to wrangle the magic and tangled feelings I could never hope to tame.

*Me.* It should have been me. I was the one who was supposed to comfort her. Hold her.

Only ever me.

It seemed the one who'd instigated her misery could not be the one to soothe it.

Self-loathing and the bitter taste of jealousy overwhelmed, a serrated blade that twisted.

This creature. This sweet and sour princess I was never meant to give two shooting stars about had upturned absolutely everything. With that first starry-eyed look, amazement giving glow to her delicate yet sharp features, she sank her unsuspecting claws deep.

I'd thought I could pry them free after gorging on her numerous times. After spending enough time with her to grow tired of her vivid mind and addictively flavorsome spirit.

Instead, I'd only grown hungry for more.

A sick jest from Mythayla, to bond me to my enemy's daughter. A creature I'd intended to humiliate and kill and deliver to Molkan as a warning of my impending final blow.

I'd spent many a night cursing the entertained goddess after my changeling's arrival.

Naively, I'd constantly reassured myself. Told myself that if I couldn't kill her, then I would at least shake those claws loose with the careful erosion of her innocent wonder. With enough sex to have my fill, and with incessant reminders of what her father had taken from me and my kingdom.

I'd thought I could use and discard her. That I would escape the cruel fate bestowed upon me.

Of course, those talons had only plunged deeper. So deep that if she were to pull them free, I'd bleed worse than ever before.

Cruel indeed.

*Fuck it.*

Tullia might loathe me nearly as much as I loathed myself for what'd happened, but I couldn't do it. I could only tolerate so much. I refused to stand by and watch another male comfort my creature when I was supposed to be the one to give her all she needed.

When Mythayla had seen to making it my damned destiny.

It didn't matter that Kreed likely had no romantic interest in Tullia. It only mattered that I wanted what she was giving him— enough trust to let go. But my intention to rip her from his arms was squashed when telling steps sounded behind me.

Closing my eyes, I inwardly cursed as Olin came to stand beside me.

He hummed at the sight of Tullia and Kreed, then sipped his ginger tea. "Progress, I suppose."

I scoffed and looked back down at my mate.

"You disagree?"

I didn't give that a response. I didn't disagree. I couldn't, and we both knew it.

"This is what she must do, Florian."

*With me.* I bit back a snarl because he was right. He was right, and I hated it because it felt so maddeningly wrong.

He seemed to read the silent roar within my mind. "Shame won't allow for it. Won't allow her to let you that close."

That pricked like a thorn. I glowered at him in warning. "Tullia has done nothing to be ashamed of."

"To you, perhaps, but to her . . ." The steward who'd served my family since my parents had married looked up at the snow-swept sky. "Every decision she's made led her to receive nothing but humiliation and brutality from the male she was so eager to find." His gaze lowered. "From the father who was supposed to protect her."

My chest burned as those gentle words enraged.

"It will pass." After studying Tullia and Kreed for another moment, Olin sipped his tea. "Soon, anger will come. The type you're all too familiar with." His lavender eyes gleamed as he turned to me. "Then perhaps"—he shrugged as though he didn't care when he cared more than most realized—"she will come back."

I licked my teeth behind my closed lips, attempting and failing to unclench my tense jaw.

"But she won't be the same creature she once was, Florian." As Olin reached the stairs, he murmured before walking down them, "You know that better than anyone."

My hands returned to the railing.

The temperature within me steadied. No ice crusted the railing. The snowfall began to slow as I watched Tullia's shoulders cease quaking.

A minute later, she straightened and wiped her cheeks. Finally, I made to leave, and she looked up.

Our eyes met and locked, her lips parted.

I could have stared at her for as long as she'd let me, but with Olin's words lingering, I tore my eyes from hers and my feet from the landing.

I needed her to come back—no matter who she became in the aftermath—which meant I had to loosen my desperate hold.

Somehow.

# 8

## Tullia

As usual, Florian delivered my dinner to his rooms.

Only this time, he didn't stay to make sure I ate something.

Puzzled, I watched him leave. But I was too tired to ask him what was so pressing that he would relinquish one of his routine guard duties.

I soon forgot to care. After a few spoonfuls of stew and a guzzled glass of water, I gave in to the exhaustion that had snuck up on me since crying into Kreed's chest.

I didn't dream, and the nightmares didn't return until dawn was stroking glowing fingertips over the manor.

The king was seated on his favored perch when I woke. Breathless and pushing strands of hair from my face, I sat up and reached for the water. *Not real*, I silently repeated while trying to control the heaving of my chest. *Over now.*

Yet it felt as if it would never end. Never stop tormenting and haunting.

There was no hiding anything from Florian.

He was wide awake and watching me with his hands clasped between his spread knees. His thumbs rubbed together. Either he hadn't slept or he'd woken well before me, as he appeared ready to meet the incoming day with a fresh burst of his woodsy caramel scent, black trousers, and a matching long coat.

The collar sat high, his long hair tied and tucked beneath.

The cliffs of his cheeks, the severe angle of his jaw, and the fierce set of his dark brows over his luminous blue eyes had been given the freedom to render me breathless anew.

I'd been naked for a week now. He'd bathed and held me while I'd reeked of blood and vomit, as well as the wine and food thrown at me. Not to mention, his eyes, hands, and mouth had traversed every inch of my body long before that.

It was therefore stupid to belatedly pull the bedding over my chest. Stupid, yet I still did.

He knew it, too. His eye twitched with his lips. But his jaw remained fixed—tight. His hands squeezed between his knees as if he were trying to talk himself out of something he could not.

"Orange-brown eyes and wine-red lips," he finally said, voice gruff.

I lacked a response as the male with the tobacco stem in Molkan's throne room flashed before my open eyes.

"You muttered it repeatedly, butterfly." Florian licked his lips and gave his gaze to his hands. "As you slept just now."

I wasn't certain what he assumed. Whether he feared the creature I'd mumbled about meant something to me, or if he suspected he'd done something to me. But it wasn't there. The desire to trap the truth behind my teeth and hold it close for fear of what it might cost to set it free was absent.

"A male," I said, toneless. My finger found the tiny scar on my cheek. "He struck me while I was . . ." Florian's head snapped up, but I couldn't look at him. I pushed the bedding away and rose to my feet. "While I was caged like a fucking animal."

I left before I could glimpse his reaction, escaping it and the confession I'd made by shutting myself in the bathing room.

When I returned, Florian was gone.

I knew why and was beyond caring that I hoped he succeeded.

The snow in the courtyard covered my knee-high boots to my ankles.

"A little too cold to be outdoors, don't you think?" Kreed asked from the door.

I'd left it open for Snow in case she wished to head indoors.

"The wolf doesn't seem to think so," I said with a glance at the tracks she'd left from bounding through the courtyard to the grounds beyond.

Kreed huffed and joined me on the damp bench seat.

Quiet settled between us, but it wasn't uncomfortable. I brushed my wet hands over my coat. After a moment of staring at the dark clouds covering the midmorning sun, I murmured, "I'm sorry."

"What in the skies for?"

My feet shifted until I could see the stone beneath the snow. "For ruining your apron with my tears."

Kreed chuckled. "It'll take more than a few measly tears to ruin this old thing." He plucked it from his chest, then folded his hands over his stomach. "You probably gave it a much-needed clean."

Despite knowing it was a lousy attempt to make me think nothing of what he'd done for me, I still snorted.

His tone turned solemn. "I haven't seen him this way in a long time, Tullia."

I knew whom he meant, and I didn't know how to respond.

"I wasn't here until after his father and sister were gone, but I saw how their absence changed him." Kreed glanced up at the sky. "In a way that made it seem like they'd taken his heart with them when they left. But you . . ."

I struggled to hold his gaze when he looked at me.

"It's as if you returned it to him, no matter how much he didn't want it, and now he's out of practice with something he has lived without for so long."

My fingers curled in my lap. I wasn't immune to the changes in the king—changes I'd glimpsed even before the heat had run its course, and I'd told him I was falling in love with him in order to gain some freedom.

I was merely unable to trust it. That, and I was supposed to hate him.

Florian had been the enemy since I'd first discovered why he'd wished to marry me, and Molkan had been the victim I'd needed to reach.

Now, there was no such thing as right and wrong. There was only murder and malevolence and monsters at every turn.

Although Kreed was not one of them, I still kept the questions I truly itched to ask about Florian to myself and tilted my head. "Are you implying I should be kinder to him?"

Kreed's brows rose. "I wasn't at all aware that you'd been unkind."

I withheld a laugh, for the staff in this manor likely heard and shared a slew of tales and assumptions.

Birdsong took my attention to the rooftop as a flock flew over the manor in the break of snowfall.

"My mother was a cook for a noble female in the western plains of Hellebore," Kreed said, quiet and with his hands remaining tight over his stomach. "Her name was Mucinia, and save for her few members of staff, she lived alone. Her parents died centuries before I was born, and though her farmstead was only an hour's ride to the nearest town, she rarely left."

I sensed this wasn't going to be an enjoyable story. So I kept my gaze fastened to our surroundings as the sun breached the clouds and the dark ivy upon the walls glimmered blood-red.

"I don't know who my father is, and my mother refuses to tell me. Eventually, she met a male in the nearby village and fell in love, so she decided to move on. Mucinia said she would allow it only if I was willing to take her place as head cook of her household. I was nearing the age of twenty, and after years of working with her in the kitchen, my mother had no qualms about entrusting the task to me."

Queen Aura's words came back to me when I was tempted to react as I once had—with shock or horror.

*We are not human.*

Kreed's mother likely felt no guilt about leaving him to pursue a new life with her lover.

"I didn't mind," Kreed said, as if sensing my thoughts. "I was already doing most of the work because Mother had been sneaking away from the farmstead for months, and she's a stoic female. She loves me, most certainly, but as far as she was concerned, I was grown, and she'd done her job well enough in raising me."

I couldn't say I disagreed with that.

Out of all the faeries I'd met in Folkyn, Kreed held the most empathy. A rarity, I'd discovered, further confirmed by what he was divulging to me. There was no mischief and deception. He enjoyed his life, and he seemed to enjoy the company of all those within it.

"I liked her," Kreed said, a gruff confession. "Mucinia. I liked how she stared at me a moment too long and touched me just a little too much. Even prior to my mother leaving, I'd liked it. Most of all, I liked that she wanted to keep me, and that as soon as my mother left, she invited me to share her bed."

I'd guessed where this had been headed, yet my eyes still widened slightly.

Kreed noticed and chuckled, but when I looked at him, he was smiling at the frosted hedges. "A touch immoral, perhaps." He shrugged. "Perhaps that is why I enjoyed her so much. Sadly, I hadn't known there were rules or certain expectations. So things went awry when I took interest in one of the horse trainers and began to like him a little too much."

"The twins . . .?" I wasn't sure if I should be so direct.

"Mucinia was their mother." Kreed nodded. "They were born some months after I left the farmstead." He scratched the dark hairs breaking through his shaven jaw. "It wasn't just the trainer. There were other females and males in town. After she caught me with him, I foolishly told her about them all. I'd been seeing others for years and always thought . . ."

"That you were merely the help she entertained herself with," I finished for him.

"Exactly," he said. "I knew she harbored affections for me, but I hadn't known they ran deep." He released a rough laugh. "We truly are despicable creatures. I should have apologized, but I was so angry that she would dare tell me to leave, so when she screamed at me, I yelled at her, too, and then I just . . ." He exhaled heavily. "I just left, and I never once looked back."

Always, it had been said that there was no creature more vengeful than the Fae. Now that I'd seen it for myself, I supposed I wasn't as surprised as I should have been. "She kept your sons from you."

"Despicable indeed." His teeth flashed, his brown eyes damp when he gazed up at the sky once more. "I wasn't aware they existed until she was murdered by her new lover, who has now taken over her estate."

"The twins." Panic rose at the thought of them witnessing that.

"They fled to the nearby village with one of Mucinia's farmers. Dillon knew they were mine." His laugh was bitter. "I would've returned to the plains to kill him for keeping such a thing from me if he hadn't gone into town the next day to ask for a way to reach the king and therefore me."

My nose creased at that. "He was after the king's coin or ear."

Kreed laughed again. "Far more accustomed to the ways of your ilk than you were a mere month ago, I see."

"I wish I wasn't." Those fractured pieces of who I once was wriggled within my chest.

"Hmm." He kicked snow from his boots. "Regardless, I'm grateful, and so he still breathes."

I couldn't imagine this gentle giant of a male harming anyone. Though as I peered at him and saw the glimmer of wrath within his eyes, that changed.

Another male had presented similarly. Had appeared nothing more than a lonely king with a tragic past and an uncertain future—all of it caused by forbidden love.

A ruse, I'd learned, and far too late.

Even so, the cook beside me wore no mask. A comfort, however fleeting. His ankles crossed. "I've never told anyone about Mucinia."

"No one?" I asked, shock raising my voice.

"Florian's pieced it together."

"Of course," I said dryly.

"That or he was informed by Dillon." Kreed's smirk fell. "I'm not saying I should have told Olin, for there was nothing to tell until the arrival of the twins. Our experiences are our own, including our heartbreaks, and by the goddess, Mucinia made sure she broke my heart not once but thrice." His chuckle lacked humor. "But maybe it would've helped lessen the blow if I'd at least told him about my life before I was hired here." He huffed. "Shit, for him and myself."

Somewhat stunned that he'd chosen to tell me when he'd told no one else, I was without words.

"I'm not sharing this so that you might share your heartbreak with me. I know enough and won't force you to divulge the details." Kreed lifted a muscular shoulder. "But you gave me a piece of you, so I thought it only fair I give you a piece of me."

"Fair play," I murmured with a smile teasing my lips.

"Fair play?" he questioned, confused.

I shook my head. "Never mind." Then I stole his hand and squeezed it. "Thank you."

He squeezed mine back. "If you tell anyone, I'll make every meal you least desire for as long as I can get away with it."

My burst of laughter shocked us both. The choked and unexpected sound loosened my jaw and some of the tension in my shoulders.

The cook grinned, as bright as the snow. I should've known when it faded that he would mention him. "He is your mate."

I took my hand back and averted my gaze to my boots.

He made an amused sound. "Only you would be bothered by a bond to an almighty faerie king."

"You have met him, haven't you?"

Kreed's roaring laughter startled me.

Still staring at my boots, I withheld a smile. "He's the reason for all of this, Kreed."

He was quiet for a moment. "I think you know that is not entirely true." I refrained from sending him a scathing look when he sighed. "Cursed is the royal with the power to provide and destroy."

I frowned. "Powerful he may be, but he's not cursed."

"Not in the way of witches, but by the gifts he inherited. All of you royals are cursed. Some just have it worse than others."

That gave me pause. "More power than others, you mean?"

A gleam lit Kreed's eyes when I met them. "As some climates are more volatile than others." He then gestured to the snow-heaped courtyard. "You made it leave, Tullia, when he'd thought he needed Molkan's annihilation to make that happen."

"Winter?" I asked, studying the frost clinging like crystals to the vines and hedges.

He didn't answer. He rose, his intimidating height blocking the sun, and only said, "You also made it return."

I was left alone with those baffling words.

Words that untangled as my mind twirled backward to the heat, and how winter had started to thaw when we'd finally left Florian's rooms.

He'd tortured and worshipped me for days with such devotion to every detail—as though there had never been a world awaiting his return. And as each night had passed, his bladed edges became less sharp.

His laughter and playfulness became less rare.

My heart and stomach dipped violently as I studied the snow-piled courtyard once more. As realization settled too deep to be ignored any longer.

# 9

## Florian

Two males stood bleeding and glaring in the cells.

Finding the first noble who was anything but noble made finding the other two toads who'd tormented my wife all the more easier. He'd given up their names, plus the names of others, with the loss of his first canine.

Who'd have thought a kingdom that frowned upon the overconsumption of blood would care so damned much about the loss of their sharpest teeth?

Our final guest for the evening stumbled into his iron cage with a punch to his jaw when he dared to try snatching the dagger from Shole's belt.

Orange-brown eyes. Wine-red lips.

Lord Hummington.

He and his wife once owned a vast amount of land in the southeast lining the border between Baneberry and the middle lands. Of course, that was before they'd sold almost all of it due to Hummington's addiction.

He drank blood more than he ate food.

Judging by the stubborn glint in the eyes that stalked my mate in her sleep and the sneering curl to his bloodstained lips, he knew exactly why he was here. Such arrogance probably made him believe he'd live to feast upon another vein.

I couldn't fucking wait to prove him wrong.

"No need for introductions," I said, withdrawing my blade from my sleeve and dragging it along the iron bars. Our guests stiffened further with each clang. "We'll get straight to the point of this impromptu meeting."

Shole chuckled.

"Meeting?" the first male we'd captured scoffed, incredulous. "You've treated us like savage beasts. Do you have any fucking idea who we are?"

"Now, now . . ." I stopped before his cage. Slowly, I grinned. "Did you have any idea who my wife was when you placed your putrid hands on her?"

"No one touched her," he lied, and with almost admirable conviction.

The male next to him, Riccard Leafglow, hailed from one of the most ancient lines of Baneberry nobles. Pity he'd yet to sire an heir. The line would end with him, though he was smug enough to believe otherwise.

He gripped the bars, then recoiled with a hiss, staring at his hands as if they'd blister from a mere touch of the iron. "Our king caged her as the evening's entertainment. So what if we looked? Everyone did. She was set on a podium, for sky's sake."

Every inch of me became nothing but molten rage.

Shole whistled low. "Keep talking, and this shall be a *very* quick meeting." He smothered a laugh behind the hand rubbing his jaw. "Indeed."

"You cannot keep us here," the first male cried. "We are nobility, and thus it is an act of war."

I tapped my temple, feigning confusion. "What was your name?"

Indignant, even in the face of death, his heavy sideburns and braided beard couldn't hide the mottling of his skin as he sputtered, "You know exactly who I am." He swiped blood from his mouth, his gums yet to heal. "You just ripped out my teeth, you animal."

Fume cleared his throat.

I ignored him and opened my hand. Ice curled over my finger-tips into sharp stones. The noble's eyes widened as I launched them at his face.

He ducked, and most shattered against the dirt wall, but a few lodged in the forearm covering his face. There was a tremor to his voice as he rose, still covering half his features as if fearful I'd attack again. "I am Jon Milstread of Appleton Heights."

"Hmm." I raised a brow and scratched my cheek. "Never heard of him."

Shole half groaned, half chuckled, and leaned against the empty cells behind me, unfazed by the iron. He'd forced himself to create a certain amount of tolerance to it when he was young and more fearless than he was even now.

Anger puffed Milstread's lips and cheeks. He wisely kept it from forming words he'd regret.

"But I am curious," I said, stalking back and forth before his cell. "What is an aristocratic male such as yourself doing prodding at caged females?"

His fists shot down to his sides and squeezed, his head close to bursting from his scrawny shoulders. "I did no such thing."

A chatty one, apparently, Leafglow said, "You did, Milstread. You pinched her ass."

"You traitorous shit," Milstread spewed, redirecting his outrage to his fellow Baneberry noble through the bars beside him.

"May as well tell him what he wants to know. I need a meal and a good wash already."

Milstread eyed Leafglow up and down. "This is about the broken clock, isn't it? I told you I'd repay you."

"It was an heirloom and over two-thousand years old, you drunkard."

"*Me?*" Milstread nearly shrieked. "Why, if you hadn't been so drunk at that ball and leering at everything that moved, then maybe none of us would be here."

"Your eyes and hands are your own problem, Milstread."

"But you touched her first and then had the gall to sell me out."

"You sold us out first."

I looked at Fume, who stood waiting at the bottom of the stairs. He scrubbed his face as if tempted to kill the idiots now to make them shut up.

As they continued to argue back and forth, I was tempted myself. But not yet.

Not until I'd made them and every other daring fuck who'd so much as gone near my wife at that ball understand the magnitude of their mistakes.

Fume dropped his hand when I jerked my head at the stairs, relief sagging his shoulders.

Shole trailed us as we walked up to the snow-piled tree line surrounding the small white hut giving entrance to the under-ground dungeon.

Fume closed the door behind Shole. Pointless, seeing as none of the nobles would live to share a thing they might overhear.

"What the fuck is in Baneberry's waters?" Shole said through a laugh. "Bunch of babes wearing the skin of grown males. Pathetic."

Nobility were always the same. Once, I'd not been much different. So I gave that no comment and said to Fume, "Nirra's still here?"

He nodded. "Awaiting information on who to hunt next."

Shole lit a tobacco stem, exhaling smoke into the frigid air. "I'm beginning to think they'll need to give up that entire throne room to satisfy you, Flor."

I grunted, staring through the trees toward the manor. "So be it." Chimneys puffed, but few windows were aglow. I wondered if Tullia had taken a nap or if she'd decided to roam someplace other than the courtyard.

"I swear . . ." Shole gestured to the door behind him and said through another exhale, "I won a game of poker against Leafglow's cousin some years ago."

Fume rolled his eyes toward the trees—wisely away from Shole's view. "Did anyone see you take Hummington?" he asked the merc.

Even after years of working together, a low animosity simmered between the two. Shole was street raised, while Fume had been raised by his mother, my father's favored general who'd retired after his death.

My lifelong friend didn't appreciate how much clout the warrior turned assassin and spy received, for he didn't believe he'd earned it.

I'd never bothered informing Fume that after the upbringing Shole had endured, he well and truly had. Neither did Shole, who tolerated my general's ignorance better than most would expect. It was the type of tolerance that often made me think he secretly liked how much he irritated Fume.

Shole took his time answering, and I was ready for them to leave. My hands itched to spill blood. That, and I had little interest in their petty games at the best of times.

"Who cares if they did?" He lowered his stem. "A message is a message, General, of which all will receive when the nobles fail to return."

"This seems hasty." Fume crossed his arms and kicked at a rock in the snow. "They are nobility. This could cause unforeseen and serious problems."

"In case you haven't noticed," Shole drawled, "we've been intentionally causing problems for years now. So what exactly is *your* problem?"

Anyone who knew Fume was aware of his reluctance to welcome newcomers, regardless of who they were. And it seemed Shole wished to unearth Fume's wariness of my wife and have me hear it.

I couldn't give a fuck if he was comfortable with my decision to keep Tullia as his queen. Just as long as he respected her.

Fume's silence was telling.

Luckily for him, my patience had officially run dry.

"Do me a favor," I clipped, drawing both their gazes. "Have no problems and don't disturb me unless it's with exceedingly good news."

Understanding they'd been dismissed, they each gave me a nod. Shole's came with a smirk as he said, "Do try not to have too much fun, your coldness."

I watched them trek through the snow toward the manor and the meals awaiting them, then I opened the door and returned to the dark.

## 10

**Tullia**

Tapping stole my attention from the snow-brightened night.

Olin entered a moment later. "You've received a letter."

I'd left the doors to Florian's chambers open, thinking I might find the courage to venture downstairs for dinner. I hadn't. The steward had long delivered my meal and set it atop the small table Florian had added to his bedchamber.

Olin gave me an impatient appraisal when I turned from the balcony door, then set the wax-sealed envelope by the dinner tray. "It arrived via sparrow late this afternoon."

"Florian inspected it first," I said flatly. It didn't shock me, nor did it really bother me. Besides Gane, who'd already visited, I hadn't anyone I cared to receive correspondence from.

Olin's mustache twitched. "It is addressed to you." The crisp words were said as if that fact meant anything.

I nodded once and turned back to gaze through the balcony door, awaiting his departure.

He didn't leave. He cleared his throat and said, "You haven't touched your dinner."

"I might soon."

Still, he lingered. "You won't open the letter, will you?"

I didn't answer. Not only was there no need but two males marched between the stables and paddocks toward the manor. The silver and white-blond hair and their dark ensembles were stark against the snow and the shadows of night.

Shole and Fume.

The steward could not see them from where he remained in the doorway. About to ask him what the two warriors might be up to, I thought better of it when they disappeared down the rear garden path, and I remembered.

The dungeon in the woods.

Perhaps they'd brought someone here. I could imagine no other reason they'd be walking through the winter-battered estate at this hour instead of arriving at the main entrance to the manor.

Olin sighed in a way that made it clear he wished for me to be aware of his irritation.

I ignored it, but I did ask, my gaze still fixed on the woodland in the distance, "Where is Florian?"

"Tending to some business," Olin replied smoothly. "He'll likely return soon."

I said nothing in response, waiting again for him to leave. After a moment, he finally did. His parting words carried an alarming hint of urgency. "At least see who the letter is from."

He closed the doors, and I peered at the table.

The flame from the candle beside my untouched meal cast the thick envelope in half shadow. With one last glance at the woods, I then left the balcony door and padded over to the letter.

My hand shook as I held it closer to the flame. There was no return address. There was only a name.

Peony Boneblood.

The curiosity I'd once carried with me like a second skin began to reform, and with it, the vivid reminders of what it had cost me. I set the letter down, drained the remaining water in the glass, and traipsed to the bathing room to wash away the incoming chill.

Afterward, I donned the same fur-lined robe I'd worn prior. It was a royal blue silk that reached my knees. I scratched beneath Snow's chin when she stirred on the bed before returning to the balcony.

No one else walked through the darkness. No lights glowed in the distance.

Still, I continued to wait.

The fire burned low, but I didn't feed it. I discarded the robe and laid it over the chaise, then climbed into bed and waited some more.

Sleep never came. Neither did the king.

Not one night had passed since my return without him eventually taking post in his chambers. Though I didn't like to admit it, it had become a comfort, knowing he would be there while I slept. Knowing he would be there when I woke, and if not, that he would leave proof of his presence.

The clock chimed from the foyer downstairs.

Midnight.

I stared at the chaise, empty of a king but covered in his clothing and my robe. Then I rose from the bed and donned it and the boots I'd left by the fire to dry.

Snow whined as I trapped her inside the rooms. I wasn't sure what I might find, should I even find anyone in the dungeon, and it was too late to hunt the wolf down if she roamed too far.

The wind whistled and danced in flurries of white. Snow fell like shards of ice, blistering as the cold wet seeped beneath the fabric of my robe. My knee-high boots were soon no match for the weather.

Uncaring, I trudged on past the stables and the abandoned greenhouse. Barren trees swayed like ghostly sentinels, tempting my pulse to spike. I shielded my eyes, my hair whipping around me and sticking to my cheeks, and pushed forward to the tree line ahead.

The door to the small hut almost tore from the hinges when I opened it and the wind caught it. I gritted my teeth against the painful spasm in my back, the flesh and muscle unprepared for such unexpected force.

A whimper followed a bellowed curse down below.

The dirt stairwell was dimly lit. Florian's scent mingled heavily with that of blood.

The whimpering turned into an unending howl right as I pulled the door closed and awaited someone's appearance at the bottom of the stairs.

If Florian was still here, perhaps he hadn't heard my entrance over the noise. It hadn't come from him. Regardless, I didn't allow myself a moment longer to linger. I hurried down the stairs.

Then I froze.

A faerie hung from the ceiling between the short row of twin cells. His fingers were missing. Blood spiraled down his bound wrists to meet with more leaving his abdomen.

The cells to the left held two dead prisoners. Males, I surmised, upon closer inspection.

One was slumped against the wall, his missing hands beside him and his eye sockets empty. The other faerie lay facedown in a spreading pool of blood and melting ice. His innards peeked out from beneath his torso. His heart had been placed within his severed hand.

I waited, though it never came—revulsion.

Instead, I studied each corpse, fascinated.

Florian didn't seem surprised by my presence. He didn't even move as he said in a cadence that would make most do as he ordered, "Return to bed, butterfly."

I looked back at the brutalized face of the male strung before him, and recognition struck. "Him." I swallowed and crossed to where Florian sat upon an upturned pail, a blood-soaked dagger twirling between his knees and fingertips. "You found him."

Orange-flecked brown eyes. Wine-red lips.

"Lord Hummington." The name was said in a cold and matter-of-fact tone, one eerily close to a voice I'd heard before. "Barely spoken since his arrival."

It was the tone of a king who'd frozen three males for dancing with me until I couldn't see straight. The tone of a male on the cusp of leaving civility behind. Or, I determined with a glance at the corpses, just now returning to some semblance of it.

I studied the lord who'd struck me while I was caged during Molkan's ball. I studied him as I walked slow circles around him, marveling at the ruination of his noble body and the fear that seeped from him—a slimy oil that seemed rather fitting for the creature he was.

"You never came," I said to Florian, inspecting the deep and oozing gouge beneath Lord Hummington's rib cage.

Florian's gaze was a weight that warmed, his words iced. "I assumed you wouldn't mind."

"Petulance doesn't suit you," I said, smiling as I came to stand between him and the male he'd been torturing.

The king stared up at me with narrowed eyes, a slight smudge of darkness beneath them. Most of his hair had escaped the tie at his nape, near-black pieces ashine with blood. It wasn't his soiled state that sparked concern.

It was the exhaustion.

Gently, and without removing my eyes from his, I took the dagger from his fingers. I dragged a nail over the jagged blade.

He frowned. The action cracked the dried blood smearing one of his brows. "Leave, Tullia."

"Why?"

More blood decorated his cheek and jawline when he swiped his soiled hand over his mouth. I didn't miss the way it trembled. "I don't think that warrants explanation." He extended his hand for the dagger.

My brow lifted. The heft of the weapon in my hand terrified, yet the leather hilt was comforting and warm. "Then you won't think this does either." I turned back to the male losing consciousness.

And I woke him up by sinking the blade into the wound in his abdomen and twisting.

He screamed.

Blood gushed over my hand, so hot it made me shiver.

The pail was overturned as Florian stood, but he didn't stop me.

Not when the lord hissed and spat at me, and I twisted the blade again. Not when I stared into the eyes that haunted like so many others, and I pulled the dagger free—only to plunge it into his flesh again and again and again.

My eyes remained fastened on his, even when they closed and his body slumped. He wasn't dead, and I was far from ready for him to be.

"Tullia."

"Don't," I warned Florian.

The sound of steel sinking into flesh, the blade nicking bone and carving muscle, became a chorus my heart drummed to keep up with. Over and over and over.

Blood sprayed.

It filmed my skin and the chilled air in a crimson mist, poured down my arm like a river I longed to see flow forevermore. The birds, the leering gazes, the pinching fingers, the revolting insults, the daring hands, and the booming voice of a father who'd turned out to be nothing but a monster . . .

I didn't know I was growling, perhaps screaming, until Florian seized me around the waist.

I turned on him, wild and desperate for more.

His fingers wrapped around my wrist—halting the raised hand holding the blade as if it were a balm to every wound inflicted upon my body and soul. He hushed me when I attempted to demand that he release me, his finger pressing to my lips.

My chest heaved. My eyes stung and watered.

Florian stared down at me, his own wildness still lingering in his gaze like stars crushed and spread across the darkest night sky. His copper-scented finger rubbed my lips. They were already bloodstained, but I wouldn't have cared.

He smoothed blood-streaked strands of hair from my face, tucking them behind my ear. "Sweet creature, look at you." But his words carried affection that melted, and his touch a reverence that matched what shone in his eyes. "Turn around."

I did, and with his hand moving to mine over the dagger's hilt, he stood close at my back. His other hand swept over the damp silk of my robe to my hip. A weight that bolstered and caused heat to crawl through my cold veins.

I should have been horrified by what I'd done. Sickened by the pulpy mess I'd made of the lord's torso.

I was only horrified that he still drew breath.

His chest rose and fell, shallow but surely, though his head hung low. He wouldn't regain consciousness, and he wouldn't leave this dungeon alive.

Florian's chin lowered to my shoulder. His whisper stirred my hair and warmed my ear. "End him." He released his hold on the dagger.

Stepping forward, I sank it into the lord's chest and pushed and pushed until I saw it move no more.

Then I stood there. I watched his lifeblood leave his body to fall to the dirt beneath his gilded sandaled feet.

My fingers uncurled from the hilt. The dagger hit the ground with a soft resonance. My hand ached. I welcomed it, opened and closed it while admiring the gruesome death I'd dealt. My lungs felt heavy, yet when I exhaled, each new breath came easier—in a way they hadn't in days.

I closed my eyes and relished it.

Florian's touch remained. When he finally stepped back, I turned and seized his waist. Gazing up at him, I found myself without words. There were none, and there were too many. "Thank you," was all I could manage to whisper.

He scowled, seeming to assess what exactly I was thanking him for.

I didn't give him time to ask me to clarify. I rose onto my toes and kissed him.

Shock stilled him, but only momentarily.

He groaned. A throaty sound of both torment and relief. Then he grasped my face and met my hungry lips press for press, my tongue ready when he tilted my head and opened my mouth with his own.

He cursed as I reached between us to unbuckle his pants. His forehead dropped to mine, his expression pained as he said, "You are not yourself."

That evoked a breathy laugh. "I haven't felt this good in weeks."

The sound stunned him, but when I sought his mouth again, he evaded me and closed his eyes. "It will fade, and then you will loathe me once more." His words deepened from the lust thickening his voice. "That I can handle, but I cannot handle your self-loathing."

"Majesty." I stroked his hard cock through his pants, my lips skimming his jaw. "You would deny me?"

His throat bobbed. His hand trembled at my cheek. "Never."

I ripped open my robe and climbed him.

He caught me, and our mouths fused again. We stumbled back toward the iron cells. "Tell me," he said, hoarse. "Tell me that—"

"Florian, I need you," I breathed.

"Where?" He nipped my upper lip and squeezed my ass.

"All over me." I moaned and rocked against him. "Inside me."

We lowered to the ground, my legs still twined around him. He inhaled a hissed breath through his teeth when I released him from his pants.

His order was strained. "Lift to your knees." I did, and we both groaned as he then fed himself to my body. His eyes came away from the sight of us joining, half-mast and sky blue. "Fuck."

His nostrils flared as he beheld me. As he soaked in the blood and the hastily opened robe exposing my breasts and torso, and the lip trapped between my teeth as I swallowed all of him with my back arching.

Clenching his hair and shoulder, I moaned long and loud, close to delirium from sensation. The type of blistering magic I'd thought I might never encounter again. His hold on my thigh and hip, his searing gaze a brand I'd gladly wear, and the pleasure of feeling so blissfully full was a fire that consumed.

My flesh and bones seemed to awaken with a hunger that howled.

Shivering, I straightened, then pushed his head to my neck. "You need to feed."

He didn't disagree, and he didn't hesitate. His nose grazed my thumping pulse as he kissed then licked at the curve of my throat. With a ragged exhale, his hand slid to the back of my tilted head, and his canines pierced.

I needn't have wondered if he'd fed during my absence or while I'd been locked away in his rooms. Though he was far more gentle, he fed from me with the same desperate ferocity I'd unleashed upon him when he'd stolen my broken body from the library.

As he did, I rocked atop him.

Drugging warmth swam through each limb and tickled beneath my skin. I moaned for more and chased the rapture. I grinded over him, my thighs shaking and my hands tangling in his unbound hair.

Release arrived with violence and a silent scream.

Florian's groan was gasped as his mouth left my neck. My hip and ass were squeezed as he moved me over him until my clenching body delivered his own release.

He licked a path of blood up my throat. Twitching beneath me, he rumbled, "You fucking devastate me."

My head lowered, my breaths leaving fast and uncaptured.

I failed to care when he claimed my mouth, and we rode the melting shivers. Hungrily, I kissed him, still starving. He was, too. Not only could I sense it but he remained hard inside me.

Before I could chase the embers and turn them into flames with sharper tilts of my hips, darkness enfolded.

He held me tighter, and my mouth slipped from his as we materialized to his rooms.

I blinked at the near-dark bedchamber Florian stood within. I was still in his arms, my legs curled around him and his body still joined with mine.

Noting my shock, he set loose a rasped chuckle that slackened my mouth. He bit my upper lip and said, "Not even the energy rifts can take you from me."

I stared at him, the hunger in his gaze shining a blue so bright in the shadowed room. Thick strands of charcoal hair framed his cheeks, as well as streaks of blood. His lips parted as we drank one another in.

"Tullia," he began.

But I didn't want to talk.

I kissed him, urgent yet luxuriating in the softness of his lips. I licked them, nipped them, moaned from the heady taste of him as a tiny bead of blood welled under my tongue.

The king gentled the kiss and turned toward the bed.

Snow huffed, claws clicking as the wolf leaped to the floor.

He lowered me to the bed, following and kissing my throat as he slowly moved inside me. His hand braced beside my head, and I longed for it to press against my mouth. Wished for his soiled fingers to enter it and brush against my tongue.

Instead, he continued to kiss my throat while his fingers caressed my nipple before skimming my side.

My eyes stung as he lapped at the punctures he'd made—as though he regretted maiming my skin when we'd both enjoyed it. And as tears threatened to fall, my heart clenched and clenched until each breath failed worse than the one before.

With a ragged gasp, I pushed at his chest.

Florian paused, then rose, frowning down at me. He searched my eyes. "Did I hurt you?"

*In numerous ways*, I didn't say.

"Quite the opposite." I smirked. "In this instance, at least."

He pushed up higher, and I rolled free over the bed to sit up. He didn't stop me, which only served to irritate me more.

"Florian, I don't want . . ." I couldn't figure out how to say it—didn't want to have to. I dragged a hand through my hair, my fingers snagging on blood-matted tangles.

Florian just stood there and watched me. A hunter unsure of what to do with his skittish prey.

The threat of tears returned, and I lowered my head as the burning in my throat intensified.

"I'll prepare you a bath," he said, the words carrying a slight rasp. For we both still felt it. The starvation for more.

We felt it, sensed it, in each other as acutely as we did in ourselves.

He knew I wasn't done, yet he wouldn't continue even though he was as hard as stone. He ordered Snow into my rooms before heading to the bathing chamber.

I slid to the floor with a frustrated groan. He was waiting for another first move from me. He was going to make me say it.

Fine.

If it got me what I wanted, then *fine*. Rushed words released in a burst of breath. "I don't want to be treated like a chipped toy that might break."

Florian instantly returned.

He didn't blink as he took measured steps to stand mere feet before me. Darkness embraced him like a lover he ignored. The sparse candlelight reached for the defined dips of his torso and the sharp crests of his face.

He said nothing.

Even covered in gore with his tight trousers snug halfway down his perfect ass, he was magnificent. And for reasons I was still trying to fathom, he was mine.

Despite what he'd done and what he'd failed to do to me, this king was all mine.

Acknowledging that, however silently, gave me the courage to give him what he needed from me—to voice exactly what I needed from him.

"I want *you*." I removed my boots and let my robe slip down my arms to the floor. "I want your hand wrapped around my hair, my throat, and my mouth. I want to wear your fingertips as bruises on my hips and thighs." My eyes swept over his pants to his exposed and hard cock. My neck curled back as I met his gaze, and my whispered words gained more sound. "I want you to fuck me without restraint."

Still, he didn't speak. He just stared. Almost seemed to glare.

But he wanted it, too.

I could see it in the violent rise of his chest. In the way he slowly released air through gritted teeth. It glowed in his eyes, the pupils expanding and lighter blue sparking.

And it was confirmed when any hint of softness to his features was wiped clean by his need to put me in my place. By his desire to take back that control he adored and needed in every facet of his life.

A need he unleashed with a smirk that hitched my breath. "Come to me." The three words were toneless.

Yet I'd never felt a command so profoundly.

I climbed to my feet, and he tutted.

My eyes widened as I realized what he wanted. But I'd asked for this. I wanted this. So I lowered to the floor and crawled to the toes of his boots.

He crooned, "Good." Then he crouched, his finger stroking beneath my chin. His eyes searched mine, hooded and aglow. "My violent little butterfly."

Not wishing to blink, I gazed at him with my heart beating hard. A whisper-soft kiss accompanied his next command. "Now go stand with those pretty bloodstained hands against the wall."

"Which wall—"

His head tilted.

My mouth closed. My pulse screamed in my ears as I rose and turned for the clearest space between the doors and drawers.

He followed, an iced breeze at my back.

My hands shook as I flattened them over the stone. Not with nerves but with a familiar trepidation layered in excitement.

"Very good." He knocked my legs open with a soiled boot, then leaned over my bare back to rumble to my shoulder, "Do you want my cock, sweet creature?"

I nodded.

He gathered my hair around his fist. I waited, growing more impatient by the second. He chuckled when I swung my eyes at him and glared, then nipped the skin of my shoulder. "Moving your head about is not an adequate answer."

The words quivered with my breath. "I want it."

He hummed against my skin, my head tilting as he tugged my hair. His lips caressed and stopped right beneath my ear. "Want what?" he whispered roughly.

"I want your cock."

His hand smoothed over the ruined skin of my back. I tensed, but for a better reason when he slid his finger through my rear until it met my wet core. He dunked one inside me, leisurely, his tone daring and too soft. "And what do you want it for?"

95

"To fill me," I said, desperate.

"So you want my cock to impale your perfect cunt?"

"Florian, *please.*"

He groaned through a laugh that made my thighs shake. "Such satisfying words, my lovely mate."

The word mate stilled me.

He noticed. Of course, he noticed. He withdrew his finger, then inserted two. "You reject it, though it's true. Though you feel within your bones that nothing has ever been more true." His fingers left my body. My hair was yanked until I turned to him. "Suck," he ordered.

I wrapped my lips around the digits, his release and my own mingling with my desire for him to give me more.

Half-mast eyes studied my mouth, my every feature. "So obedient." He returned his fingers to my body. "So wonderfully greedy." His lips closed over mine. "My mate." His eyes held mine as he licked my upper lip. "My wife." He dragged his fingers free to rub my clit. "My fucking queen."

I fractured.

As he grinned with feral delight and crooned, "Your body eternally betrays you for me," release swept through me so swiftly, I nearly fell.

Florian struck while I was still asunder.

He indeed impaled me, his arm banding around my stomach and his hand gripping my hip. He cursed viciously, his head rolling back. Veins and muscle corded. A rasped, "Fuck," whispered from his lips.

My hands slipped down the wall, and I concentrated on remaining upright while he ground into me. Then he reared back.

And gave me exactly what I'd dared to ask for.

A wicked chuckle washed over my skin as he leaned over me to sink his teeth into my shoulder, his thrusts striking deep. He licked the blood drawn, groaning as he eased back to fuck me without a drop of mercy.

I couldn't moan. I could scarcely breathe as he relinquished his hold on my hair to grip my ass so hard it would certainly bruise. I might have cursed. *More*, I might have panted, held up solely by his punishing hold and thrusts.

Another orgasm loomed, and I would've feared falling to the floor if I had any room to care. I didn't. His hands, his powerful body, and the throaty noises he made, coupled with his precision and unfaltering determination to render me undone, caused me to explode when he did.

He emptied inside me with an animalistic sound akin to a low roar and pulled me to him.

Bent at the knees, he rocked into me and fed from the curve of my shoulder as he groaned with contentment.

When he finally spoke, it was hoarse and between laps of his tongue over the punctures he'd made. "Better, butterfly?"

"Close enough, Majesty," I rasped, gripping his forearm at my waist with a smile I was glad he could not see.

He must have sensed it, for he hummed in amusement. Lazily, he licked and kissed my neck before hauling me into his arms and setting me on the end of the bed. He then went to draw the bath he'd promised.

In a blissful daze, I caught my breath while catching glimpses of him through the door.

Resisting the urge to surrender to exhaustion was a struggle as he washed blood from my hair and body once more. But after asking who the two dead males in the dungeon had been, I wanted to know more.

"How did you find them?"

"I didn't." Before I could roll my eyes, he tipped my chin and poured another cupful of water over my head to rid the last of the suds from my hairline. "Shole found them."

"Your hunter," I remembered. "Assassin."

Florian swiped water from my forehead with his thumbs, then left me to lower into the pool. When he emerged, he smoothed his hair back from his face and scrubbed blood from his cheeks.

I was far too tempted to do it for him. But it was one thing to have him tend to me and another to return such intimacy. I wasn't as accepting of this as he seemed to be. That he was still dumbfounded and unnerved me.

*My fucking queen*, he'd said, and with such potent conviction that denying he'd meant it—that I meant something more than vengeance and an enjoyable body to him—was impossible.

His long lashes caught tiny beads of water. Some sluiced over the cliffs of his cheeks to fall to his hewn jaw when he blinked. Mesmerized and still dazed, I watched their journey. I watched him with a hollow ache that resembled yearning.

A hunger for more than his body.

He cleansed the death and destruction from his physique with care to detail, though his eyes never once left me.

I didn't mind that he could probably see the rapt spell he'd cast over me.

But I was somewhat relieved when he spoke as he waded to where I sat on the stone step in the corner of the pool. "Once Milstread was caught, the others were easily hunted."

"You're not done." I wasn't referring to his body, which was clean although he hadn't soaped his hair.

I was referring to hunting the rest of the swine who'd tormented me during my father's ball, and this husband of mine knew as much.

"No," he said.

Maybe I should have, but I didn't care to protect them. Any creature capable of deriving pleasure from the terror I'd suffered that evening was capable of far worse deeds.

"One of them even had a spouse or lover," I confessed, staring at the dark ink that spanned his broad chest.

The tattoo of his sister's name written in the old language.

The memory of Molkan's revulsion over his obsession with the princess he'd killed twined tight around my bones.

*Lilitha was an obsession, an addiction I could not quit.*

So he'd murdered her. Robbed the world of a color that had filled the heart of the male standing between my knees.

Florian lifted my chin, thumb stroking my lower lip. My eyes met his as he wished. Though his jaw was clenched, the words were gentle. "You need not trouble yourself with remembering details. But should it make you sleep better to ensure those we hunt deserve it, then I will inform you when they're found, and you may check."

I searched his darkened gaze. "You mean that?"

His head lowered for his lips to touch the tip of my nose. "You know I do," he whispered.

I scowled. Not from his words, but at the way my heart jumped from the sweet action.

Noticing, as always, he gently nipped my nose before he climbed out of the water. "Better, butterfly?" Humor drenched the question.

As I left the warmth of the bathing pool, I fought back a smile and decided not to give that a response. Instead, I snatched the awaiting towel he'd spread, and I wrapped it around my body.

Florian huffed and trailed me into the bedchamber to build a fire, his towel clinging to his mouth-drying hips.

I sat at the table, my hair dripping, and ripped at the mound of bread beside my untouched dinner. It had grown hard, but I didn't mind. I chewed a piece and poured another glass of water, admiring the muscles aglow in the king's back as he stoked the growing flames.

Though I already knew the answer, I asked, "Will you sleep on the chaise again?"

"No." He fed the fire another log from the small pile by the hearth.

It needed restocking. Idly, I wondered how many trees would be felled to endure this eternal winter. Then I wondered more over what Kreed had divulged in the courtyard.

A curse, the winter running through this king's veins, though not in the traditional sense.

I set the water down and padded across the patches of carpet over the stone to the balcony doors. Peeling back the drapes, I wasn't surprised to find snow had ceased falling after what Kreed had said.

Yet the reason for it still jolted. A spark felt deep within my bones.

*You made it leave.*

Florian's arms encased me from behind.

Before I could break free of them, he murmured to my hair, "Sleep, butterfly." Then he retrieved my soiled robe and entered the bathing room to put our ruined clothing in the basket for collection.

I let Snow back in and crept into bed, pulling the bedding high and staring through the gap I'd left in the drapes. The mattress soon dipped with Florian's weight, and I braced for his embrace. Half of me craved it, while the other half refused to want it.

He remained on his favored side of the bed where I'd usually lay, as the fire crackled and sleep gradually stole me from the clearer view of the night sky.

# 11

**Tullia**

Despite my inability to allow the king privileges he'd once had, I woke in a baffling position.

Florian was on his back and carving away at another ice sculpture, the scratching of his blade what had caused my eyes to flutter open. His hands worked over his chest in that diligent manner I'd come to assume was soothing for him.

All the while, my head was in his lap. His very hard and unclothed lap.

He released a low and sleep-thickened chuckle when I pushed up. Snow was not at the foot of the bed, nor was she at the doors. I surmised she'd been let out some time ago.

The sight of his smile reduced my self-loathing. Only by a fraction. "You found your own way there, sweet creature."

The sun danced through the gap I'd left in the drapes, bright and glorious, but not nearly as magical as the ruthless creature who'd tricked me into marriage.

"First my chest," he said, peeling a layer of ice from the sculpture and flicking it to the floor. "Then you tucked your head into my neck before complaining that I snore. Then, well . . ." He grinned down at his lap. "It seemed that wasn't enough for you to leave entirely."

"I don't remember any of that," I said, and too sharply.

He gave me a look that said I'd seen the proof. A look that softened, his brows dropping and his mouth slackening, as his dark blue gaze lightened while traversing my sleep-crumpled state.

Warming rapidly, I flopped to the other side of the bed, where I'd fallen asleep before I'd decided to use him as a pillow.

"You snore, too, I'll have you know." Seeming far too pleased with himself, he added smugly, "Like a fly trapped beneath a teacup."

I glowered, unsure if I believed him. "You tell me this now?"

"It seemed unwise to do so before."

"You mean when you were trying to make me believe in your false intentions?"

He dragged his teeth over his lower lip. "Precisely."

I groaned and turned my face into the pillow. The space I'd put between us did nothing to alleviate the temptation of him as I studied his hands and kept glimpsing the hair beneath his lower stomach.

His erection tented the bedding. Perhaps my snoring wasn't so bad either.

He appeared content to ignore it. "You didn't whimper. Nor did you sweat."

I blinked profusely at his face. His eyes remained on his sculpture. Another rose, I determined, as more ice gathered beneath his fingers. "I had no dreams at all," I realized aloud.

Finished with the rose, Florian admired it for mere seconds, then set it upon the plate on the nightstand.

"May I see it?" I asked.

A dark brow arched, but he retrieved it and placed it in my awaiting palm.

Sunlight slid across the ice, sending spirals of crystal light over the bed and the king's chest. I stayed on my side and flattened my hand to keep my body heat from melting it too quickly.

"You carve them when you're unsettled," I said, knowing I was right. "Anxious."

His lack of response confirmed. He watched as I traced the petals unfurling from the bud. Then he murmured, "Lilitha was fond of them, even when she grew, as she never had the patience to sit still long enough to learn how to make any."

Those affection-riddled words drew my gaze to his. The violent severity of his features was stark with his sleep-touched state. He waited, long lashes lifting when his eyes left my mouth to meet mine.

The princess had possessed winter magic too, then, or at least some form of it. I had so many questions regarding Lilitha. So many lies and truths to untangle.

Though I found I could ask nothing more than, "And how old were you when you learned?"

"Twelve years."

I scoffed. "Of course."

"I am also a hands-on learner." The purred words taunted and tested.

But I remembered. It was unlikely I'd ever forget.

I stroked the ice, then brought the cold and damp pad of my finger to my lips. "Oh?" It had no taste, yet I could still taste him. Winter with a hint of whiskey, although I hadn't seen him drink any since my return.

Florian's gaze narrowed upon my mouth.

I crawled over him and tried to keep from smiling as I reached for the nightstand to place the rose back upon the plate. "Apologies, Majesty," I whispered, my breast right near his chin.

I snatched the glass of water and took my time draining it. Then I set the glass down and swiped my mouth with a breathy exhale.

He was so very still. Our skin didn't even touch.

Finally, as I crawled back over him, he snarled softly and rolled atop me. Above me, he loomed so close his dark hair tickled my cheeks. His eyes brightened right before my own. They moved through layers of blue until they settled upon a light cerulean.

His eyelids lowered when I pressed a finger against his supple mouth. "This doesn't mean I've forgiven you, Florian."

He grinned. "Exquisite creature." He nipped, then kissed my finger. "I don't want your forgiveness." Our lips grazed with the edged whisper. "I just need your surrender."

Before I could form a response to that, his mouth claimed mine.

Hard and merely feeling, he breathed me in and groaned. The bedding was taken with him when he pulled away to snatch my nipple between his teeth. He licked and tugged, then inhaled with a throaty rumble. His exhale accompanied his gravel-coated words. "Smells like you need me."

"Florian . . ." I reached for his head, all that thick hair awaiting my fingers.

But he dragged his parted lips over my stomach and down to my thighs. Evading my hands, his eyes sparked. "I'll bet you taste like it, too."

My legs opened wide. An invitation he took with a pleased glance given to me.

His gaze returned between my thighs, and a harsh exhale shook his shoulders. "Already so ready." It didn't deter him, though. His head dropped, his nose rubbing and his lips pressing to my swollen core in a deliriously soft kiss. "Better than I dreamed."

My breath caught. "Monsters do not dream, Majesty."

"Is that so?" His tongue flicked, and my hips bucked. He curled his arms around my thighs and seized my hips, holding me to the bed. "Then why is it that when I close my eyes, all I ever seem to see is you?"

Like so many from these perilous lands, this king was exceedingly adept in the art of manipulation. Heat still coiled tight in my stomach. My heartbeat became a song in my ears, dancing for more.

I melted just enough to say, "You once said you'd never done this before." I swallowed thickly. My back arched when he flattened his tongue and licked me slowly. "Before me."

A low hum caused a shiver. "And you believe I lied." He parted me, and I gasped, sensation ridding my mind of coherent thought. Another slow lick, then he stopped right beneath my clit. "You likely believe many things you shouldn't. Right now, I cannot change that." His voice had roughened, his fingers digging into my hip bones. "But . . ."

His tongue swept through me once more, and my hands sank into his hair.

"Like the monster I am, I can make you come." He finally gave my clit three languid laps of his tongue, then kissed it, and he did.

Skies, he fucking did.

Sunlight and darkness collided behind my closed eyes.

My thighs captured his head, my own turning into the pillow and my fingers winding through his hair. They tugged, but he wouldn't relent until he was done. I moaned louder—failing to smother the sound.

The sound of surrender.

Dizzied, I opened my eyes when Florian crawled over me. He gazed down at my heaving breasts, intently absorbed the flushed state of my skin.

His nostrils widened, his glowing eyes heavy with need. "My father once told me to save something," he said, almost ragged. "To have my fun but to save something for the one I wished to keep."

Breath was forgotten as I gaped up at him while his confession seared through my chest like a remedy and a blade. Surely, he couldn't have known that he wished to keep me when he'd first placed his mouth between my thighs back in his pleasure house. I still struggled to believe he wished to.

He'd intended to kill me.

*The moment I laid eyes on you was the moment I knew I could never end your life.*

He didn't wait for a response. Didn't wait for me to call him a liar.

He lowered his head and his hips. The taste of myself blended with the taste of him on my tongue, a potion that drugged.

Again, I moaned, my legs twining at his lower back. I held his face to mine, fingers curling into his cheeks and hair when his cock entered my body. He seated himself with a groan I swallowed, and my hand left his face to roam the smooth expanse of his upper back.

He sucked my bottom lip before he rose above me. "You need to feed."

I frowned. "I don't—"

He kissed me, firm and unyielding, and glared. "It wasn't a request."

I stared up at him, then at his heavily whiskered jawline. I licked it, whispering, "You need it, don't you?" Though the words were teasing, they were dipped in venom. "Me, wholly at your mercy." His head lifted and his cock pressed impossibly deeper as my tongue moved to his bobbing throat.

I was rewarded with a deep groan when I licked his Adam's apple before he said, "Fair play, my lovely mate." That word made me tense until he slid his hand beneath me to the back of my head. He pushed my mouth to the curve of his shoulder and neck. "If I am at your mercy, then you will be at mine."

I couldn't have moved if I'd wanted to.

He was all over me, inside me, warm and cold and overwhelming every sense. And I didn't want to. My eyes closed, and my lips searched his skin. Right as they peeled back, he began to thrust.

My teeth pierced his flesh with a drawn-out and smothered moan.

The forearm braced beside my head clenched as he cursed, muscle trembling beneath my hand at his back.

His essence was a poison I welcomed. My taste buds tingled with recognition and glee as I drew the cold heat of him from his body into my own. I sucked and licked, stars crawling across the dark behind my closed eyelids when his hips jerked and his cock nudged exactly where I needed it.

The king's throaty approval emboldened, my tongue lapping as I sucked harder.

"That's it, butterfly." His lips and low laugh brushed my ear. "Drink my blood and take my seed, my fucking lifeforce, like the defiant yet greedy little creature you are."

His hips worked alongside his crass words, ruining me.

I came again, my body shaking and utterly trapped. A prisoner, willing and mindless, I writhed beneath him though I never wanted to leave. Tears singed my eyes, the intensity of the orgasm crashing into the pleasure still sparking from feeding.

His laughter was wicked, the kiss he pressed to my erratic pulse adoring. "Look at me." He drew away. "Perfect." Delight shined in the hooded eyes gazing down at my glaring and tear-streaked face. "Fair play indeed."

I failed to speak, and wouldn't have even known what to say.

Those pleased eyes explored my features and paused on my bloodstained lips. "So fucking perfect." Then he licked a tear from my cheek.

And I couldn't stand it—his tender cruelty.

Still shaking, my words were bitten between the slight chattering of my teeth. "Stop that." I attempted to grasp his face when he licked the other cheek and something fissured in my chest. "Florian," I growled, or tried to. The sound was more of a plea as my weak arms fell.

He kissed my nose, and I did growl. He chuckled, raw and genuine. "I love it when you bare those fucking teeth." Then he sealed our mouths as he hooked his hand at the base of my neck and began to fuck me in earnest.

It was best he didn't allow me to speak. As I melted with every claiming caress of his lips, and every powerful thrust of his hips, I didn't want to. He made me forget, perhaps intentionally, that I'd ever dared to want anything other than this.

Dangerous, certainly, yet there was safety in forgetting.

## 12

**Tullia**

Afterward, my mind blissfully empty, I washed blood from my face and readied a cloth to clean between my thighs.

Florian roused quickly from where I'd left him sprawled on the bed, his chest heaving and his forearm covering his eyes.

"Futile." He braced his hands atop the doorframe to the bathing room. Muscle flexed. Everywhere. "We're far from done."

*Indeed*, I thought, unable to keep from noticing his hard cock in the mirror as I squeezed water from the cloth. It was still damp from our coupling, and my attention seemed to make it twitch. "I think we've done quite enough."

"Enough what?" His teeth caught his lip and dragged with his smirk. "Fornicating, perhaps?"

Though seeing more of this side to him—the playful side people spoke of that I'd only glimpsed in rare moments—was something of a treat, I wasn't sure what to do with it. Enjoy it, of course, and I was, yet with too much caution to wholly do so.

Still, I smiled down at the cloth while recalling how mortified I'd been after saying such a word to him what seemed many moons ago in that pleasure house. "We're married, apparently. That word no longer applies."

"Apparently." His iced heat neared my back. "Fucking, then?" he suggested, rubbing his lips over strands of my hair. My eyes closed when his mouth reached my temple. There, he inhaled my scent with a tight breath I felt within my own chest. My eyes opened as he whispered, "Fine," and the cloth was taken from my hand. "Allow me."

There was no use in protesting or feeling embarrassed when he'd cleansed me of far worse after my return from Baneberry.

He crouched low. "Hold my shoulder and lift your foot to my leg."

I gripped it and placed my foot on his knee. Arousal arose swiftly as he took more care than necessary in wiping me clean.

"I wouldn't let you," he said, husked. "If it weren't for the fact that I still linger inside you."

My cheeks heated, but the rapidly growing need was soon doused.

He set my foot on the stone. My hand slid down his hard chest when he rose to rinse the cloth. "Your aunt sent you a letter," he said, and so simply. "That you have not opened."

Ice began to drip from each newly warmed heartbeat.

I blinked at the rushing water. "Aunt?"

He wrung the cloth, dark brows crinkling when I met his eyes in the mirror. After a moment, his features eased into their usual apathetic state. He exhaled a dry sound that was not quite a laugh. "I take it he didn't tell you much about her."

"About this aunt?" I asked, knowing he was referring to Molkan. "Nothing. Who is she?"

"Your mother, Corina . . ." Florian set the cloth over the rim of the wash basin and turned to me. "She had a younger sister who keeps far removed from the royal family."

I stared at him, without a word to say as so many questions yet again plagued and paralyzed.

A knock came from outside.

He unhooked a fresh robe from behind the bathing room door and handed it to me. "Come, we'll eat and talk."

While he saw to the delivery of our breakfast, I brushed my

teeth and wild hair and failed to find a reason for this aunt's correspondence.

Florian was dressed in all black when I left the bathing room. His silk shirt gaped, gifting me a glimpse of the chest I'd had pressed against my own, as he opened lids and removed bowls from the silver tray.

He untucked one of the two chairs, and when I was seated, lowered into the other. His hair was still unkempt. I half hoped he'd leave it that way when he exited these rooms—tangled from my hands and carrying my scent.

As he fussed with dishes, I sipped the water he'd poured, then stared at the unopened letter from an aunt I wasn't sure I should wish to know. I wasn't sure what I really felt about it at all, but I asked, "Where is she?"

Florian set a bowl of blueberries before me. "Eat five of those, and I'll tell you."

"You're bribing me?"

"You've not been eating nearly enough since you came back to me."

*Since you came back to me.*

To better ignore the startling effect of those words, I stabbed a blueberry with my fork. "You mean since you stole me?" I chewed and smirked at him, eyes narrowed beneath my fluttering lashes. "*Again.*"

His own eyes narrowed, and his lips quirked. "If believing that makes you feel better, then I won't bother correcting you."

I snorted. But my smile fell as I ate more fruit and studied the elegant curl of Peony Boneblood's handwriting. "What could she possibly want from me?" The question wasn't supposed to be whispered. It wasn't supposed to sound jaded and fearful.

"We'll inevitably find out, but perhaps . . ." Florian stirred his tea. "To share some truth. From the little I know, she doesn't seem the type for games."

At that, I looked up, sensing he'd braced for it. I still said it, though it was with more humor than scorn. "Like you, husband."

He pushed the bowl of oats toward me without taking his dark gaze from mine. "Eat, *wife*."

I hid another smile behind the glass of water. Setting it down, I couldn't resist the urge to finally ask, "How *did* you do it? I read that contract multiple times."

"I know," he said, amusement curving his divine mouth. "So adorably thorough." Noting I had yet to touch the oats, he conceded, "It was double-sided, butterfly."

And my blood had bled through the parchment.

More impressed than angered, I found no response. So I ignored his smug satisfaction at my confoundment and began to eat.

Another knock arrived before he'd so much as looked at his own oats. This one was louder. Almost urgent.

"Enter," Florian called, still watching me as he sipped his tea.

Snow raced into the bedchamber ahead of Fume, who blinked at me before looking at his king. The firm set of his jaw as he closed his mouth and stiffened in the entryway made it obvious he was hesitant to share what he'd evidently been in a hurry to say.

But I didn't take it to heart. Not when I observed his drawn features and the pallor to his typically bright blue eyes.

Fear. It permeated from him with gentle lethality.

I bid Snow to sit when she came to my side, and placed my hand upon her head as Florian too sensed Fume's troubled state. He tore his gaze from me and set his teacup down with care that didn't fit his stern question. "What is it?"

"Outside," Fume said, and he didn't wait for the king before leaving.

Florian followed, a cloying cold mingling with his scent in his wake. His worry was such that he didn't close the door Fume had opened.

Whatever happened was bad enough that the two males didn't make it to the stairs to discuss it. I needn't have moved to eavesdrop, but I did pause in chewing to ensure I didn't miss anything.

"The eastern post at the border has been decimated." The king didn't respond, so Fume spoke again. "Wiped clean from existence, Florian."

Florian's question seemed far away, as if he couldn't believe what he was being told. Couldn't imagine it. "The entire post?"

"Yes, Flor. Gone. Tents, horses, even most of their damned belongings. Fucking gone."

Silence descended.

Snow groaned and flopped to the floor, her ears pricked.

Florian's next question was clinical—detached, even. "Witnesses?"

"One of the survivors was on duty close to the clearing," Fume said.

"Ready and guard them. I'll meet you there." A moment later, Florian returned and marched straight for his dressing chamber.

I dropped my spoon with a clang and followed.

He was stepping into knee-high black boots. A matching crimson-fringed cloak was ripped from a hanger. He froze when he saw me in the doorway.

I gripped the frame, unwilling to back down no matter how bleak his features. "Take me with you."

"You heard." He licked his teeth behind closed lips. "Of course, you did." He threw the cloak over his shoulders with a dry laugh. "Your aptitude for eavesdropping is exceptional, butterfly."

I didn't let those words sting. "One of the doors was left open, Majesty."

He pinched the bridge of his nose. His hand fell to his side as he exhaled roughly. "Then you know I have no idea what we'll find."

"Nothing," I said, not unkindly and stepping closer. "By the sound of it."

He stared at me in a way that made me wonder if he saw me at all. As if unable to digest that we were having this conversation. That something so horrible had befallen him—had befallen his people.

Just when I'd thought he'd materialize right then and there and leave me behind, he said, "Get dressed. We leave in two minutes."

There was no time for shock, and it was not the time to smile. But I couldn't deny that I was relieved he was allowing this.

I raced through the adjoining door to my rooms, Snow trailing as I hurriedly entered the dressing chamber and pulled clothing from hangers.

Florian stopped me from tossing another garment to the floor, his hand curling around my wrist. He brought it to his mouth and inhaled, then said, "Sit and put your boots on," before he instantly found something suitable.

He helped me into the simple yet elegant wool-lined blue gown that hugged my torso and fell with gentle weight to my ankles. Then he maneuvered my arms into a coat of black and gray fur.

He checked I'd buckled my black boots while I refrained from rolling my eyes. "We need to go," I said, which was unnecessary.

These were his warriors. He felt the gravity of urgency far more than me.

But despite the news Fume had delivered, Florian smirked as he rose to his full imposing height. It faded when he eyed me, a hint of concern tightening his mouth. "Perhaps you should—"

"Perhaps you should not finish that sentence." I clicked my fingers at Snow, who'd curled upon the cream linen of the bed I hadn't slept in for weeks. "Unless, of course, you want to piss me off."

The wolf followed us out into the hall, then vanished down the stairs.

"Troublesome creature." Florian stole my hand atop the stairs, tugging me close. "If you truly wish to run from me, this will evidently not be a safe place to try." His tone was mild, near playful, but when I looked up at him, the storm brewing in his gaze warned that he'd meant it.

I nodded, and he scowled as he took my other hand, so I said, "I know."

We materialized as soon as the promise left my mouth.

The instant scent of spring wafting from the border we stood near was a punch to the senses that cleared the dizziness caused by materializing.

Florian's hand gripped mine tighter as he released the other. "Butterfly?"

He accepted my nod, perhaps knowing I needed a moment to shake the instinct to flee as far from the border as possible.

Stone and wood and chimney smoke peeked through the woodland to our left. A village. Trees that stretched for miles surrounded the rest of the clearing. A clearing that was eerily empty, save for what looked to be metal gleaming beneath the sun.

"Julan," Florian informed. "The closest village to the border of Baneberry. So close"—he walked forward, taking me with him—"they share creeks with those in a town of Baneberry called Riddlen." He stopped a safe distance from some weaponry when he scented it—a strange aroma with an almost acidic bite.

Behind us, Fume was in quiet conversation with the warriors who'd been on duty during the disappearance of their encampment. Whispers and murmurings of witches and scents and other terms I knew little about carried easily due to the low-lying landscape.

Florian released my hand, his order stern. "Wait here."

I watched with a new terror, sudden and suffocating, as he walked among the remnants of his warriors.

He kicked at a shield, turning it over, then crouched down to pick up a blade.

It took strength I wasn't aware I had to bite my tongue. To keep from demanding that he drop the weapon and move away from where this strange scent lingered so potently. My hands curled before me, my nails digging into my skin, while he perused more objects.

"No pommels," he said, loud enough for all of us to hear. "No leather and no straps." He surveyed the grass that swished at his booted feet, the breeze throwing his hair across his cheek. He paid it no mind, lost in thought as his brows gathered and his fingers rubbed together. "Just metal crests and flasks and scraps of weaponry."

My eyes caught on the rows of tent pegs.

The warriors hadn't simply left, and though I didn't know how many had been stationed here, the sheer amount of remaining pegs suggested there'd been too many to capture and kill without leaving bloodied evidence behind.

Not a speck of blood could be seen. Not even the slightest scent.

It itched at my skin, prompting me to search the skies and treetops encircling the clearing. No birdsong. Even amid the harsh climate of Frostfall Mountains, there was always birdsong. Always life outside of the manor.

I strained to listen, scarcely allowing my eyes to leave Florian. Only faint scuttles and calls deeper within the woods.

Breath came easier when Florian finally returned. But although a spark of knowing gleamed in his gaze, every trace of the king who took endless pleasure in tormenting my heart and body within his rooms had been erased.

I didn't take his offered hand, but I did walk alongside him to meet with Fume.

The warriors behind the general bowed and lowered their heads. I blinked when they did so to me, my hands clenching tighter as one of them stared at us with a horror I knew all too well.

One that chased and clawed and devoured no matter how safe you were.

Only four of them were left. Four out of goddess knew how many. The blue of their uniforms was stark in this bright place that had been visited by darkness.

"Melaina." Florian's gaze fell upon the stricken female. "You saw what happened."

In similar uniform but with the markings of his rank, Fume stepped aside and gestured for the warrior to come forward.

The willowy female did with a slight tremble to her pointed chin as she inclined her head again. "My king, it was unlike anything I've ever seen. I don't know if I can even describe it."

"Try," Florian said. "For we must develop some idea of what transpired here if we are to stop it from happening again."

The cold authority in his voice brooked no room for further hesitation.

Melaina's gray colored gaze roamed beyond her king to where she'd last seen her comrades. "The entire encampment was wreathed in fog, which was nothing too unusual. But then it thickened, covered absolutely everything . . ." Her mouth quivered, and she closed her eyes. "That's when the screams began. I ran to help, but as I neared, I sensed it was no fog."

Grief shrouded her like a heavy cloak, waning her words and her delicate features. It wasn't a relief to be shown that some of these creatures were not without souls. If anything, it only made it more clear that some hadn't any souls at all.

"The others returned, but by then, it had started to take color as it faded with the screams. We could do nothing but watch and wait until it dissolved." Again, she looked at the clearing as if seeing what had once been. "It turned crimson f-from their . . ."

From their blood.

Wildflowers in yellows and golds swayed with long blades of deep emerald grass, seemingly untouched. Drops of metal and the slight flatness where tents had resided appeared to be the only disturbance to the landscape.

"And when it did dissolve?" Florian pressed, his tone only a fraction softer.

"Gone." Melaina swallowed, a lone tear sliding over her cheek. "The tents, the horses and livestock that couldn't escape . . ." Her head shook, as did her shoulders as more tears fell and strangled her words. "Gone, as if they'd never existed at all."

## 13

**Tullia**

We returned to the manor right after Melaina's haunting statement.

Florian released me and strode to his study with Shole, who'd been waiting in the foyer, his features grim as he'd straightened from the wall holding the portrait of Florian and his parents.

As none of them had the ability, Fume had been told to see to materializing the surviving warriors to the barracks here in the mountains. Another warrior arrived mere seconds after Shole and Florian had tucked themselves away.

Not merely a warrior, I noted when she bowed deeply upon seeing me. A red crest, that of a general, decorated her coat. Her plum-colored hair was short, framing sharp cheekbones and a prim jawline. Hazel eyes outlined with dark lashes twinkled as she straightened and smiled.

I failed to return it, but I nodded once before she vanished behind the study door.

I sat at the bottom of the staircase, unable to hear what was being said behind the spelled door and uncaring.

He'd shut me out.

It wasn't as if I'd attempted to follow him into his study. Still, I'd been excluded. I shouldn't have been surprised. It was what Florian was accustomed to—dealing with matters of extreme importance with those he trusted.

A smoky scent accompanied Fume's arrival in the foyer. He paused only briefly to glance at me, then marched into the study. The door closed behind him with a volume that made me flinch.

There was no use waiting for something that wasn't going to happen.

I stood and dragged my feet upstairs.

Olin's steps clacked behind me. "Where are you going?"

I would have thought that was obvious, and my flat tone and stare conveyed as much as I peered over my shoulder. "To wait for Florian to finish with his meeting."

"Of which you were not invited to attend," he said, the amused curl of his lips shifting his mustache.

I squeezed the railing to better refrain from cursing at him. "I'm not in the mood for your mood, Olin."

His eyes widened, then he scoffed. "And here I was, believing things were different now."

Stiffening, I took the bait. I stopped halfway up the last flight of stairs. "What is that supposed to mean?"

"You are a queen"—he inspected his elegant fingers—"and queens do not wait for scraps." He tipped a shoulder. "But what would I know, being in a mood and all." With that, he stuck his nose in the air and sauntered up the stairs to the second floor.

It wouldn't have surprised me if he'd made a tiny hole in the room above Florian's study to eavesdrop and keep the estate's rumor mill running steady.

Not a terrible idea, actually.

Irritation prickled, but only because he was right. For although I didn't feel like one, a queen was what I was. Even if I couldn't see it becoming *who* I was. Who I was now was nothing I recognized. A creature afraid of everything I'd once been so willing to embrace.

A fool afraid of rejection from my husband should I attempt to fit into places he'd spent years filling by himself.

The rows of glass displaying the courtyard captured my gaze.

Snow had well and truly ceased falling, workers clearing the melting mess.

I had more power than I ever could have dared to imagine. Yet my bones rattled at the thought of marching back downstairs to entrench myself deeper within this kingdom and its king's affairs.

And I hated it.

So much so that I let that self-loathing flood my limbs—the cracks within my heart—until my shoulders rose and my feet were moving.

I didn't knock. I opened the door to the king's study and closed it behind me.

Then I froze.

The female warrior I'd seen minutes ago looked from the maps upon the wall to me, her hazel eyes agleam and her mouth spreading into a grin her king could not see.

Fume scowled and seemed poised to rise from the armchair he sat in. Not to offer it to me but to send me on my way. Beside him, Shole smirked and eyed me curiously.

I ignored them all and stared straight at the king, who stood facing one of the windows beyond his desk. Hands tucked behind his back, he continued to gaze at the pebbled drive as he said, "We will be finished here shortly, Tullia."

The words left me with unexpected ease. "I wish to stay."

Fume failed to hide a shocked laugh with a cough.

Irritation bubbled my blood, further steeling my spine.

Florian said nothing. But he closed the drapes and turned to give me the full weight of the displeasure within his dark-blue gaze.

I remained by the door, clasped my hands before me, and gave him my best attempt at an unbothered smile.

A brow rose. He kept his attention fixed on me as he returned to the conversation I'd interrupted. "Thin and spread them out, Nirra. Make sure they're prepared while we make plans to bring them home."

"Home?" Fume questioned. "Florian, we cannot stop here, or it won't end."

I tilted my head at the king, curious about what had been said before I'd let myself in.

Florian sighed and looked at Fume. "I won't have more of our warriors killed by a foe who doesn't even have the courage to show his damned face."

"A witch," Shole said. "Has to be."

"It was faerie magic," Fume said as if he'd done so already.

"Name a faerie with the ability to decompose that many warriors in one clean sweep." Shole waited, then spread his hands. "Right. You fucking can't."

"So it was more than one, then," Fume argued.

Shole shook his head. "You even said it doesn't smell like faerie magic."

Fume reluctantly admitted, "It smelt like both witch and faerie." He paused. "And iron."

Such bickering made me wonder if the general and the mercenary were often not allowed to work with one another. At least any grievances about my presence were forgotten, as the two males leaned over the arms of their chairs to argue about the differences between witch and faerie magic.

"Due to my vast worldly experience, General, I've learned witch magic has a *very* specific reek to it," Shole taunted.

"As do you," Fume grunted.

"Now that would be the lack of a stick up my ass," Shole said with a menacing grin. "Remove yours, and you might live a little more, too."

Unable to help it, I snorted.

Nirra bit her lips, her eyes widening when Fume slowly turned to glare at me.

Shole noticed, and his smile stretched. "Our new queen is owed far more respect." He tutted and stood, then gestured to his chair. "Here, take my seat, Majesty. I'm quite done being so close to this cranky fuck anyway."

"I'm happy to stand," I said. "But thank you for the offer."

Shole inclined his head. "Wise choice." As he neared me, he whispered, "Care for a walk in the gardens, then?" He extended a large and calloused hand. "I hear they thaw rather nicely."

Withholding a laugh, I unlatched the tight lock of my hands to give him one. Humoring him might provide more information to put with what I'd gleaned thus far.

"Shole," Florian said far too softly.

Shole immediately released my hand. He winked when I stepped back for him to open the door and leave.

Fume stood. "Suppose there's little more to discuss."

"Oh, but there's plenty," Florian said with a look that was unmistakably a warning to his general.

Fume's stiff frame tensed further. But he nodded once.

Looking elsewhere, I gave him a wide berth as he exited the study. I was about to follow when Florian said to Nirra, "You have your orders."

"Indeed, my king." She bowed and materialized from the room, presumably to see to the outposts.

Once we were alone, Florian sat in the high-back chair at his desk. "Come to me, Tullia."

His tone told me I was going to be reprimanded. I didn't care to receive any such thing. I stared at him, studied those expressionless features, while he stared back.

He didn't stop me when I left the study and went in search of my wolf.

# 14

**Florian**

Tullia's rejection became a fist squeezing the disobedient organ in my chest.

I did my best to ignore it, as well as the impatience to return to her to discuss what the fuck had just happened.

Autumn, a witch from one of the few covens residing in Hellebore, walked the perimeter of the landscape that'd been filled with my warriors only yesterday. Her grandmother had been a dear friend to my mother for many years. I'd made sure to keep that connection after her passing for remedies and resources my own folk lacked the talent to supply.

The witch studied some of the metal lingering within the grass, her orange hair whipping around her wind-bitten cheeks. She looked at the sky, then at the treetops surrounding the clearing. "Do you hear that?"

I strained, but nothing was out of the ordinary. Wolf and birdsong floated in the distance, and noisy breaths of large beasts within nearby caves. The citizens of Julan were quiet, keeping indoors after what transpired so close to their quaint village. "I hear nothing."

"Exactly."

I refrained from scowling, awaiting the witch's assessment.

"It took the wildlife within reach," she finally said, kicking at a metal canteen. "The rest would've scattered upon sensing the fog's arrival. It appears to take those with hearts and anything soluble to feed to the soil."

"A decomposition mist, then," I confirmed. "Wielded by one

of our own." The ability wasn't common, which would assist us in finding the culprit.

"Yes." Autumn crouched to brush at some blades of grass. "It grows brighter here where the magic fed the land." She rose and gestured to where I stood. "Dim over there, and there's traces of iron."

"We scented as much."

"Faeries don't work with iron magic because of the obvious, and because it involves great sacrifice."

"It seems our enemies will sacrifice whatever they must to gain an advantage," I said coolly.

The witch curled her dancing hair behind her ear. "I've heard what he did to her," she said and stepped closer. "Could that have something to do with this?"

Cold blistered my blood and seeped into my low words. "My wife has nothing to do with this."

Although Tullia had yet to admit as much, her allegiance was undeniable at this point. She'd found her family, and the beast had ripped her soul in two before discarding her for the second time in her short life.

Autumn kept distance between us, her floral scent heightened by a spike of fear. "I'm not suggesting she was willing or aware, my king."

I absorbed that momentarily. Remembering how I'd found Tullia, the screaming as we'd removed the blanket stuck to her wounds, and the nightmares I feared might never cease . . . "It doesn't seem possible."

"Anything is possible with the right magic and ingredients," the witch said, careful. "Whoever has the ability to decompose did not act alone. Unfortunately, this fog eradicates even the scent of the wielders."

"Making them the perfect assassin." If things had been different, if they hadn't destroyed a unit of my military, then I'd consider hiring these sneaky assholes myself. I gazed around the clearing, rage curling my fingers. "I have grieving families who want answers. Retribution."

"We'll keep searching, but for now . . ." Autumn came to stand beside me, and we both observed the clearing. "We know it was a faerie who has amplified their magic with the help of a witch."

Tullia didn't move from the balcony door when I returned and shrugged off my cloak.

I tossed it over the chaise, and still, she just stared through the glass to the melting estate beyond. Anxiety ripened her sugary-sweet scent. But the stiff set of her shoulders and the stubborn height of her delicate chin told me she wasn't merely anxious.

My changeling-turned-queen was royally pissed off.

I took a seat at the table now emptied of our unfinished breakfast, and I waited.

Though it often thrilled me to see her riled, excited me even, I hadn't the desire to poke until she unleashed her adorable wrath upon me. Not when the reason behind her anger was not fear but hurt feelings.

Feelings always fucked things up.

The state of my kingdom was a prime example of that, as workers frantically scraped at sludge and hoped the winter would retreat long enough to allow the land to bloom.

But I couldn't do it—harness the ability to feel nothing as my father had when my mother died. He hadn't merely done so for the sake of the kingdom, as many of our people loved to believe. No, those closest to him knew he'd done so out of necessity.

He wouldn't have survived those two decades without numbing himself to the pain.

It was Lilitha's passing that had created a chasm no amount of concoctions and methods of escapism could hide. My sister never did do anything in half measures. Not even in her death.

Finally, Tullia deigned to acknowledge my presence. "You're annoyed because I interrupted your meeting."

She was right. I had been annoyed.

Though now, I was glad she'd disobeyed me by leaving the study. It had given me time to realize I hadn't been annoyed with her. I'd been annoyed with myself for the way I'd left her in the foyer without so much as an explanation.

"I was shocked," I decided on.

"As was I." Turning from the door, Tullia gathered her white-blonde hair over her shoulder. The wild curls covered one breast. "Shocked that I would so much as consider doing such a thing." She twined her fingers together, her teeth pinching her lip. She sighed and released it. "It wasn't like me, and it was disrespectful."

Mother of fucking skies.

It was as if I was wading through water without knowing how to swim. Yet even with my lack of experience with such typically frightful things like romance and shared lives, I knew it was wrong to say, "Is that an apology, butterfly?"

Tullia was not capable of appreciating my scathing humor right now.

She leveled me with a glare that might have sent me to my knees had I been standing, then turned back to the balcony door.

I almost swallowed my drying tongue.

A changeling she may have been, but at that moment, wearing the gown I'd selected and the displeasure that deemed me unworthy of a response, no one would know she'd ever been anything other than royalty.

I knew how to deal with royalty. I had no idea how to deal with the panic that tugged me to my feet and across the room.

Uncharted territory, indeed.

As I closed in behind her, relief bruised when I clasped her upper arms and she allowed it. "You have nothing to apologize for." I felt her shoulders drop a fraction. My lips roamed the soft skin beneath her ear, and I inhaled her scent deep before whispering, "I left you, and after including you in the discovery of something horrific."

Her silence was a knife dragging over my chest. But what she finally said sliced through skin. "You forgot me."

I nearly laughed at the absurdity. "Do I treat you like you're forgettable?"

"You did then." She turned to gaze up at me. "And I just watched others help themselves to access to you without any intention of trying to do the same." Before I could ask what had changed her mind, she pressed her finger against my lips. "I don't want to play games."

The sadness in those words singed. "I'll tell you anything you wish to know."

She took her touch away. "Yet you won't have me by your side as you deal with these things. Things that pertain to me, to all of us, and things that I wish to help with."

Oh, I knew exactly what this wife of mine wished to help me with—knew *exactly* what she wished for and what she needed— even if she wasn't yet ready to voice it. I'd known it since she'd mounted my cock in that dungeon, covered in gore, her thirst for blood still luminous in her dark gaze.

There was no hiding her hunger for vengeance when she wore it so well.

But now was not the time to force such an admission from her. "You have endured so much . . ." I trailed off when her head tilted and she released a bitter laugh.

"You really don't trust me, do you?" Her eyes dampened as they searched mine. "Perhaps you want a dutiful wife and an obedient mate to meet your needs, just as you first described in that rotting pleasure house, but you cannot have either if you're not willing to share more than scant pieces of yourself, Florian."

My chest tightened. My question incredulous. "Meet my needs?"

"You're not understanding what I said." She stepped back and carved me in two with the resolute darkness in her eyes. "You might have your queen right where you want her, Majesty, at your mercy once more." Her head shook. "But you cannot have me." With that, she dared to leave me to bleed.

Ice sealed the doors before she could reach them. Before I could think to control myself.

But I didn't want to, and I wasn't capable of realizing I'd trapped her when all I could feel was the wound she continuously deepened.

Tullia stared at the blood she'd drawn as it crawled up the wood, her hands forming fists at her sides.

Slowly, I stalked across the bedchamber as anger and fear warred with the foreign mess she'd created within me during the first skies-damned evenings we'd met. I flicked off the stopper to the whiskey on the shelf and poured a small glass.

"Unseal the doors, Florian."

I sipped and felt the burn join with that already scorching my throat.

Tullia marched to me and snatched the glass. I smirked down at her, but it fell when she tossed it across the bed to the fire. Glass crashed against the wood. The flames flared, yet she stared only at me. "Unseal the fucking doors."

I brushed my knuckles over her cheek.

She flinched, her heart thundering as she waited to see what I was playing at.

For I was always playing at something, and no one knew that better than the creature I enjoyed playing with most.

It didn't deter me. "Trust has nothing to do with it, butterfly." Confusion furrowed her golden brows. I spoke before those glorious lips could fully part. "I simply won't always know what to do with you because I've not done this before."

Realization crept into her delicate features. The result was breathtaking as her whiskey-colored eyes glossed and her cheeks stained a light pink.

I closed the small distance and stole her chin. I tilted it until her wet eyes swam with mine. Amusement etched my voice. "I trust you, though I likely shouldn't yet. I trust you because I want to." My thumb skimmed her lush lower lip. "Because never have I craved anything in all the ways I crave you."

She swallowed, her soft fingers wrapping around my wrist. "You've been given no choice, then." Though she might have intended it, the words lacked her sweet venom.

I fought a shiver as her fingers traveled down my wrist and forearm. "Precisely."

She stepped so close that when she lifted to her toes, her nose brushed mine. "Then *trust* me, Majesty, when I say the feeling is mutual."

Knowing she wasn't merely referring to the surrender of trust but as to why, my hard cock twitched, and my heart gave a giddy thump. I'd already known that she felt all I did—could feel it and see it during every exchange and touch, no matter which way she was heated.

But to hear a confession close to the one she'd given me before she left me . . .

I crushed her mouth and body to mine, my arm a bruising band beneath her ass as she climbed me, and my fingers disappearing into that snowy hair. The doors clattered when I pushed her against them and her skirts to her waist.

She reached between us to free my cock, but I couldn't wait.

I stole it before she could tease me with her touch and eased into the magic of her warm and wet cunt. Her exhale broke across my lips, tinged with the sweetest sound of victory, as her body welcomed mine with a greedy clench.

I remained still and deep for seconds that both relieved and blinded me with murderous desire. Being inside this female was unlike anything I'd felt before. It was not merely pleasurable; it was vital. A necessity that strengthened and weakened all that I was.

At first, I'd thought it merely the mating bond that made it so. But it hadn't lessened after days spent seeing to our curiosities and insatiable appetites. Bonds could be placated. After the wild surrender, they could be tamed and, sometimes, even rejected.

But this poison I couldn't live without had only worsened.

It wasn't the sex that sated and left me starved anew. It was her. The dark innocence. The sly confidence. The curious hunger. The stubborn determination that matched my own no matter how different the shade of our souls.

With a tug at my hair, her lips tore from mine. Her breaths panted. "This is madness, Florian."

"You do not seem the least bit concerned."

Tullia laughed, and I reclaimed her mouth to taste the intoxicating sound.

# 15

## Tullia

Florian returned with dinner and Snow, who waited for her meal to be set upon the floor with an impatient flick of her tail.

Freshly bathed and wearing a robe, I sat at the table while Florian washed up in the bathing room. He shook his wet hands on his way to his seat, then lowered with that eye-drawing grace. "Many of the encampments now journey back to the mountains," he informed, removing lids from dishes.

I watched steam rise from the green beans and mounds of beef, pondering if that was wise although I knew it was for the best.

A glass of water was poured and placed before me. He sensed I wasn't bothered by his absence but, rather, lost to this dangerous turn of events. I'd told him to tend to what he must after he'd fucked me against the doors, as he'd seemed poised to either do so again or crawl free of his skin.

Florian needed control, and Molkan had now broken the tight grip he'd held for almost two decades.

Twice.

There was no doubt Molkan was responsible for the decimation of all those warriors. Only one creature would dare to make such a bold move against Florian.

And it was likely he hadn't even left the safety of his palace walls to do so.

I'd spent the afternoon in the courtyard with Kreed. He'd had a friend in the unit erased from existence by the fog. So I'd sat with him for as long as he needed while we watched new buds unfurl upon the thawed hedges and vines.

Florian carved at his dinner as though it were my diabolical father's head.

"You don't feel at ease with your decision," I surmised.

Often, I treated my food the same way. Tonight, I took my time with slicing, imagining the meat was Molkan's unmerciful hands, clasped behind his back as he preferred, and he was trussed like a pig.

Comfort was now but a memory, so the small tastes my imagination provided were a luxury I quietly relished.

Florian didn't deny nor agree with what I'd said. "Molkan's revenge is cowardly but also frustratingly perfect."

Indeed. I'd thought no creature on this goddess-cursed continent had more patience than the male seated across from me. I'd thought wrong.

"Earlier, I met with a witch." He sipped his water and stared unseeingly at the fire. He set it down and licked his teeth. "Autumn. Her grandmother and my mother were close friends, and she inspected the site."

I continued slicing my meat. I wanted it in pieces before I ate. "What did she have to say?"

"She believes a faerie has sought amplification methods from a witch. No way of knowing who, exactly, for the fog erases scent." There was a pause before he said, "Well, most. A residue of iron was detected."

That made me look up at him. "Why would they use iron?" Surely, flesh-eating magic was plenty enough on its own.

"I'm assuming because of how it interacts with our skin. Therefore, combined with magic, the two can incapacitate completely." He studied my slack features. "And kill far more creatures."

I blinked down at my plate. But I was no longer so hungry, lost to how it might feel to die in that way—trapped and burning and then . . . gone.

Perhaps it wasn't as ruthless as other ways, I grimly thought. Ways that hadn't killed, but had made me wish for death countless times. Perhaps compared to most deaths, the fog was not so terrible. When compared to the gouging scrape of—

"Look at me."

The gruff order snapped me free of my spiraling thoughts.

Florian's gaze was dark. He nodded to my meal. "You've murdered it enough now, butterfly."

He was right. I'd created a small pool of bloodied meat. I stabbed some of the minuscule pieces and made no excuse for it. He didn't need or want one.

I chewed, and so did he, and we watched one another in silence.

It was a warm quiet. Snow tended to her feet before the crackling fire, her dinner long demolished, and the bowl licked clean.

"How many?" I eventually asked, sipping some water.

He knew what I'd meant. "Fifty-three."

I shook my head, fury curling my fingers tight around the glass.

"I've begun the visits with some of the families," he said.

It was hard to comprehend how anyone, even someone as vengeful and apathetic as he, could deliver news of that magnitude. "How do you manage such a thing?"

Most of his dinner finished, Florian set his cutlery down. "It's indeed not enjoyable." He looked over at the flames. "Once, quite some years ago, someone's brother tried to be rid of me with a pot of hard-boiled eggs as soon as I entered his restaurant to inform him."

I held back a smile, knowing it was not appropriate.

"Kent had been that young warrior's name. He was duped by one of Molkan's spies. Half of him was found in an old well of a nearby village a few days after his disappearance. The other half sent back to the encampment he'd foolishly strayed from after a night of too much ale.

"I suppose Kent's brother thought if he could just keep me from saying it, then it didn't happen." He continued to stare at the flames. "But this afternoon was different. It was . . ." He frowned and looked back at me. "These three families were so very quiet."

Before I could squash the impulse, I rose from my seat and rounded the table.

My hands clasped his, but he didn't allow me to pull him to his feet so that we could forget all the increasing horrors, even if for a short time. He pushed his chair back and tugged me between his spreading knees.

A shocked half laugh lightened my dry tone. "And here I'd thought you were heartless."

His lips curved as I lowered to sit across his lap. "Not entirely, it would seem." He shifted heavy strands of hair behind my ear, his thumb tracing the arch and his voice a deep whisper. "Disappointed, butterfly?"

"Extremely," I whispered back, then dodged his nearing lips before they muddled every thought and indeed made me forget anything but him.

He feigned a loud sigh.

I toyed with a button on his shirt as he reached for his water. "Regardless of who this witch might be, the ability to decompose comes from a faerie. We should simply go to the source." I watched his throat dip as he swallowed and set the glass down, my finishing words carrying much less volume. "Or who knows how far they might take this."

"Simply," Florian murmured, as if unsure such a word existed. "If this keeps up, we won't have the power to move against the source, butterfly." The arm curled around my back tightened. The fingers brushing my upper thigh crawled to my stomach as his hold turned from relaxed to possessive—worried. "We act now, when we know far too little, or we retreat and regroup until we know what we're up against."

I scowled at his chest. "We're up against a coward who now has a way to reach us whenever he so desires." I tried not to let the gravity of that unbending fact seep too deep beneath my skin. "He must be stopped."

He asked though he already knew, his eyes aglow, "What are you poking at, sweet creature?"

"You once said you would go to war." I took his hand when he reached for my chin and opened it in my lap.

Even his tone was knowing. "It is difficult to battle an enemy who refuses to engage, and though allowing his cowardice is likely what gave him the time to enact this plan with the fog, battle is now not enough to stop him."

I studied the length of his fingers compared to my own, the thickness and the slight calluses. "You did march." I remembered the message delivered while I was chained to the cold metal table warmed by the endless spilling of my blood. I would never forget. "You intended to attack Baneberry in earnest."

Florian went so incredibly still. "And how might you know about that?"

"The poisoned messenger you sent," I said, toneless, and met his eyes. "Word arrived while Molkan was . . ."

His features creased, then turned to stone.

I looked down at our hands. "I'd thought I was the excuse you needed." Yet, in the end, there had been no battles. No war. I'd heard nothing of any bloodshed. Just as Molkan had predicted, Florian had pulled back.

Continuously, I failed to confront what that could mean.

"The excuse," he repeated, as if tasting something sour. He gripped my cheek and jaw, and forced my gaze to his. Sincerity roughened his voice. "For you, I would do far worse than wage war, and I do hope you're finally beginning to understand that."

As I stared at him, my heart bruised with erratic beats. "I did not think you were one to believe in hope."

His thumb brushed the corner of my lips. "A troublesome changeling might have poisoned me with her sweetness."

I laughed, but as he stole my mouth with a kiss so soft it threatened to bring tears to my eyes, I pushed at his chest. I could no longer keep my suspicions to myself. "Would many faeries have the ability to decompose?"

As with any immense magical ability, it had to be inherited from somewhere important.

Florian confirmed as much. "Though it's somewhat rare due to descending from ancient royal and noble lineage . . ." His teeth skimmed his lip, his eyes glazed with lust. "I'd wager at least a few hundred."

That failed to change what I felt deep within my tired bones. "I think I know who it might be, Florian."

His eyes darkened as his head tilted. He released my face and dropped his hand to my thigh, waiting.

I felt nothing for it. I couldn't allow myself to. Avrin might have helped me, but he'd also done nothing to stop the horrors unleashed upon me. If anything, he hadn't even tried.

"A mist was used when the hunt visited Crustle." The memory of it, the ease in which my guardian had simply ceased to be, was as bright as the night it had happened. "Used on Rolina."

The king tensed beneath me. "Used by whom?"

"Avrin. Molkan's adviser," I said. "Right-hand. Whatever he might be."

"He is whatever Molkan needs him to be." Setting his elbow on the table, Florian rubbed at his bristle-covered jaw. "Such a position now makes more sense." He searched my gaze as if he saw the confliction within, no matter how small, from handing the name over. "He has a brother in the hunt."

I nodded. "He told me that, yes."

"He told you that," he repeated, his contemplative state now one of intrigue as his eyes narrowed. "Just offered it to you in passing, did he?" he asked coldly. "Or maybe while he was torturing you?"

"Over dinner, actually."

Though the words had been matter of fact, they still made Florian's fingers curl away from his chin and erased his features of expression.

"Interesting," he finally said.

I held his gaze—allowed him to see that I had nothing to hide. He could ask me anything he wished.

He didn't.

He said, "Let's say it is Avrin." His intense stare strayed to the fire again. "He does not roam far from Molkan's side, and when he does, he has the protection of the hunt and the ability to materialize."

He knew his opponents well. Before I could wonder or ask just how well, he looked back at me as he decided, "I need to speak with Shole."

Of course he did. Yet I held no resentment, only an understanding I should have rejected.

Given everything, I couldn't. His people needed him to act. I was unable to deny that I did, too. Nor that perhaps he was no longer the tyrant I'd once believed him to be. Not entirely, anyway, and not without reason—of which I'd been shown by his enemy.

"Then go. I wish to sleep."

He stopped me from leaving his lap and assessed my face with lowered brows. Then he gripped my throat and kissed me, whispering to my mouth, "You're a lousy liar, but I'll deal with you when I return."

"Don't make threats you might not keep."

★　★　★

Florian did not return until dawn painted the horizon with light.

His presence was made known by a brush of his fingers over strands of my hair upon the pillow.

Through the filmy haze of sleep, I watched him change before leaving again, then I took my time rising. I washed the residue from the nightmares down the drain, wishing the water would carry them away forever. Wishing it would eradicate the sound of Molkan's voice from my mind.

*Just look at you. Weak and filthy creature.*

My hold on the hairbrush slipped.

I put it down and made my way into my rooms to find something to wear. It was odd to still think of them as mine. None of this was mine. Yet all of it was, and it would be for as long as I drew breath.

Once, I'd naively accepted what marrying Florian would entail. Now, I could scarcely think it, let alone believe that I was his wife.

That I was Hellebore's queen.

Snow's claws clicked against gaps of stone between the carpets. She sat upon the curtained bed while I selected a burgundy gown with long sleeves that flared at the wrist.

The rich velvet was a soft embrace, molding to my torso and rising high at the neck to my chin. I had no plans nor the energy to venture far. I wished to eat breakfast in the kitchen with Kreed as I once had, so I chose a simple pair of black ankle boots and told Snow to follow me downstairs.

Doors opened down below.

Voices carried as I hesitantly descended the stairs, feminine and somewhat familiar.

Olin turned in the foyer, appearing almost relieved as he noted I was dressed in something suitable to greet our unexpected guests.

Queen Aura and Queen Mercury.

Shockingly, the steward bowed his head to me. Maybe after his scolding on how I should act like a queen, he'd realized it might be time to treat me like one. "Tullia, you've met Queen Aura, and this is her wife, Queen Mercury."

A brown gown that lovingly hugged numerous curves shimmered gold within the morning light as Mercury stepped forward. A sharp yet somehow fitting contrast to her wife's ensemble. Aura wore a long gown of sea-green netting, and a slip of turquoise silk beneath that reached mid-thigh.

Mercury's amethyst eyes gleamed as bright as the jewels drowning her wrists and ears. Wheat-colored hair swished over her shoulders as she inclined her head with a ruby-lipped smile. "I've heard much about you, changeling."

Snow remained at my side as I ceased gaping and continued down to the foyer to greet them.

"Including rumors that you might need some military assistance." Aura met me beneath the stairs and took my hand. With a knowing squeeze, she pulled me close. Her green eyes darkened as her whisper chilled. "To make sure he pays."

# 16

## Florian

Three corpses gave audience to the carving and consuming of my breakfast.

An apple.

I'd rather be enjoying a meal with my wife, who was beginning to warm to me in splendid and much-needed ways. But I could no longer sit still due to the state of things. I could scarcely enjoy anything without remembering.

He'd mutilated my mate's heart and soul.

And now, more than fifty warriors were simply . . . gone.

I tossed the core at Lord Hummington. It hit his decaying cheek with a fascinating sound, then fell to the bloodstained dirt.

The reek of death seldom bothered me. In the past, I'd even found it comforting. To know that it was real, no matter how long we carried on like indulgent and untouchable assholes.

Chewing with unnecessary vigor, I pondered what Tullia had divulged for the hundredth time since the words had left her divine lips.

Avrin.

She'd had dinner with him. Which, after what he and Molkan had done to her, likely meant very little. I could have pressed her to tell me more. She'd seemed to expect me to, and I certainly should have.

Something had stopped me. Fear, maybe. For there had been some hesitance in surrendering his name.

Instead, I'd met with Shole to discuss Molkan's puppet. And I'd tacked on an order before we'd parted ways—to find out if Avrin was whom Molkan had intended to wed Tullia to before they'd discovered she was all fucking mine.

Fume arrived and whistled. "Someone got a bit carried away."

"She did, and it was glorious." It was almost a shame to get rid of the art my wife had made.

Flies and other less-than-lovely critters crawled from the numerous gaping holes Tullia had given Lord Hummington. He was nothing but a head and limbs, really. But if you looked closely, you could see it.

The beautiful markings of unleashed grief and rage she'd bestowed on him.

In my humble opinion, he didn't even deserve that much from her.

I rose from the pail I'd perched upon. Fume stared at the corpse as if unsure he believed Tullia was capable of such brutality.

Admittedly, I had been shocked as shit myself when she'd taken that blade from me to hack at the lord. I'd also been shocked to feel so instantly and immensely aroused.

I sure as fuck wasn't confessing any of that aloud, and certainly not to Fume. "I took some of the fingers," I told him. "And his canines, of course."

"Of course," he said absently.

I chuckled, then sighed and clapped him on the shoulder. "Fear not, I'm sure your queen will forgive your hostility all in good time. If not, I won't let her hurt you." I paused for emphasis. "Too much." I clapped him harder for extra emphasis.

My general and friend received the warning loud and clear.

"I harbor no ill will toward her, Florian." He finally blinked, rubbing a hand through his fluffy hair. "I just didn't want any of our careful planning, all these years of work, to slip from our grasp." His hand fell as his jaw set. "Like it now has."

"Be that as it may," I drawled tightly, as he was right, and we needed to work faster to find a way to regain control. "That's not Tullia's fault." I looked back at the corpse still hanging from the rafter in the dirt ceiling. "It's my own."

Fume did not refute that.

Footsteps crushing the wet grass outside infiltrated the silence. Henron's voice followed as he skidded to a stop atop the dirt-packed stairs. "Majesty?" His breathing was labored as if he'd run circles around the estate searching for me.

Fume stuck his head into view. "He's down here."

"Skies." Henron whined with relief. "Merciful Mother."

Fume waved his hand. "Just spit it out."

"His Majesty is needed at the manor urgently. Oleander." The stable hand paused to suck in a large inhale. "The queens. They're here."

Fume looked at me with wide eyes.

No time for walking, being that I had no idea what Aura was playing at with this visit.

As I materialized, I said to Fume, "See that the nobles are disposed of, and I'll consider letting you breathe near my wife."

## 17

**Tullia**

An iced breeze followed Florian through the arched entryway to the courtyard.

Mercury turned from where she'd been admiring the birth of new roses in the hedge. "He deigns to bless us with his presence."

Beside me, Aura lifted her teacup to her painted lips and snorted. "You stink of death, darling."

That drew my eyes to the king's. He brushed his hands over his long black coat. They were clean. At least, they appeared to be. Bending his towering frame, he clasped Aura's hand and brought it to his mouth.

He kissed it, then gave Mercury the same greeting. But it was accompanied by a dry question. "Should I be concerned about your presence?"

She smacked his arm and pulled him to her with strength that shocked to hug him. "You will be if you do not give us the recipe for Kreed's miniature cakes."

"Indeed." Aura took one of the last from the tray between us and spoke around the sugared fluff with a slight moan. "So fucking good."

Releasing Mercury, Florian huffed. "He'll never surrender it."

Mercury scowled up at the king in a way that might intimidate most. It only made him smirk as he stepped back and cocked his head toward me.

"Shame." Aura licked her fingers. "Perhaps we'll need to reconsider our offer, then."

Florian's gaze burned a violet blue beneath the glow of the autumn-flavored sun. I hid my smile behind my cup of tea. His eyes narrowed, his shoulders pulling taut as he looked back and forth between the two queens.

Mercury resumed her inspection of the winter-ravaged garden, feeding warmth that seeped from her fingertips like a ball of moonlight to the buds. "Oh, don't be so nervous, dearest. Have we ever delivered you bad news?"

Florian raised a brow at Aura. "Shall I answer that honestly?"

Aura feigned exasperation. "We've decided that we're ready to assist you in your efforts to squash Molkan."

Florian's eyes widened ever so slightly, then he blinked at me. He didn't ask them what had changed their minds, though I knew the desire to do so poked behind his teeth when he flashed them at Aura. "You're ready," he simply said.

"That is what she said," Mercury sang, close to laughing as she moved down the line of hedges.

"Your lovely wife," Aura said with far too much enjoyment, "has been chatting with us about this fog that ate your warriors. The decimation of so many souls in one strange sweep cannot continue."

"And continue he will," Mercury said. "Another regiment will certainly fall all too soon, if not all who occupy this very manor."

My hold on the teacup tightened.

Florian was not so shocked that he reminded them that this war between Baneberry and Hellebore had nothing to do with Oleander, like I had some minutes before his arrival in the court-yard. But he began to pace the path from the door to the arched tunnel leading to the rear gardens.

Aura slurped her tea while giving me a fluttering sidelong glance.

Mercury stated what had already been said to me—what Florian now understood. "With such a weapon in his grasp,

145

Molkan might not stop with Hellebore's military," she said. "Nor with you."

Florian halted at the archway and stared into the shadows. "He could try to take so much more."

My father could have every realm of Folkyn at his mercy, eating out of the palms of his cruel hands.

We soaked that in for a silent minute, and a shiver straightened my spine. It was not so hard to imagine, given the lies and the brutality I'd experienced from Molkan and those close to him.

"He's likely realized this, too," Florian surmised.

"If he hadn't before he conducted his first test." The clash of porcelain meeting was sharp as Aura set her teacup in the saucer. "So shall we move indoors?" She didn't wait for a response.

Mercury ceased fussing with the roses and joined her wife at the door.

I watched them enter the manor, then stood and gazed up at Florian when he neared. "You've already given the order for the warriors to return home."

He grazed his knuckles over my cheek, then gently splayed his hand on my lower back, prompting me to walk ahead of him. "We've yet to decide on anything, butterfly."

I smiled as I headed inside. "Of course."

A decision was indeed made, and with far too much ease to provide comfort.

Perhaps I'd merely grown too cynical. Repeatedly, I mulled over the conversation I'd witnessed in Florian's study. Seated before the fire, I searched the gaps between things left unsaid and those that had been.

Snow snored upon the bed, exhausted after a day spent exploring the melting estate for treasures hidden beneath the sludge. I'd watched her from the balcony after Mercury and Aura had left, the weather crisp but not so much that I remained behind the glass doors.

Five hundred warriors awaited the order from Aura and Mercury.

A small portion, Aura had informed, of what was available should we need more. Given their previous reluctance to partake in the hostility between Baneberry and Hellebore, it was more than generous.

It was a powerful display of allegiance, regardless of Oleander's agenda.

And though I was fond of the queens, I'd learned in more ways than one since that inciting visit from the Wild Hunt and Rolina's death that an agenda always stood behind any act of decency from the royals of Folkyn.

"This can't just be about the fog. They must want something else," I said when Florian exited the bathing room.

He entered the bedchamber with a comb in hand and a towel clinging to his defined hips. "I would be disappointed if they hadn't any ulterior motive."

I smiled at the flames.

His energy cloaked before his body, as he lowered behind me and spread his legs astride my thighs. My hair was gathered at my back, his fingers tickling the bare skin above the towel loosely covering my torso.

As he combed and untangled the strands, my own fingers twined in my lap. "And what is your ulterior motive, Majesty?" I'd meant to ask teasingly, but it was whispered instead. "Ensure I'm well and truly drowsy before you skip away to find more darkness to play within?"

"You said you wished to sleep," he reminded me, gently tugging at a tangle. "If you must know, this morning I was spending some quality time with the nobles we butchered."

That roused me from my rapidly relaxing state. "Why?"

"I had a message to send." He said no more, and sensing he didn't want to, I didn't press. But he added, "And I do not skip, *wife*."

I laughed.

He hummed, slowing as he dragged the comb through the strands at my lower back. "That sound."

Though he couldn't see, I smiled and closed my eyes, relaxing once more. "What do you think the queens want?"

"We'll eventually find out," Florian said, and so calmly.

"Why wouldn't they just state it?"

"Birthing a negotiation requires careful skill and patience," he said, a touch of cold humor to his tone. "One is always better off withholding their full desires in case they end up duped or"—he paused to lay his lips upon my bare shoulder—"discover something they want more."

The heat of his mouth and his words elicited a shiver. "How long did it take you to learn such a skill?"

"Many decades of watching my father deal with folk who tried endlessly to pick at the life he'd made until some of our treasure bled into their own lacking lives."

Recalling what Molkan had said about Florian's parents, I nearly shivered for different reasons and opened my eyes.

Florian resumed untangling my hair as I said, the confession barely carrying sound, "He spoke of them. Molkan." He waited while I found the courage to fight the chilling memories of walking through those spring-washed gardens. "Of your mother and father and how the three of you were the source of much envy with your seemingly perfect fairy tale."

The teeth of the comb were more gentle over the traitor mark, as if he'd memorized each scarring curl of the snake I'd wear forever. He didn't speak for so long that I began to think he wouldn't.

When he did, his voice was rough. "It was perfect."

"Until Lilitha," I said, not unkindly. "That is what they say."

"And they are not entirely wrong to, though I still loathe it."

"So many have spoken of her, Florian, yet I've seldom heard what you have to say."

Maybe time was responsible. Maybe he was doing as he'd vowed—beginning to earn my trust. I didn't know. But it seemed I'd encountered a confidence to dig for things I once wouldn't have. At least, certainly not without restraint.

So although he was silent for another stretched minute, I didn't brace. I didn't fear rejection or redirection. I merely waited.

"It's difficult to speak of something more powerful than words." His admission held a weight that sank beneath my skin. "Something that both saves and destroys."

The fire blurred as my eyes grew damp.

Knowing exactly how it felt to have no desire to speak of matters of the heart, I chose not to say anything more. I watched the fire, luxuriated in the warmth and each tickling swipe of the comb.

"She was born in the in-between." The low words fractured the silence. "In the fleeting moments between night and dawn upon the week of the great thaw. Fitting," he said, quiet and somewhat distant, "for a creature who never wanted to fit into any defined space."

His combing slowed, as did my heartbeat.

"She didn't cry, but my father did. His agony trembled the very mountain this manor resides on. Some even say they felt his anguish from the barracks in the city outskirts. He was desperate with despair, upon the edge of life and death himself, as my mother faded in a pool of her own blood."

My eyes caught the scrunching of his toes before he bent his knees and flattened his giant feet over the floor.

"It wouldn't stop." He swallowed thickly. "It was everywhere. I'd known the dangers of birth. That such a significant creation robs strength and drains bodies faster than they can replenish, yet I'd never seen it . . ." He cleared his throat, a slight shake to his hand as he kept combing.

My hair didn't need more attention. I doubted it had ever been so smooth and detangled in my entire life. But I didn't dare stop him.

"I promised her. While my father roared at every grieving soul in the manor to help him, to save her, I promised my mother that I'd take care of them. I took Lilitha from the crook of her arm, and it was as if she'd held on for just that."

"She needed to know," I rasped.

"A mere moment later, her unseeing eyes still upon the blood-ied babe tucked against my chest, she was gone. My father knew. He was still downstairs, but he knew. And his bellowing and roaring . . ." He exhaled sharply. "It stopped. Then I watched from their rooms as he fell to the grass outside. Birds were shaken from treetops and lingering snow from the mountains."

He finally ceased combing. "When he returned, it was as if his soul had left his eyes. He took one empty look at his new daughter in my arms, and he made us leave. He remained with my mother for days until I enlisted help to have him restrained and her body removed. Even then, he stayed in their rooms." A harsh huff. "And he rarely ever left."

"Where are their rooms?" I asked, though I had a feeling I already knew.

"We're sitting in them." Noting my shock, and lack thereof, he released a rough chuckle and pressed his mouth to my shoulder. "The bed has always been my own."

I turned to scowl at him, as that wasn't why I'd asked, and he took the opportunity to seize my face. He kissed me, once and lingering. His eyes closed as he drew away and licked his lips. "Sweet indeed." He rose and walked to the bathing room, comb in hand.

I traced my lips, still feeling the touch of his. "You did raise her, then."

"I did," he said.

Out of all the questions to ask, one I hadn't expected pushed free. "Did you name her?"

He returned and readied the bed. "My mother suspected she was carrying a female, and she'd already chosen her name." The pillows were fluffed, then he padded into the dressing chamber. "Not once," he said when he emerged in a pair of tight pants and tugged on a dark gray tunic, "did I blame Lilitha for what happened to our family."

"It would have upset her," I surmised. "That others looked at her as the reason for such heartbreak."

"It would upset anyone, no matter how dark and depraved the soul, of which hers was not."

I tried to match that with what else I'd heard of Lilitha, yet as I studied her brother while he secured his thick hair at his nape, I was confronted by something I'd tried to ignore. The undeniable proof that one could be monstrously ruthless and cunning, but that did not mean they were without heart.

It meant they'd once had too much.

"I've never met a creature so vivid and daring who loved more than Lilitha. Wild, most certainly"—he chuckled, adjusting his sleeves—"but with a zest that often makes me wonder if she'd known her life would be cut short."

Though I craved more, Florian evidently had other places to be. Likely many after our meeting with the queens.

"Rest." He stepped into his boots and snatched his dagger from the drawers. "If we're doing this, then weeks of terrible sleep and food await us."

I crawled to the side of the bed and laid my chin upon it. "You won't ask me to stay behind?"

He stilled, then slowly turned. "There's no glory in victory if you're not present for it, sweet creature." Firelight flickered over his features as he watched me. "Besides, you're safest with me."

Once, I'd have thought that to be a tremendous lie. Once, I'd have told him he was a monster for what he was planning to do.

Now, I hoped he truly heard me when I whispered, "I know I am." Some of the heaviness within my chest dissolved as I then confessed, "But I don't want glory, Florian."

"I know exactly what you want."

I smirked. "And what makes you so certain?"

Unmoving and swathed in golden light and shadows, he stared at me from across the bed. He left his assessing trance with a murmured, "I recognize the look in your eyes. The swelling cadence of your heartbeat when you so much as think of it."

Said heartbeat faltered. "When I think of what?"

"Vengeance, of course." His teeth flashed with a half grin. "Sleep. Tomorrow, you learn how to ride a horse."

Then he vanished.

# *18*

**Tullia**

Three days passed in a flurry of preparations.

Beneath it all, trepidation lurked throughout the estate. I didn't doubt that everyone wanted the threat we were facing extinguished now that news of the deadly fog had spread, but there was something more to it.

An undercurrent of impatience that I sensed had nothing to do with Molkan.

An edginess, perhaps, that spoke of a desperate and tired desire to see this through after years of seldom broken winter and potential warfare.

Arryn disappeared with Snow as soon as we'd arrived in the kitchen for breakfast, barely pausing to bid me hello.

Thistle remained, assisting his father with cuts of meat while I ate. When he asked if the traitor mark still hurt, he was immediately dismissed with an order to return within the hour. "Don't make me send anyone for you," Kreed warned. "There is too much to do."

My imaginings and the tales I'd read of journeys and war had been nothing like this.

I'd envisioned a mass of darkness ready to battle, not a household of staff readying provisions for the long journey and a king bouncing from one meeting to the next. It made sense, I supposed, yet I wished those tales and my naive imagination had proven true.

I itched to leave. To also see this through.

After cleaning my breakfast bowl and glass, I joined Kreed before the array of dried meats, fruits, and nuts. "Are there more pouches?"

The flustered cook blinked at me.

I gave him a look that said not to waste time by arguing.

He gestured to the storeroom on the other side of the kitchen. I found the pouches in a hessian sack that made me think of severed heads. Of Fellan, Zayla, and the driver. Of my blood ceaselessly dripping from a metal table to the floor.

"You may as well bring them all out," Kreed called, effectively extracting me from the coppery haze.

I picked up the sack and ignored the numbness in my fingers beneath the rough fabric. Choosing the wall where my breakfast stool once stood, I set it down and plucked a handful of the soft little bags from within.

They fluttered to the countertop. I snatched one and opened it, dropping almonds within. "What will you do while we're gone?"

"Protect the manor and staff alongside other warriors. They're mostly veterans. The rest are needed to watch over the city since it holds the largest portion of Hellebore's population."

And such devastation would be colossal with a decomposing fog on the loose.

"But I think I'll take a quick nap first," he said, his big fingers struggling to place dried meats into a pouch.

Thinly, I smiled. "Good idea."

"Winter isn't merely thawing," he whispered after some soothing minutes of working in silence. "Even with all that's transpiring, many say they've not seen the king like this in years."

"Like what?" I foolishly had to hear it.

"He'll never be who he once was." The gentle gravity behind that statement hit me in the chest. "But this is the closest he's been since, well"—he shrugged—"since before."

Since his father and sister died, leaving nothing but a barren heart and endless winter in their wake.

Unsure what to do with that and unable to meet his eyes, I frowned at the pouch he struggled with. I took it from him and set it on the counter. "I'll do these. Go tend to something else on your gargantuan list."

"You're no queen," he said, already hurrying away. "You're a fucking goddess."

I snorted, feeling so very far from both. But the simplicity of the task he'd entrusted to me was somewhat comforting as my mind whirled with what-ifs and memories and future fears.

In four days, we would be on our way to Baneberry to knock Molkan from his perch of lies.

Just four more days of waiting, and then I might finally taste it. That freedom I'd unknowingly once had. That I'd so recklessly abandoned for foolish dreams of finding a place to belong and family who wanted me.

I wasn't sure what Molkan's death would bring. If it would even return that freedom, or if it would only grant relief that he could never again touch me. All I knew was that I needed it. To breathe without feeling the brutality of his betrayal. To fall into sleep without being afraid of dreams turning into nightmares.

To look in the mirror and know that, despite all of the stupid decisions I'd made because of a desperate hope, it was not my fault, I would be okay, and it would *never* happen again.

Judging by the amused glint in his midnight eyes, I sensed him far later than when he arrived.

Florian leaned against the wall by the door, his booted ankles crossed and his open coat brushing the sack of pouches beside him. His near-black hair was bound yet anything but tidy, a piece falling across the violent crest of his cheek. "Hiding, butterfly?"

155

The twins burst through the door from outside, bringing noise and cool air into the musty room.

They froze at the sight of Florian, then bowed. All the while, Snow strutted past them to deliver the king her fresh kill.

"Should've seen it, Florian," Thistle said, gesturing to the ceiling. "She flew over a log three times the size of her and snatched it midair before rolling to her feet."

Florian removed his attention from me with a slowness that said he'd indeed been pondering my state of mind and crouched to greet my wolf.

Perhaps she was his now. I didn't know, nor did I mind.

Snow pawed at the poor hare's lifeless form, evidently proud of herself as she gazed at the king with her tail swishing. "We should bring you with us," he said to the wolf, scratching behind her ear. "Save us some work."

I crinkled my nose at the dead creature, then returned to my task as Arryn tried to show his father what Snow had done, and Thistle tried to convince Florian to bring him on our journey south.

"You're needed here," Florian said, and with a gentleness I'd seldom heard. One that was different from the taunting softness he bestowed upon me in private. "Someone needs to keep Olin's panic under control."

Kreed snorted, then halted as he exited the storeroom to find the hare suspended right before his nose. "Skies, Arryn, get that fucking thing out of my kitchen."

His son laughed. "But it's what they'll eat on their travels."

"Should they run out of provisions because you and your brother were fluffing about, maybe," Kreed chastised, dumping a slab of meat to prep for cooking on the countertop. He sent me a sidelong glance. "Pray to the goddess that you don't."

Florian huffed. "Hare is still considered a delicacy in some places."

"Perhaps in the mortal and middle lands, Majesty," Kreed responded with a shake of his head.

Florian did not argue that, but he sent Snow upstairs before saying, "I fear hare may be present in our future regardless."

Kreed tensed, giving the king his whole attention at the same time I did.

"Come, butterfly." A grim hardness now sharpening his jaw, Florian extended his hand. "I need to speak with you."

I wiped my hands on a dish towel and crossed the room. But I could only stare at that offered hand. It would be so easy to take it, to allow others to believe he was truly my husband and that I was truly forgiving of his actions.

Easy, yet I couldn't seem to do it.

Certainly not in front of Kreed, who pretended to be absorbed in feeding the flames of the stove.

I'd given him so much more than my hand that rejecting him felt asinine. Even so, Florian knew he did not have all of me and that, despite his ruthless determination and beliefs, he might never. Not entirely.

His clenched jaw ticked, but he said nothing as I walked by him in silence and upstairs.

Staff did not cease their rushed activity for more than a nod as we passed. Florian caught up with me at the grand staircase. He didn't speak. We veered right at the landing to the second floor.

The ballroom contained packs housing extra tents and bedrolls, other supplies stacked around them in small trunks. We trailed the hall surrounding the stairs to the other side, walking by an empty sitting room and a handful of closed doors.

At the end of the hall, directly beneath my rooms, Florian stopped before another closed door. A rusted key was procured from a pocket in his black trousers. Dust-sprinkled sunlight splashed him as the wood creaked open.

He waited, and I walked in ahead.

A giant bed stood center. The wooden frame had been left in its natural state and the four posts painted white with vibrant flowers upon them.

I knew without asking that we were in Lilitha's rooms.

More dark and white wood decorated the vast space so similar to what had been gifted to me. "Were the rooms you gave me once your own?"

"They were," Florian said, a smirk lilting his voice. "I refurnished before your arrival."

I withheld a sharp retort. It was wasteful when I seldom spent time in them now. His efforts were also unbearably thoughtful—the care he'd taken in selecting my clothing, the books, and even the supplies in the bathing room.

Unbearably thoughtful and incredibly calculated.

I smiled down at the white dresser I trailed my fingers over. Only he could make such a contradiction seem to work.

Yet I couldn't forget that those rooms had been a pretty cage for a creature being prepped for slaughter.

The twinge in my chest stilled my feet.

It worsened when my finger paused upon a book with a piece of parchment poking from the center. Out of all the belongings flooding this chamber, that nicked at my heart the most. Lilitha hadn't known how the story ended.

Carefully, I picked up the novel and blew the dust from it.

A fairy tale from the mortal lands. Well loved, I deduced, hoping the signs of wear were not merely due to its age but that they meant the young princess had read this book cover to cover countless times.

Knowing what I was thinking, Florian said quietly, "She left many stories unfinished."

I placed the novel back where Lilitha had left it and followed him deeper into the room to the light wooden shelving stretching beneath the row of arched windows.

Atop them, dried inkpots and quills collected dust and sunshine. Gilded hairbrushes of every size sat in a basket next to spilled tins of what appeared to be rouge. It stained the wood a blushing pink and ruby red, hair pins scattered amidst the color.

Florian gazed through the last window, hands tucked within his pockets. "She would rarely finish anything she started." He smiled wryly. "Including that of forbidden relationships with males who sought only to use her affections until she was wrung dry."

"Molkan was not the first, then," I surmised.

"And he was not the last, as much as he wishes differently."

Confusion struck, and I was glad he wasn't facing me as I absorbed what he'd said. It didn't fit with what I'd been told. Then again, everything my father said had likely been nothing more than elaborate lies—like those he'd told his guests during his ghastly ball.

"Which is why we're all here and she is not." Those dark words slithered through the cold air of his sister's bedchamber.

Sensing I might need to should he divulge anything more about the father I didn't want to talk about, I was tempted to take a seat on the bed.

Unlike everything else, which appeared to have been kept exactly as Lilitha had left it, it was tidy. The vibrant green sheets and emerald blankets were tucked tight at each corner, and the frilled pillows perfectly placed before the headboard.

Then I saw the map beside Florian.

A map covered by a large ruined painting of a sunlit house that stood atop a cliff looking over the sea. "She wished to live there, wherever there is." He set the painting with three jagged rips through the canvas against the wall. "I never found out. She destroyed it not long before she died, and now"—he leaned against the windowsill, ankles crossed—"it's where I keep this."

159

"The real map," I said, studying the wax markings on the land-scape depicted.

I'd seen such a map before, only far smaller. At this angle and size, the continent of Mythayla seemed different from what I'd studied in books. "It almost resembles a squeezed lemon." I tilted my head. "And the wax markings mildew."

Florian hid a grin, maybe even a silent laugh, behind the hand he rubbed over his jaw and mouth.

I scowled, my cheeks warming. "It does."

"I don't disagree, but that you'd notice that first . . ." His hand fell as his teeth scraped his lower lip.

My toes curled. I returned my attention to the map of Mythayla. "What did you need to speak to me about?"

"There's been another visit from the fog," he said instantly. "Last night."

The heat unspooling within me turned cold. My eyes closed. "How many?"

"Just shy of thirty. More than half of the unit managed to outrun it." I looked at him as he crossed his arms and stroked the bristle at his jawline. "Twice now, they've struck at night."

"What have the survivors had to say?"

"They couldn't see anything. The mist was too thick, and just like last time, it left too little."

I was beginning to understand why he'd said we might need to eat hare. "Shit," I breathed.

Florian huffed, gazing up at the map. "Shit indeed."

"What do these marked locations mean exactly?" But it dawned when I looked back at the wax spread across the stenciled outline of the continent upon Lilitha's bedchamber wall.

The crimson splotches were thinly grouped throughout the northeast of Hellebore, growing thicker as they headed south—as they neared the Baneberry border. The warriors would be split into smaller factions before meeting later in the journey to push forward as one.

Florian confirmed as much. "They mean our troops have their orders, and we cannot dawdle any longer." He straightened and made his way to the door. "Ready or not, we leave at first light."

# 19

**Florian**

"Again." My command rang sharp through the farthest paddock.

The distance from the manor and any curious eyes didn't matter, nor that everyone was frantic with preparations. My reluctant mate was still more interested in her paranoia than learning how to wield a blade.

After another glance at the trees behind her, she licked her lips. Then she leaped toward me as if she were training to be a professional dancer rather than an efficient killer. Blade raised far too soon, and glinting under the sun, she slowed and lunged.

Sidestepping with ease, I kept my laughter caged behind tight teeth.

Tullia saw it in my eyes. She growled, the noise akin to a feral kitten, and whirled upon me with the dagger strangled in her fist.

"You cannot simply stab someone. It's—"

She lunged again. "Yes, I can."

"Butterfly." I caught her wrist and brought us nose to nose. "Your foes won't be bound and ready to mutilate. They are warriors with years of experience and burning hatred."

Her shoulders rose and fell, breasts brushing my chest. I was ready to steal her lips to kiss away her dismay and to punish her for the rejection in the kitchen until she whispered, "I don't want to be a warrior, Florian."

I fought the desire to promise she need not become one. To promise I would protect her and slay anyone who dared to creep too close to her with ill intentions.

I would mean it, yet it would still be a lie.

I wouldn't always be there to keep such a promise in the weeks ahead. Knowing that, feeling that fear hollowing deep within my bones, had caused me to drag her into this paddock after lunch although there was an ever-growing list of shit awaiting my attention.

"Too late, butterfly." My mouth trailed her cheek to her ear, her shiver curling it. "A warrior you already are." Before she could recoil, I swept my hand up her back into her hair. A fluttery breath washed over my neck as I pulled her body against mine. "Regardless of your pitiful skill with a weapon."

She huffed, attempting to push out of my hold, but it was feeble.

I released her, though I knew she didn't truly desire it, and stepped back. "Again."

"Florian . . ." Tullia poked at the dagger's sharp tip, the breeze stealing thick curls from her braid to dance across her exertion-warmed cheeks. "I want to know what will happen when we get there." The question was soft, but the feeling beneath it could have knocked me sideways.

I resisted the urge to comfort and ordered, "Look at me."

Slowly, she did, her pinkened lips battling the amusement shining in her dark eyes.

The order was a mistake, as was taking her with me, though I couldn't imagine anything different. Her tunic sat tight around her breasts and hips, showcasing the vast temptation of each. Her pants were even worse. They were not slacks but something akin to leg warmers, molding to her thighs and calves.

*Mother maim me.* If these past few days were any indication of what awaited in the weeks ahead, then I was so perilously fucked. Might as well stay behind, for all the damned good I would certainly *not* do.

My curse breaker and affliction used the toe of her boot to nudge a small rock. Teasingly, she said, "I'm looking, Majesty."

Those husked words made my hard cock throb. Tilting my head, I feigned good humor though I was torn between taking her to the grass to devour her and taking her inside to dress her in something much less form-fitting. "I can see that." I grinned. "Very fucking well, actually."

Tullia glowered, then raised a brow.

"Fine." I forced a sigh. "Do you wish to know what will happen? Or how it might happen?"

"No games, Florian," she said, adorably stern.

"It's a question, sweet creature." Her heartbeat pattered faster when I neared. "Molkan's defenses are a problem or he would've ceased existing after your return."

I let that sit there as she frowned at my chest.

Then I took her wrist, turned her hand, and readjusted her grip on the blade's worn hilt. "He will keep hiding behind that wall and the wards. So we must reach the palace, but it will be no easy feat."

"He never leaves."

I nodded once and turned her hand until the blade was poised at my chest—right over my heart. Her grip was now unyielding yet sustainable. "If there's no opportunity to sense for the heart-beat, then you push here and—"

"Send me in."

The temperature of my blood dropped, the air cooling with it.

Louder, she said, "Send me in to Molkan."

Ice feathered through my veins and chest. I waited for her to explain herself. I waited, barely breathing, barely leashing the need to punish her until she screamed my fucking name to the sky for saying something so foolish.

But as rational thinking overpowered the beast she constantly awakened within me, I understood it wasn't foolish at all.

And I understood she hadn't been making a suggestion. "You've thought on this."

Her hand lowered, as did her eyes. They returned, lashes spreading as she surveyed my features when she said, "His wards can't keep me out when we share the same blood that made them. At the very least, I can get in and get Avrin's ear. I can—"

"Why would he humor you?" My baser instincts reared, scenting a threat.

Tullia was unperturbed. "He left my shackles unlocked when I was cast out of the palace, Florian, so I could remove them and materialize. He might be loyal to Molkan, but that doesn't mean he agrees with all he does."

"One might say that is awfully presumptuous of you." I couldn't have kept the cold from drenching my voice if I'd tried, and I didn't care to. "What makes you so confident it wasn't a mistake?"

My creature didn't cower. She just smiled.

Then she poked my fucking nose.

I snarled, and her rich bout of laughter reduced my possessive instincts to their typical smoldering state. Her cheeks colored more with mirth, bright flecks of brown glinting within her whiskey eyes.

"It's not enough to hope to scale those walls. If we intend to end Molkan, we need a reliable way to reach him." Her humor died as she said with terrifying confidence, "I am that way."

After all she'd endured, such boldness made me even more reluctant to agree to this asinine plan. "I'll consider it."

"You'll consider it?" she repeated, golden brows raised high in disbelief.

That she was surprised at all rankled. If she only knew the depth of what she'd done to me, she wouldn't have dared to so much as think of offering herself without hesitation.

"I'll withhold what I truly wish to say to you right now and instead"—my glare was glacial—"tell you that you're fortunate to be getting that much from me."

Groaning, she said, "He won't kill me. We both know that."

Indeed, but Molkan's concern over his soul provided no relief.

I looked skyward, pondering all the many thousand ways this could destroy her more—destroy *me*. She had no idea. None. And if she did . . .

Then perhaps she would do this just to spite me.

Fair play.

Soft fingers touched the chilled tips of my own, luring my gaze to drop. A rush of warmth spread down my back and straight to my pained groin.

Tullia scraped her teeth over her lower lip. "What is your plan to get to him?"

It gave me unspeakable delight to shock her by divulging, "There are tunnels beneath Bellebon. We need only reach the heart of the city, where one leads to the woods deep within the palace grounds." The confession was edged and quiet, despite no one else being near. "Coupled with brute force against the palace gates."

"Those tunnels would be sealed."

"We know." And we knew how to unseal them. Our primary focus was surviving the threats that would greet us beforehand. Her tone made my eyes thin. "But what makes you so sure, butterfly?"

"He told me you stole from the tunnels."

Out of all the things he would've told her, she believed that, and she wasn't wrong to. I took the opening with a grin, wolfish and uncaring. "Care to share what else he told you?"

My request was ignored. "Molkan wants you stopped." Her long lashes drooped as she said, "Dead. He will use me to accomplish that. He'll want you to come to him, of course. He'll be distracted by us, by what you might do, which will give your warriors more room for a quicker advantage."

I'd guessed where this had been headed. That didn't mean I liked hearing it.

Molkan would not be the only one distracted.

"But if we could break those wards," she said. "Perhaps my blood—"

"Stop." My teeth gnashed. I pushed through them, "I'm still trying to digest the mere idea of you being used as bait."

Tullia stepped close enough for me to kiss her forehead, her scent a potent sweetness and her fingers stroking the length of mine. "I'm not being used if I'm willing."

The near-purred words almost got me. Before I was defeated by the animal she turned me into, I smirked and retreated.

My clever creature wasn't escaping this lesson now.

"Even if he won't kill you, you need to know how to defend yourself against fates worse than death." I adjusted the dagger in her hand once more. "So that's enough talk. Try again."

There was comfort in taking action.

Yet apprehension was a constant since our departure from the manor and meeting with awaiting warriors outside of the city. We would convene with more along the way.

I could only hope that they would avoid the deadly fog.

That we all would.

My anxious creature had packed little, so I'd packed extra for her. But among the few things she'd chosen to bring was the letter from her aunt, which had been left unopened for days atop the nightstand.

"I'm still failing to see it," Tullia said, the first words she'd spoken in nearly an hour. A relief and a welcome distraction from my plaguing thoughts.

"Dare I ask what you're referring to?" I sniffed her hair, inhaling her scent deep into my lungs. My nose nudged her thick braid out of the way to skim her neck.

She scrunched her shoulders and released a low laugh that ended far too soon. "My own horse, being that I'm now an expert at riding after one very intense lesson."

A lesson that'd been spent attempting to fuck upon the stallion's back before we'd climbed down to finish in the grass of the woods while the beast plucked at blooming wildflowers.

"There will be time to give you plenty more lessons," I murmured, eyeing the formation of warriors before us.

She hummed, feigning consideration.

Truthfully, I had no intention of humoring her unless it involved making her come undone again in the woods. I'd decided she was just fine where she was—tucked between my arms and against my body upon my horse.

Safe.

If Tullia was aware, she made no comment. Perhaps after all she'd endured, she felt most secure riding with me. Especially among so many warriors.

We traveled with a band of sixty. Many of our warriors had already left or returned to their posts. Hundreds more were to depart in the hours after we had. All had orders to split into assigned factions.

Should Molkan's spies be lurking, then it made us more difficult targets for the fog. It couldn't reach us all at once.

There were no fancy carriages or flags. No sign that I traveled amongst my brethren. We kept it simple with mandatory supplies and as few wagons and trunks as possible.

Despite knowing that none of them would harm her, I still recognized that Tullia was surrounded by strangers. I still felt the unease in her tense posture. Noticed the way she didn't merely soak in the scenery as she once had—with exuberant delight and wonder.

She watched everything around her with a scrutiny that said she was marking the warriors who might pose the greatest threat, as well as the weapons strapped to bodies and glinting from saddle bags.

And though I doubted she realized it, nor was she capable with her senses preoccupied elsewhere, as her anxiety drew birds and other critters closer to the road we traveled.

Hopefully, it would soon ease. Her affinity with wildlife could very well make more than our movements known. If the creatures didn't piss off, they could let her father know exactly where she was.

Exactly where to strike.

Not that he would ever see to anything personally. The coward wouldn't leave his precious palace even if he was gifted an easy shot at my throat.

My stallion huffed, and without taking her eyes from our surroundings, Tullia reached forward to rub his neck. I refrained from telling her not to pet him while he was on duty, as when she did, it seemed to soothe both her and Hemlock.

We moved at a brisk pace, yet not quite fast enough.

As soon as we cleared the winter-ruined road and met the fields before the awaiting woods, relief loosened my muscles. "Hold on," I warned Tullia, as we all spurred the horses into a gallop.

# 20

**Tullia**

We set up camp along a stream outside of the woods.

Well, Florian and the warriors did.

I watched while standing against a tree, my hand pressed to the bark as tents were erected and horses were tended to at the water. Within minutes of arriving, bedrolls were prepared and there was talk of deciding on shifts for sleep.

It was barely midafternoon.

Florian had warned me that we would not be stopping for long during the night. To avoid an encounter with the fog, we must move throughout the night and rest during the afternoon.

No matter how difficult it might prove to rest, I still understood.

Warriors took post. Some walked deep within the woods, and others crossed the narrow river to keep watch from the trees on the other side.

It was no comfort. Despite my belief that embarking on this journey would offer some, I now had a feeling that comfort would not be found until this was all over.

My thighs were sore and my ass was numb from hours upon Florian's stallion, but there was too much adrenaline and open air to even consider sleep. It wasn't going to happen until I was exhausted. I peeled away from the tree and walked along the stream, keeping my distance from the numerous warriors.

Their conversation and laughter, though low, pricked at my skin.

There were discussions of taverns they hoped to pass, foods they wished to trade with others, and the odd and embarrassing items loved ones had sent with them for our journey.

They were not discussing me. Certainly not with the king present. I didn't much care if they did, but they watched me.

Everyone fucking watched me.

At the edge of the water, I made to gather my gown before remembering I was wearing riding pants. If it weren't for the way I'd separated from our group, I supposed I could pass as one of them with the dark blue material and matching thick tunic.

But although Florian had made me their queen, I was not one of them.

I was a changeling who'd been branded a traitor by the kingdom who'd rejected me not once but twice.

Leaning over the water, I tugged up my sleeves to cleanse my hands before scooping handfuls to drink. As the ripples settled, my reflection cleared. Dark eyes and bright wind-swept hair. Much of it had escaped my braid, so I sat among the reeds upon the bank to fix it while listening for nearing footsteps.

"Does it hurt?"

My heart ceased beating, then screamed in my ears as I jumped to my feet and reached for the dagger Florian had given me. It was a simple blade, no jewels or etchings in the hilt, but it was light and well-worn, which seemed fitting.

Though I still had no idea how to fight, I'd learned I wouldn't hesitate to stab something.

The warrior reclining against a giant tree tipped up the brim of her blue hat, and I sank back down to the bank. Nirra, I believed her name was. One of Florian's generals. She'd been part of the meeting I'd interrupted in his study after the first attack from the fog.

Her sharp hazel eyes twinkled in the shade cast by the hat as she smiled. Letting it drop back over her eyes, she clasped her hands at her stomach. "Please don't stab me. I'm rather important."

Almost snorting, I sheathed the blade at my hip, needing to look as I did, unlike all of these trained creatures. I peered through the trees, then to the encampment. "Why are you sleeping over here?"

"Answer my question, and perhaps I'll consider answering yours." Seeming unfazed that anyone could advance upon her with half of her face covered, she tacked on with her mouth curving, the only feature I could see, "My queen."

"You needn't bother calling me that."

Her smile widened. "Why?"

"We both know I am no such thing," I muttered, turning back to the water.

"Interesting." Curiosity lightened her tone. "Was there no blood-binding contract? I hear differently."

I didn't answer that. I studied the slow-moving stream, the frogs and tadpoles hiding among the moss-blanketed rocks. Leaning forward, I dipped my fingers into the water. Nothing happened, so I wiggled them.

The frogs and tadpoles darted away.

Shaking the wet from my hand, I turned back to the general. "Does what hurt?"

"The traitor brand."

I stiffened as if the mere mention of it was another blade nearing my back. It no longer hurt, but the skin was tender at times. Yet I had a murky feeling she wasn't referring to physical pain. Even so, I only said, "It's healed."

"Hmm." She crossed her ankles, horse muck and mud caked beneath her boots. "I've only ever seen one before."

"Is that your way of asking me to show you?" I wouldn't, and my tone implied as much.

The general laughed, a hoarse yet pretty sound. "No, Queen. But by all means, should you wish to share, I won't say no."

Irritated, I said curtly, "You can answer my question now."

"Perhaps after my nap."

I bristled, glaring though she couldn't see.

Another laugh. "I can feel your royal glower blistering my skin." Licking her lips as she smiled, she murmured dryly, "Queen indeed." I was ready to march back to those I'd been trying to avoid when she finally deigned to indulge me. "I cannot sleep with canvas floating right above my head. Our tiny cottage caught aflame when I was young, and now I suffer from a lovely curse called claustrophobia."

"You need open space."

"I won't even sleep in the barracks. I've made a home in an abandoned barn a half mile beyond them. The holes in the rotting roof let me gaze at the night sky until I fall asleep."

Although it shouldn't have, it did sound a little appealing.

"Your reasons might be different, but I think you will desire the same." She tipped her hat to give me a pointed look, then glanced at the nearby warriors. She lowered the brim again. "If you do not already."

For some minutes, I just stared at her, unsure what to say but carrying a slight inclination to say more.

Sticks crunched, my frosty husband approaching.

I rose to my feet, though I would have preferred to stay. I would rest easier near one stranger rather than a large group of them.

The king glanced at Nirra, then looked at me with raised brows.

"Our queen has a need for stargazing, Majesty."

Florian cocked his head. "Does she now?"

Nirra didn't respond, as he wasn't asking her. He was still staring at me.

I was close to refuting that, but I wasn't sure I could. Instead, I gave Florian a small, close-lipped smile as I joined him.

He didn't return it as he murmured, "I fear you might be disappointed with my efforts, then." Before I could ask what he meant, he led the way through the small smattering of trees to the cloud-shaped clearing.

Eyes fell upon us like brambles, conversation lowering.

I kept my chin high and looked nowhere but the king's back as he navigated the many tents and bedrolls to the trees on the other side of the clearing.

A large yet simple tent stood within them, a healthy distance from the rest of the camp. It was not triangular but square, and tall enough for us to stand within. He opened the flap, and I ducked inside, then straightened, my stomach tight.

Two bedrolls were spread over the canvas-covered ground. Beside them were canteens of water and pouches of food.

"It's certainly not the manor, but I thought it would do. However" —he reached for the dagger strapped to his side—"if you want stars, then that can be arranged."

I grabbed his wrist before the blade was taken to the tent's ceiling. "This is just fine."

"Fine," he repeated as if the word meant foul. He turned to me, dark blue eyes scrutinizing my every feature. "No one here seeks to harm you. They've all been thoroughly assessed and warned. You have my word. That, and your allegiance has now been made clear. No one would dare."

I wished I was as certain as he seemed to be about that. "I know," I said, for the rational part of me understood. It was the larger parts of me, those which had been so tampered with that I was still trying to figure out where they now fit, that did not care for logic.

Logic and heart seldom coexisted.

Florian frowned when I released his wrist. I looked down at the bedrolls. My chest pinched at the sight of the small throw pillow he'd smuggled within our packs. "When do we leave?"

"Six hours."

Not long. We were keeping things precise to make sure we met with the other units on time, including that of Oleander, near the border.

Yet six hours felt like a small eternity.


Florian didn't sleep.

Almost two days had passed since our departure from Frostfall Mountains, and neither of us had slept. I pretended, knowing he was well aware, and he sat at the tent opening, alert to every tiny noise.

Save for our journey through Lurina, there'd been nothing but villages between bouts of heavy woodland. I'd studied Florian's map each time we stopped, learning what might lay ahead.

We would keep to the woods and avoid towns and main thoroughfares until we needed to restock supplies. Not only to remain better hidden and make our movements less predictable but also to avoid spies lurking in well-populated areas.

In the hours spent trying to sleep, I'd often think back to the city of Lurina and the awakening citizens who'd rushed from their homes and opening businesses. They'd waved, accustomed to seeing warriors passing through or patrolling. Upon realizing the king marched with them, their curiosity became unmistakable excitement. Some of the watery gazes even hinted toward relief.

They'd known.

And the florist I'd never made it to on Ashen Street meant that Molkan also knew.

Florian hadn't been concerned when I'd told him. "The florist is no longer there," he'd said, seeming unbothered by the secret I'd kept from him. "They closed the day after you were taken. My informants found that curious, so we checked. Nothing."

It was unsettling, to say the least, that his enemies could set up shop in his royal city—right beneath his nose. Until I acknowledged that whatever amount of spies Molkan had lurking throughout Hellebore, Florian would have twice as many, if not more, in Baneberry.

He'd proven to be unapologetically calculating, this king I'd been bound to, and as manipulative and merciless as I'd first discovered. Skies, maybe worse.

But it took a monster to defeat one, and the only comfort I'd found came from knowing I'd somehow tamed the bigger beast.

One that never roamed too far from me. Even while in deep discussion with Nirra and two other warriors, he watched me while I knelt upon the bank to wash the clothes we'd been wearing since leaving the manor.

Other warriors had been given the task. I'd refused when they'd tried to collect our clothing. If I couldn't sleep, then I wanted something to do.

It was oddly satisfying and sobering to do a chore I hadn't in months. To reminisce on washing Rolina's gowns and my own in the apartment while lost to daydreaming about being exactly where I now was.

I hung the clothes next to other washed items slung over a line of wire stretching between two trees.

It would have been nice to bathe, but there was no privacy to do so. I'd caught glimpses of bare asses and wet chests more than I'd cared to. No one seemed to mind. Of course, they wouldn't when they were used to it.

It wasn't because I was shy about potentially revealing my body. I just didn't wish to show anyone the brand I knew they were curious to see.

I also had a feeling Florian might remove me from the water before I fully entered it.

The clothing was still damp when we set up camp again the following afternoon, so I hung it right away. This time, there was no clearing. Each tent sat next to a giant tree, and fires were kept to a minimum.

While warriors slept and patrolled the woods, Florian sat in his preferred place at the opening of our tent. We hadn't talked as much as I'd expected. It wasn't due to the reservations I clung to as if they might cure me when I was already irreversibly poisoned.

It was because we were seldom alone, even while sharing a horse.

I tucked the hairbrush back inside the pack and stared at his broad back. He hadn't bathed in days either, but the odor added to his scent hadn't made him any less appealing. Rather, the new musk only made my legs clench tighter around the horse when he would say something into my ear.

I could only hope my own unwashed state wasn't so bad.

His hair was now long enough for the strands to be curled into a small bun at his nape. A few rogue pieces slipped free. I wanted to touch them. To touch him. To place my hand upon his tense back to see if it might soothe some of his many concerns about what awaited us.

Nothing would.

At the very least, I could ignore my fear of being overheard. I whispered, "Did you think you would find yourself here?"

As if shocked I'd spoken of anything other than our journey, Florian jerked slightly. He peered over his shoulder, his knees wrapped in his strong arms. "Married to a mate who wishes to despise me?" he teased. "Or on my way to war?"

Unable to resist, I smiled at that. "I do not despise you, and you know it." I had to wonder if I ever truly had, or if I'd merely tried to in order to hide my loathing for myself.

He resumed his watch of the camp. "You want to, butterfly, and though it is unspeakably bothersome, I will endure it." Crickets

177

chirped, and a wolf howled deep within the woods. Eventually, he said, "No. Truth be told, I'd thought I might need to avoid it."

"To set aside your plans for total humiliation and simply assassinate Molkan," I surmised.

"Precisely." The word lacked his usual ice.

For long moments, I stared at him. The percussion of early evening lulled, coaxing the haunting question to finally leave me in a barely-there whisper. "Do you believe my mother really died after giving birth to me, Florian?"

He tensed even more. "Yes." He rolled his neck, adding with quiet conviction, "But not because of your birth."

That made me scowl. "You've never said anything." He could have undoubtedly used that to better sway me numerous times.

"Because I have no proof."

The letter tempted yet again, and I ignored the urge to look at my pack. "Is it possible that Peony might know what happened?" I asked. "Is that what you meant when you said she might be writing to share the truth?"

"I think if anyone knows, it would be her."

Even as his murmured words lingered like another taunt he perhaps hadn't intended, I couldn't bring myself to open that pack and read the letter. And I could no longer believe any of the stories Molkan had hand-fed me. I'd revisited each one over and over until they'd fallen apart like weathered bones turning to dust.

I didn't need to see it written in ink to know what I felt was true.

"How long have you been stewing on this?" Florian asked.

"Mostly since we left the manor, though I think I knew before then. He said he loved her," I whispered. "My mother. But how could you do that to someone you love?"

"I believe he did love Corina." There was a pause before he said, "I also believe he resented that love, for it led him to unleash his frustrations upon my sister in a way that couldn't be undone."

Molkan had spoken of his father with a hostility for his actions that was to be expected. My grandfather had murdered my grandmother. Yet it seemed Molkan had done the same thing to his own wife. I couldn't help but wonder if he even recognized he was just as despicable.

Then again, monsters so rarely believed they were monsters at all.

If it weren't for our mutual burning desires to see Molkan pay for all of his atrocities, I'd consider asking Florian to find another way to end him and be done with it. The sooner he was dead, the better.

But that burning raged into an inferno at the mere thought of him receiving an easy death.

The king continued his studious study of the growing dark. With slight turns of his head, he marked everything that moved and made sound. The return of the stiff set to his shoulders made me realize that conversation helped him relax. Even if only marginally.

Just because I couldn't allow myself to trust this didn't mean I liked how our mission had him so on edge.

So I asked quietly, "What did you think when you first saw me in your pleasure house?"

"That I couldn't wait to get my cock inside you."

The instant honesty evoked a laugh I smothered against my knees, pulling them tight to my chest.

"The correct answer would be that you were the most magical thing I've ever laid eyes on."

"No," I said, smiling at his back. "Your first answer said that just fine."

He hummed. "Suppose it did."

The call of night birds and more howling gave increased volume to the incoming night. Snoring sounded from many of the tents. Soon, we would ready to leave and ride through the darkness once more.

I considered attempting an hour of sleep beforehand when Florian said, barely audible, "And what did you think?"

Surprised that he'd asked, I sat stunned. "I do believe you remember my reaction." Yet as I thought back to how nervous I'd been upon bursting through the door to the private room to meet my first client, I moved down the bedroll, closer to him. "I thought you were the most terrifying thing I'd ever seen."

He snorted softly. "Now that is saying something, considering the guardian you were stuck with."

I smiled again, grateful he couldn't see. "And far too beautiful," I conceded, for I knew he wanted more, as I placed my hand upon his back like I'd longed to.

Florian stilled, as if he'd ceased breathing at the touch.

A moment later, his shoulders loosened with a rough exhale. He said nothing in response, and I didn't try to fill the quiet, content to feel his addicting heat beneath my palm until it wasn't enough.

Then I moved closer to rest my head upon his back where, finally, I fell asleep.

**Tullia**

It would be two more nights of riding before I realized what Florian already had.

We were being followed.

Not by our foes, nor merely the unit miles behind us, but by creatures that lived within the woods. Howling grew closer, though not so close that we moved on. Snarling of larger beasts gave us pause, so we remained alert and did our best to keep from tempting them.

At long last, I was able to bathe.

A small creek dribbled through the woods toward the stream where we'd pitched camp. Florian showed me to it, likely because I'd grumbled about the itch of my tunic.

He kept his back to me while I bathed in the deepest portion of the creek. Not to give me privacy. Which would have been laughable after all we'd done together. No, he was making sure no one came near, although camp wasn't even in sight.

Biting back an insistent smile, I soaped up then set the bar upon a stone. "Guard duty seems highly unnecessary, Majesty."

"Just wash yourself, butterfly."

I bent lower in the water to rinse the suds from my body. "What about you?"

His answer was clipped. "I'll do so after you're done."

Huffing at his emphasis on *done*, I lathered my hands in soap to scrub my scalp, wishing it were his fingers instead. I ducked underwater a few times to wash it from my hair. Squeezing the long strands, I asked, "Does this mean I can guard you?"

His arms remained folded, and his towering physique strung as tight as his words. "If you wish."

"You know . . ." I bit my cheek, enjoying the freedom to admire his impressive form unabashedly in the glow of afternoon. "I'd do that better if you were in here."

Florian tensed further, then peered over his shoulder. His narrowed eyes brightened as he surveyed me. His jaw was rock-hard, his warning hissed through his teeth. "Cease toying with me, Tullia."

Unable to keep it trapped any longer, I laughed, almost giddy from it.

His features softened. Only marginally. "Right. You're clean enough." He placed the towel he'd been strangling in his clenched hand upon the bank. "Get out."

"Fine." I sighed with feigned annoyance. But I was indeed done, and I didn't want anyone glimpsing my back.

He grumbled something I didn't catch, snatching the towel and opening it. His eyes lightened even more as he wrapped it around my naked body.

I waited until he entered the creek with an angry splash to inform him, "You brought one towel, Majesty."

He swiped the soap. "I'll wear my trousers."

Orange light dripped between the leaves and branches over-head, swathing his wet skin and luring my eyes to every soapy indent and muscled peak.

He noticed, of course. His snarl was low, throaty. "You're going to get us killed."

"Me?" I asked, incredulous. But I turned to do my duty, watch-ing to ensure no one neared although I knew damned well that hadn't been what he'd meant.

Florian finished what felt like a mere minute later. Water crashed as he launched onto the mossy bank.

Stark naked.

182

Then I truly did watch, each muscle stiff and my hands clutching the rough fabric of the towel, to make sure no one saw him. If this squeezing combination of worry and jealousy was a sampling of what he'd felt, then I regretted teasing him.

Florian prowled toward me, mouth watering even with menace sharpening each goddess-carved feature. Too focused on sensing for threats, for wandering and feasting eyes that weren't there, I didn't expect it.

His hand latched mine, and I squeaked as I was tugged behind him. He dragged me toward a brush-bordered tree, the towel almost slipping.

It did slip—upward when he lifted me against the tree. His whisper was rough, eliciting gooseflesh. "You might very well be the death of us."

I grinned when his nose dropped to my collarbone. He inhaled, then licked the damp skin, and I twined my legs tight around his waist. "But what an enjoyable end it would be."

"You make a convincing argument." He kissed my desperate pulse, and my head tilted to give him better access. He licked my jaw. "So fucking convincing."

I took that as a loud yes and uncurled an arm from his shoulder to reach between us. As soon as his cock touched me, he pushed inside my body, and I gasped. It had only been a matter of days, yet I was instantly aflame and hungry for release.

"Troublesome creature." His head rose, eyes as bright as the residual blue staining the sky. "You cannot make a sound."

I shifted over him—desperately needing him to move.

His features creased, as if it pained him to keep still. "I mean it. No one hears you, or this doesn't happen again until we return home."

Home.

An ache bloomed within my chest. Hellebore Manor was not my home. It never would be. Yet nowhere had ever felt more like home than the winter-laden estate that had served as both a refuge and cell.

I ignored the panic the realization brought forth by nipping at Florian's lower lip. "Then you'd better make sure I'm quiet, Majesty."

Understanding, he clapped his hand over my mouth. The other squeezed my ass. A feral gleam lit his lust-changed eyes. "Gladly, butterfly."

Then he gave me what we'd both been starved for.

My back arched against the rough bark, the towel falling to my waist, as he drove into me with thrusts that deepened each time. Relief, and something quiet yet powerful in its restlessness, coursed through my veins. It thickened when he seemed to sense it.

His nostrils flared, a groan leaving him as he then pounded into me over and over. His eyes held mine. His hand smothered the moans I failed to suppress when I unraveled into trembling pieces.

He followed, teeth clenched and groaning low.

With my fingers tangled in his damp hair, I gripped his neck. His hand slackened at my mouth, allowing my head to drop to his shoulder as breath heaved from me.

"Fuck," he rasped. Bracing his arm above me against the tree, he finished filling me with spasmed jerks of his hips.

My eyes opened to find a bright green pair among the foliage across the creek. "Indeed," I whispered, fear spiraling down my spine and locking it.

Sensing it, Florian tensed. "What is it?"

"Wolf," I said, unable to remove my gaze from the creature as it slowly stalked toward the water.

The setting sun cast the forest in shadows, illuminating the pack in the brush behind the wolf.

"Across the creek," Florian guessed.

"Yes."

He cursed again, then said, "Fix the towel."

I covered myself as best I could while squashed between the tree and his chest. Satisfied, he slowly eased me down to my feet.

The wolf halted when Florian turned. It seemed the gray and black predator now recognized that he'd encountered a larger one. A low grumble conveyed his displeasure as he retreated a step. The enormity of him . . .

I blinked. "Snow is but a babe in comparison."

"Snow is a runt, and that is why she should've died."

Scowling, I hissed, "Yet I hear she was forced to stay with you while I was gone." I smacked his arm without thinking, the sound stilling the wolf and bringing some of his brethren forward from the trees.

"Be that as it may, these beasts are not domesticated." Florian kept his voice quiet. "Nor are they in need of rescue."

Lips pinched, I leaned around his muscled arm and withheld a nervous laugh. "You're not wearing anything."

"Thank you for reminding me."

As I failed to trap my laughter, the alpha wolf leaped over the narrow center of the creek.

Florian kept me behind him, but he hadn't any weapons. Neither of us did. They were with our clothing by the creek.

Ice formed in rapid cracks within his fist. A shard reminiscent of a dagger now in hand, the king stepped forward.

The wolf ceased his advance, his companions mercifully still beyond the creek.

The dark beast gave his green eyes to me, and I felt a twinge of it again—that strange warmth that calmed and eased my tense limbs. I touched Florian's back. "Wait." Still staring at the wolf, I said, "Maybe we should just leave."

"They've been stalking camp for days, butterfly, just waiting for easy prey to fall away from the group."

"Or they're curious."

"About meat," he said. "Which has been slim throughout years of winter."

"But winter is thawing." The grass grew greener, more lush, the farther we traveled from the mountains. Fauna more abundant. "There's plenty of food, Florian."

He finally seemed to understand what I was saying. Without taking his eyes from the wolf, he stated, "You believe they're only interested in you."

"Perhaps," I said, shrugging and forgetting my volume. Another wolf leaped over the water. This one was all gray with black eyes. A female, judging by the smaller size and her scent as she stood just behind her alpha. I studied them and smiled. "They're mates."

Florian also studied them.

I wondered what I'd do if he decided to harm them, as that restless quiet within balked at the thought of any of them being injured, or worse.

Relief settled the rising wave of tightness when Florian finally murmured, "Walk backward with me."

He kept the ice blade ready as we did.

The wolves remained where they were until we reached the outskirts of camp. Then they immediately bounded over to the tree we'd fucked against, snouts upon the ground and sniffing at the bark.

I crinkled my nose.

Florian noticed and chuckled.

The delicious sound ended abruptly when a familiar voice chimed from behind the tree we'd stopped next to. "Nice ass, my king." Her face half shielded by her hat, Nirra reclined against the trunk, unbothered by our visitors or unaware they'd roamed so close to her resting spot.

I folded over with laughter that stunned the general and the wolves, as Florian refused to pay them any more heed and stormed back to the creek to collect our clothing.

The beasts retreated and scattered into the trees.

The wolves continued to follow us.

The alpha made his presence known each time I stepped away from camp to clean myself and our clothing or stretch my aching limbs after riding for hours.

The following evening, he sat beside a burrow, his patience infinite as his mate joined him, and they waited for some unfortunate creature to leave their home and become their next meal.

As long as they weren't too interested in eating us, I didn't mind. But I headed back to our tent before I witnessed it.

"They're drawn to your energy," Florian said when I informed him upon returning. "Your emotions. Maybe your needs, too, as they're all connected."

He was studying the map we'd both looked at countless times, a cup of broth growing cold beside him. Shadows pressed beneath his eyes from lack of sleep, rendering the dark blue reminiscent of rare and priceless jewels.

He hadn't slept at all. Not that I'd seen.

I wasn't doing much better, but I managed to steal an hour or two when night loomed before we readied to leave again. My offers to take over his compulsive watch duty so that he could rest had all been brushed aside with murmurs of, "Next time."

Soft lies. I'd known, yet I hadn't argued. I hadn't thought he'd let it get this bad.

His innate stubbornness and need for control would see him falling from the back of his damned horse. Not ideal when I wasn't ready to ride one by myself. I needed him alert and rested, as did the rest of our unit and those we were to meet.

So I crouched beside the bedroll he sat on and snatched the map from his fingers. Ignoring his scowl, I folded and slipped it inside the breast pocket of his tunic. Then I clasped his chin, tilting it side to side. "Look at you, Florian."

His brows jumped, a smirk quick to follow. "Am I no longer so terrifying, butterfly?"

My lips twitched. My fingers began to crawl over his thicker stubble toward that soft mouth. I released him and handed him the broth. "Drink and sleep. Right now, the only thing that will kill us is your inability to stay on your horse because you've been too stubborn to rest."

"I believe you meant to say too *worried*"—he sipped the broth—"so I'll let that be."

Withdrawing my dagger from the sheath at my hip, I took a seat at the tent opening before he could.

He huffed, and I heard him set the tin cup down. "As if I'll sleep with you seated there, ripe for the plucking."

"No one will touch me," I said, meaning it.

He was silent for a moment. "You seem rather certain about that."

"You told me so yourself, and our new friends are now encamped behind our tent in the trees," I said, referring to the wolves.

Florian cursed.

"You'd have noticed them if you'd rested," I teased, then shrugged. "Perhaps."

"Perhaps," he shot back, snide yet too soft to suggest he was truly irked. "You believe they're guarding you."

I twirled the blade between my fingers, admiring the glint of the sharp point. A reminder that I wasn't as powerless as I'd once felt, no matter how little skill I had. "I don't know what they're doing, but the horses are unbothered. They've not attacked any of us, nor have they made us think they will."

A minute washed by, the crisp breeze rustling my hair. It carried a calming mixture of pine and smoke and a hint of damp.

Drowsiness deepened Florian's voice. "Tell me what you feel from them."

"Their heartbeats, mostly," I said. "At the moment, they're soft, just like any other." His silence prompted me to say more. "But when our eyes lock, they get louder." The desire to keep the frightful memory to myself was strong, yet it left me with unexpected ease. "The carriage horse saved me on that mountain road."

"From the guards," Florian said, almost tentative, as if I might not elaborate if he pressed too hard.

"Yes. I thought I was going to die. Felt it, even." My nape chilled with the slithering cold fear and certainty I'd experienced—before it had been replaced by something else. "I didn't want to look at any of those guards, to give them more satisfaction," I said. "So I looked at the horse behind Fellan. When our eyes met, I felt a calm unlike any other. My terror, everything, seemed to drip away."

"Your energy touched," Florian said. "Combined in a way that made the beast feel your desperation as though it were his own."

That made sense, even as it still mystified.

"What happened then?" the king asked, groggy.

"The horse reared, knocking Fellan to the ground as he tried to slit my throat." I licked my drying lips. "He stomped on him, and Zayla tried to help him, then the driver . . ." Mercifully, I didn't need to say much else.

Sensing I was done describing it, Florian whispered, "Then you materialized."

"Desperation," I whispered back, a smile forming from what he'd once told me.

"And did this desperation take you straight to Molkan?"

Hesitant to confess that I was taken from Crustle, and unsure why, I simply said, "No."

He seemed to deduce as much anyway with a hum.

It didn't really matter how I ended up in Molkan's grasp, so I let him. Though perhaps, I thought, when Florian said nothing more, it mattered to him.

Some warriors slept. Others meandered through camp in quiet conversation while they ate. A few glanced at our tent, perched upon an outcropping of rocks four or five feet above the rest of them.

Aside from Nirra, no one had spoken to me. I'd begun to wonder if Florian had told them not to out of concern for my well-being or because he was more possessive than I'd first thought.

I peered over my shoulder to ask him and smiled.

The king lay sprawled over both bedrolls, hand slack by his head as if he'd been dragging his fingers through his tormented hair before he'd succumbed to sleep. As I looked back at the camp and the trees on either side of us, he mumbled, "Promise me."

Those words squeezed my heart. I studied the blade between my fingers, whispering, "I promise to wake you at the first strange sound I hear, Majesty."

## 22

**Florian**

The deep blue tunic and tight pants were a fucking crime committed to doom me.

I'd had too little sleep, too little blood, too little of her, to endure the sight. The thick cotton molded to the curves of her thighs, ass and hips—stretched over her luscious breasts in a way that made me offer her a cloak numerous times.

Tullia saw right through me.

Sometimes, she'd humor me. Mostly when we were riding and the wind was a cold lash that pinkened her cheeks and left tendrils of hair in fluffed tangles that refused to stay tucked in her braid nor behind the delicate arch of her ears.

Other times, like mere minutes ago, she'd simply ignored the cloak I'd set beside her in the tent.

My creature kicked at stones and crouched every other skies-damned step to peer at an insect in the grass or to inspect the rare coloring of a wildflower.

To say it bothered me was a gargantuan understatement.

Mainly because I liked it, the slow but sure return of her curiosity for the world she'd once hungered for but had since left her in ruins. I liked it so much my chest burned, the sensation pushing clipped words between my teeth. "We're not here to admire the scenery."

Her fingers stroked the giant petals of an orange wildflower. "Then why do you keep ogling my ass?"

I rubbed my mouth to hide my smile. Pointless when a huffed laugh escaped me.

"Majesty, are you jealous because I'm not spending all my free time admiring you?"

I didn't give that a response. She didn't need one. Instead, I cleared my throat and said, "We have little time before we need to move on, and you need to sleep."

"I've slept far more than you," she said curtly, as she rose and walked deeper into the field with me.

Sleep was impossible. Making myself vulnerable was one thing, but to leave her for even a moment when that fog could creep out of nowhere was inconceivable. Not to mention, the fucking wolves were becoming a problem.

They continued to follow us, no matter how fast we rode nor the terrain. Birds, too, I'd come to notice after waking from my nap some days ago to the chorus of their presence drowning all other sound.

Even if Tullia were more educated in her abilities, I knew it would still be so. Just as the winter running through my veins had tormented my kingdom for years on end, her ability to attract wildlife would not be quelled until her own torment was dealt with.

So we would work on the ability we could control.

I stopped walking. Tullia did, too, keeping a few feet between us as she turned to face me.

Torment indeed, I thought.

But I brushed aside my longing for her complete surrender and folded my hands before me. "Each time you've materialized, you were afraid," I needlessly said, the words colder than I'd intended, for just imagining such a thing rendered me murderous. "You felt threatened."

As if lost to one of those memories, her dark eyes stared past me to the trees we'd left behind, unseeing. Her hand rose, fingers drifting toward her neck. To the scar there, given by Fellan—the mongrel now rotting in the pits of Nowhere.

I didn't make her aware. Seldom had I witnessed her touch the scar unless she thought no one was watching.

I was always watching.

"Do you feel it?" I asked, the burn in my chest lowering my voice. "Remember how it felt."

A slight nod, her hand falling and those huge eyes meeting mine. I waited, and she conceded with a whispered, "I'll never forget."

Goddess fucking take me.

I swallowed thickly, the taste of my rage acidic. "I want you to hold and dissect it." I began to walk a slow circle around her to better ignore the imaginings of what she'd gone through. "Within it, you'll find a glimpse of what you're seeking when you materialize. It's there, no matter how hard it might be to see."

Her eyes closed, as if she might better find such a thing in the dark.

Perhaps she would, but I still withheld a smile as I paced. "It's a kernel of warmth amongst the coldness of fear. It's the rope all with this ability latch onto when we first start materializing."

"Safety," she whispered, eyes still shut, long brown lashes cresting her regal cheeks.

"If that's what you wish to call it, then fine. Feel that. Pull it forward to feel it without the fear. Without the terror of danger. Take your time and lean wholly into it."

I waited, prepared to fetch her from the apartment she'd fled from multiple times.

After mere moments, she said, "Nothing is happening."

"It will," I promised. "For now, you will find yourself taken to this place of refuge, but with enough practice, you'll be able to call upon that warmth as if it were always sitting right beside you, waiting. Then you can imagine any destination and, so long as there is a strong desire to assist in pushing you into the energetic fields, you will materialize there."

"But what if it's not warm at all?" she murmured. "What if it's cold?"

I frowned, pausing beside her. "Cold?"

"That tether you speak of." Her eyes opened. "It feels cold."

I pondered that, perplexed momentarily. Ultimately, I didn't think it would matter. "As long as a distinct difference awaits you beyond the extremes of your fear. Pull the cold forward, seize it." Though it unnerved me, I said, "See what happens."

Her eyes closed once more.

I resumed pacing, studying the curves of her plush lips and the freckles beginning to dust her cheeks.

She asked, "How long did it take you to learn?"

I pushed through the haze of memories, many blurred by age, liquor, narcotics, and far too many bodies. Recalling it delivered an ache that sank into my soul with teeth too sharp to extricate. "I was seventeen years, I believe."

I'd intended to leave it at that until Tullia's lips pursed. She wanted to know more.

Fine. A good sign, so I would gladly indulge. "I ended up in my mother's favorite room. A room she spent most of her time with me in."

"The library," Tullia said.

I raised a brow, though she couldn't see.

As if sensing my curiosity, she said gently, "A female's scent lingers on some of the books. Similar to yours, but rather than caramel and woodsy, it's just like caramel." Her hands joined and twisted before her. "Just sweet. Lilitha's scent was more . . ." Her nose crinkled slightly while she pondered her answer. "Honeyed."

My heartbeat became a blade striking at my chest cavity. I couldn't speak. I didn't know what I would have said even if I could.

Tullia opened her eyes and looked at me.

I'd stopped in front of her, my chest tight.

Concern lowered her brows and pinched her mouth. She tilted her head after attempting to read the features I'd kept void of emotion. "So you materialized to your mother."

I stared a moment longer, the breeze colder and knocking strands of hair around my cheeks. Tullia didn't prompt me again. She waited with a smile slowly lightening her dark gaze.

Fairly certain I had my heart tamed, I finally spoke. "My father was irritated that it always seemed to be her and not him." I paced again as the bittersweet memories invaded. "He was competitive, and though my mother was not, she endlessly enjoyed celebrating my arrival in her library by informing him as soon as I'd done it again."

Tullia blessed me with a low and stomach-cinching laugh.

"Eventually, perhaps a month or more later, I was able to materialize to him by drawing upon that feeling of warmth. By using that tether as a means to deliver me to any place I envisioned."

"And was he happy?"

"He was always happy to come second best, so long as it was to my mother." I remembered the high arch of his brow as he'd peered over top of his document and drawled, *well, better late than never.* The gleam in his eyes was as bright in my mind as it had been then.

"More than anything, he was proud." I slowed my pacing. "Always so fucking proud of me, even when I'd least deserved it." Which had been the case so many times, I couldn't dare to count.

"You were his son," Tullia said, as if that meant he had to be.

"You know better than anyone that fathers, and even mothers, are not always loving." She had no response for that, and before I could punch myself for being tactless, I sighed. "I shouldn't have—"

"Don't do that," she said.

Tensing, I halted next to her. "Apologize?"

She shook her head, casting her gaze toward me with a sheen coating it. "I don't want you mincing words. I want you to say what you mean, and with the lack of restraint I'm accustomed to."

I nodded once, but I had to ask, "Why?"

Staring straight ahead, she squeezed her hands and swallowed. "Anything else feels like a lie, and I don't want lies." She paused, then whispered, "Not from you."

I'd indeed already withheld so much from her, and what had happened as a result would haunt me forevermore.

For if I'd been more forthcoming, then—save for the marks she'd eternally wear from my teeth—perhaps she would have no scar to reach for at her throat. She would have no traitor brand. No shame and self-loathing she should not feel.

Her heart and soul would still be whole and unbearably hopeful.

Before I could open my mouth to attempt broaching the many things I might never find the courage to wholly say, Tullia closed her eyes and inhaled deeply.

As she exhaled, I knew she was done talking.

Again, I paced, the circle growing wider to give her more room, and I watched the trees in the distance. My senses remained alert, awaiting a shout from camp or a violent rustle in the brush and foliage beyond the field.

We stood in a small valley surrounded by giant rock formations, woods behind us to the north and ahead to the southeast where we'd made camp. The rocks and cliffs were not so close that I expected trouble from the villages beyond, but not so far that I was comfortable stopping here for long.

There were too many ways for the enemy to gain an advantage. Too many hiding places.

Energy pricked at my nape and lower back.

Squinting, I studied the rocks. Shadows unfurled over the field as the sun dipped lower. Indeed, it would be wise to move on early. We'd rested enough to make it to our final layover before we made haste to the meeting point. An outpost astride the border.

We would reach the town of Harmony tomorrow. A risky yet much-needed stop. We were running low on provisions, and we needed plenty more to see us through the rest of the journey. A journey that, within a week's time, would be nearing its end.

Whatever end that might be.

Distracted by the sensation of being watched and all the various what-ifs awaiting us, I didn't see it happen. But I felt it—the shift in the air a split second before her sugared scent exploded.

Wind was knocked from my lungs, and my feet from beneath me. Eternally the case where this creature of mine was concerned, apparently.

I hit the ground with a grunt as she landed atop me like a laughing bird that'd fluttered down from the sky.

Laughing. She was laughing harder than I'd heard in weeks. A true laugh. The type that sent blood rushing to her high cheeks and bronze stars into eyes of darkest brown.

A lone butterfly with blue wings bobbed behind her toward the trees.

I didn't need to say it. As that laughter faded, she knew exactly what she'd done. Her cheeks were a shade of crimson I hadn't seen in too fucking long—burning as hot as the fading sun.

Despite all I'd done, despite all she still refused to give me, it was me she'd materialized to.

I was her place of refuge.

I gazed up at her, her perfect face framed by wild hair freed from her braid and aglow with afternoon light. Her smile waned, but her lips remained parted. I reached up to brush my knuckles over the joy in her cheeks, my chest tightening as her smile slipped from her eyes.

Ridden with sudden panic, with the need for it to stay—for her to stay, I murmured, "If you wanted me on my back, all you had to do was say so, butterfly."

Her scowl was delightful, but my dry words had returned her smile.

She splayed her hands over my chest, pressed the tip of her nose against mine, and purposely dug her cunt into my aching erection. "Something obviously went wrong, Majesty." Pushing up, she grinned when I groaned from the extra torture given to my cock. "Let's try again."

Nothing went wrong, and she damned well knew it.

Another laugh blessed my ears when I rolled us and pinned her hands above her head. Before her smile could leave, I claimed that mouth and nudged her legs wide open with my knees.

Tullia moaned when my cock met her warm core through our pants. My teeth dragged over her lower lip as she turned her head. "I never told them anything, Florian." The confession was a rushed burst that hinted at both a reluctance to set it free and a need to ensure I was aware. "When they gave me . . ." She swallowed, lashes dipping.

When they'd branded her a traitor because she was mine.

Horror lanced through me.

My hold on her wrists tightened. My foolish creature writhed, a spark in her eyes as she squirmed against my pained cock. "And you think that pleases me?"

My tone made her still.

But I couldn't have kept the cold within me from seeping into my voice if I'd tried. Imaginings, each one more sickening than the last, scraped across my mind and pulverized my chest.

"You should have told them whatever they wished to hear, Tullia. What shape the fucking moon was each night, how many cloaks I own, what stupid soaps I use—anything. You should've made a pile of shit up." I pushed the words between my teeth and my forehead against hers. "*Anything* to keep them from harming you."

My eyes closed when tears glistened in hers.

I kept them that way as her whisper croaked, "No, I shouldn't have." Her dark eyes swam into mine when I opened them, a defiant smile alleviating some of the churning within my gut. "They would have hurt me anyway."

"Not as much," I said, gentling my hold on her wrists.

She pulled a hand free to reach for my jaw, fingers brushing over the thickened bristle. It loosened under her touch—until her rasped statement flayed me to the bone. "The severity is all the same in the end, Majesty."

If she was attempting to soothe me, she was far from succeeding. My head lifted as I glowered. "Tullia—"

She pressed her finger to my mouth, then pushed up on her elbow. So gentle it ruined me anew, she molded her lips to mine. Pulling back, she whispered, "I've been doing some thinking."

I sighed. "You do know what they say about that."

She couldn't hide the smile she refused to give me from her whiskey eyes. "The guard towers encircling Baneberry Palace."

My poor cock throbbed as I waited for her to take this where I knew it was headed.

"Molkan said items infused with his blood to ward the palace were stolen." A knowing look accompanied her soft words, although camp was not so close that anyone would overhear.

Which was likely why she'd waited until now to voice these particular musings.

"They were something of a test," I admitted. "But it was a mistake to take them, for their replacements are infuriatingly superior."

"The guard towers," she said again. "They are now the wards."

Slowly, I blinked, awaiting the inevitable suggestion that was bound to make me immensely unhappy. At least my cock might cease pleading for attention.

"If one is taken down, then it would cause a gap in the wards." Exasperated by my silence, a frown puckered her lips before she huffed and said, "We need only demolish one, Florian."

And I was officially done with being patient. "No."

"No?" she repeated, brows high. "No, I'm wrong?" She glared. "Or no, you will not allow me to attempt such a thing when I'm the only one who can materialize onto the grounds?"

I tried to rise, and she seized my tunic in her fist. Eyeing it, then her with a smirk, I drawled, "Adorable, butterfly."

"Do not patronize me, King. We've already spoken about this. I *want* to do it."

Her sincerity made me almost regret saying, "And I want to fuck the defiance out of you, then return you to the manor for safekeeping."

Her tongue poked at her cheek. Through her teeth, she exhaled and said, "We had a plan."

"We didn't," I said, not to further rile her but because it was true. "You had an idea that would guarantee getting yourself injured or worse, but now . . ." I nipped her chin. "We have the makings of a plan."

Her lashes fluttered wide as her eyes darted between mine. "You mean that."

She knew I did. "We will need to fortify it with the generals once we meet with the rest of them." Worry gnawed like a parasite as I gazed upon her features, now softened with relief. "But you're not going in there alone, and that's not up for debate."

Even without thorough training, with my assistance, she could materialize me into Molkan's den of cowardice with her. A fact of which Fume had pointed out more than once since Tullia's arrival in Folkyn.

A fact I'd vehemently ignored and then dismissed because I wouldn't risk her—not when I'd first met her, and certainly not now. Never, if I could help it. Though it now seemed unavoidable when she was this skies-damned determined to ensure Molkan's ruination.

"I know." Her head tilted, her smile coy and her cheek cushioned by that snowy hair. "My overbearing husband will accompany me."

My heart jumped, as if it would leave my chest to reach her. But my dazed grin fell when that prickling awareness returned. It watered down my spine, turning it to steel.

I took Tullia with me as I leaped to my feet.

An almighty shriek I hadn't heard in decades drained the blood from Tullia's face before the scaled beast appeared atop the hills of rocks beyond the field.

I pulled her tight against me, and we materialized back to camp.

## 23

## Tullia

As soon as we appeared before the trees housing the tents and horses, I asked Florian, "Is that a scalon?"

Fear and adrenaline smothered the effects of materializing as the grass shook with the monstrous creature's hurried pace.

It scuttled across the field toward us on short legs, a salamander-shaped head bobbing close to the ground. Without taking our eyes from it, we moved backward into the trees. Scales, dark green and brown and as large as shields, covered the beast. Spikes glinted from a long tail and down its sides.

"Indeed." Florian withdrew his dagger and another I hadn't seen him carrying. "Typically placid unless provoked."

We retreated farther, my heart a swelling weight that made each breath pained. "Well, it certainly seems provoked." Though why, I didn't know.

The warriors awake came running just in time to greet the giant reptile as it reached the woods. Trees and foliage were crushed. One warrior made a strange hissing noise and threw his arms up at the scalon.

The creature paused only a moment before opening its mouth and releasing another shriek that had the horses rearing and attempting to flee.

"Hide, but don't run." Florian stopped and stepped in front of me, saying with enviable calm, "Stay with the wolves if you must."

He was out of his mind if he thought I would simply leave. Even if I wanted to, I couldn't move, as the scalon's advance was again thwarted. This time, by bursts of wind and swinging metal.

"Tullia," Florian said rigidly. "Go now."

Realizing he was torn, unable to decide where he was needed most, guilt needled, and I considered leaving.

Then Nirra darted forward between vicious sweeps of the spiked tail.

"The sides are soft," she bellowed to her warriors. "Beneath the scales. Aim there." But as Nirra lunged, the scalon struck, and the general's sword was knocked into the air by the creature's tail.

Warriors roared and rushed forward, a closing circle of blue fury and readied weapons.

The scalon paid them no heed and sank its teeth into the general's leg.

Nirra screamed, a howl of rage and pain. The breeze unfurled into a harsh wind as if she were gathering it. With another shout, she flung her hands toward the beast.

The scalon released her with a shriek that was cut short. Yellow eyes bulged. Black veins appeared and protruded, crawling rapidly up its throat. Teeth the size of arms were exposed, rows of sharpened swords glinting in the late light of day. Its maw opened impossibly wider, forked tongue stiff and long neck thrown and twisting—

The creature was in pain.

"What is she doing to it?"

Nirra's hands were still raised. Two warriors ran forward. One hooked his arms around her torso, then dragged the general back, while the other blocked them with a shield and narrowly avoided a flick of the tail.

Florian advanced. "She's choking it."

Horror gripped me. Unreasonable given what a creature this size was capable of. Yet it worsened as the ground shook again.

"Florian," I yelled in warning.

Of course, he already knew. Over his shoulder, he ordered, "Do as I said," as another scalon crashed into the brush, small trees snapping and bending in its wake.

This one was furious.

A single step backward was all I could manage. My hands opened and closed at my sides, empty and trembling. I'd never felt more useless as Nirra was hauled into camp and every warrior converged upon the two beasts, Florian taking Nirra's place as their leader.

Horror and a strange sadness were instantly snuffed by the weight of my heart sinking into my stomach.

The force of it sickened and propelled me from my paralyzed state as my insane husband grabbed one of the numerous spikes upon the writhing scalon's side. He used it to pull himself up onto the creature's back.

Warriors attempted to stab the beast from beneath as Florian, catching a sword thrown to him, readied to drag the blade across the scalon's twisting neck. "Watch the tail," he hollered. "The poison will spread before we reach aid."

Growling from the wolves joined the screeching coming from the second scalon, and Florian's orders to distract it while he swung for a clear kill on the first.

But he was jostled. The scalon's entire body twisted now, bucking to be rid of the king when Nirra's magic released its hold.

The tail rose, scaled with a barbed tip.

I didn't think. I just ran.

Wolves snarled, advancing faster from the western side of camp where they'd chosen to rest. Their glowing eyes studied the chaos, then looked at me as they slowed.

I stopped when the second scalon's gaze latched onto mine and, in its haste to get to me, the creature nearly crushed one of the warriors attempting to push it back.

My hands lifted high, for all the good it might do, my heart silent yet screaming in my ears. I tripped backward, my fingers shaking as I slowly reached for the dagger at my side.

Florian cursed, and I spared him a glance that should have been fatal. He ducked, scarcely avoiding the barbed tip of the scalon's tail. It rose again, too quick to evade—

I screamed.

The scalon nearing me froze.

Time slowed, then came to an ear-piercing halt. The echo of my anguish faded into the dying breeze. The tail mere inches from Florian's back fell to the grass with a thump.

Everything just stopped.

I wasn't certain how or why or what possessed me to look up at the creature before me and hiss, but I did. My distress twined into a knot of vehement disapproval. Absurd, yet I ignored the curdling temptation to cease looking like a fool and continued to glower at the scalon.

It wouldn't work, I knew, if I gave in to any other feeling.

Seeming to receive the message, the scalon scuttled back, bumping into its companion as I hurried to Florian.

One hand on the hilt of my dagger, I kept the other raised before the beast he'd climbed, and said to him, "Get down."

His stunned expression might have been comical if he weren't seconds away from death. Florian shook his head and gave a tight glance at the scales beneath him. "Tullia, get back—"

"You won't harm him, and he won't harm you."

The monstrous mixture of frog and lizard blinked, his tongue unfurling and nearing my chin. A reek of damp and sulfur made my nose twitch, but I remained still.

"Him?" Florian scowled. "You are far too confident and far too fucking close for my liking."

Avrin's taunting words returned to me then. *A form of communication where no words are required—only feeling. A useless gift, really.*

The hand raised in front of me wavered. Before the doubt and other hopeless feelings wholly crept in, Florian acquiesced.

He tossed the sword, then jumped to the ground, startling the beast he'd climbed with the thud. I stepped closer, and the scalon once again focused on me until Florian moved. He retrieved the weapon, eyes trained on the creature watching him retreat, forked tongue flicking.

Perhaps not so useless after all.

For although they wouldn't understand anything I said, the large reptiles could understand what I felt. So even as my stomach roiled with fear, I covered it with my relief—with immense gratitude. Then I forced that calm I'd felt once before to return. The peace I'd met when I'd gazed upon the horse that had saved me.

I forced it until I didn't need to. Until it enfolded me completely.

Realizing, the king looked between me and the scalons. Quietly, he gestured for the warriors to retreat. They did so, reluctant to move too far behind us, as Florian remained at my side—mere feet from the scalons.

The creatures watched and studied us all, but their barbed tails slowly ceased swishing. Their wide snouts rose, the slits quivering as they sniffed the air for more threats.

I stood still with that calmness, now a cold caress that whispered soothingly beneath my skin to settle my heart. Their heartbeats were as loud as my own in my ears, the combined pounds a drumbeat that relaxed all three of us. The swaying dance of tree branches and the percussion of wildlife became a cocoon of tranquility.

The temptation to stay there, in that place of peace, was so strong that tears burned when the scalons began to retreat.

Nirra's cursing echoed, further fracturing the bubble, then grew in volume with the crunching and snapping of the creatures' departure through the brush. The trance broke, leaving me bereft within the heaviness of reality.

The wolves grumbled and returned to the other side of camp.

I closed my eyes, Florian's voice too loud when he asked if I was hurt. Only when I'd wrangled myself into some type of order did I open them.

I ignored the king and swept through the thick line of warriors at our backs, heading for Nirra. "We need healers," I needlessly said.

Blood seeped through the bandage being wrapped around her thigh.

"Harmony is a day's ride," Nirra said through gritted teeth as a male with golden-brown hair did a terrible job of tying the bandage.

I looked at Florian when he walked over and said, "There's nothing but villages nearby. To reach them, we'll need to back-track by a handful of hours, and we risk encountering more scalons in the passes."

All those giant rocks. We'd avoided them for a reason, waded through the muddy banks of the marshes astride them to camp in the valley.

"They won't have healers there," Nirra said. "None that'll make me any use to you any time soon."

Florian stared at his general's bitten leg, almost vacantly.

"Harmony will," the male warrior said, inspecting his handi-work with a wince. "We could materialize her there."

Nirra laughed at his expression, then winced, too. "Too risky. We visit as a group or not at all." She cursed. "You should've killed the giant toad, Florian."

The king smirked. It failed to mask the concern tightening his jaw. "Brink," he said. "Get her set up in the wagon."

The warrior who'd bandaged Nirra nodded. As he rose, hold-ing the general, his hazel eyes darted to me. A touch warily, perhaps.

Florian tracked Brink and Nirra through camp to the horses tethered by the stream, his command to his people echoing with urgency. "We leave now." He then turned to me, his gaze dark as night. "It would seem you're in need of another lesson on how to do as you're told."

Despite all that'd just transpired, warmth uncoiled in my stomach at the thought. I hid it by smiling when his hand stole my hip. "And if you'd been poisoned, I would have needed to find someone else to teach me anything."

He tensed. His glower and energy made me regret my choice of words. "Sweetest creature." His mouth caressed my cheek, the heat of his hand branding my lower back. He inhaled deep, then released it with, "Nothing, not even death, will keep me from being the only one who can see to your greedy needs."

He stepped away and looked toward the field, where the scalons now munched on wildflowers.

I watched him stalk to our tent, his ripened scent and the soft graze of his threat and mouth lingering.

**Tullia**

The town of Harmony was a small circular community backed by rocky cliffs and dense woodland and gently embraced by the Heartline River.

Camp was set up in the trees along the river while a group of us crossed the arched bridge into town, Nirra towed in the wagon.

Stone and wood homes sat squat and perfectly aligned astride thin cobbled streets. Morning frost clung to leaves of vines crawling over homes and shopfronts, as well as flower petals.

Despite the fading winter, varying breeds flourished in myriads of color from tidy wooden boxes beneath windows and garden beds separating properties. Civilians poked their heads out of doorways and windows, and halted their activity on the street to make room as we passed.

"Legend states this is where Mythayla found peace," Florian said. "Before she was murdered in the middle lands."

His soft tone after hours of nothing but wind and pounding hooves had my grip tightening on the saddle. "I once read that the land was surrendered with significant ease because of that."

"Small communities of faeries resided there," he said. "Most moved on with a bribe from the human queen, as she didn't trust they wouldn't be resistant to the wards. They were glad to have the means to do so for they believed the land is damned."

"Damp," I remarked, thinking back to the bustling town I'd been trapped in with an unexpected nostalgia. "And somewhat of a prison, certainly, but not damned."

The king released a breathy huff and sniffed my hair. "Those wards could very well be the reason it keeps the taint of a long-ago past."

The brief touch of his nose on my neck hunched my shoulders and forced a smile I knew he could sense, though he couldn't see.

We returned to silence as we trotted through the charming town that once gave refuge to a goddess.

We seldom talked while riding. The pace we had to maintain made conversation difficult, the wind often the only sound to be heard over the thundering of hooves and the clang of small wagons. But the arousal that pressed into my back had me expecting some type of teasing when our pace had slowed. Not to mention, the energy of his hunger—an iced heat that serenaded.

Alas, he'd said nothing lewd at all.

That I'd ended up materializing straight to him hadn't been a surprise. Not to me. Suspecting it might happen had been the reason I'd stalled. Since the shock and adrenaline had faded from our encounter with the scalons, I'd repeatedly recalled how stunned he'd been upon the ground beneath me in that field of wildflowers.

It was futile to keep hiding from the truth it had exposed.

It had proven that I cared more than I was willing to admit. That I more than cared for this king. He knew it, though he also knew I was reluctant. That I was reluctant to trust in anything the way I once so naively had.

Especially him.

Nirra's groan interrupted my thoughts. At the end of the long street stretching through the center of town, we came to a stop outside of a large two-story home.

Squinting up at the pale-blue shutters aside each arched window, I asked, "Who resides here?"

Florian dismounted. "Lord Jedworth and his three nuisance daughters." His tone was apathetic at best. "A necessary evil. I'd hoped we might avoid him, but he has access to the best healers in town."

I frowned at that, but I could ask nothing more.

Florian walked to the wagon carted by two patched stallions, and I took Hemlock's reins. Carefully, he gathered the grumbling general into his arms and carried her to the door at the end of the short stone drive.

Behind me, the warriors waiting atop their horses wore a mixture of curiosity and contemplation as they eyed me while their king kicked the door of the home, his hands full.

I offered them a small smile, of which the female closest to me returned with a nod. Then I turned back as a member of the lord's staff opened the door and gasped. He bowed, muttering apologies about not expecting Florian's visit.

"For the love of skies, just fetch your precious lord and find me some fucking booze, *please*," Nirra complained.

Her bandage was now covered in crimson. My eyes fastened to it. Even after I blinked, all I could see was hessian fabric and blood-spattered boots.

A pity, as I would have liked to glimpse the flustered male's reaction to Nirra.

"Of course," he clipped. "Do come in." I heard him say from inside the home, "You may take her downstairs to the kitchen, Majesty. An old table in there is easily cleaned if spoiled."

The door slammed.

Hemlock huffed, and I ran my fingers through his mane. Though he tolerated it, he didn't like being scratched behind the ears, nor did he like being idle without something to graze on or drink.

Lace drapes covering one of the upstairs windows shifted, exposing a bright blue eye and a rouged cheek.

A glance at our small entourage ignited unease, my thighs locking around Hemlock. More residents now peeked through windows of the neighboring bungalows beside us.

The giant stallion stood alert, ready for me to command him though I still wasn't confident I could.

I'd need to learn to accept it, being watched and studied, and I was. But it was a discomfort I never thought I'd experience. Therefore, I struggled to navigate it—feeling ridiculed and assessed and prodded like a caged bird who wasn't caged at all.

I was free.

Yet this ageless paranoia screamed differently.

I drew in a deep breath, releasing it slowly as I began to silently recite my letters. Mercifully, Florian returned by the time I'd reached the letter M, his cloak sailing behind him with tendrils of his wind-swept hair.

The lord exploded through the door and hurried down the drive after the king. I wondered if Florian had made haste due to us waiting outside.

The fog was unlikely to find us here. Of course, nothing was truly unlikely in this place of endless magical and violent possibility. Something else could decide to pay us a visit if we outstayed the time required to tend to Nirra.

"Give me but a few hours, Majesty. I have that whiskey you like," the lord was saying as he trailed Florian to the street. He was short for a Fae male, his unruly brown curls falling into sideburns at his ruddy cheeks.

Upon each finger was a gold ring, jewels winking in the morning light as he gesticulated nervously. "We'll provide you with the finest refreshments. Goddess knows you and our brave warriors deserve more than that, so let's make it a feast . . ." He blinked when his muddy eyes found me. "Skies, you look just like your mother."

Florian reached Hemlock, his features tight with that typical stillness. He dug his boot into the stirrup and mounted. His weight and heat immediately eased some of the tension within me. He took the reins, fingers intentionally brushing mine.

"Tullia is your queen, Jedworth," Florian said coldly. "You are undoubtedly well aware of this."

The lord's nod bobbled his thick chin. He lowered into a bow. "My apologies, my queen."

It irked. The title and the way he'd been forced to address me. But I wouldn't undermine my infuriating husband.

At least, not too much. I offered a faint smile to the lord. "Tullia."

"Beautiful name for a beautiful queen," he said, eyes ashine as he straightened and tugged the lapels of his chestnut waistcoat. He flashed his teeth, revealing browning canines that threatened to take me back.

Back to a throne room with another lord. One who'd thought me so far beneath him that he could touch me. Hurt me.

*Dead now*, I reminded myself. I swallowed, relief a soothing liquid rushing through my limbs when I remembered how it had felt to end his life.

Like I'd reclaimed a stolen piece of my soul.

Florian snorted softly by my ear, plucking me from the memory. He said to the lord, "Very well." Hemlock turned, forcing the lord to trip backward out of the way. "We shall return this evening, so long as you see that Nirra is cared for, Jedworth. I need her ready to leave at first light."

Glee rounded Lord Jedworth's eyes. "Of course, my king."

As we trotted back down the cobbled street toward the glinting lamps at the bridge in the distance, I asked Florian quietly, "Is it blood that causes someone's canines to brown in such a way?"

"Tobacco, too," he said. "Mostly, gorging copiously for many years with a lack of hygiene and care." I made a face. He sensed or saw it, as he said with velvet indulgence, "Near-immortality does not exempt one from rotting teeth."

"Stop it." I bit back a laugh. "And what of this feast? Is it a good idea?"

"Absolutely not," he said instantly, as if already pondering all the ways it could go wrong.

Citizens were now standing outside of their homes. Some bowed and curtsied upon our passing, others waved or merely stared, gaping.

"Very reassuring," I drawled dryly. "Thank you, Majesty."

"You're most welcome." His lips whispered over my ear. "My beautiful queen with a beautiful name."

I snorted, then smiled when he chuckled.

Fitting all of the warriors within the lord's small estate would have been a near impossible feat, given the number of guests he'd invited.

More than half of our unit remained at camp, content to rest and keep watch. A few warriors patrolled the town as per Florian's orders, eagerly soaking up the affections and awe from citizens offering treats and greetings.

The horses also remained behind. And though we were exhausted, the freedom to move our bodies after the arduous journey from the valley awakened and loosened muscles.

But I couldn't shake the tension entirely.

People were everywhere. In frilled and bright frocks and coats, they floated about in buzzing groups, a swarm of liveliness.

The long yard stretched from an enclosed courtyard adorned in twinkling lights toward a small lake. Lanterns aglow with fireflies were strung above tables teeming with delicacies and fine wines along the fence.

The warriors who'd accompanied us stood around them. Some slipped food into their pockets for later. Others watched the growing crowd of guests who'd come to glimpse their king with wariness and amusement.

Half a day didn't seem nearly enough time to put together a gathering of this size. Then again, the town of Harmony wasn't big, and the citizens still arrived in droves.

A shapeshifting faerie appeared to be the evening's entertainment, attracting attention from a podium in the middle of the yard. In mere seconds, the blue-haired female morphed into a mirror image of the muscular female warrior standing before her.

Fascinated by the gentle yet rapid growth and change of her petite body, I snapped out of my trance only when those surrounding her clapped and laughed.

Florian stood stiffly beside me at the back of the yard, drinking whiskey he'd brought himself and observing. I noted he'd picked our spot intentionally. The grass skirting the edge of the lake provided a quick escape to the streets at either end of the long row of houses.

In our tunics and cloaks, we were immensely underdressed for such an occasion.

I couldn't find the desire to care, after helping myself to another sweet cake and a lemon water. I didn't touch the wine, knowing that to let my guard down, even slightly, was a bad idea among a crowd that continued to grow.

As I licked my fingers, Florian's eyes shifting to my mouth, I realized he'd placed us here for another reason. The warmth that came with that knowledge sealed a fissure in my chest. "Thank you," I whispered.

Florian's gaze narrowed.

"For keeping me away from . . ." Struggling to voice it, I decided on muttering, "So many of them."

He studied me for a moment that further warmed my chest. He then sent his gaze to the lord, who was grinning and close to shouting as he told his guests a grand tale of our arrival that was hardly reminiscent of the truth.

"One day," Florian said quietly, still staring at the lord, "you will talk of it with me, butterfly."

I made no promises. Instead, I forced my eyes to wander over the many people dotting the grass.

Surprise chased me from the fear of uncertainty—from not knowing if I'd ever be able to talk about it all—when I locked eyes with a scaled faerie. A female similar to the male who'd denied Rolina what seemed so long ago in that trading tent.

Looking deeper into the crowd lit only by lanterns and colorful clothing, I found more scaled faeries. "The scalons," I whispered to Florian. "The scales on those faeries darken to a similar hue."

The airy strain of flutes took flight, floating from three players standing in bright blue waistcoats in the courtyard.

The king moved closer and kept his voice low. "Some eons ago, a faerie betrayed his spouse by laying with another." His arm brushed mine when he took a sip from his goblet. "And so his mate, who'd been half faerie and half witch, cursed his bloodline with a potion crafted from scalon blood. Any babe he sired without her would bear scales."

My brows leaped high. "Is that true?" Surely, it was but another faerie fable.

Florian looked pointedly at the reptilian female who threw her head back, laughing as the warrior charmed her with some type of story. "Never doubt the power of a scorned lover, butterfly." He sipped his whiskey again. "Especially one with exceptional talents."

His suggestive words fell flat when a gaggle of females pushed through the crowd toward us. Each one wore a bright gown that revealed much of their impressive breasts.

He groaned. "Fuck."

I looked from them to Florian. "Who are they?"

"Lord Jedworth's daughters." He cast me a shockingly startled glance. "Dance with me."

It wasn't a request.

He tossed his whiskey over his shoulder, the goblet reaching the lake with a splash, and grabbed my hand. He pulled me so close, I felt his shoulders loosen. All the while, every part of me turned to stone from the heat and hardness of his body against mine.

"They're gone?" I asked, my hand trapped between us upon his chest and my mouth dangerously close to his throat.

"They've halted their advance, but they're watching." He grumbled, "Strategizing, no doubt."

As he slowly rocked us side to side, I hid my smile against his collarbone.

"So tense, butterfly," he crooned to my hairline. His fingers splayed at my lower back, tickling. "One might think you prefer the woods over civilization." His mocking tone implied knowing the reason was not merely the people surrounding us.

The bridge of my nose brushed his jaw. The bristled graze of the thickened growth elicited gooseflesh. His scent flooded, softening my limbs against my will. "Do you prefer it?"

He'd been anxious, certainly, and so intensely alert. But there was no denying the difference in him since leaving the manor for open skies. His restlessness had settled. His need for control appeased by the action he was taking.

As if the question stunned him, he took a moment to respond. "Sometimes. Right now," he huffed, "absolutely."

I withheld a laugh, and as we turned, caught a glimpse of the three females standing mere feet from us by the table's end. One appeared to be on the verge of storming over to her king—his dance with his queen be damned.

Unable to stop it, and I didn't care to try, my hand moved from Florian's chest to his back.

If he knew why, he said nothing, and I decided I'd rather look at his hair-dusted throat.

Perhaps it was because I was able to hide from his eyes while tucked against him. I didn't know, but truths better left alone pushed free on a whisper. "You could've materialized to the border to oversee the downfall of Baneberry, Majesty." His hand tightened around mine, our gentle swaying slowing. "You could've spent all these nights dining on proper meals, resting in your bed and gazing up at your chandelier."

The rough question held a notch of humor. "*My* bed and chandelier, wife?"

Deciding to leave that taunt without a response, I waited.

He surrendered with a whisper that warmed my temple. "You needed this, and although I didn't know it, I suppose I also did. It's been too long since I've seen this world in this way."

"And what way would that be?"

"In color."

That gave me pause. "You've seen so much." He might not have told me all of it himself, but I'd heard enough about the indulgent prince he used to be to know it was true. That, and he was one hundred and thirty-seven years old.

"Everything yet nothing. Unless it provided me with enjoyment or furthered my plans, I've rarely noticed much of anything."

The silence that followed caused my fingers to link with his.

"Well," I said, my tone more tentative than I'd have liked. "When this is all over and you no longer need to spend your days plotting and scheming, you'll have a lot of free time on your hands."

"My days of plotting and scheming are far from over, butterfly."

I laughed as he turned us sharply, the sound drawing eyes that pricked into the skin of my back. "Dare I even ask what's next on your agenda?"

He held me impossibly closer. "You," he whispered to my ear. "Me." He kissed the crest of my cheek. "Venturing to any place you wish to see."

My heart was unable to be tamed, thudding painfully hard.

Hearing it, he hummed, lips rubbing my forehead. "I intend to show you everything this world has to offer, butterfly, if you'll let me."

The question was weak, all breath. "And if I don't?"

"Oh, Majesty," a feminine voice sang at a volume not even an army of flutes could battle.

Florian went still, muttering, "Goddess have mercy." Before I could laugh, he clenched my hand, then brought it to his mouth. He bowed, blue eyes piercing beneath his dark lashes, as he pressed his lips to my skin and warned, "Don't go anywhere."

An unexpected cold embraced when he released me.

Arms spread, he hurried to Lord Jedworth's daughters, as if he'd catch and keep them from walking any closer.

From reaching me, I realized, as one in a peach frock pouted my way before grinning brightly up at my king.

As my possessive thoughts jarred, a harsh crack sounded.

Florian's head whipped to the side. A brunette in a blue gown that matched his eyes glowered, as if she might slap him again.

My curled fingers drew blood from my palms. My fists shook. She'd actually fucking slapped him.

My teeth gritted while Florian said something I couldn't hear. Whatever it was seemed to work. Lord Jedworth's daughters then laughed and hugged him.

Shrewd and kohl-lined gazes found mine over his broad shoulders. The female in a gown of violent purple even had the audacity to cling to his arm as though he were not a king at all.

As though he were not married. Not mated.

I wasn't certain how many people were aware of the latter, and I didn't care. Red covered my vision. Thorns sprouted from somewhere deep within my chest, slicing each quickening breath.

Florian shook his head, attempting to remove the hands climbing him like slithering serpents determined to get beneath his clothing to sink their teeth into his skin.

I heard one of them say, "But it's been so long," and, as another looked at me, "She can join if you choose me. I don't mind middle land outcasts."

And I'd heard enough.

As I marched along the length of the table, guests and warriors quickly moved out of my way. Perhaps due to my expression or the cloying cloud of rage born from jealousy. I didn't care. But I paused upon spying a basket of blue cakes, stars piped atop them in a yellow cream, and snatched the handle.

Inside the gold-bedecked home, more guests mingled among the excessive amount of fine furniture. Some gasped upon realizing who I was. Some even bowed and curtsied.

Squeezing between them all, I paid them no mind.

My chin remained high. My anger kept my fears and paranoia tucked deep in a dark place that made me forget I'd ever been afraid of anything in my life.

Nirra was downstairs in the kitchen, as the lord's steward had instructed earlier. The general lay sprawled upon a bench seat behind a small wooden table in the corner of the stuffy room. She drank straight from a decanter, eyeing the staff flitting about the overloaded counters with unveiled irritation.

Nirra lowered the wine, and her drowsy hazel eyes widened when she finally noticed me. "Oh, thank fuck." She made to rise, but I held up a hand and slid onto the stool opposite her. A scowl joined her whined question. "We're not going?"

"You know we can't until that leg heals." I set the basket of cakes upon the table. "Florian said it will be sunrise before you can move it without disrupting the stitching and the potion's work."

"Florian says, huh?" A lazy drawl. She sipped more wine. "Well, I say we get out of here before we regret visiting." A narrowed glance was given to the staff behind me. "Something feels off."

"Might be that you've had too much wine when you probably shouldn't be drinking any after taking that potion." I pushed the cakes closer to her. "These should help soak some of it up."

The general was slow to drag her gaze from the fogged window above the stove. Shadows of moving bodies from the courtyard swayed beyond. "Might be that I've not drunk enough." Taking another swig, she set the almost empty decanter on the table and reached for a cake. She sniffed it, then shrugged and pushed the whole thing into her mouth.

She moaned her approval, causing one of the cooks behind us to cluck her tongue.

The cook realized who I was when I turned. Her eyes rounded and her knees bent as she and the others in the kitchen curtsied and murmured soft greetings.

I could only stare. Though it unnerved me to give them my back with so many blades in the room, I frowned at Nirra. "How are you feeling?"

She mumbled through the cake, "Like a giant toad-beast tried to rip off my leg."

I nodded. "Good, then."

"Fantastic," she said, attempting to push herself up from the cushioned seat. "So let's go."

Knowing her claustrophobia was likely getting to her more than her fear of sabotage, I placed my hand over hers on the table. She stilled, sinking back down with a groan. I squeezed her hand. "Won't be long."

Nirra looked at it, then at me, but waited until the cooks behind us hurried up the stairs with food to deliver outside before saying, "What's bothering you?"

"Nothing." I removed my hand. "Just thought I'd check on you before I head back to camp."

She glanced at the window again, her glazed eyes clearing a little when they returned to me. "Where's Florian?"

"Outside with Lord Jedworth's daughters."

"Skies, no," she gasped and smacked her face, her fingers sliding down it as she laughed. "You *must* go get him."

"He's fine."

"You don't understand. They're relentless. He made the mistake of entertaining two of them over the years, and now they won't quit sending him letters." She snorted. "I'd pay good coin to read them, actually." Noting my growing annoyance and the anger that hadn't abated, she laughed once more. "If you want him back unscathed, you really should go." She gave me an impatient glare when I didn't move. "Honestly, hurry."

"He's a grown male with winter at his fingertips. He knows how to fend for himself."

Biting her lip, she tipped a shoulder. "If you say so, Queen."

I prompted with a wave of my hand. "But . . .?"

"But what?"

I half rolled my eyes. "I'm sensing you've more to say on the stupid matter."

"Stupid, is it?" she questioned, grinning wide. It wilted as I waited, and she sighed. "If I had a mate, I'd be out there in a heartbeat, removing their fingers or taking their eyes."

Though I tried to hide my shock, I must have failed.

Nirra chuckled dryly. "I've spent nearly two weeks with you both. Not a soul in our unit isn't aware of it by now."

Fair enough, I thought, but didn't say. "You don't want one, trust me." I reached for a cake and sniffed it. Biting into it, I mumbled, "Far more trouble than they're worth."

Nirra was silent for a moment. My chewing paused when I glanced up to find her staring down at the table.

So quiet, I almost had to strain to hear, she said, "To find a mate, one would need to be interested, and though I've tried, I've so far been unsuccessful."

The cake stuck to my throat. I stole her wine and took a swig to wash it down. "You've never been with anyone?" I asked, possibly far too loud. I eyed her up and down. "You're a general, so I know you can't be too young."

"Fifty years next full moon," she said, taking the wine back and sipping. It was put down without care, her pointer finger tracing the glass base of the decanter over the wine-splashed table. "I've been with everyone." Sensing my confusion, she explained with a slight laugh, "I've been with males, females, humans, and everything in between."

Realization cemented. Finally. "You're not interested in any creature, then."

"Nope, and I've tried desperately to change that." A minute passed after those sorrow-tinged words, and she studied me intently. A smile slowly curled her lips. "But I've never been with a queen."

I laughed, cake nearly flying from my mouth when I took another bite. Swallowing, I shook my head. "Though I'd like to help with your tests, I don't think you need it." I licked frosting from my fingers. "I think you know that, too."

"I know," she said, softer now. "But sometimes, I can't help thinking it would be nice, you know? To share some type of connection like that with someone."

"You don't need sexual attraction for connection." I swept crumbs from the table. "If anything, it just makes what maybe shouldn't be harder to escape."

Nirra pondered my words as she again scrutinized me. Steps tapped toward the stairs.

"Try to get some rest." Brushing crumbs from my tunic, I stood. "I'll see you in the morning." I didn't wait for a response.

As I reached the stairs, Nirra gave one anyway. "You cannot escape him, Tullia. I've watched him with you. Watched him watch you. He won't let you. Should we survive what lies ahead, he will be your fate."

Those words were claws scraping over wounded flesh. A familiar ghost I'd been ignoring. Acknowledging it would mean facing more than I was ready to contend with—that I was still just as trapped as I'd always been.

And that Molkan's death would provide little more than a fleeting taste of the freedom I craved but was never destined to possess.

The cooks returned and curtsied.

I gave them a smile that was probably more of a grimace, then hurried up the stairs and into the hall, accompanied by Nirra's haunting warning.

## 25

---

**Tullia**

Citizens of Harmony, and even a handful of warriors, sang and stumbled through the streets.

None of them paid me any mind as I walked toward the river. The hood of the cloak Florian ceaselessly tried to make me wear kept my telling near-white hair out of sight.

Some other time, I might have wished to soak in the bawdy ballads and my surroundings. The beautiful homes, from small cottages to boastful two-story structures swallowing much of many side streets. The fireflies dancing in and out of streetlamps and the scent of autumn and celebration on the crisp air.

Unable to decide when a time like that would be, my senses remained heightened. My ears were sensitive to every noise, even as I neared the river.

Rather than cross the stone bridge to head back to camp, I trailed the bank until I encountered a small waterfall downstream. It crawled from a creek in the forest above into a growing rush over a cropping of rocks, no taller than eight or nine feet, to crash into the river.

Carefully, I wended down the worn river-lined path between spiky and reaching shrubbery to get a closer look.

Reeds stood tall on either side of the falls, the group of rocks almost as large as the torrent of water falling over them to travel through the heart of Folkyn. Vines draping over the stones curtained a darkness beyond the falls.

A cave.

Though I sensed nothing within, I couldn't be sure from where I stood on the opposite side of the river. Foolish, maybe, to even dare. But the curiosity I'd seldom felt since leaving Baneberry bloody and bruised poked. It prodded and pleaded to explore, and to distract.

To cast aside thoughts of possessive feminine hands and blue-eyed kings.

The river was not so violent that I couldn't cross it. I wanted nothing more than to be rid of my soiled tunic and pants and the feelings that scraped like talons over my chest.

After ensuring I was in fact alone, I peeled off my clothing and left it upon the embankment. But I took the dagger.

The iced water stole my breath. My teeth met and threatened to chatter. My feet slipped over slimy and sharp stones until I reached the middle of the river and needed to swim. I'd never been taught, but I managed to kick and push my arms until I once again felt rocks beneath me.

I waded toward the giant stones, skin sprayed from the waterfall. Smooth, mossy, yet there were crevices. Enough of them that, if I grabbed a fistful of vines, I could probably haul myself up into the cave.

First, I tucked the blade in a gap between the rocks and dug my toes into the riverbed. Pulling the vines back, I peeked into the darkness.

A low rumble, followed by the snap of foliage, had me dropping the vines and pushing away from the falls.

But it hadn't come from the cave.

I hesitated in reaching for the dagger when a hiss echoed like steam over the river.

The water falling from the creek hindered my view, spraying into my eyes as I peered up to the forest above. Two sets of giant eyes, yellow with thin black pupils, glowed through the trees and shrubbery.

The scalons.

My heartbeat slowed as I strained to hear. As I watched them watch me.

They didn't move.

Minutes passed, howls and hooting and scuttling mingled among the crash of the waterfall next to me, and still, they merely stared. Unsure what they wanted, I decided to see by taking my time to wash the past two days from my body.

Aside from the occasional flick of their tongues, the scalons did nothing. They seemed content to remain where they were. The wolves, if not already roaming the outskirts of town, were likely not far behind. Unless, I thought, they considered the scalons a threat, and so they'd finally ceased their stalking.

"From now on . . ." Florian's calm voice was a startling blow at my back. "I think rather than tell you not to move, I shall tell you to run and hide from me naked and alone in a river in the dead of night." His clenched jaw rose when I whirled in the water to find him standing beside my discarded clothing. "Then you won't move a fucking inch."

My own ire made it impossible to feel concerned about his, regardless of his scolding tone and the energy wafting from him like a harsh wind from a nearing blizzard.

I then realized the scalons had been here for some time. Perhaps since I'd left the town aglow in the distance. And the hissing sounds they'd made had been a warning of Florian's approach.

A brief rise of his gaze to the forest told me that the king knew they were there. He evidently assumed the same as me—and deemed them no threat. That, or he was too angry to care.

"I don't need to tell you how reckless you've been," he said, removing his cloak. His hands lowered to his pants, and my stomach to my curling toes. "But perhaps I need to show you."

My tongue was stuck to the roof of my drying mouth, speech and breath robbed from me as he kicked off his boots and finished undressing.

Moonlight washed over his physique. A physique I hadn't seen in all its powerful glory in days. Glimpses when we'd bathed, when he'd fucked me against that tree what seemed far too long ago, had left me starved in ways I hadn't been able to appease.

"I hunted you," he said, rough and low as he stepped into the river. "I trailed your scent, my heart in my fucking throat as it led me here." He didn't so much as flinch from the temperature of the water.

And he wouldn't.

He was winter personified. A storm given the body of a Fae male.

Midnight-blue eyes brightened to dawn-touched morning. His nostrils flared, starlight brushing crevices between muscle in his broad shoulders and dripping over his defined chest. He waded toward me, a beast who'd finally found his prey. The gleam of his gaze, the twitch of his plush lips, and the tic of his fixed jaw said he was pleased that I'd realized and hadn't fled.

That I'd surrendered.

Breath burst from me as soon as his hand hooked around my waist. He pushed me to his chest, his other hand smoothing damp hair from my face as his hungry eyes devoured me. After a thorough study of my features, he tilted his head and concluded, "You're upset."

I escaped his embrace with a hard shove at his chest. He hadn't expected it, enabling me to push backward into the water.

He seized my ankle.

A yelped laugh left me and echoed. I was tugged back to his chest, this time with my back to it. His arm banded around both of mine—around my breasts—as his hand slid over my hip and straight between my legs.

"You ran." He cupped me, the hold possessive and his lips at my ear. "Just left me without saying a fucking word."

"You seem far too surprised."

"Oh, I'm not." His fingers curled, hugged my core tight. "Furious, butterfly, is what I am."

Pleasure struck, unleashing a desperate desire for more. "Release me," I whispered, the order weak as I tried to resist riding his hand.

A laugh dripping with menace evoked a violent shiver. "You don't want me to do that."

"Don't I, Majesty?"

"No." His mouth tickled my ear, then lowered to my thrashing pulse. "You want me to fuck the disobedience out of you until we both forget how foolish you've been."

"What else should I have done, Florian?" I asked, incredulous. "Wait there with everyone watching while you went to entertain yourself with one of Lord Jedworth's daughters?" I laughed, quiet and dry. "Skies, perhaps all of them."

He turned to stone, save for the hand cupping me. It clenched, as did my core in response. The silence screamed with cascading water and wildlife and the earth I continually scorched between us.

A shuddering exhale quaked his body. "You truly believe I would do that."

It wasn't a question. I wouldn't have walked away if my jealousy and doubts and self-loathing hadn't gotten the better of me.

It had been wrong to leave, and it was certainly foolish. But he was a king. He could have whatever he desired. He was my husband. But not because he'd chosen to marry me from a place of love that necessitated commitment.

He might have set our fates in motion, but we were now bound by a force beyond our control. And Florian Hellebore was a male who demanded complete and utter control over every facet of his life.

He would not fold because of a goddess-ordained bond.

He did not share the dreams I'd concocted and carried. Dreams I'd since seen so thoroughly crushed that I was still fighting the temptation to dream again.

He would always be this way. Ruthless, cunning, and so coldly complicated that he could never be tamed.

Tense minutes passed, neither of us moving.

Then his harsh hold on my body gentled a fraction as he finally broke the silence. "I can tell you that I have no desire for anything that isn't you until the sun and moon cease to rise." Silken soft, those words grazed my shoulder, a burn he soothed with his lips. "You won't believe me until you let yourself see it."

Half delirious with the need he'd reawakened, I dared to ask, "See what exactly?"

He huffed. "Precisely." His mouth pressed to the curve of my throat. The whisper was close to a taunt. "You're still upset."

My head fell back to his shoulder. The words left on a weary exhale. "I'm not."

"Lies no longer fit between us, sweet creature."

As much as I loathed it, he was right. "I was just so . . ." I couldn't deny it, and I didn't want to when he began to rub me, and my thighs opened wide. "Angry, and I won't tolerate anything I don't have to again."

"Good," he praised with a hum. "Very good, butterfly. Now tell me . . ." He slipped one finger inside me, and my forehead met the coarse hair covering his chin as my eyes closed. "Which part was it?"

Wanting more, I bent at the knees. Wanting that finger to move, to curl, or for him to add another. "What do you mean?"

His embrace firmed until straining to move pressed his finger deliciously deep. "Tell me what ignited your fury."

My head flopped. I failed to answer, and he withdrew his finger—waiting.

"One of them slapped you," I breathed, then moaned when he rewarded my response with a deep thrust.

"What else?" His lips skimmed my jaw, followed by his tongue.

His finger moved in and out of me slowly, torturously, rubbing and retreating. My eyes fluttered closed. Moonlight, bright behind the darkness of my closed eyelids, danced with sparks of pleasure.

Then he stopped. "Tullia, what else?"

Desperate, I almost whined. "One of them clung to your arm," I said through my teeth. Yet again, he waited, forcing me to admit, "As if she had the right."

A kiss so soft was given to my temple. "Good," he rasped, then rewarded me by inserting a second finger. "And did she have the right?" When I failed to respond, he rumbled, "Answer me."

"No," I snapped, instant and ravenous.

His pleased smile was present in the gentled question. "What else?"

"And you . . ." I was close. So close I would probably tell him anything he wanted to know. "You just let them."

Desire and something I couldn't place strangled his voice. "Let them what, Tullia?"

"You let them fucking touch you," I nearly shouted.

His chuckle sounded relieved. "And how did that make you feel?" He stroked deep, and kissed my temple again, as he whispered, "Tell me, my jealous creature."

The words left me in a slight growl as I began to contract around his fingers. "Like I might murder them if I didn't walk away."

He stilled, then groaned and fucked me with his fingers. His hips jerked against me, his erection steel at my back. I clutched his forearm over my chest, my nails scoring into his skin, and came apart.

With a violence that hurt, I unraveled.

A gasped cry was stolen by Florian's mouth. His kiss was bruising, unmoving, as he held me trapped within his embrace and filled with his fingers.

He broke it to watch me, and my head slumped to his shoulder. "That's it." He licked my exposed throat. "Let your body scream every word you refuse to say." He withdrew his fingers and cupped me hard, his palm digging into my clit. I trembled, and he grunted. "Fuck, you destroy me."

I was still writhing over his hand as he moved through the water to the bank.

Grass and stones and mud met my back, reeds tickling my cheek. Unable to think clearly, I lay there while he remained in the water and opened my legs. He trailed his finger through me, and I jerked. He cursed, ordering, "Cover yourself."

I swallowed thickly, my voice as weak as my limbs. "No one is around."

"Cover your fucking tits, Tullia."

I did, and he pushed my thighs wider. "Now squeeze them." His groan of approval vibrated against my core when I did as I was told and he dragged his tongue through me.

My thighs clamped around his head, but his hands were stronger. He pushed them wide again—spread me so far, my knees met the bank. "I can't," I rasped. "Florian."

"Your lies are sweet," he crooned to my swollen flesh. "But your truth-telling cunt is far sweeter."

He licked me slowly. Devoured every drop of pleasure his fingers had wrung from my body with throaty grumbles. Taking his time, he savored and swallowed me like a rarity he might never taste again.

Only when I quivered, pleading to the stars for the orgasm he intentionally delayed to tear through me, did he stop. "I think you're ready, sweet creature."

I wasn't sure what he meant. I was ready to come, and he knew that. I was more than ready for him to climb atop me and fill me, but he knew that, too.

As I tried to rise on my elbows, I slipped.

His mouth latched onto my clit. Stars swirled in the inky-dark sky as he flicked and sucked, then held me pinned to the bank when I released a near-silent scream.

His chuckle was wicked as he gathered me into his arms and moved back through the water toward the cave. I clung to him, useless and still quivering, my breaths coming fast against his neck.

He stopped and eyed the blade I'd left between the rocks. "At least you weren't completely blinded by jealousy."

I said nothing, but I squeaked when he lifted me to the vine-shrouded cave. My hands slapped against the slippery moss. One of his slid to my ass, squeezing before he pushed, and I laughed as I pulled myself inside and crawled into the dark.

He followed, ice crusting the rock in a large shard he gripped to haul himself up in one shockingly graceful swing. The dark space brightened from his lust-stained eyes as he stood there, dripping wet, neck bent to keep his head from hitting the rock above.

I stayed where I was, seated on the stone. My hands pressed against it as I stared up at him with far too much awe.

An awe he deserved, his shadowed and moonlit form overpowering and his cock twitching, as he gazed down at me. "Come to me."

The soft command was a tug at that force outside of our control, luring me to my hands and knees. I crawled to him, pleased by the way his nostrils flared with his hooded eyes, then sat back on my knees beneath him.

He stared, that blistering blue gaze framed by damp and dark strands of hair. A finger stroked as it curled under my chin, his thumb brushing my lower lip. Lust might have shined in his eyes, but there was no escaping the adoration in them, and in his touch.

A touch I'd received countless times since I'd met him.

His mouth parted and his brows furrowed slightly, as if he were about to attempt to say something he didn't quite know how to voice.

Before he could, I gripped his cock.

All of him seized.

From head to toe, he went startlingly still. Then he groaned as I rose onto my knees and took him into my mouth.

There was none of the hesitation and insecurity I'd had when I'd tried this before. There was no curiosity to explore the thick veins and his tightened testicles. As I drew him deep into my mouth, then moved my hand down his shaft and squeezed, there was only the need to make his knees quake because of me.

As his groans grew more ragged, and muscle strained and bulged in his shoulders and neck, there was only the desperation to pump him faster. To lick and suck him harder and take him even deeper.

As his hands clenched my hair, pulling my mouth on and off his cock, there was only the urgent desire for victory. To make him spurt down my throat until I choked and the sound haunted him after that inevitable moment came.

The moment when he would break me again by proving he was the same as he'd always been—what everyone I'd dared to care about had always been—just another liar who would only break my hungry heart.

For it was inevitable.

Realizing that, surrendering to it as Florian groaned and braced one hand upon the rocky ceiling, filled me with an unexpected freedom.

If doom was to be my destiny, then I would do as I wished until I collided with it again.

And I was tired of resisting that I wished for this treacherous male I'd been chained to.

Especially when his throat bobbed and his eyes opened. They were still aglow as he gazed down at me while I licked his softening cock clean. A shiver rocked his enormous frame, and it thrilled me even more.

His chest rose and fell with deep heaves. He released the fistful of my hair to gloss his knuckles over my cheek. I wasn't prepared for the tender touch, nor the rasped question. "Why?"

My mouth unlatched from him. "Are you complaining, Majesty?"

A brow raised, he swiped his seed from beneath my lower lip. He fed his thumb to my mouth as he lowered to his knees. I licked it clean, too. "Sweetest creature." He traced my front teeth, then slid his thumb across my upper lip. "I've never had my cock so fucking ravaged in my entire existence."

Jealousy flared, a winged monster scraping talon-tipped wings throughout my chest cavity.

The king's smirk quickly wavered. He frowned, his calloused palm sliding over my cheek and his fingers into my hair. "Answer the question, Tullia."

I couldn't find words to do so. Not when I'd made a habit of withholding so much from him since returning to Hellebore.

But the way he'd gazed down at me, the way he continued to stare at me—it took me back. Back to when he'd fed me strawberries and whispered the same words I whispered to him now. "You make me want to kill anyone who's ever looked at you."

His eyes flashed, blinding in the dark. He remembered, too.

Then his mouth met mine, hard and unyielding. His other hand curled around my lower back to my waist. My chest was squashed against his, my mouth to his, as he held me prisoner for seconds that melted my reservations.

They were erased completely when his lips left mine, only enough to say, "Tell me." He dodged my attempt to quiet him with my mouth. "Tell me that you see it."

Annoyance, and perhaps something like fear, threaded into my voice. "What is it you're wanting me to see, Florian?" I opened my eyes, and they crashed into his.

A mistake, for I could see it swimming within the stormy sea of his gaze. I saw it all before he released those poisonous words to my lips. "That I'm so wretchedly in love with you, it's both saved and damned me."

With vivid violence, I saw everything.

The frozen and mutilated males in the manor drawing room. The possessive tenderness during the days we'd lost in mindless bliss to the heat. My blood speckling Avrin's boots as the messenger delivered news of Florian's advancing armies. A severed head rolling from a sack containing two more. The constant guard of me while I healed. The bathing and the combing and the feeding. The destroyed bodies of nobles who'd dared to touch me . . .

I saw it all in undeniable color—felt it invade the coldest parts of my heart with warmth.

And as I stared at him, I heard his heart thudding in tandem with mine. "I do see it," I rasped.

Perhaps it wasn't right. Perhaps none of what he'd done was right at all. That didn't matter. Not to him, and it no longer mattered to me. It was his way. So much of what he'd done was his way of caring far more than he'd ever intended to care about anything again.

"You've shown me," I said, reaching up to clasp his face. "I just didn't know what it meant." Tears stung my eyes, thickening my confession. "I didn't want to know, and now that I do, I still don't know how I'm supposed to trust it."

His head tilted, his fingers curling into my hair.

"But I want to." I swallowed. "I want to trust it, Florian."

He scowled at the tear that fell to my cheek. Then he licked it and placed his forehead against mine. "I know."

My fingers tightened at his cheeks. It was expected that I would say those words back to him—words I'd hinted at feeling once before. But that was then. Now, my heart refused to let them go.

Sensing as much, he whispered again, "I know." He hushed my attempt to apologize with his mouth, and lowered me over the moss-blanketed stone.

He kissed me with a gentleness so lethal that more tears burned.

Each one was captured by his lips and tongue before he whispered, "You can hold on to your fears." My legs climbed his back. He entered me, slow and keeping himself deep as he loomed above me. "For now." His forearm curled by my head, his hand cushioning it against the stone.

His other braced near my ear, muscle flexing as he gently rocked his hips. He didn't withdraw. If anything, he pushed impossibly deeper, the sound of our meeting mouths and sighed breaths hidden beneath the rush of water beyond the cave.

"Just tell me that you're mine," he said.

"You don't need me to tell you that."

He stared into my eyes, a gleam I recognized sparking his own. A warning of what he intended as he kissed me once and lifted my head to his neck. "Then show me."

Happily, I obliged. My lips roamed, finding the vein I longed for near the curve of his shoulder. I licked it, luxuriating in his throaty groan when my teeth took their time piercing his skin.

His scent was heady, his heat everywhere yet never quite stretching far enough. Until then.

Until his taste collided with my tongue, and I swallowed his essence into my body with a moan. My legs tightened, a foot pressing into his perfect ass as I writhed against him, in need of friction. Needing to gorge on him as my mind was rendered empty of all else.

He circled his hips, murmuring husky approvals into my ear. He kept me lingering upon the precipice of immense satisfaction for mere moments. Then he lowered his mouth to my throat and licked the skin in preparation.

For his teeth to puncture.

Florian drew my blood from me with a harsh suck and violent shake of his body.

My mind was no longer empty. It overflowed with the synchronized beat of our hearts as we fed and he began to move inside me. That beat was a golden tether in the darkness. A song I'd never tire of hearing. And the fire that burned through my veins . . .

My lips unclasped from his neck as it spread straight to my core.

It was too much, yet I gyrated against him. *More*, the furious force screamed. Pleasure assaulted in waves—in what felt like thousands of miniature orgasms striking all at once—a prelude to the overwhelming connection being forged.

He felt them, too.

His entire frame was racked by tremors. His seed spilled into my body in small spurts with each thrust.

An animalistic noise, growled and almost desperate, left him when his teeth released my flesh. He gently pushed my mouth back to his neck. "Drink, butterfly," he said, sounding so different, so far away, although we'd never been closer.

His tongue caressed my skin before he fed in earnest again, and only when I did.

I understood what this was. I needed no explanation for the feelings that overlapped and cemented until I didn't know if they were his or my own.

They were both.

*Then show me*, he'd said. His earlier words about being ready now made sense.

A consummation of the mating bond. Again, this maddening creature had tricked me into falling at his feet in surrender.

Even if I had the ability to feel as much, I wouldn't be shocked. He'd proven time and again that he would do whatever he must to get all that he desired, and he would do it without shame. Without a shred of guilt or mercy.

I had to wonder if I even wanted mercy when he wasn't capable. I'd known all along that he wasn't. I'd known, and my hunger and affections for him had continued to grow regardless.

He moved with the primal pace of the beast he was, thrusting slow and deep as he drank from me with the same lazy yet powerful rhythm. His tongue lapped, his cock aimed with precision that tortured and shook my legs.

Beginning to fray into tattered threads, I tore my mouth from his neck, the words a gritted moan, "You tricked me."

Florian licked a path up my throat and over my chin. His bloodstained lips glossed mine. My ears rang with our racing pulses.

His voice was too loud and too soft, ricocheting off the stone and water surrounding us. "You seem so incredibly disappointed." He rammed into me to emphasize his point, his grin feral and devastating. "Go ahead," he taunted. "Lie to me, wife."

I fractured.

He watched me come undone. "My sweet butterfly." Stars danced upon the rock ceiling of the cave. He kissed me, then licked my upper lip. "My queen." I grasped the back of his head when he dropped his mouth. "And now . . ." Pain mingled with pleasure as he once again feasted on my neck, emptying inside me with a gravel-coated groan. "Forever my mate."

I held him to me as he trembled and suckled at my skin, accepting that this creature I was now bonded to in every unbreakable way would never change.

Accepting that I didn't want him to.

## 26

**Florian**

A clack against stone woke me.

Tullia, nestled in the crook of my arm, nuzzled her nose into my neck. Our consummation marred her own and still leaked from her body. Slowly, she stirred awake as I pressed my mouth to her forehead.

I kept it there when she licked my throat with a groan of exhaustion and hunger, and smoothed my hand down her back to toy with my seed in her beautiful cunt. But I paused at her ass, squeezing it.

Another clack.

A strike against the rocks outside. Prickling unease traveled over my skin. Of course, something was fucking amiss.

Confirmed by a call muted by the flow of water splashing into the river.

Silently cursing the goddess for seldom allowing me the time to overindulge properly, I carefully moved Tullia from my arms. Futile. She sat up when I did, pushing hair from her face and blinking drowsily.

I gritted my teeth against the urge to lay her back over the stone and sink my cock inside her while I kissed every sleep-crumpled feature.

*Mine,* that beastly bond between us crooned—smug and so fucking satisfied, my very bones shivered with pleasure.

No matter how far she ran nor how long she clung to her fears, she was now unchangeably and irrefutably mine.

Well and truly distracted, I crept to the entrance of the cave and nearly fell face-first into the river when I peered down to find plum hair. "Nirra?"

"Fucking finally. I've been trying to get your attention for half a lifetime," she hissed, but it was whispered as she waded closer to the cave with our clothing. "We need to leave immediately."

As I took it from her outstretched hand, Tullia asked what was happening behind me. "I smell Nirra," she said when I handed her the clothing.

Without the time to care about our nakedness, I extended my arm to Nirra. Her healing leg made climbing as high as we were without assistance impossible, hence the throwing of stones.

She gripped my arm, and I hauled her into the cave. "Speak while we dress," I clipped. "Jedworth?"

The general averted her gaze as she did, peeking through the vines to the town in the distance. "Right now, he's likely shitting his pants. He had two of our warriors poisoned and taken by Molkan's spies to the cellar beneath his kitchen. I searched as soon as I heard the muffled screaming, but it was too late. By the time I found them and broke through the door, Melk was dead and Jennis was wishing she was."

*Fuck.*

I'd known Jedworth couldn't be trusted.

He'd been an associate of Molkan's before Lilitha was killed. I'd heard reports they remained in touch, though he disputed them regularly. I hadn't cared due to his proximity to the border. He resided far enough from me that I never thought him much of a threat.

That, and I'd foolishly thought his fear of me would keep him from acting like a skies-damned spineless moron who wished to have his head removed.

"How many spies?" I asked, fastening my pants.

"Three."

"You killed them?" A pointless question. The general's infamous temper would've guaranteed their end. But I hoped I was wrong. We needed at least one of them alive.

"Had to," Nirra said, rubbing her leg, which was still bandaged. No sign of fresh blood, thankfully. "Given the state of Melk and what was left of Jennis, they could have known something of importance."

"Where's Jennis now?" I asked.

"I dragged her to the healer's hovel." Her features were grim as she turned to me. "They punctured her heart with iron splinters. I don't know if she'll make it, but she stands far more chance in this putrid town than with us. Then I sent the remaining warriors back to camp with an order to move."

This just got better and fucking better.

Noting my expression, she said, "We'll meet them five miles downstream. We need to hurry. The horses on the bank are a dead giveaway to whoever's watching." A look was given to Tullia, who was dressed and pulling her hair into a tangled braid. "Those rotting giant toads, too."

Tullia made a face and shrugged slightly.

It was glimpses like that—of the female who'd unknowingly deconstructed every plan I'd spent years crafting—that gave me comfort like nothing else could. Slowly but surely, she was breaking free of what had tried to break her.

Her time within these lands had changed her. As was to be expected. But it had changed her in ways that made it an honor to witness the unveiling of who she was becoming. An honor I was determined to be worthy of.

I helped Nirra and Tullia into the river and across it to the grazing horses. Sopping wet, we stomped into our boots, then mounted.

Nirra groaned. "Where are you going, King?"

"To pay the lord a visit," I said, Hemlock already trotting

toward town. As I urged the beast into a gallop, I yelled, "Go. We'll only be a few minutes."

We slowed upon reaching the entrance to town, and Tullia asked what she'd already sensed. "He stands with Molkan, then? This lord."

Debris from the celebrations of the previous evening clung to gardens and gleamed within puddles beneath pipes. Goblets and sodden tobacco stems, mostly, but there were the occasional items of clothing stuck to hedges or draped over fences.

"He has sworn seven ways from the skies that he doesn't." Hemlock avoided an open copper tin, toadstool dust surrounding it on the cobblestone. "I've never believed him, but I also believed he lacked the testicles to betray me so overtly and with such short notice." I dug my heels into Hemlock, spurring us into a gallop again. "He will pay dearly, but for now, this will need to do."

My anger unfurled, and I let it.

I allowed every scathing feeling to permeate my blood. My bones. My fucking soul.

Civilians gasped. Some lurched out of the way. Others ran indoors as gusts of wind gathering in our wake blew out windows of homes and businesses in the street.

By the time we reached the two-story home of the lord, my fury rushed over the cobblestone. I sent it down the drive and marching up the door and stone exterior of the house—until the entire structure was covered in ice.

Ice that thickened and creaked beneath the wind now forming a blizzard above. We stopped a safe distance from the drive. There, I let the howling force descend to tear the tiled roof from Lord Jedworth's home.

Only when we were riding back down the street did I relinquish my hold completely, and my fury with it.

The ice swallowing the lord's home exploded in our wake. Stone and glass, too.

Much of the structure caved in, judging by the sound and Tullia's expression when she glanced behind us. Her words were breathless from Hemlock's increasing pace, and the hint of desire that tinged her scent and cheeks. "I probably shouldn't be so aroused right now."

The final dregs of my rage left me with a rough and unexpected chuckle.

We met with the unit downstream, but we didn't stop.

They were ready, horses rearing and hollering as we left Harmony and its audacious lord behind.

The breeze tossed around scents of ale and wine and sex. Not from Tullia or myself. Many of the warriors, especially those who'd accompanied us to the lord's gathering, appeared to still be inebriated. Much of the rest were simply without adequate rest.

It seemed that wouldn't be changing any time soon.

As the sun began to wane beyond the trees and hills in the distance, we reached our destination. The outpost where all troops were to convene before crossing the border.

Tents and wooden huts came into view. Before we reached them, Shole stepped out from between the trees.

We slowed, Hemlock protesting the late warning. Tullia stroked his neck to comfort him. He'd never been so spoiled. If this journey had taught me anything besides unbearable restraint and something resembling patience, it was that I could be jealous of a fucking horse.

Shole neared, a tobacco stem in his fingers. His rugged features gave nothing away as he bowed to Tullia with an irritating smirk some might dare call charming. "The journey has served you well, my queen."

I'd known him long enough to recognize the concern dulling his gaze when he looked at me.

Tullia smiled but remained upon Hemlock when I hit the ground. "You'll bow to her, but not to me."

Shole's expression was impassive, even as he said, "I'm afraid now is not the time for jealousy, your coldness."

He joined me as I wove through horse and rider and wagon. I didn't ask. That he'd made his presence known right away had been warning enough.

Warriors began to dismount. Those who'd realized before me chose to remain with their steeds. Shock and fear mingled with that of beast and soil and unwashed bodies, spreading fast until it nearly overpowered the scent.

The unforgettable scent of witch and faerie magic.

Those arriving from the north and west, and those who'd already arrived, avoided the clearing that once contained my most populated outpost. A vital hub of warriors who'd dedicated years to training and rotating brethren for the outposts along the border of Baneberry and Hellebore.

Few huts and tents remained. The ones that did encircled the vast clearing.

And there were even fewer warriors.

One of them stepped forward. A barely matured male. "General Polk is gone," he said, his chin set as if it might keep his mouth from quivering. It didn't. "They're all just . . ." His drawn features grayed with the threat of sickness as he twisted his hands around the leather pommel of his sword. "Many were sleeping, sire, but many were still awake. It got them, too. It seemed to come from everywhere."

"When?" It was all I could think to ask.

A female warrior came forward and clasped the young male's arm when his shoulders shook. She nodded to me, and informed, "Early last evening, my king."

Not Lord Jedworth's doing, then. And the feast he'd insisted on throwing not a distraction.

It was but a tentative attempt from a spineless shit to learn what he could to gain more of Molkan's favor.

Besides, Molkan didn't need Jedworth to know how important this encampment was to my cause against him. He'd known for as long as it had existed. If I were him, this outpost would have been first on my list of places to send that fucking fog.

Which led me to ponder his next move. As I'd thought I was target number one, and our army a bonus in this new game.

I asked, "How many of you remain?"

"Twelve," she said.

*Twelve.*

The number cleaved through me to flay my blistering chest.

Shole came to stand beside me. "Fume's units should start arriving within the hour."

I looked up at the gathering stars and refrained from pinching the bridge of my nose. Almost one-hundred warriors. Many of them new recruits. Many so fucking young. Many with families and many now without the chance to make one . . .

Gone.

Tullia's gaze was a burn at my back. One that kept the winter frosting my blood from exploding into our surroundings as everyone looked at me. As they all awaited an answer, a fucking cure, for a horror none of us could fix.

Not yet.

I lowered my gaze to the haunting clearing. "Everyone remains alert and ready to leave."

Metal gleamed within the clover and grass. I studied it, my entire chest cavity on fire with growing rage and something I refused to let unspool.

Fear.

## 27

**Tullia**

I hadn't known what to expect when we finally crossed the border.

Awaiting Baneberry warriors ready to attack, maybe. I hadn't known we'd even crossed it until Florian told me, his voice raised to carry over the wind.

There was only more trees, more waterways, and more vibrant valleys between. Some of the latter were speckled with tiny villages, a few younglings staring wide-eyed as hundreds of warriors burst through the trees and converged upon a land that wasn't their own.

But it was mine.

No matter how conflicted I felt over that fact. No matter what Molkan had done to my body and soul.

Some of the remaining warriors from the outpost decimated by the fog had joined our unit. Depending on the terrain, other units only briefly came into view now and then. We traveled in our original factions, some amounting to one hundred or more, and kept a minimum of one mile apart.

There were too many of us now, so we stopped only when we had to. Florian's anxious anger and concern over the fog was evident, but perhaps only to me.

Nothing had changed. Yet everything had.

I could better sense his emotions, and he my own. I could feel his energy brush over me like a hovered hand hesitating to caress. It touched my own, I realized, the woolen warmth of the sensation alarming at first, and now something close to a necessary comfort.

We were mates. This I'd known.

But now, that connection had been sealed by the coupling and dual feeding within that cave. During the long hours of riding and amid the brief respites, I chased away my fear of the deadly fog by immersing myself in thoughts of it over and over.

His heated declaration sat at the forefront of my mind to dance with every memory that reinforced those words.

*I'm so wretchedly in love with you.*

It seemed wrong to find hope within that which had played a part in robbing it from me. Though that hope was small, I still clung to it. I wrapped it around me like a sheet of soft silk that didn't only cover my scars but embraced them.

And for moments that stretched farther than any other upon this journey, I felt no shame. No self-loathing. For no matter what awaited us, Florian had meant it. There was no disputing his confession, and for once, I didn't even want to try.

He'd asked, but I hadn't wished to join the meeting with the generals.

Instead, I chose solitude. I tended to my needs and quickly dipped into the tiny creek hidden beyond the giant ferns near our tent.

Afterward, I dressed and donned the cloak in dire need of washing and sat before a fire someone had left unattended. The air still carried a bite of winter, though beneath it was the scent I tried not to recoil from.

The scent of spring.

Its nearing touch stroked the grass a brighter green, the blades softening. There was no sludge and no frost. There was a vivid change in the mottled leaves, too.

I wasn't sure where my wolf companions had gone, nor the scalons. Perhaps they drew the line at stalking faeries into other territories. More likely, they hadn't been able to keep up with our hurried and rarely broken pace since we'd left Harmony a few days ago.

Boots crunched over sticks and flattened the grass.

My eyes trailed the black pants that resembled leather, and I knew who it was before confirming with a look at his face. Only one creature among us wore no semblance of uniform. Although he was a warrior, he seldom did, and he didn't visit our stops long enough to be considered a part of Florian's royal army.

He was sent ahead to check on scouts and do some spying between his other missions.

Missions, Florian had said, that were commissioned by the wealthy and desperate of Hellebore. I'd been tempted to ask him if his friend was merely ensuring he did not miss out on any of the action as we drew closer to more of it. For a creature with an occupation such as his did not do what he did merely for the coin.

Shole gestured to the log on the other side of the fire. "Is this seat taken?"

I looked from the barren log to him, squinting slightly against the glare of the dying sun behind his head of thickening silver hair. "Unfortunately, I'm rather in demand."

He grinned, stabbing a finger at me and shaking it. "A sense of humor. Good." Then he bowed. "I would be honored to join you, my queen. Thank you for the offer."

I bit back a smile as he sat and spread his hands before the flames I'd been feeding.

"The scalons are a half day's journey behind," he informed. That grabbed my whole attention. Noticing, he explained, "Nirra requested I check after her gruesome encounter."

I nodded. "I don't know how to stop them."

"You should, being that you're the one luring them across realms." His head cocked, and he appeared to ponder it. "An attachment must have been made during that attack."

249

"Seems to be the case," I said, for I knew that much. I just wished I knew how to make them detach. Something told me they wouldn't until I ceased emanating an energy that called to theirs—until I found that peace I was seeking.

Yet that was looking different with the dawn of each new day.

Shole interrupted my befuddlement. "They speak highly of you, you know," he said. "Especially since then."

"Who?"

He jerked his head to the warriors dotting the riverside clearing. "Your travel companions, of course."

Many of them slept on their packs. Only a few bothered with tents we would need to tear down in a mere couple of hours. No one wanted anything hindering their senses right now.

"That traitor mark might be something you don't wish to live with, but to them, it makes you more than a changeling they once had to tolerate because of their king's vengeful plans," he said so quietly, I might have missed it if I weren't stunned. "It makes you their true queen."

My heart pounded, and I knew he could hear it. In an effort to keep from peering at the warriors he spoke of, I ripped a leaf in two. "Most of them barely speak to me."

"As if Florian would give them the chance." He punctuated those words with a glance at the hills in the forest aside us.

Florian, Nirra, and Fume were in talks with the other generals about our next moves. There would be three, that much I knew, which meant little to no stopping until we'd reached the city outskirts of Bellebon.

Where we expected an army would await us.

Florian, hand on the hilt of his sword at his side, was looking down at me. I wriggled my fingers. Even with the distance, I knew his expression remained unchanged, stoic and still.

Shole huffed, curled mouth drooping as he stared at me. "Looking forward to seeing Father dearest?"

His casual lack of tact straightened my spine. I blinked at him, scowling and uncaring of whom he was. "Are you truly expecting an answer to that?"

He made a face, as if tempted to laugh but deciding it was best not to. "It is but a question, my wounded queen."

My eyes narrowed. "I am no longer wounded."

He pushed his lips out, seeming to silently refute that.

Rather than indulge him, I asked, "Is it curiosity or merely boredom that landed you in your line of work?"

"My line of work?" he repeated, lips curving once more. Otherwise, he appeared unbothered by the blatant subject change and my own incredibly direct question.

"You know"—I tossed the leaf pieces onto the fire—"being hired to kill and spy and goddess knows what else."

His chuckle was a low and stalking smoke. "Goddess knows indeed."

I waited, selecting some twigs by my feet and snapping them.

He knew exactly where the tactic came from. "Florian has rubbed off on you in ways I believe we've yet to wholly appreciate, my queen." When I only smiled and threw the sticks onto the fire, he chuckled again and said, "I was born with a need that turned into a desire to move, if that answers your question."

"Survival," I surmised, somewhat shocked he'd answered but unwilling to show it.

He hummed. "You have indeed learned a thing or two about that, haven't you?"

"I have indeed," I said, giving my gaze to the flames.

"It changes you," he said. "But instincts born from darkness are always better." I met his ice-blue eyes at that. "Those scars can be molded into weapons that will serve you well, no matter how horrifically earned."

I stared at him, my heart scarcely beating and my fingers twisting into the worn fabric of my cloak. Unable to form a response, for I did not wish to lie and I did not wish to give truths, I simply nodded.

We sat in silence for some moments, my smile growing genuine when his smirk spread into a crooked grin.

"What's your favorite part?" I expected it would be the murdering.

He assumed as much and released a full-bodied laugh. The rough melody drew eyes toward us. "Gathering intel, my blood-thirsty queen." I waited again, and he cursed through lingering laughter before explaining, "It allows me to travel."

"To move," I said.

He nodded. "To explore and study this vast continent. Whenever I return to a place I've been before, I find something new to appreciate."

"Even the middle lands?"

"Especially the middle lands."

"Were you ever asked to spy on me?"

The fire brightened the gleam in his eyes that told me he likely had been asked. "I'll never tell."

I tilted my head, giving him a look that said I knew the answer.

He laughed again, the sound attracting the attention of warriors patrolling along the river.

Shole waited until they'd moved on.

Then he changed the subject with an ease I didn't see coming. "Forgive my unending curiosity, dear queen, but I often wonder what one might do with two crowns." He scratched at the growth marring his square jaw. "You could use them both, of course. Perhaps wear the gold with something red, and the silver with—"

I interrupted him. "Two crowns?"

He surveyed me carefully, a brow raised. "I take it you've yet to digest exactly what this journey means should we meet our desired end."

But I knew exactly what it meant. "It will mean Florian will possess two kingdoms, and most importantly, that Molkan will be dead."

His lips pouted once more before he looked at the hillside containing the conversing generals and king. I didn't need to look to know that Florian was still watching. I could feel it. He was always watching, and I no longer minded.

Truthfully, I never had. I'd merely loathed how much I enjoyed it, the constant caress of his icy attention.

Shole clucked his tongue. "Faeries are not as barbaric as humans." He lifted his bent knees, his muscled arms folding around them. "That kingdom won't be his, winter queen. He is wed to the Baneberry heir." His next words were stones flung at my skin. "It will belong to you first."

A suffocating weight pressed upon my chest.

The merc chuckled, disbelieving and dry. "Florian's no longer doing this solely for his family and our snow-haunted kingdom." Again, he swept his eyes to those hills, then looked back at me. "His hunger for vengeance now extends to you."

"He's not doing this for me," I said far too defiantly.

His brows rose. "Sure about that?" They fell as he explained, "Winter thaws, my queen, inviting autumn and making his need for revenge less vital." A slight shrug. "This murderous fog is a nice excuse, but he didn't need to accompany us in finding the culprits—nor to ensure Molkan's ruination."

"But . . ." I couldn't trap my panicked honesty. "I don't want him doing this for me."

Shole stood, his height staggering. "It's far too late to change that."

Before he walked away, I murmured to the flames, "You intended for me to be made aware. Why?"

I thought he wouldn't answer. That he would just leave me stewing over all he'd said. But when he finally spoke, his tone was gentle. "My only intent was making sure the mate my friend has found is not merely forgiving his betrayals because she seeks her father's crown."

His truth struck a bruised nerve.

So much so, I glared up at him—giving pieces of myself away.

The spy and assassin studied me, a silent laugh creasing his features. "Looking at you now, I cannot help but think I was not entirely wrong to assume that after all." The stilling of his harsh edges swiped the humor from his face. "To some extent, you did desire this opportunity."

"I haven't forgiven him," is all I chose to say.

Florian was well aware, perhaps even before I had been, that I craved the demise of Molkan's rotten soul.

I wouldn't explain myself to his friend. I certainly wouldn't make declarations I'd yet to give Florian. I wouldn't try to voice the conflictions I still couldn't manage to untangle enough to put voice to.

I didn't need to. Somehow, this nosy creature managed to simplify it in a few measly words.

"You might not forgive him, but you've fallen in love with him anyway," Shole said, tone gentling again. I still flinched, which only further mollified him. He backed up with a smile that seemed unmistakably genuine, rendering him more handsome than fearsome. "And perhaps that is enough to comfort us all."

With that, he stalked into the darkness gathering between the trees.

I'd meant to ask Florian about his discussion with the generals— about the plan regarding the palace guard towers.

His return to the tent ripped a different question from me. "What will you do with Baneberry should we succeed?"

"*Should* we succeed?" he questioned, dropping his sword by the entrance and discarding his coat. "I'll forgive your error if you explain what caused you to make it."

I wasn't in the mood to spar.

I stared down at my clasped fingers in my lap, uncertainty making all the what-ifs and questions blur into a storm too chaotic for words.

Florian watched me. "You had a lengthy conversation with Shole." He crouched over the bedroll. "Am I to assume he's placed doubts in your whimsical mind?" A gentle tap was given to my forehead. "He might be my friend, but that doesn't mean I won't hurt him for troubling you."

Despite having no desire for humor, I smiled. "He's a good friend, and I've learned those are rare. So I must advise against it." I looked over at our packs beside the bedroll. We would need to leave soon, and the letter inside my own continued to haunt me.

He shifted closer on his knees. His finger curled beneath my chin to lift it until I met his piercing gaze. "Did he or did he not trouble you?"

I shook my head, and he waited. The cold within me melted beneath his infuriatingly patient stare. "He didn't. I'm merely feeling . . ." I failed to find the right word for so many feelings. "Now that the end of this journey nears."

Florian's eye twitched. He knew I spoke true, yet he also knew there was more. "You will have your vengeance, Tullia."

"A kingdom, Florian," I whispered, fear hitching it from the enormity of such a thing.

"A kingdom," he reiterated carefully, "that is rightfully yours."

Not his or ours to claim, but mine.

Mere weeks ago, it gave me more than endless pleasure to daydream about holding what Molkan held dear in the palm of my hand as I slowly squeezed my fingers closed. It gave me purpose to carry me through the dark.

So now that it was real, why did it terrify me? And why did it no longer feel like enough?

I wanted Molkan to suffer. I wanted to look down upon those who had looked down upon me. I wanted to reclaim the pieces he'd stolen from me, and with them, my freedom.

But freedom no longer looked the same as it once did.

"What if I wish to stay in Hellebore?" I struggled to hold his gaze, tentatively adding, "With you."

Florian's brows lowered. "There is no wishing required, butterfly." He laughed, incredulous, then glowered and tightened his hold on my chin. "With me is where you will always be."

"Plotting and scheming," I breathed, my smile trembling.

"Plotting and scheming," he repeated. He studied me, his lower lip drawn between his teeth as he searched my features. He released it and me with a slow exhale through his nose. "*We* will decide what to do with Baneberry when the time comes. For now, get some rest. We leave within the hour."

I refrained from reaching for him. From begging for the return of his touch. "I won't be able to."

Lowering to the bedroll behind me, he removed his boots. "Then come to me."

He didn't wait for me to wriggle back to his spread legs. He hauled me between them. One arm looped around me. He splayed his hand over my breast while the other scooped my hair over my shoulder so that his mouth could rest upon the curve of my neck.

For moments that soothed and heated, he just held me.

I reached for the dagger I'd had sitting beside me, tracing the worn hilt. "You do want Baneberry, don't you, Majesty?"

"I want the same as you." He released my breast with a squeeze and stole my dagger. "I want Molkan and his daring ilk to suffer. For them to rot in the pits of Nowhere, and to let this goddess-fearing realm know that such atrocities will always be met with devastating repercussions."

"Though you paint a beautiful picture, it doesn't answer my question."

He hummed a near laugh against my neck. "I would love to take Baneberry from him," he said with both conviction and a trace of hesitance. "Of course."

It didn't upset me to hear him say it. I'd known it all along. We all had. More than anything, it was a comfort to know his original desires remained.

Until he claimed, "But it must be me, Tullia. You mustn't try to kill him." He brought the dagger toward my chest, the sharp point mere inches from my tunic and angled toward my heart. "For you cannot."

"Do not underestimate me," I said, not fearing the dagger but curious as to where he was going with this conversation. "If given the opportunity, I won't hesitate to stick a blade in his heart. Just as you've shown me."

"That simple, is it?" Florian teased.

I rolled my eyes. "Obviously not."

"I've not shown you nearly enough." His low voice became edged. "Do you know how difficult it is?"

"I know what it is to end a life, Majesty." And he knew it. He'd been there, and we'd fucked like animals in the aftermath.

As if remembering with vivid detail, a throaty noise left him. He kissed my neck. "But you don't know how difficult it is to kill someone who means something to you."

I tensed and almost shouted, "He means *nothing* to me."

He dropped the dagger and hushed me, smoothing his hand over my stomach until I relaxed against him once more. "Even hatred makes a home in the soul, butterfly. That is why we seek to eradicate it with indulgence and vengeance."

At that, I couldn't help but think of Rolina. She'd certainly hated me, but not for reasons that were any fault of my own. Whereas Molkan was entirely to blame for my hatred of him.

Regardless, Florian was right. No matter the justification, hatred was but another curse with very few cures.

"You thought it would save you," I whispered, remembering the ears all around us, even if our tent was set apart from the rest of camp, as usual. "That killing Molkan would help you garner control of the power connecting you and your kingdom."

"*Our* kingdom," he corrected. "Yes." His tongue flicked at my pulse, earning him a slight giggle I tried to keep trapped. "Then I met a changeling in a ghastly frock who showed me another"— he nipped my skin—"far more perilous way."

"Had you not considered this particular way before then?" I played along, all breath as his hand swept over my stomach and beneath my breasts with warming slowness.

"I hadn't any heart left, butterfly, so never would I have considered such strange magic."

"Strange indeed." I placed my hand over his. "I can do it, Florian." When he said nothing, I pushed harder. "And what if I need to, just as you once believed you did?"

His sigh heated my skin. He grabbed my breast again, thumb rubbing my nipple over my tunic. It hardened beneath his touch, and I bit my lip but didn't encourage him to tempt me further. His other hand tickled my stomach. "You read much during your years in Crustle."

My heavy eyes closed. "Much."

"I'm assuming you've never stumbled across tales of the heir curse."

My eyes opened, blinking at the growing dark sprinkling through the crack of the tent opening. "I haven't, and Gane has never told me of it."

"It's not commonly written about, as it has never needed to be. It's widely known among royalty, and that is why such a curse exists—to keep an heir from usurping their parents." He amended, "At least, by their own hands."

"What happens if they do?"

"Supposedly, they are rendered barren."

"Male and female?"

"Yes. A pact was made eons ago. We may be viciously immoral and greedy creatures, but we need our royal bloodlines to continue in order to feed our land and therefore reinforce our own strength. However, there was a time when the rulers of Folkyn refused to create any heirs out of fear of their offspring taking their kingdoms from them."

My eyes closed again as his voice dropped even lower, the deep and crisp cadence one I could happily fall asleep to for the rest of my nights.

"A powerful and sought-after witch, who held a close association with some of the royals, put forth the suggestion of the curse when her friend, a late queen of Oleander, wished desperately for a babe, and so the courts convened and agreed."

He went quiet, and I feared there would be no more. So I asked, "What did they do? To make this curse."

"I am not entirely certain." His fingers slid beneath the waistband of my pants, teasing. "My father once told me the blood of each ruler was spilled and bound with the witch's, an incantation cast as they stood in the center of Folkyn and fed it to the Heartline River."

The silence that followed began to bite as his fingers dipped lower. "You want an heir," I said rather than asked. He was a great deal older than me. Not to mention, a king who evidently understood the importance of them.

And he wouldn't have told me I couldn't be the one to kill Molkan otherwise.

"I won't lie and say it doesn't terrify me," he murmured. "After witnessing the death of my mother due to Lilitha's birth, it fucking petrifies me. So although I would like to constantly swell your stomach, I cannot bear the thought of being too daring."

"You would like one heir, then," I surmised, even as a fear I'd never expected began to invade the bruising beat of my heart.

He sensed it and pressed his mouth to my skittish pulse. "One."

My fingers twined around his wrist when he began to distract me with his own sliding over my core. "I'm so young, Florian."

His scoff was almost groaned. "I am well aware, butterfly, and though I adore defiling you, I would never pressure you into that."

"That is but a nicer way of saying trick," I said dryly as relief washed in. He'd already tricked me into fulfilling his desires more than once. I would not be fooled with something like this.

As if he'd heard my thoughts, he took my chin and turned my head to vow to my lips, "You have my word, even if you're still deciding how much that means to you."

I stared into the depthless blue of his eyes, my own damp. Softly, I kissed him, once then twice. Upon the third, he rasped, the promise sparking in his gaze, "But I'm afraid I must make you come."

I smiled against his mouth. "We leave soon." Yet I turned into him and seized his face in my hands.

His whisper was scathing, his teeth nipping my lip. "Then you'd best get on your hands and knees."

The order shot through me to my clenching core, rendering me instantly aflame. He ripped my tunic over my head, then cupped my breasts in both hands. He groaned as he squeezed and dropped his head to lick and suck them.

He scowled when I pulled away. Smirking, I got rid of my pants to do as I was told.

He kept his clothing on, which made me burn hotter when I lowered to my hands and knees over the bedroll, and he whispered, thick with want, "Arch your back for me, butterfly." He then swiped his finger through me from behind. It was dunked inside me and slowly dragged out. He sucked it with a savoring groan. "So sweet and ready."

More than ready, so he indeed didn't waste the little time we had. I heard his pants unfasten before he aligned himself and immediately impaled me.

A rumbled sound climbed his throat as he ground into me.

I moaned. A mistake I was glad to have made.

He forced me down onto the bedroll, his chest hovering over my back. He plunged deep, and we both moaned softly. "I know you like being punished, but . . ." He reached beneath me, tilting my hips by pushing my lower stomach. Against my shoulder, he warned with a lethality that contradicted his silken kiss, "Not a fucking sound."

He withdrew then entered me, slowly and accompanied by a rock of his hips that quaked my thighs. Again and again, he tormented me as if we had all the time in the world.

His breaths grew harsher, warm against my neck and shoulder blade. Veins and tendons pulsed in the hand braced next to my head. His forearm, too, as it flexed with every mind-numbing thrust.

Rapidly, I neared release, and his thrusts quickened. Not enough. I was taken over the precipice with a slowness that caused him to leave me—as he was unable to hold my useless body and keep my moans from echoing into the trees and ears beyond the tent.

He didn't seem to mind.

Breathless, I sprawled upon the roughened fabric of the bedroll as his hand uncovered my mouth, and he pressed his lips to my shoulder. My eyes finally opened when I realized what he was doing. When his mouth didn't cease its gentle ruin over my skin.

He was kissing the traitor brand.

Tears threatened. Every inch of skin was lavished in adoration from his mouth.

I closed my eyes, wanting it to end and needing him to never stop touching me in any way he desired.

"Perhaps I shouldn't think so," he whispered, "but you wear it so fucking well."

"Don't," I rasped—wanted to scream and crawl away. The tears escaped, sliding down my cheek to my hair. "It's hideous."

He exhaled a low and disbelieving laugh. Another kiss was given to the snake I would forever wear, this one right above my ass. "You haven't seen it, have you?"

"I do not want to."

"Why?"

I'd thought that would have been abundantly obvious. Maybe he wished to hear me say it, though. Fine. "It's a reminder of what a fool I've been."

The warmth of his mouth immediately vanished. I felt his eyes probing me, his energy sparking and flooding the tent.

"It should remind you of one thing only, butterfly." His hands brushed over my ass and down the back of my thighs. He pushed them, forcing my knees to rise and my ass to tilt into the air. His hoarse words washed over my swollen core. "It should remind you that you're forever and irrefutably mine. That you will always belong with me."

Then, lowering behind me, he licked me.

He devoured every drop of pleasure he'd wrung from my body, producing more with each languid swipe of his tongue until I was desperate, my hands squeezing the bedroll.

As I came undone, he rose and pushed his cock inside me.

He remained deep, prolonging the pleasure coursing through me, and gripped my ass in both hands. The darkness blurred when I opened my eyes and turned to find his head rolling back with his rumbled groan that was probably far too loud.

It dropped, his nostrils flaring as our eyes locked.

I watched him as he began to move, still clothed yet seeming utterly naked when his features softened the longer he watched me in return. The call of night birds and hushed conversation muted. Our surroundings dripped away until the only sound was the matched rhythm of our hearts, and the only color was the blue of his eyes.

It pleasured better than any orgasm. It burned worse than any brand.

I turned away, rising onto my elbows and arching my back.

He didn't stop me, though his thrusts sharpened in response. His hold on my ass turned bruising. "Defiant creature, you will give me another." As I tried to protest, he reached beneath me to circle my clit. "We both know you can."

I wasn't sure I could. Not when it still held me prisoner—my previous orgasms and the guilt and regret and shame that battled a want that wasn't want at all.

It was a furious longing of the soul. A need to keep this forevermore.

All I had to do was reach out and take it. Close the final gap and forgive him although there was no longer anything to forgive.

It was merely myself I couldn't forgive.

He drove up into me from behind and beneath. I felt him everywhere. He'd made sure of it. In every breath and wild beat of my heart, he would remain.

He rubbed, and as I erupted, he gently smacked my clit. "Good, little butterfly," he gritted between his teeth. He caressed the swollen flesh with a groaned, "So fucking good." His deep and coaxing pace disappeared as he slammed into me, over and over. Our skin slapped, his long growl of satisfaction loud enough for the entire camp to hear as he bucked and spilled inside me.

Then he collapsed over the top of me.

I laughed, flattened beneath him but uncaring. "Everyone will know."

"Worth it," he grumbled, kissing my shoulder. He nuzzled his nose into my neck as he rose, still twitching inside me. I was taken with him when he rolled to his back, half splayed over his chest. "Kiss me."

I leaned over to give him my lips.

He captured them with his, fingers curling strands of my hair. I dropped my chin to his chest, exhausted but never more alive. He lifted those dark lashes to reveal the cloudy sated blue of his eyes, and my bones ached with the explosion of that longing in my soul.

I wanted to have this always.

I wanted his punishing devotion and his gentle wrath. I wanted the possessive captivity and the future riddled with freeing adventure. I wanted every inch of the soul he shared through his eyes and the heart he'd forced into my uncertain hands. I wanted all he was beyond his forgotten dreams and the nightmares that had delivered me to him.

I wanted everything I'd been too afraid to want.

I wanted it so badly it hurt. So desperately, it caused more guilt to nudge at my chest. Not because I shouldn't want it when he'd married me with the intention of humiliating and murdering me. But because of what I had done as a result of discovering those intentions.

I hadn't betrayed him. Nor the kingdom I'd never expected to find myself loyal to, and perhaps even one day ruling in earnest.

But I had kept so much from him.

There were still many things I hadn't shared, including something he would be displeased to hear. Displeased was likely far too mild a word.

But as night deepened around the canvas covering our naked souls, and his fingers toyed with my hair until his eyes closed, I told myself it could wait.

Florian apparently thought differently.

Even on the cusp of sleep, he sensed the rise of my inner turmoil. "Say it, butterfly." His tone was too gentled from drowsiness to suggest he had any idea what I'd been considering sharing.

He had no idea.

Soon, we would be departing once again, making it difficult to talk, let alone confess anything. Yet I had to. To better close the gap I kept between us—to one day claim this entirely—I had to. And by the unmerciful goddess, I wanted that day to arrive already.

A whistle cut through the percussion of the woods around us.

Time to leave.

Florian was up in an instant, holding me to his chest as he reached for his weapons. He blinked when he realized it was merely time to move on. "I need to find Fume." He nuzzled and bit my cheek, then kissed it. "Leave the tent. I'll return for it."

My heart sank, but I crawled out of his lap to don my tunic and pants.

He snatched his boots and left, and a thorny sensation trickled down my nape.

I rolled the bedroll, tying it closed and hauling it outside to the grass with our packs. That was when I realized I was utterly alone—save for the warriors filing into assigned positions in the growing crowd of horses downhill.

Quickly, I reached into the tent for the last pack and my dagger. A rustle in the brush nearby tightened every muscle Florian had relaxed. With my hand clenched too tight around the weapon's hilt, I dropped the pack and turned as the rustle came again.

From behind our tent.

"Princess," a familiar voice called, a touch above a whisper.

My heartbeat slowed as I searched the dark swimming between trees, knowing what I'd find before I did.

Gold eyes.

Avrin.

## 28

-----

**Tullia**

Fear stampeded through my chest as my father's beloved puppet crooked his finger, beckoning me to where he hid in the foliage.

I shouldn't have moved an inch, but although this creature had been a participant in giving me wounds that might never wholly heal, I knew he did not wish me dead. I was almost certain that was the reason I still drew breath.

Molkan might not kill me, but I didn't doubt he'd have no qualms if someone else wished to do so. Yet Avrin hadn't. Perhaps he'd even convinced Molkan to let me live.

Regardless, I didn't walk too close. I stopped and glared, my heart a rock in my throat.

He cocked his head, his brown cloak blending him with our surroundings. "Fine," he said.

It was then I realized what he was here to do. That he indeed wasn't here for me.

I glanced beyond our tent, the only one erect, to the mass of awaiting warriors downhill by the river. There was no sign of Florian. Still, I would wager Avrin knew exactly where my husband was.

My mate. My ruination and my salvation.

My pulse roared with panic in my ears. So loud, I couldn't ignore it. But I could do something.

"Fine," I repeated, wearing a smirk I feared he'd see right through. This was an opportunity. To stop or delay him, maybe, and to find out if he was in fact responsible for the existence of this deadly fog.

Acting on what I felt was true, I kept my steps quiet as I crept into the trees. My voice even quieter as I kept a healthy distance between us and whispered scathingly, "You've been busy."

He feigned exhaustion with a sigh. "Exceedingly."

"The fog." His gaze left the dagger in my hand when I stated rather than asked, "It's yours. Born from your ability to decompose."

He didn't deny nor confirm. Instead, he surveyed me from head to toe. His slightly crooked nose twitched. "It's true, then," he said. "That he's been enjoying you more than his beloved vengeance."

He could smell it. What Florian and I had just done.

I didn't allow the color rising up my neck to leak into my cheeks, though the dark might have kept him from seeing it anyway.

Florian called my name. Avrin's hand rose.

His folded hand. He looked at it, then at me. "I merely wanted to give you the courtesy of a warning."

"Why?" I asked to buy time. "So that my father's lovely artwork upon my back was not in vain?"

Avrin lifted a thick brow.

Steps sounded. Florian's encroaching energy invited a terror that hurt more than any weapon or iron tearing through the skin.

Horror thickened my tongue. "Don't do it," I pleaded—would have dropped to my knees to beg. "You cannot possibly want all these people dead." A bold assumption, yet one I couldn't help but believe despite all he'd helped Molkan achieve.

"Go," Avrin simply said.

I couldn't. I ran at him.

As predicted, he evaded me. His shocked bark of laughter rang through the night. "Just what are you going to do, Princess?" He circled me slowly. "Wrestle me to the ground?"

My hands clenched, fingers bruising around the hilt of the dagger. "Avrin, *please*—"

"Tullia," Florian called, close.

Too close.

"Go on, then," Avrin said, delight brightening the gold of his eyes. "If you manage to succeed, perhaps I'll consider letting you kiss me again."

"*You* kissed me," I hissed, though facts were far from important right now.

"Semantics." Avrin halted and looked beyond me, tone taunting. "And if I'd known she was your wife, Florian . . ." A mist, silver and so light it was nearly translucent, wreathed his unfolding hand. "Well, then I might have kissed her sooner."

Florian's unsheathing sword cut through the screeching of my heartbeat. His silence was a storm that curled the branches above with a harsh and icy wind.

He didn't know the ingredients to form the fog laid in Avrin's outstretched palm. That all he'd need to do was add his own magic. A magic that had turned Rolina into nothing but food for the land.

"Run!" I screamed, the sound breathless yet echoing.

It carried through the trees and downhill. An answering scream from Nirra to flee was followed by cursing and the anxious shifting and grunting of horses.

But Florian didn't run. He advanced upon Avrin with his sword raised.

The tendrils encircling Avrin's hand stirred the cream-colored dust in his palm. He released it as he retreated, and it was carried into the air by his silver mist.

I hurried to Florian. He stopped and sheathed his sword when he realized—when he saw that dust dancing toward him.

Avrin materialized. Vanished behind the forming fog and left us to decompose, just as he'd intended. Even if his target hadn't been me.

It hadn't even been our warriors.

Florian seized my hand and tugged. We ran, though it was futile. We weren't going to escape it. There was no time to materialize. It stalked us, growing and spreading and reeking of an unnatural magic that shouldn't exist.

But it did, and soon, we wouldn't exist.

The reality of what was happening weakened my legs. We tripped downhill, Florian also understanding that we wouldn't outrun it. Understanding that it would chase until it found something to eat—something to feed to the land.

Shouting echoed from warriors. Horses whinnied, sensing the approach of a predator. Nirra screamed incessantly, ordering the warriors to go. They were unable to help us, and hooves pounded as they began to flee.

We were going to die.

We were going to leave this life, and should we enter the next, it would be with the knowledge of my betrayal. With the stain of a secret I hadn't shared.

I stopped and almost fell when Florian kept running, his hand wrenching mine. "*Tullia*—"

He didn't expect it, which was the only reason I succeeded in shoving him to the ground. He cursed when I covered his body with mine. Panic and rage glared up at me from eyes of darkest blue.

I kissed him, words rushing from me. "I didn't tell you, I know, and perhaps I should have, but I didn't, and I'm sorry."

"Perhaps?" Florian gritted.

Then he rolled, the scent of the fog so close. So acrid, it singed my nostrils and snuck into my lungs. Cracking sounded when I attempted to cover him again. My reaching hands were pinned above my head as he seethed, "Don't fucking move."

My wrists burned. Not from his hold.

From the ice.

It crept over Florian's arms and wrapped around our legs. It stabbed into the soil atop my head and hugged my hips, blistering as it cocooned us entirely.

My heart stopped as we both felt it, that strange essence cascading over the ceiling he'd made above us. Florian flinched, his teeth meeting with a clack. The fog might not be reaching our flesh, but he still felt it.

His magic felt it.

He groaned. Our iced shelter cracked and then thickened.

He was reinforcing the ice. Replacing the layers the fog absorbed, I noted, in awe and engulfed by a relief so painful, my heart restarted with a spasm.

An eerie hissing penetrated our hideout—the fog constantly touching the ice as it passed over us.

All the while, Florian gazed down at me.

My relief faded as my heart shriveled beneath that gaze. A gaze focused on keeping us alive, yes, but also darkened with fury. So much so, I couldn't help but think that fury was responsible for his strength in reinforcing the ice the ever-rolling fog tried to infiltrate.

"Florian, I—"

"Quiet." His jaw was so tightly clenched, the demand was a growled breath through his immovable teeth and lips.

His eyes closed.

Somehow, that hurt worse than his refusal to let me talk.

Moments that seemed a decade later, the hissing ceased. The ice exploded as Florian rose above me. I blinked up at the blurred stars, tears flooding. Swallowing thickly, I pushed them back. He was angry. I'd expected as much. But he would calm down.

We'd almost died.

It was a goddess-damned miracle that we hadn't.

That no one had died, I discovered upon walking downhill to join the warriors reconvening at the river's edge. The only victims appeared to be a few packs of belongings, a bundle of clothing someone had left on the bank, and our tent.

The letter.

I ran back uphill, Nirra cursing and following. "Tullia, there's nothing there. We need to go."

"No," I said, staring at where our tent had been. At where we'd lain just minutes ago, content and sated and daring to hope. I spun in a useless circle. Nothing was there. Our packs had been decimated. "I didn't read it," I gasped. "I never read—"

"Turn around, Queen," Nirra said, and in her hand was a pack that had fallen downhill.

The letter from my aunt laid upon the grass at her feet with some of our clothing.

I hurried to her, collecting it all and stuffing the letter inside the pack with the meager belongings we now had.

"Who's it from?" Nirra asked quietly, bending beside me as I kept checking the letter was still there. My hands shook. Gently, she knocked them away and carefully tied the cords into knots.

"My aunt." I took the pack from her with a mumbled, "Thank you."

We rose together. Nirra's brows scrunched as she looked from my face to the awaiting army below. Exhaling heavily, she murmured, "We got lucky."

We had indeed been lucky.

Yet I couldn't seem to agree as we trekked to the river, and I met Florian's cold gaze.

Nirra found me soon after reaching our next destination. "What in the goddess have you done?"

Oleander's warriors had been waiting.

In bronze and gold uniform that both blended and glinted, they'd set up camp hours before our arrival. None of them had

271

been sleeping. All of them remained awake, though some took respite beneath the shade of trees and by the creek.

No tension existed between our two groups. Quietly fascinated and a tad uncertain, I'd watched our warriors clasp hands and arms with Oleander's. Even those who appeared wary still gave nodded greetings as we all settled among the trees.

Four more days, I'd heard someone say, until we would reach the city of Bellebon.

The general set her pack by the trunk of a tree, but she didn't intend to sleep. Untying it, she reached in and plucked out an apple with an endless amount of bruises.

I didn't need to ask what she was referring to, nor whom.

The king's mood pressed upon the looming spring air—seemed to push it back with flares of chills that had many of us reaching for something warm to wrap ourselves in. I welcomed it, for it was the only touch he'd given me save for the necessary embrace upon his stallion.

He didn't want me sharing a saddle with another, and our unit had no spare horses. I had a feeling even if there were, despite how furious he was, Florian would've insisted I remain with him. To punish me, maybe.

We'd traveled until the sun dipped low, and we would soon be leaving. At dusk, Nirra had warned everyone upon our arrival.

"You probably don't want to know," I finally told her.

Chewing a bite from her apple, she looked at me, then over at the king.

Along the narrow creek, Florian walked in quiet conversation with Fume and who I assumed was a general from Oleander, judging by the cerulean markings upon her uniform.

Fume looked downstream at us, and I averted my gaze from the scowl I could feel more than see. I doubted he knew, but I didn't doubt he knew I'd done something to upset his king. His friend.

Nirra waited until I'd finished washing the day's journey from my arms and face. I attempted to braid my hair and gave up. It was too windswept and tangled. I hadn't checked, but I suspected the hairbrush had been lost in the grass at our last stop.

Florian wouldn't be tending to my hair any time soon.

The thought sent a spark of panic spearing straight to my heart, which hadn't stopped bleating with sharp thuds since we'd survived Avrin's ambush.

Nirra tore a chunk from the apple. "Whatever it is, fix it." Urgency darkened her hazel eyes as she chewed. "We need his head clear, and your own for that matter, before we meet with Molkan's armies or end up in another encounter with that fucking fog."

She was right.

"How's your leg?" I asked, peering over my shoulder to Florian. He walked back through camp, wending between groups of warriors upon the ground. He paused when some of them spoke to him.

I could imagine his responses were clipped, his head indeed elsewhere, as he moved on quickly and headed toward Hemlock.

"It'll do." She tossed her apple and ordered, "Go."

"General indeed," I drawled, but I sighed and rose to my feet, folding my fingers at my sides when my hands shook.

My sullen husband sensed my approach and stiffened.

But when he left Hemlock and walked away, my fear became anger with one pained heartbeat. "Don't do that, Florian."

He ignored me, heading deeper into the shrubbery.

I followed, glimpses of other warrior factions and the village we'd passed winking through the smattering of trees. "Do you plan on never talking to me again, then?" I said, glad my voice remained steady.

He stopped, and I understood he'd walked farther from camp so we could do just that—talk with some semblance of privacy.

My relief was short-lived when he began to pace. His hair fell from behind his ear to curtain his clenched jaw. "Is Avrin the reason you won't forgive me?"

"What?" I nearly shouted. A disbelieving laugh softened my tone. "Florian, no. I'm not remotely interested in him."

"Yet you kissed him. You kissed him, and you planned to keep it from me."

"I tried—"

He laughed bitterly. "You didn't."

I stepped closer. "I was about—"

He whirled, and I tripped backward as he loomed above me. "Why would you fucking do that?" he growled, and so sudden, I flinched.

A hint of what might have been regret creased his stony expression.

I stabbed a finger at his chest. "Don't you dare yell at me."

His brows rose high at my audacity. Feral fury honed his features into a severity I'd seldom seen. And when I had, nothing good had followed.

I didn't care. He was behaving like a beast, but he wouldn't hurt me.

"You seem to be forgetting important details." My finger slid down his chest to my side. "I'd just discovered that you were more of an enemy than I'd first thought after your guards tried to kill me because *you* had failed to."

He stepped back. "You and I both know I haven't been your enemy for a long time, Tullia," he said, guttural. "If ever."

While I knew that was true now, I hadn't known it then.

I said as much. "All I knew with certainty was that you'd intended to kill me because I woke each day with the proof healing upon my damned throat." When he resumed pacing, apprehension had me speaking in an irritated rush. "It was just a kiss, Florian."

274

"Just a kiss," he repeated, his laughter rasped. "Just a fucking kiss." He rubbed his mouth and jaw. "Just you letting someone who isn't me put their filthy fucking lips on yours." His voice became a gravel-coated growl again. "On what is *mine*."

"I didn't just let him, and I didn't expect anything like that to happen. He just . . ." I threw my hands out, exasperated but mostly with myself, as I had no idea how to explain it.

Florian froze with his back to me. "He just what?"

"He just did it."

"He just did it," he said with a calm that gave me gooseflesh. Then he turned, his glacial glare pinning me in place. "And how many times did he just do it, *wife*?"

I almost flinched again from his gaze and the scorn soaking that one word. "That's not fair. I didn't know we were married."

"Fair?" His eyes flared, as did his energy. His scent spread upon the crisp breeze surrounding us. Cold glossed my skin and drenched his voice. "You mean to say you might have avoided such a situation had you known?"

Wisely, I didn't answer that.

"You knew who you were fated to," he continued. "With or without a blood contract. And you knew right down to your bones that I would never fucking harm you."

"But I also knew you'd planned to," I said, loathing the vulnerability within my gentle tone.

He dragged his hand through his wind-ravaged hair. The iced breeze caught his cloak and fluttered it. "How many times?"

"Only once."

He immediately followed with, "How long was it?"

Almost laughing, I shook my head. "Florian, please."

He enunciated each word with venomous grit. "How. Fucking. Long."

"I don't know." I tried to quickly recall. "It was brief. Maybe three or five seconds?"

"Three or four or five?" He began to pace again. "There's an extremely vast difference there, Tullia. Pick one."

Frowning, I tried to argue. "There is not—"

"I need a skies-damned number."

"You need a number," I repeated dumbly, for this now seemed so very stupid. "Why?"

"Because otherwise imagining it will send me to the edge of insanity repeatedly for the rest of my fucking existence. *That's* why."

I understood then that it wasn't stupid. If he'd kissed another, regardless of the extenuating circumstances, I would want to know the details as well.

And I would want to kill them both.

"Four seconds," I decided on, unsure if that was true. It was likely close enough, so it would do. I'd tell him anything he wanted if it would erase that stricken look upon his face every time he paused in his pacing to stare at me—to glare at me as if I'd attempted to murder him in his sleep.

"Where did it happen?" he finally asked next.

*Goddess save me.*

I withheld a sigh. "Outside of the room I was staying in." I muttered belatedly, "Not long before they made it abundantly clear I was no longer welcome there."

"Molkan was going to wed the two of you," he stated.

That he was aware stunned me, though it shouldn't have.

"But you knew that," he surmised while surveying my shocked expression. "You knew that, and you kept it from me, too."

"I overheard them talking about it, yes, then the ball happened right after and . . ." Still, I could not find words for what that evening had been.

How in the skies could I summarize a nightmare I might never leave behind?

Florian stopped. He stared at me, this husband—this goddess-given mate—of mine. *Mine*, that bonded beat echoed. He was mine, and I was his, and if I could only remind him of that, then maybe I could keep him from looking at me as if he weren't sure what to do with me.

As if he weren't sure where to put me now that I was no longer a treasure discovered only by him.

Words, useless and not enough, sat behind my teeth. Sorrow battled building panic and an inferno of anger.

For how dare he stand there and judge me when he'd hurt me, too? When he'd upturned my entire life with deception and deadly plans, and all I'd ever wanted was to find a place in which I belonged.

When he'd forced that place to be him, and now I was left destitute without it.

Before I could unleash any of that, he walked right past me.

I remained, blinking back tears until his command to ready the horses echoed throughout the trees.

## 29

**Tullia**

Florian helped me on and off Hemlock. He held me as we rode.

Otherwise, he had little to do with me over the next two days.

I stared longingly across the field of swaying lime-green grass and wildflowers. Florian was talking to Nirra, a map spread across the ground between them. Despite his unwavering anger with me, he was focused. Perhaps too focused.

I would need to talk to him about the plan he'd promised to put forward to his generals. Of course, I could ask Nirra, but that seemed cowardly. It was one thing to give him his space yet another to intentionally avoid him.

Shole had arrived, then disappeared again with no warning. Nirra said he was gathering intel on the city of Bellebon. But who really knew.

Boots entered my line of vision. Fume.

"Did you receive a sparrow?"

"Weeks ago," I said, folding the parchment and tucking it back within the thick envelope. "It's from my aunt." There was no need to tell him, but after what I'd read, it felt good to tell someone.

It felt good that she was real.

Even so, it was scary to let myself hope. Only time would tell if Peony was just another creature who intended to use me for her own gain or if she was someone I could one day consider family. Providing we escaped this war unscathed.

As it was, a steady tension began to overpower the eagerness that had accompanied us on our journey. It wasn't quite fear, but rather, a restless and edged energy that spoke of nervousness.

Florian was still staring at the map. Still ignoring me.

I worried even if we did escape what awaited us, we wouldn't be unscathed.

*Florian is as cold as the unforgiving winter haunting he and his bloodline, but he is right in his deeds, no matter how wrong. Stay with him,* Peony had written, *and far away from Molkan. Should you choose neither, write to me. I will come for you.*

I'd stared at those words the most.

*I will come for you.*

Fume hadn't moved.

Shielding my eyes from the glare of the sun, I peered up at him beneath my hand. "You can read it if you don't believe me." I didn't want to share the letter. It was mine. A tiny piece of something for me to keep when everything else seemed skies-bent on fleeing from reach.

But I had nothing to hide.

I'd memorized most of the letter already, and the return address included within. Should the general choose to take it—or worse, destroy it—then I was certain I'd recall the rest and memorize those words, too.

*Corina suspected he would kill her,* Peony had written. *She wrote to tell me she feared it might happen, but by the time I received the letter, word soon followed that she'd given birth to you early. Mere days later, I arrived at the palace gates to discover I was too late. Molkan sent me away with a warning that should I speak a word of my asinine beliefs, then he would see that it was the last thing I did.*

Our assumptions had been correct.

My birth was not responsible for my mother's death. My father was.

The knowledge settled within me like a bone my battered body had been missing—irrefutable even without proof.

Fume plucked the letter from my extended hand as one would an insect from their clothing, his gloved fingers holding it primly.

I folded my lips between my teeth to withhold a snort.

He turned away to rid the glow of the sun as he held my aunt's correspondence suspended. Pinching the corner of the envelope, he read, "Peony Boneblood."

My hands linked in my lap, itching to snatch it from him.

The general looked down at me again. "I met her once."

Shocked by his admission and that he was handing back the letter without so much as reading it, I took it carefully.

"I'd just been recruited. We celebrated too hard and fell asleep in a wagon of hay, only to be woken by the threat of a pitchfork before we explained." He needn't have bothered telling me whose wagon it had been. "Then she offered us refreshments and teacakes. Her cottage is lovely and not too far from here."

"You knew the letter was from her." I'd had enough of faerie trickery and had little desire to play along.

He shrugged and didn't bother denying it. "Had a feeling, being that she's your only living relative besides Molkan."

I'd deduced his unusual interest in me was for good reason. Now I knew what that reason was. "You wish for me to leave." I swept my gaze to my lap, unsure why I was even the least bit surprised. "You believe I'm a distraction."

Fume said nothing.

I blinked at his boots, crusted in mud and other unseemly things. As were all of ours by this point.

"I have considered it." Again, I looked over at Florian. "But would that only distract him more?" I asked, not waiting for an answer before adding, "Or make it easy for Molkan to capture and use me?" Fume's eyes narrowed when I met them. "For if you know of Peony's whereabouts, then he certainly does, and he will be quick to learn that I have separated from you."

The general still said nothing.

"I know you've thought of this, too," I said quietly, gently. "And you still believe it's the best course of action."

He finally spoke. "You have learned much from your time here."

Not nearly enough, I knew, and considering how much I usually enjoyed it, I was so tired of learning. I wanted to step off this gameboard as much as Fume probably wished I would. But I wanted Molkan's demise more.

"Yet you still sit here, awaiting forgiveness he will not give you."

That caused my head to snap back, my eyes watering from the sun when I shielded them too late. "And what would you know of it?"

"Enough," he said. "I do not need details." He crouched before me, almost nose to nose, his light blue eyes searing into mine as he whispered harshly, "If he were capable of forgiveness, if our species were more capable, then we would not be two days away from attempting to topple a kingdom." He straightened to his full height, staring down at me as if expecting a response.

I had none.

He walked to a nearby group of females sleeping upon their packs. Gently, he nudged their shoulders with his boot. I heard him say, "We leave shortly," then nothing else as he moved on to where Florian and Nirra still studied the map.

My heart cracked, a fissure worse than any I'd received yet, as Fume's words stayed with me.

A tear splashed the letter in my lap. I looked down at the ink it blurred until I was certain no more would fall, then I lifted my head and rose to my feet.

My fingers clenched the envelope containing a truth that only strengthened my resolve.

Florian could keep his forgiveness.

I wasn't going anywhere until I'd seen Molkan bleed.

There would be no more respites.

The following dawn, a scout sent warning. Molkan's encampments had moved.

Some of our units were southbound, including warriors from Oleander. They would see to the armies now flanking the southeastern side of the royal city. The remaining factions now formed one giant army.

No one seemed scared. No more anxious energy could be detected. There was only haste and anticipation and pounding hearts and hooves.

It didn't happen as I'd expected. Perhaps I should have expected that it wouldn't. That no horns would be blown. No drums would be beaten. No meeting of two opposing forces waiting in tense silence moments before violence was unleashed.

There was no waiting. No hesitation at all.

As a new dawn scattered darkness from the sky, less than half a day's journey from the southwest entrance to the city of Bellebon, we collided with Baneberry warriors. Far earlier than originally planned, as we'd been forewarned.

Any intention I had to talk to Florian before battle was squashed.

With an order to remain in the trees, I was dumped from Hemlock, and the king galloped ahead to join the fray.

War cries split through the valley. Warriors rushed forward as one giant wave of multicolored darkness.

Shocked that Florian was going to fight, that every warrior was going to fight, I stood stunned by the sights and the explosion of sounds.

The priority was reaching the city. The palace. Of course, that had been my understanding before. Before Florian had decided he wanted little to do with me. Before we'd discovered Molkan's military movements had changed.

Our plans had since changed, and quickly. I understood but failed to comprehend why I hadn't been told a rotting thing, regardless of how fast we'd had to act.

There was no time to surrender to the sting of such a betrayal, nor the broiling anger. An ambush had always been expected before we reached the city, but this . . .

It seemed far too soon.

My fingers scrunched into my tunic over my chest.

The bellow of injured horses, the impact of some hitting the earth with horrifying force, tore into my flesh to scrape over the bone. The screaming from injured faeries and clashing steel rose higher alongside the scent of blood rapidly staining the air.

I stumbled back against a tree. My shaking hand reached behind me, fingers finding bark. *Real.*

This was real.

It was truly happening. For weeks, we'd anticipated this exact moment. I'd even longed for it, but now that it was here . . .

Fighting the urge to recite my letters, I concentrated on searching for glimpses of Florian amongst the myriad of blue and brown and gold uniforms and the bright flashes of armor. Finding him was impossible. As was attempting to sense where he might be.

Crimson flew through the air in raining arcs of finality.

Bodies met the ground. Many didn't rise. Some were stomped on by steeds or caught in the crossfire of arrows and erupting magic. Wielders of water drew moisture from the soil, using it to distract and cut their opponents down.

I ducked as arrows began to soar over heads and shoulders, powered by more than the usual strength of a well-crafted bow.

Wind, I realized, as they hit the dirt along the tree line. One of them embedded by a stone next to my boot.

It still shook. Still carried the scent of the Baneberry soldier who'd nocked and launched it—who launched more and more at our warriors from somewhere across the vast plain and—

A cold and sharp point dug into my lower back.

The blade cut through my tunic to my skin, a male voice whispering, "Keep quiet and come with me, traitor heir."

## 30

### Tullia

The wild cacophony of battle became a buzzing in my ears, submerged beneath the pounding thud of my heart.

In seconds that felt like precious minutes wasted, I tried to decide whether I should materialize or scream for help. Materializing was risky when I'd only just begun to learn how to do so at will, and with a blade already digging into my skin.

And I didn't need help.

I sensed one heartbeat. One presence only.

They thought me that weak. That useless and easily overcome.

My anger unfurled, spreading deep within the dark cracks of my heart. Everything went eerily quiet as I let it flood and rise and warm. As I let the sound of my enemy's heartbeat and his sour scent surround me until I grew comfortable with it.

And it was decided.

I would be just as they all expected. I'd become the creature I feared more than anything in these treacherous lands.

I became the inexperienced changeling who didn't know nearly enough of anything to know how to save herself.

I hadn't much skill in combat. But I had enough fury to carefully loosen my dagger from the sheath in my sleeve as I let my fear inch into my voice—let it make me appear meek. "What do you want?"

"Your husband's head, and you're going to help us get it."

"Indeed, I can help you," I lied, using the volume and wavering of my voice to distract from my fingers closing around the blade. "Please, just don't hurt—" I stabbed blindly over my shoulder.

The male released a cry nearly as sickening as the sound of steel meeting his eyeball.

His knees hit the ground, and I whirled, dagger ready. His state was enough to gain leverage, his hand clutched over his eye. "You traitorous fucking whore, you'll—"

His head left his shoulders before I could decide where to stab him next.

It thumped to the dirt mere inches from my boots. As I blinked and looked up, his gushing torso was kicked aside.

By Florian.

The Baneberry warrior's blood gathered in a puddle around my boots while I was inspected from head to toe. Florian's eyes were a shade closer to purple with the blood smearing his face. Not his, I realized, inspecting him, too.

Seemingly satisfied, he then surveyed the trees around us.

No one else was here, and if they were, I was prepared. Adrenaline coursed through my veins and heightened every sense. I welcomed it, almost wanted to find someone else lurking, and to cuss at him for taking the warrior's life before I could. "I handled it."

"Just . . ." Florian swallowed thickly. "Stay where I can see you."

Then he was gone.

I tried to keep track of his movements. But within seconds, he'd disappeared.

So many of the warriors I'd spent weeks traveling with had disappeared beneath the explosion of steel and blood and magic.

Energy rose from the ground, pulled from it, I discovered with distracted awe, and also from the sky. Color and darkness swirled and separated, blinded in sparks and shadow. It was horrific.

A work of art crafted from years of pent-up hatred between two kingdoms.

And I was inexplicably drawn to it. To the carnage of divine creation.

Beyond it all, the sun crested as midday neared. Hours that'd seemed mere minutes, and the brushstrokes of brutality began to slow. The screams began to fade to pained moans. The numbers dwindled. Mercifully, not our own.

Before I knew what I was doing, I'd left the trees. Walking across the flat terrain, soaking the last vestiges of battle in, I squeezed the sweaty hilt of my dagger and stopped when I felt it.

Stopped and looked down.

*Bodies.*

Dead underfoot.

My head lifted, eyes singed from the violent malevolence and magic staining the spring air.

Living up above.

". . . isn't a victory," Nirra shouted between cupped hands. "It was only the first wave, so get your shit sorted so we can move."

This first dance with death drew to a close. The living were cut down if they wore brown and green. Some were bound together in small groups if they put both arms up and tilted their faces toward the sky—a plea to the goddess to breathe another day.

A beast huffed beside me.

The horse was bleeding. Everywhere.

I looked around me, but no threats remained. It was then, the air clearing, that I realized how few Baneberry warriors had been awaiting us. Which could only mean there were far more encounters to come.

I crouched beside the injured horse and splayed my hand over her cheek.

Then plunged my blade into her struggling heart.

287

I did the same for the next I found, ignoring faeries who begged for the same mercy because they wore no blue or gold. I glimpsed two in Hellebore uniform who were dead—one appeared to have been choked with dirt.

Halfway across the field, I found a patched gray mare with an arrow in her thigh. Not too deep. I plucked it free and waited to see if the bleeding would cease and she'd rise. Mud and blood soaked her white patches. Not her own, I determined after closer inspection.

She stared at me without blinking. Terror glossed her dark eyes and clouded her energy.

I moved back, and sure enough, she released a mighty grunt as she rose high above me. When she didn't move on, I neared again to look at her thigh. The bleeding had slowed.

Nirra walked over, then stopped when I held up a hand and swept the other down the mare's neck.

Feeling her racing heartbeat as if it were my own, I bid the creature to calm with firm strokes of my hand. She settled, and I righted the saddle, ignoring the flare of energy that warned of the king's rapid approach.

"You barely know how to ride," Florian said.

"The horse will take her regardless," Nirra interjected, impatient. "We must send the wounded back to Hellebore with the transporters and move."

A good sign. If the faeries with the ability to materialize could be spared for a short time, then that meant there weren't too many dead and injured.

"Tullia," Florian said, gruff. "Come. We need to discuss the strategy."

"Oh, now we do?" I said, petulant and uncaring as I fixed the mare's bridle. "Let me guess, the tunnel."

Nirra huffed and left us, and I managed to haul myself into the saddle. Albeit clumsily. The horse shifted beneath me until I seized the reins.

"Tullia," Florian said again. The words sounded bitten between his teeth. "Come with me."

Finally, I gave him my full attention. "No."

Atop Hemlock, he'd halted mere feet from me. Freed strands of his bound hair curled over his bloodstained cheeks. "No?" he repeated, so low and so heated that I almost shivered.

"You heard me, Majesty." I dug my feet into my very own horse, perhaps too softly. Thankfully, she understood.

We left him glaring behind us.

He remained there for hours, his eyes poking holes into my back as we inspected the dead and the wounded, and as we journeyed toward the southwest entrance of Bellebon.

Maybe it was cruel of me to deny him. Maybe he was more cruel for refusing to acknowledge me unless he had to for days that felt like an eternity. Maybe we were both stubborn idiots.

But I couldn't fix something he didn't want to forgive. And what he'd done since I'd tried to, since I'd put every reservation I'd clung to for weeks into a box I would have tucked away just for him . . .

My own fault. All of it.

I'd known better than to think I could claim anything that could be so easily taken from me.

# 31

## Tullia

While we'd anticipated more Baneberry warriors, the city of Bellebon had expected our invading forces.

Businesses were closed. Homes had been boarded up. Steel and thick layers of wood covered windows and even the cracks beneath doors. Understandable.

It was the absolute quiet that caused hair to rise upon my nape.

Florian now rode ahead of me, back straight and his shoulders high and tight. "We should send half back to the entrance," he said to Nirra.

The general, stiff upon her horse next to him, said nothing.

My unease unfurled into trepidation with every second of passing silence. I wasn't alone. The horses nickered, many shifting over the stone street as if reluctant to move forward. There was no calming my own beast. Not when I couldn't calm the instinct within myself.

The instinct to flee.

"Stop," Florian ordered.

We'd reached a large quad with abandoned shelving and wagons. Baskets swayed atop tables in the breeze. A market square.

"We leave the horses," he whispered to Nirra. "Now."

I understood why we had to. Should we meet another battalion, we would find it hard to fight upon horseback—to survive—as the streets grew tighter. But that he'd said to leave them right here and now meant he felt something was indeed amiss.

It carried in the silence only broken by the murmurs of horses and the clops of their hooves.

So much silence, the warming breeze whistled down alleyways and streets.

We separated from the horses and a large portion of the warriors filling the city behind us. They were given orders to split into two groups. One would scope out the northern quarter of the city, and the rest were to head back to await possible ambush near the entrance we'd taken.

On foot, we proceeded through the streets toward the river.

Florian slowed, seemingly to fall into step beside me. Before he could, a screech that threatened to draw blood from my ears struck the city. Via some type of amplifier, a voice boomed as if the words were sent down from the sky.

A voice that turned my blood to ice.

"Welcome home, daughter. May your flesh and bones feed the land of which you betrayed."

Florian stopped. Dark blue eyes locked with mine. Though his features were void, I still saw it within that gaze. Concern.

It both softened and angered.

Molkan wouldn't kill me. He'd made that clear numerous times. But it appeared he was now done treading carefully. He would no longer stop someone else from doing it for him.

Or *something*.

The shout came from the group of warriors we'd left. "The fog!"

"Split up and run," Fume's holler echoed. "Climb if you must."

If the fog had been unleashed at the entrance we'd taken to the city, then there was no telling how many had succumbed.

But it wasn't only coming for them.

It was stalking us all, as if sensing the blood rushing through our veins and the sound of our panicked heartbeats.

Many dropped in the crowd behind me, disappearing with screams cut short.

The rest of us ran.

Florian looked from me to those clambering for escape. With a twist of his features, he ordered, "Stay close to Nirra," then raced behind me.

Within seconds, he was lost in the crush of desperate warriors.

I had no doubt he would be fine. I knew he was either helping or materializing to a higher vantage point to assess the situation.

Knowing couldn't stop the hurt I carried from abating beneath an onslaught of worry.

More fell in the stampede as we ran and pushed amongst the streets narrowing into alleyways. Eyes peeked out of tiny holes in boarded windows. They retreated as we surrounded their homes in a giant moving mass.

There would be no enemies to fight. None were needed. The Baneberry warriors in that valley had been a sacrifice to distract us from the true threat.

We were trapped.

Trapped within a maze of squat and giant stone buildings behind, aside, and before us. We could climb, but many wouldn't make it. Only a handful of us could materialize, and they were already taking friends to freedom.

I slammed into Nirra's back when she stopped suddenly. "Shit," she hissed, panic stealing color from her skin as she turned, and we all crashed together in a squashed halt.

Cursing and pleas came from those who'd tripped and fallen, roiling my stomach as we all stood helpless.

A stone archway loomed up ahead, vine-wrapped and giving entrance to a wider alleyway between two tall townhomes, and it was filling with a cloudy and acidic substance. A fog that grew thicker the longer we stared and panted.

Utterly trapped.

Defiant fury widened the cracks within my chest. Filled them so fast and so high that I would choke on my rage long before Molkan's murderous fog even reached me. Nothing was fair. I'd always known that, no matter how much hope and wonder had once been in charge of my heart. But only a coward would stoop so low as to—

His gaze was a tug at my energy, luring me to turn and seek his whereabouts.

My eyes met Florian's across broad and armored shoulders. "Breathe," I thought he said, too far away to hear over the emotional voices and vicious cussing of the souls wedged between us. He jerked his head to the stone wall of wisteria beside me.

I scowled. I wasn't leaving, although warriors tried.

They scaled the windows of homes. Some had made it to rooftops.

Others hadn't.

In horror, I stared down at the busted head of a male who'd once offered me an apple he'd plucked from a branch hanging over a village cottage fence.

My stomach clenched as a female from Oleander stuck her sword into his heart to end his suffering.

Farther down the alleyway, behind Florian, warriors had made it to the street on the other side. Arms were extended to help others climb, too.

For many, it was too late. They vanished beneath the advancing fog.

Screaming sounded from the north side of the city, dragging my eyes from the deadly white and silver.

Screaming from more warriors.

"It's everywhere," I rasped; defeat crawling into my bones and voice.

Steel and numbers were useless when we were penned like cattle being led to slaughter.

A harsh wind nearly sent me to my knees until it was wrangled by Nirra. She pushed it toward the fog creeping through the archway ahead. Her eyes were brighter, her scent and energy a flare of hope that failed to spark when she said, "Climb, Tullia."

She could hold it back, though not for long.

As more had discovered behind us with similar magic. Fire was unleashed from a few desperate faeries with the ability, but it only managed to create more panic. The misty fog curled around the flames and licked at them.

Then extinguished them with a hiss.

"Tullia."

Florian's voice was clear, prompting me to peer over the jostled bodies around me. He was close. I could push toward him, apologize and tell him I hadn't meant for this. That I knew none of us had meant for any of this to end so fucking badly.

"Materialize," he barked. "Get out—"

Another screech, this one ear-piercing and chilling the blood, echoed from the other side of the home I'd pressed against to keep from falling under the pulsing push of bodies.

A cry of desperate and unending rage silenced those near me. It matched what lived within me—within us all—but couldn't be unleashed for it was stuck like we were. Emotion was the root of magic, yet it now seemed a useless blessing.

A boom rattled my teeth.

The warrior bellowing his grief was kicking the wall behind Florian. A gust of magic unfurled, a burning breeze. Stone flew through the air as the warrior unleashed his strength again and again.

My ears popped, then rang with a familiar cadence.

Through the swirling spray of dust, through the gap forming in the stone wall, something moved.

Warriors ducked. The injured fell, dragged to their feet at the sound of that screech. We all froze when a glowing yellow eye peered through the hole. A forked tongue flicked, almost licking the warrior who'd broken the stone.

Someone grumbled, "Goddess, we're so fucked."

But that eye met mine right before the creature disappeared.

Florian was shouting at me. Nirra told me to move. Bodies pushed and pressed, some climbing over the wall and scaling homes while others squeezed through the hole and others tried to widen it.

Yet I focused on that presence, the energy that touched my own, and I gazed up at the two-story home above me.

The scalon climbed it, barbed tail swinging and destroying one of the carefully sealed windows. Wood and glass crashed into the street below. Screams came from inside the home. The creature paid none of the commotion any mind. It crawled up the stone, giant scales and spikes gleaming in the fading glow of day, and its eyes never leaving me.

I kept my own trained on it. Welcomed the beast's advance. "Get back," I warned, barely registering that I'd spoken. Then when the scalon reached the rooftop . . .

I smiled as it leaped down onto the wall beside the home.

The stone collapsed beneath its weight. As did some of the warriors who'd failed to retreat in time.

Nirra cursed, her grip on the wind slipping.

Florian roared, "Everyone out!"

Then he reached my side. Before I could say a word, he pulled me with him while ordering warriors to move out of the way. He stopped and splayed his hands against the barricaded side entrance to the home. Ice covered the wood and steel, then cracked.

The barrier splintered with it.

More screaming came from inside, prompting me to remind him, "There are civilians in there."

"Fuck the civilians," he grunted. Sharp shards of ice punctured the ruined barricade until it was in chunks at our feet and half the door was revealed.

The handle was frozen and the lock ruined when Florian turned it. He barked to all who remained trapped between the destroyed wall and the fog-infested archway ahead, "Get out to the street."

He gave me no choice.

I was plucked from the ground and all but tossed into the home.

As everyone entered, I waited though I couldn't see him. I waited until I heard him close the door behind Nirra. I wasn't sure what good it would do without the extra barrier against the fog, and I had no room to care. The family would be wise to just leave.

The lower level of the home was a mixture of stone counters, rusted stoves, woven armchairs, and a dining table beautifully painted with aged flowers. I spared a brief glance at the stairs, guilt ensnaring, then I rushed to Florian, who was destroying the barricaded door in the kitchen.

Light exploded into the dim, and we all spilled onto the street filling with our people.

The scalon was there, tail flicking. The male, I realized as I walked closer. He didn't appear poised to attack anyone. He simply watched me, as if waiting to see what I'd do next.

Cries echoed from the alleyway we'd escaped, the scalon moving when I made to walk over to assist the warriors in saving those who were still stuck. An injured male cursed, freed from the hole and almost stabbed by the creature's barbed tail.

I stopped. The scalon blinked as he did too.

Survivors from Fume's unit had arrived. But the general and Florian's attempt to regroup was interrupted.

"You monsters," a female shouted, the knife in her hand catching the waning sun and my entire attention.

The scalon hissed as the brunette faerie charged from the house we'd broken into toward Fume and Florian. A male quickly followed, his brown eyes stricken as he searched the street for who I assumed was his wife.

The female was blocked from reaching Florian, who hadn't seemed to even acknowledge her approach. She swung the blade at the warriors attempting to restrain her, as her husband hurried over and put his arms up. "She means no harm. She's just frightened."

"Of course I mean them harm. They've caused harm to all of us."

At that, Florian turned. He stepped between the warriors to warn the female, "If you wish to live, you need to move on."

"Or you'll kill us too?"

Nirra finally exited the home, her face drawn. Squinting toward the commotion, she muttered, "Skies, we should've locked them upstairs."

"Not us." Florian looked pointedly at the destroyed wall, faeries struggling to get through as the fog reached them.

Others tried to help them. Bloodcurdling screams came from those who weren't going to make it.

My heartbeat was a storm that wouldn't calm.

We were free, yet we were still trapped in a maze controlled by a foe who wouldn't show his fucking face.

Everything fell into a distant hum when the creature before me took a lurching step forward. I reached out to touch the cool skin between the wide slits in the scalon's snout. "Thank you."

He swung his long neck, giving a look that could only be considered a glare in Florian's direction. It seemed he remembered the king had tried to kill him.

Florian was staring at me. All the while the fog now crept through the carnage of the wall and onto the street.

I returned his stare until Nirra reached him, and they began to strategize with Fume and the warriors surrounding them. Another wind-wielder was attempting to hold the fog back. The couple from the home argued with one another.

I watched it all and made sure all were not watching me.

Then I snuck back inside the house.

I hurried through the kitchen into a small sitting area, feeling the fog's heavy and coppery menace even through the stone. Swallowing hard, I looked around, but it hadn't entered. It was hunting for flesh.

The lone window in the room had been broken, likely by our warriors, but I didn't need to use it.

I drew in one deep breath after another, each exhale quieting the chaos outside until I felt it. The tether I'd only ever associated with fear and danger. Relying on those wouldn't work now. Not when fear and danger were to be my destination.

Rather, I did as Florian had taught me. I sought the cold comfort, used it to ignite my desire to be materialized elsewhere, and I hoped I'd been right to believe wards wouldn't refuse that of the same blood who'd created them.

I held that hope, the longing attached, and I pulled my dagger from the sheath in my sleeve.

Gentle, like that of a summertime breeze, energy split and darkness arrived. They then combined to set my feet upon the wooden planks of a guard tower at the palace gates.

Two guards stood within it.

One hit the floor, my blade in his chest.

The other seized my arm. Smiling, I reached behind me for the blade I'd taken from the saddlebag of the horse I'd left behind. "Hello." I fluttered my lashes. "You wouldn't happen to know where my father is, would you?"

The green-eyed male scowled.

I smiled brighter. Before he could speak, I dug my knee into his groin.

As he crumpled, I plunged my dagger into his back.

He went still, but his friend at my feet stirred. He reached for my ankle.

I wrapped my hand around the hilt of the blade in his chest and twisted. Bronze eyes bulged as his back arched. I held them, my chest and eyes burning, until the light left them and I heard my scaled companion's screech.

The scalon was hunting me.

Wrenching my blade free, I waited.

# 32

## Florian

The civilians were restrained.

With rope binding their wrists at their backs, they were sent into the streets to escape the encroaching fog unleashed by their cowardly king.

I reiterated to Fume and Nirra, "Find them. Retreat only if you sense its approach." Peering up at the sky, I added, "We have an hour, if that, before we lose the advantage of daylight."

Nirra nodded and began to bark orders.

Fume remained at my side, his hesitance another smog we hadn't any time for. "We won't have enough warriors by nightfall, and we need to end this now."

Before we lost more lives. Before we were forced to retreat from the city entirely. I didn't argue. I couldn't.

The tunnels beneath the city were a perfect trap for the fog, and Baneberry warriors ready to protect the palace supposedly filled the one leading to the palace grounds.

Even so, what Fume was suggesting was unimaginable. It wasn't a sound plan, but it appeared to be the only viable option.

Yet as I searched for the one creature who could materialize beyond the wards that had surrounded Baneberry Palace since Lilitha's death, I felt it.

Her absence was a forceful kick to the gut.

Never again would I use her. I certainly didn't want to risk her, and it would be a gamble indeed—to run with the plan my mate had vehemently put forward. To accompany her in creating a gap in the wards by taking down one of the towers from within.

She would be ripped from me, and goddess only knew what they'd do to her.

So we would destroy a tower from beyond the palace walls. A plan that might no longer work, due to spreading ourselves thin to survive the fog. We lacked the numbers to withstand the onslaught of arrows and magic that would be launched our way, many shields lost and extra weaponry left behind with the horses.

But every eroding concern vanished beneath the most pressing. Tullia was nowhere to be found.

I'd given her ample reason to do more than kiss someone else.

I'd stolen her. I'd wed her without her knowledge. I'd had every intention of snuffing Molkan's daughter's existence between my fingers after I was done enjoying her. And although that'd changed the second I'd laid eyes on her, I'd held on to my plan like I had the grudge that caused me to form it in the first place.

I'd held on to it for her safety. To protect her from her people and my own. Perhaps even for my own protection. A desperate attempt to believe I could do without her. To prove I didn't need her.

A lie.

One I'd let everyone I trusted believe. In the end, never making the change in my desires known, never wanting to admit how much had irrevocably changed—not even to myself—was what had led Tullia to end up here.

Tortured and tormented, her soul bruised and her lips touched by another's.

It didn't matter that she'd kissed Avrin. Not in the way she believed it did. What mattered was that I'd put all of it in motion.

Now, I was tempted to fall to my damned knees because the only thing that mattered was laying eyes upon her again. Over the past few days, it was the only thing that'd kept me sane. Watching her. Knowing where she was.

Reassured that she was right there—safe—while I failed to find a way out of this unfamiliar spiral of jealousy and self-loathing.

She was no longer here. I knew that, yet I kept searching— pushing and shoving and shouting her name until my voice grew hoarse. The street we'd moved down to keep clear of the fog became so silent that I swore my panicked heartbeat could be heard by all.

Everyone had gone still. Warriors looked at brethren beside them. Behind them. She wasn't there.

She wasn't here.

Neither was the scalon. Its screech echoed from the river separating Molkan's palace from the city.

Fume found me again. "What is she doing?" More shock coated the question than his typical dry displeasure.

"The guard tower," Shole shouted as soon as he materialized to the street. "The queen is in the tower."

The screeching lowered in volume as the scalon crossed the bridge. Dying sunlight bounced from its scales as it scuttled toward the queen who'd lured it to the palace.

A fist wrapped around my heart.

It squeezed and squeezed as I beheld the guard tower holding my wife. Made my voice rasp as terror unspooled within my blood. "She's given us a way in."

## 33

***

**Tullia**

The scalon reached the top of the wall, and it buckled.

Stone crumbled then collapsed beneath him.

The wall wasn't just damaged. A gaping arch, too large to block for long, was left in the scalon's wake. Shaking sandstone from his scales, he then attempted to climb one of the four posts supporting the guard tower.

Guards converged. I hurried down the ladder before I was killed.

I'd rather die on the ground, though I had a feeling it wouldn't be that simple. I'd counted on it not being that simple, even as my back tingled with the reminder of what not killing me meant to my father.

Before panic over what awaited me arrived, my legs were seized and tugged.

I met the dirt, mercifully only mere feet from the ground.

A crack sounded, and the scalon hissed his outrage as he fell from the snapped post and the structure teetered, pieces of wood raining. Guards backed up while others still dared to advance upon the creature.

The guard tower groaned.

Flying blades and arrows bounced off the scalon's scales as the tower came down. Scrambling away, I covered my eyes as dirt sprayed, guards shouted, and wood exploded.

Before the dust settled, I climbed to my feet.

Escape was futile. I didn't come this far just to run. Retreating farther from the debris, I waited as guards charged through the cloud of chaos toward me, then frowned as they continued past.

To the scalon.

More hurried across the palace grounds in blurs of brown uniforms and glinting weapons. Blood traveled on the breeze.

The guard who'd pulled me from the ladder lay trapped beneath half of the wooden lookout. The rest was in ruins around him. Dark green eyes gazed up at the sky. I flinched, my chest tightening when he blinked slowly, although I'd killed two of his comrades.

A mighty shriek from the scalon halted his attackers and slowed their approach.

The scalon retreated, only to climb the wall again.

A handful of guards stood near me, weapons drawn at the beast I'd lured into their royal home, yet it seemed I'd been forgotten.

But the scalon remembered.

Bright eyes locked on my location as he climbed along the top of the destroyed wall. More rock disintegrated beneath the creature's weight. More holes were left in his wake. Exactly what we needed, and right where we needed it—at the gap in the wards.

I threw my hands up. "I'll just take myself to see my father then, shall I?"

Heads twisted my way, and finally, I was given the treatment a delinquent daughter deserved. The scalon followed when I stepped back toward the terrace, effectively wrecking more of the barricade separating Molkan from the world beyond.

I smiled, even as my arm was gripped so tight, my shoulder screamed.

The scalon continued to follow. He would trail me until the wall was so ruined, Molkan's military stood no chance at stopping the advancing Hellebore and Oleander warriors from entering the palace grounds.

Their battle cries were as sweet as morning birdsong—close enough to suggest they'd neared the river.

"What a lovely mess you've made."

Avrin.

The guards remembered their duties then. I couldn't keep from tensing as the one holding me unhooked manacled chains from his weapon belt.

"I'll take care of her until her husband arrives." With a smirk that said their incompetence was showing, Avrin drawled, "See to the giant frog."

The guard with the chains sneered at the mention of Florian. As he released me and eyed me up and down, I smiled again, but it drooped quickly. This was what I'd intended.

My heart still quivered in my chest when Avrin clasped my wrist, and I was taken away from the screeching scalon and the struggling royal guards.

More roaring echoed from deep within the palace grounds.

Baneberry warriors. As we met the terrace, hundreds of them charged through the gardens toward the gates.

They'd been waiting.

"Where are we going?" I asked, the fear in my voice not feigned. It was all too real.

Memories seared with remnants of torn flesh.

"I think you know." Pulling me close, Avrin whispered while glancing across the grounds to the commotion, "I think you even hoped for it."

I didn't deny it. I just met his gold eyes and waited until his stony expression cracked with that familiar smirk. It was brief before he sighed. "You should've stayed in the middle lands, Princess."

Mere weeks ago, I'd have agreed so vehemently it would have delivered tears to my eyes.

Now, defiance rose at hearing him say that. "And your precious king shouldn't have cowered behind wards to better hide his misdeeds and play the victim while allowing his kingdom to be attacked."

Avrin paused at the stairs, a look cast down at me that hinted at curiosity. Perhaps a desire to have me explain why I'd said that. But he had to know.

Surely, he knew.

In case he didn't, I talked some more as he escorted me up the stairs into the palace. For I had nothing to lose in doing so, and unlike my father, I certainly had nothing to hide. "I received a letter," I whispered. "From my mother's sister."

Avrin only said, "Peony belongs with the hunt. She's a staunch non-believer in our ways and conformity."

"I cannot fathom why," I said dryly. "Those who disagree with tradition aren't always wild or wrong."

"Believe me, Princess," he huffed, "I know. But no one cares, and you'll find fighting battles you cannot win is a dangerous waste of time."

I snatched the treat dangled before me without thought. "Is that why you remain loyal to a monster?"

Avrin stopped in the hall above the stairs.

It was so quiet. Just as quiet as it had been during my time here. Fear, maybe, of my father and what was happening outside. That and many of Molkan's servants hadn't the ability to talk.

Avrin seized my shoulder when I searched the hall, but I sensed nothing. No one. I knocked his touch away. "You've earned me enough trouble."

"Oh?" he said, amusement loosening his clenched jaw. "I was trying to save your life, of which you've now surrendered, but do tell me more."

Warning shouts ensued. Our warriors had arrived.

Bloodcurdling screams and bellowing confirmed a mere moment later.

"You speak of monsters," Avrin said, glaring at the sandstone stairs. "Yet you've dragged one to your own people's homes to make a meal out of them."

"They are not my people." I tore away from him and began to hunt.

He was here somewhere. He never fucking left.

Avrin seized me again. "There is only so much I can do, Tullia. He knows you're here, and now I must deliver you." As he pulled me down another hall, he said, "Even if I gave you the chance, I doubt you're smart enough to leave."

We entered a stairwell, my laughter echoing. "Just a filthy, weak, and traitorous changeling, right?"

He froze, his eyes bright in the dim. "Vengeance won't heal you."

"I don't expect it will." I stepped close and vowed, "But I will have it all the same."

"You truly believe that, don't you?" He almost laughed— seemed to stop himself as something akin to pity narrowed his eyes. He shook his head, and we continued down into the dark antechamber. "Not weak," he murmured. "Just plain fucking stupid."

My heart began to slow, the whooshing beat filling my ears as we neared it.

The throne room.

Avrin noted my hesitancy. He tugged me forward as he pushed the curved oak doors wide open. "You asked for it, Princess. Don't complain about the way it's given to you."

Dust sprinkled the air from the disturbance of our arrival.

My eyes caught on the portrait first, halting me mere feet into the room. White-blonde hair, regal features, and knowing eyes.

My mother.

Birds flapped by the glassless windows. Some lowered to perch and dance upon the stone ledges.

From his throne, the king of Baneberry eyed them. His fingers brushed over his beard, as if he were deep in thought and an invading army wasn't outside. He was so silent, so still, I didn't expect it.

I flinched when Molkan tossed a silver bowl of nuts at the birds.

It struck one, and they all scattered with sharp twitters. My teeth met as the injured bird toppled to the gardens below.

Avrin apparently thought it best to make our arrival known, though his king was already aware. "Florian's nowhere to be seen."

Molkan finished chewing. The crunch of nuts curled my hands at my sides.

Then he straightened in his throne of gold, the leaves twining around the arms and legs matching that of his absent crown. "He won't be far behind." An arm rose, a click of his fingers given to the dark doorway beyond the dais. "Ready the weapon."

The fog.

Surely, he couldn't mean to unleash it within his own palace? Then again, a male who'd murdered his own mate in a jealous rage, and his lifelong friend and wife, was capable of just about anything.

I said nothing, though the urge to ask about their intentions became hard to ignore as my pulse ticked in terror.

Sensing that, or perhaps merely enacting whatever plans they had, Avrin said, "We don't want you, changeling." He sealed the doors, returning with hardened features. "We want this nonsense to end, so we merely require your husband."

"The fog won't work," I said, although I wasn't entirely certain of that. "Not on him."

"Brilliant, isn't it?" The question was empty. The king continued to stare at the windows as the birds lingered but at a safe distance from another flare of his temper. "So utterly horrific and yet you cannot help but admire it." Finally, Molkan looked at me.

"You are no stranger to admiring horrific things, though. Are you, traitorous daughter?"

The weight of his gaze threatened to bring forth all he'd done to me. The dreams he'd turned into nightmares. The hope he'd turned into fear. The death of the life I'd thought I should have.

My shoulders began to curl. My heart slowed to a violently quiet beat. But I held his eyes and kept my chin high.

He smiled ruefully. "In fact, I would wager you admire your husband so much that you might fail to see how horrific he truly is."

"It seems cowardly." Avrin intervened. "But we needed a way to end it, Tullia. An unstoppable method to cease his torment. We met with many and discovered little until my brother referred us to a witch he'd met during his travels with the hunt."

I wondered if Avrin knew that it felt like iron grazing wounded flesh—the heavy darkness of Molkan's gaze. And I wondered if that was why my father refused to shift his eyes from me.

"Upon the evening of your welcoming ball, she attended," Molkan said, so casually, just as he'd done while telling me truth-speckled lies in his gardens. "She said we needed iron-infused blood to enhance Avrin's ability to decompose, and of course"— he spread his hands—"we were not going to harm ourselves now, were we?"

He chuckled as if this were just another day that would end like every other. He spoke as if what he was saying was nothing but reasonable. As if I should understand and empathize with his struggles. But he'd caused these struggles himself.

And I'd ceased empathizing with tyrants after making peace with Rolina's death.

Appearing deep in thought again, or perhaps guessing at my own thoughts, Molkan studied me with those same whiskey-dark eyes as mine. His mouth quirked when an alarming crash came from the palace grounds.

Avrin shifted, what might have been concern heightening his pine-like scent.

But if Molkan were troubled by the battle outside, and what sounded like the booming demise of another guard tower, he showed no sign of it at all.

He seemed the epitome of calm as his puppet cleared his throat. Slowly, Avrin walked toward me. "She spelled it to mask her magic, as she is to remain anonymous."

"Lovely," I said, tearing my eyes from Molkan when his brows jumped at my response. "Let us get to the part where you chain and torture me so that my screams can draw every creature outside of these walls into your home."

Molkan chuckled again. This time, it was humorless and short. "Unless that brand has given you a tolerance for iron, no creature will come when it touches your skin." He taunted as memories of that cold table and his hot rage weakened my resolve, "But you remember that just fine, don't you?"

At my lack of response, he rose from his golden throne.

Just as they had been during my stay, his feet were bare. His olive tunic pulled taut over his broad shoulders. "Fear not. We won't torture you, daughter. It would be futile when your use will soon run dry."

Avrin stood beside me.

But I didn't dare take my eyes from Molkan as he neared, his hands clasped behind his back. For some reason, that was the blade that cut through my courage.

It snapped, my teeth baring when he came too close.

Another chuckle was followed by a sigh as he tilted his head and surveyed me once more. "Your potential was intriguing, Tullia, but it has since been so abhorrently wasted." Molkan clucked his tongue. "You'll find sharing a bed with a blood-feeder never ends well. What in the dear goddess shall you do when your cravings can no longer be satisfied, hmm?"

I didn't answer.

He circled me, slow and predatory. "When your husband dies, you will wither. You will search tirelessly throughout these lands for a worthy substitute, and you will find none, foolish creature." He stopped, his words a whisper beside me. "It will force you to become someone you no longer recognize."

"Is that what happened to you?" I dared to ask. I smiled, unable to help it, though it felt anything but sincere. "When you killed your own wife, was it because she lacked the ability to satisfy your cravings after you murdered the forbidden mate you fed from?"

Avrin's curse was the only warning.

The blow was a rock thrown at my cheek.

Blood filled my mouth as the room turned dark. My body swayed. I stumbled, then dropped to my knees.

I didn't need to clear my vision to know Molkan had paused on his way back to his throne. Nor to sense my husband's arrival.

The temperature dropped. Ice crawled across the floor toward Molkan.

Pushing to my feet, I moved back against the window-lined wall. My father's shout and the thunderous boom of the upended throne ricocheted throughout the vast room and worsened the ache he'd caused in my skull.

Avrin's sword unsheathed with a ringing *ting*.

Florian paid the adviser no mind.

He stood over Molkan, pinned him to his fallen throne with one boot against his throat and the other upon the hand holding a dagger. "I do hope your sick soul enjoyed that." Florian rolled his neck, his voice deadly deep. "As it was the last time you'll ever fucking touch her."

The ice on the floor impeded Avrin's advance by creeping up his legs. It kept climbing until it reached his knees, and he ceased his attempts to reach his king.

A crack locked my spine.

Molkan groaned, his wrist snapping beneath Florian's boot. "I want no part of her," he rasped, face mottled as Florian's other boot pressed harder against his throat. "Certainly not after you've sullied her."

I refused to flinch, to feel anything but that hatred. Which deepened as I cupped my cheek, my eyes flitting between the kings and Avrin. The latter was mercifully still stuck, but he was trying, his teeth gritted, to carve at the ice with his sword.

Florian laughed, a song of wicked delight. He removed his boot from Molkan's throat. "Then you won't mind me saying . . ." He crouched nose to nose with the father who'd disowned me countless times. "That I've never enjoyed anything more in my entire existence."

Molkan roared.

Florian laughed as he leaped back, then lunged. The two of them collided and rolled behind the fallen throne.

Molkan's fist rose. It failed to connect with Florian's face when he clasped it and squeezed until Molkan's entire hand was covered in ice.

"She won't leave here alive," Molkan growled. "And should you manage it, all that is mine will *never* be yours."

"Kindly cease talking," Florian said with that eerie calm. "It's all you ever fucking do." He flipped Molkan to his back. "Never mind." He reached behind him for his sword. "I'll hack at your putrid lips and tongue first."

A scratching sounded. Not from Avrin, who'd managed to cut one leg from the ice, but from the window behind me.

Molkan grunted and cursed as Florian landed a blow to his mouth, then seized his throat. He pulled his arm back, sword glinting in the final rays of daylight, to press the tip to Molkan's jugular.

Avrin tore free.

I shouted in warning, "Florian!"

The adviser didn't spare me a glance as he marched toward my mate, those silvery shadows wreathing his hand.

I launched into a run.

Only to hit the stone so hard, black nothing threatened once more.

The thud of my heartbeat drowned all else, filling my ears. Jaw smarting, I pushed up—right as something coiled tight around my ankle.

A vine.

The scratching I'd heard.

More crawled through the open window behind me. The thorn-covered snakes twined around my other ankle. My wrists. My dagger remained embedded in the guard's back. The other fell to the stone floor with a hopeless clang when I pulled it from my sleeve, my fingers slackened from the squeezing grip of the vines at my wrists.

Horror morphed into instant panic when they met my throat. They looped and hauled me back beneath the window, my knees beneath me and my hands behind me.

Avrin cursed, his advance halted by more ice that swept across the throne room floor. It rushed up his legs. Within seconds, from his feet to his chin, he was covered just as those three males had been in the drawing room of Hellebore Manor.

"Release her," Florian growled to Molkan, his advantage foiled as the vines tightened and tightened around my throat. "*Now.*" Torn between finally getting to kill the king who'd stolen so much from both of us, Florian made the mistake of looking from Molkan to me.

"Don't," I choked out, my airways struggling—but not as much as my pounding heart when a thick vine slid between my lips.

Molkan's grip on the vines loosened. Just enough to allow me to breathe.

And to release a muffled scream as Florian was taken to his back, his sword seized by my father.

The stone behind me shook. Sprinkles of rock rained from the ceiling and the windows. Not from the kings.

From the scalon who'd leaped against the throne room wall outside. His barbed tail scraped against the sandstone as he reached the open window above me.

My relief died rapidly.

The creature did nothing but flick his tongue through the arched window, watching me watch him. Pleadingly, I gazed up at those giant yellow eyes, but he seemed content to know where I was and perhaps that I wasn't going anywhere.

I writhed against the binds, so agonizingly helpless that I could've wept.

Florian roared as vines attempted to loop around his wrists.

Molkan was sent flying against the wall opposite me. Shards of wind-hurled ice peppered the floor and walls and my father's still body.

Avrin groaned when Florian's rage blistered into an icy gust that tore down every portrait and tapestry. The chandelier followed, crashing beside Avrin into endless pieces of gold and glass.

And Avrin's cocoon of ice . . .

It didn't just crack—it exploded.

I couldn't tell if Florian's or Avrin's magic caused the ice to break. But he wasn't unscathed. Molkan's adviser fell to his knees, a curved piece of ice embedded and wrapped around his bleeding thigh.

Sword reclaimed, Florian prowled toward Molkan's crumpled form with painfully slow grace. A laziness that said he intended to savor every moment of his demise.

Avrin's teeth met and bared as he attempted to pull the ice from his flesh. It was too deep. Good. He needed to stay out of this, just as I'd been forced to.

As if sensing who had my attention, Florian made sure he would. A dark look was thrown at Avrin. Florian's hand and fingers twisted, coaxing the ice upon the floor to break.

Avrin ducked. Mist spiraled from his palms, but too late. His magic fizzled as boulder-sized chunks of ice rose.

And slammed into him repeatedly until he was silent and bleeding upon the floor.

A twinge of concern annoyed me. I shouldn't have cared if Molkan's precious puppet was dead. A part of me still hoped he wasn't. The part of me that couldn't forget the small yet huge ways in which he'd risked himself to help me.

The scalon had apparently grown tired of the commotion in the throne room.

With another flick of his tongue, he climbed higher up the palace. Claws scraped against stone, and I winced when his barbed tail curled through the window above me before he disappeared.

"Now," Molkan bellowed through bloodstained teeth, bleeding from his nose and mouth. "Send it in now." He braced his hands behind him to rise, but he teetered. The blast from Florian seemed to have knocked him so hard that he was failing to even regain balance.

But Avrin couldn't obey his king when he was wounded and unmoving.

Florian chuckled. "I'm afraid your lackey is a little incapacitated at the moment, so it's just us." He crouched before my father and murmured with menace that made me shiver, "Just as it should be."

Avrin stirred, and with a low groan, he shifted slightly. He could try, but he certainly couldn't do anyone's bidding. He could barely move, yet . . .

He pushed to his knees when the door beyond the overturned throne opened.

But Molkan hadn't been giving Avrin the order.

A slim male servant delivered a raven-haired female through the dark doorway, her familiar blue eyes widening upon the scene before her.

The weapon was not the fog.

It was Lilitha.

# 34

**Tullia**

The distraction worked.

Three missed heartbeats were all Molkan needed. Vines swept in from the windows and leaped across the room. Florian sensed them too late.

He moved too late.

His sword clattered against the stone as they twined around his wrists and ankles. Tightened and turned him toward the windows until the only thing holding him firm on the ground was Molkan.

I screamed as Molkan plunged Florian's own sword into his side.

"The last thing you'll see before the pits of Nowhere take you will be your sister's beautiful face." Molkan pushed the blade in deeper.

My mate hissed and cursed. The ice crawling up Molkan's legs stopped at his waist, as if the blood loss and pain had weakened Florian's magic.

Molkan sneered. "The last thing you'll learn is that I kept her all to myself." His laughter was a darkness from every nightmare, but his words were an iron fist pounding at my gut. "For two decades, I've had her. I've fed from her, and it's her own fault because she *made* me do it."

*Mother maim me.* Maybe the female frozen beside the throne wasn't a shapeshifter at all.

A groan squeezed between Florian's clenched teeth when the blade was removed from his side. Molkan brought the sharpened edge to his throat.

Avrin rose to his feet.

I writhed within the vines, my pleas muffled. I begged the goddess, Avrin, even Lilitha—who retreated from the remnants of daylight slashing sections of the room.

I groaned and writhed for someone to do something.

"She forced my hand the moment she had me feast upon her blood like the forbidden nectar it is. She sealed my damnation, and then *you* had the fucking gall to wed her to another." Molkan dug the blade into Florian's neck.

Lilitha's shaking hands lowered from her mouth. But though her lips parted, she said nothing. Hesitantly, she stepped forward as if she'd attempt to make Molkan release her brother.

Metal scraped across stone.

"I warned you, Florian," Molkan growled.

Avrin lifted his sword.

I screamed, my teeth biting into the vine between them.

"I fucking warned you not to interfere with a gift from the goddess, yet you still did. Over and over, you just had to exert your tiresome need for control over what is mine." He punctuated each word with a press of the steel against Florian's throat. "And now, you will die knowing that I won. That I've spent all these years feasting upon the creature you failed to keep from me."

Again, I looked at the weapon Molkan had used.

Lilitha.

Florian's sister was truly alive. Alive and staring at Avrin, a limp slowing his advance behind the two kings.

Molkan seethed, "The creature made solely for me."

Fury reddened Florian's face. His efforts to escape the vines had scraped his wrists raw. Blood trickled from them, but it was working. He could snap the binds. If he just kept tugging, he could . . .

Molkan dragged the blade across Florian's throat, unhurried, as if enjoying the gradual tearing of his flesh. The steady gush of his blood.

A throaty sound of pain fled my husband's gnashed teeth.

All the air left my lungs on a muted scream.

"Take these last breaths and hear me when I say I've had her this entire time. Every day . . ." Molkan moaned with perverse pleasure. "Every glorious day, I've stuck my cock into her willing cunt and—" Molkan went completely still.

A flash of silver blinded as Avrin's sword arced through the air.

Florian snapped free of the vines at his wrists right as Avrin struck.

My heart seized.

The blade tore cleanly through Molkan's neck.

And removed my father's head.

The vines immediately loosened and unraveled, thorns scratching as they receded across the floor and curled through the windows.

For moments that felt suspended, no one moved.

The scent of magic and blood permeated. Not merely from what had transpired here, but from outside. Screaming and shouting and another explosive shudder flooded the throne room in the silence that quaked alongside our four heartbeats.

Avrin stared down at Molkan's severed head in unveiled horror. But something else was in that pained expression. Something far darker than guilt or regret.

Florian cursed but still didn't move.

He remained pinned beneath the weight of the dead king who'd sired me. Who'd stolen his sister and kept her for the entirety of my life.

I pushed to my feet. They refused to hold me, so I lowered to the floor and crawled to him. My hands slipped in a cold puddle, and I paused to look down at Avrin's ice-crusted blood.

Then, with a hoarse roar of unmistakable pain and rage, Florian shoved Molkan's body hard enough to send it halfway across the throne room. It hit the wall, a smear of blood painted across it when the torso of the dead king settled upon the stone with a chilling thump.

Florian tried to rise. The wound beneath his ribs had created a small pool of blood, and his attempt to sit up caused even more to leave his body.

Sickened, I watched it spread over his tunic and upon the ground.

I continued to him but stopped again when I noted what had made him so desperate to stand. What had him forgetting Avrin stood above him—his teeth clenched as he bled from a myriad of wounds—ready with that sword still in hand.

Molkan's blood dripped from the blade.

I could have sworn I heard it hit the stone between each hollowing beat of my heart in my ears. My eyes remained fixed on that half-raised sword as I asked, "Why, Avrin?" I wanted to know, and I wanted to stop him should he decide to move against Florian.

Avrin blinked, seeming to exit the haze of bloodlust and shock. Then he glanced behind him.

To Lilitha.

Her bright blue eyes lacked the vivid spark I'd seen winking at me from her portrait within the manor. They were murky, rapidly overflowing with tears. As her hands fell away from her face and the tears slid down her cheeks, Avrin tried to reach her.

He managed one step before dropping the sword and stumbling backward. He met the wall with a ragged curse and slid down it.

Though he'd managed to sit up, Florian was pale. From blood loss, perhaps. Shock, too. A storm of emotions broke the cold veneer of his features. "Lil," he rasped.

But his sister hurried to Avrin. Crouching before him, she lifted his chin to inspect him.

Florian stood, a hand at his bleeding neck and the other holding his sword.

Lilitha rose above Avrin—protecting him—her cerulean gown bloodstained and a perfect match for her eyes. Her stance and expression said what I began to fear she couldn't. That Florian was not to harm Avrin.

My mind whirled. My eyes bounced between Molkan's head and Lilitha again and again. She was really here.

The princess everyone had thought was dead then threw herself at her brother.

The sword clattered to the ground as Florian caught Lilitha. Her shoulders shook, her hold around his neck tightening. He held her just as tight, his hand cupping the back of her head and his own tucked in her shoulder.

He seemed to be scenting her, the hand at her back feeling for the beat of her heart. An odd and tear-inducing laugh escaped him as he held her impossibly tighter.

His sister—of whom he'd sworn to avenge by tearing down a kingdom.

All this time, she'd been right here.

"Say something," Florian said thickly, pushing her back and gripping her face.

Tears collected over Lilitha's high cheeks, her chin wobbling. Half a head shorter, she gazed up at her brother, searched his face, then framed it with her hands. Her near-black hair rippled in the glow of nightfall when she shook her head.

She couldn't speak.

Just like Molkan's servants.

*Would you keep help in your household who might one day be captured and forced to tell the enemy every secret they've heard within your walls?*

My gaze met Avrin's across the room.

"He took her tongue," he confirmed.

"You tried to hint at it." I voiced the realization. "When you said that none of the servants could speak, nor read or write." The memory burned my eyes, the room twirling through the wet.

Avrin shrugged with a grimace of pain.

*I do have eyes.*

*Doesn't seem like they work very well.*

Looking from him to Molkan's head, I couldn't resist asking again, "Why did you do that?"

The question was left unanswered in the battle-struck silence. It didn't need answering when I knew. When I'd witnessed what he'd just done.

Avrin had wanted Lilitha free. No matter the cost.

Lilitha retreated from her stricken brother to glance down at Avrin. Urgency twisted her features. Her hands moved, the gestures too fast to understand what she was trying to convey.

Avrin seemed to understand just fine. "You stay here."

With a stomp of her foot and forgetting that everyone thought she was dead, she disobeyed and stormed out of the room. "Litha, wait," Avrin said through a groan. "The fighting might have moved inside the palace." He cursed and pushed up from the wall.

*Litha.*

They were indeed familiar. Maybe too familiar.

Avrin left the throne room and a bloodstained mark upon the stone.

Florian looked from the open doors to me. I shook my head when he neared. He ignored me, crouching and assessing every inch of me. "I'm fine," I said, peering behind him. "You need to go."

His lips parted. Even with the cries and volcanic clashing of magic and steel outside growing louder in the quiet of the throne room, his rapid heartbeat was a violent comfort.

"Come on." As if just now remembering kingdoms were at war, his gaze flicked to the windows. When it returned, the depthless blue was a relief so beautifully calming, washing through me as he stared and waited.

I stayed where I was and reached for his throat with trembling fingers. It still bled. As did the deeper wound in his side. But he was here. He would heal.

So I smiled, though it felt out of place. It wavered as I said, "It's really her." He swallowed thickly, and I knew he was without words. He needed to digest all of this. To lay eyes on Lilitha until it settled deep.

I felt similarly but for different reasons, which made it unbearably easy to say, "Go, Majesty. I promise I won't climb any guard towers."

A huffed breath left him and twitched his lips.

His eyes crawled over my face, narrowing with a brief touch of his fingers at my bruised cheek. He stood and retrieved my dagger. His jaw was granite, ticking as he wrapped my bloodied fingers around the hilt and gave me one last perusal. "Don't leave the palace."

He didn't wait for a promise I wouldn't give. He hurried from the throne room in search of his sister.


The fighting came to a slow close outside of the palace as word spread of Molkan's demise, and Florian and Avrin delivered orders via their generals to stand down.

I watched it all from one of the highest rooms.

From the same chamber I'd been tortured in.

The scalon was nowhere to be seen. I'd heard no screeching and felt no disturbance from the palace walls. I hoped he lived. That he'd simply retreated from this war-touched city and ventured home.

Starlight washed through the window to glimmer across the metal table behind me. Down below, a sea of brown and blue uniforms covered the palace grounds and spread beyond the bent gates. Now and then, a flash of gold could be glimpsed from Oleander warriors.

Crimson and metal glinted. Spilled blood and forgotten weapons.

Many warriors lay still. Gone. Many more were injured, the full moon granting better view of their twitching bursts of movement and absorbing their cries for assistance.

The table was a cold presence at my branded back. It taunted now as it did every time I closed my eyes.

I feared Molkan's death wouldn't change that.

But I turned to it, pressed my hands against it, and allowed the tremble within them to rise up my arms to meet with the thudding beat within my chest.

Until the tremors stopped. Slowly, my heartbeat settled. My wet eyes dried.

And it became exactly what it was—just a table.

Just a metal bench harboring my blood and who I'd once been within each grain and mark of rust.

The axe was a welcomed weight. After Florian had vanished with Lilitha and Avrin, I'd found it next to a deceased Baneberry guard. I'd made sure the adjoining halls were empty, then dragged it up the stairs with me.

It was lighter than it should have been when I raised it over my head. Over and over.

Again and again, I swung as tears blurred my eyes and my ears rang with the clash of metal.

My grief drew some of the warriors roaming the palace.

I didn't care which kingdom they belonged to. I ignored their presence in the doorway, and they didn't dare try to come closer as I hacked at the metal until the bolts were torn from the stone. Until the table was a dented mess bowing in the center.

Until it was shoved onto its side by my boot and too mangled to collect anyone's blood ever again.

Nirra arrived with a curse.

The axe slipped from my sweaty and stinging palms. I pushed my hair back from my face, my hands numb but steady. My heart in need of more—so much fucking more—but steady.

The general looked from the table to me, understanding smoothing her creased features. Then she told the warriors behind her to keep searching for our wounded.

"Been looking for you." Carefully, as if worried she'd startle me into picking up the axe by my feet, Nirra approached with a wry smile. "Feel better?"

I scowled, but when she shrugged, it eased.

All of the tension I'd brought with me into this haunting room dissolved.

I laughed, the sound wet and cracked, and swiped the perspiration speckling my forehead. "Actually, yes." I noted the dark patches of blood coating her stomach, hands, and face. Some of it had yet to dry. "Any of that yours?"

She scoffed. "Don't fucking insult me. My pride is still recovering from your giant toad's audacity." Mirth faded from her hazel eyes when I stepped over the axe and rounded the destroyed bench that'd played a role in too many of my nightmares. "I hear the princess lives."

"I'm hoping that's a good thing."

The general agreed with a nod. "Time will tell."

I walked ahead of Nirra down the stairs, shaking my arms as if it would help after abusing the axe. She'd left people in need of aid to check on me, so I smiled over my shoulder. "Let's see who else does."

Healers had arrived from across the city of Bellebon, and as midnight neared, witches from the villages beyond.

The halls were still quiet when I returned to the palace.

Everyone was outside, scattered in clumps across the battle-ruined grounds, wounded or attempting to create some semblance of order in the wake of Molkan's death. Many of our warriors remained in case tensions flared again. Just as many—mainly those who couldn't materialize—were already beginning the journey back to Oleander and Hellebore.

I drained the first pitcher of water I came across in a sitting room, ignoring the flecks of rocky dust upon the surface. Then I went in search of Florian and Avrin.

Wherever Avrin was, I deduced he was still with Lilitha, for I found Florian standing alone in the throne room.

Molkan's head and body had already been removed, but the bloodstains and damage remained. I didn't ask where he'd been taken. I didn't much care. He was gone, and that was all I cared to know.

A bandage embraced Florian's lower torso, a large patch of blood soaking it.

He'd sensed my arrival, but he didn't turn from the arched window. "We need to take Lilitha home."

*Home.*

Lilitha.

Both words were a shock.

Yet I questioned a different one. "We?"

Hands clasped before him, Florian turned with that familiar winter stone to his features and that tic to his jaw. His hair was freshly bound, revealing his crimson-covered throat. Although the wound hadn't yet healed, the blood appeared dry.

Those dark blue eyes absorbed me from head to toe for moments that thickened with tension. "You do not wish to come?" he surmised.

I walked deeper into the throne room, the desire to reassure him strong.

Pushing it down, I stopped before the overturned golden throne. "I do, Florian. I just . . ." He waited while I tried to explain it. In the end, I couldn't. I could only say, "There are things I need to do."

"Things?" he repeated, distaste dripping from his tone.

"Yes." I tried not to smile. "Many things."

He finally blinked. The first fracture in those breathless features. "And you require . . ." His tongue poked at his teeth. "Space," he decided on, as though the word tasted foul, "to do these things?"

I couldn't seem to say it. I didn't want to.

Once more, he waited but not long enough for me to find a response. He didn't need one. His stride was intentional, giving me ample opportunity to reject his intention to touch me.

I wouldn't—knew I could never.

Gently, he cupped my cheek, thumb brushing the crest. "You ask the impossible."

"I'm not asking, Majesty."

His brows lowered. "I cannot leave you here."

"Florian," I whispered. "You must."

His eyes closed momentarily. When they opened, he searched my own. "Tullia." My name was an exhaled breath. His eyes traversed my face, every blemished inch of skin, before returning to mine. "I have shared lovers in the past, but you know you are not merely my lover."

My inhale hitched when his thumb grazed the split in my lower lip.

"You are a light in my soul that unearthed my heart. You now hold it in the palms of your perfect hands, and to say that has been an adjustment is a fucking understatement." His thumb stroked the corner of my mouth, fingers firming over my jaw and cheek. "I will get jealous, butterfly. I will always be territorial. I will get this wrong far more than I will ever be willing to admit, but mark my words . . ." His head lowered until our foreheads met. "Every realm will freeze over before I allow you to believe that I want to do this without you."

Unable to stop myself, I gripped his wrist. "Do what?"

"Live," he said, and so simply, this bloodstained world shouldn't have brightened around us.

My voice cracked. "Florian—"

"The heart you hold is not rational, but it is yours." His lips whispered over my cheek. "So essentially . . ." His smirk entered his voice. "What I'm trying to say is that I'm somewhat sorry for my behavior."

I failed to keep from returning his smirk, even as tears singed. "Somewhat, Majesty?"

His groan was throaty. Tormented. "I'm one twitch of my cock away from throwing you over my shoulder and taking you home to fornicate until you forget all else."

My hoarse laughter stunned us both.

I longed for exactly that, for nothing more than that, as every reason I had not to go with him frayed, and I struggled to remember why I wasn't begging him to take me right now.

A soft smile darkened his eyes. Apprehension, too. It erased the gleam within as he stared down at me and swallowed, the harsh sound constricting my chest.

Then, with a lingering kiss to my forehead followed by a rasped inhale, he was gone.

And I was left clutching frosted air.

# 35

## Florian

Lilitha studied everything as though it were new and not exactly as it had been when she was taken from us.

A tiny smile graced her mouth when she came upon her hairbrushes. She lifted one, pointing at the dark strands still tangled in the golden bristles.

"I didn't want to," I said, at a loss for how to explain it. "Couldn't," I settled on.

She'd spent the day roaming the grounds, not wishing to be indoors. It killed me to know why, as I accompanied but gave her space to feel the wide-open and awaiting world.

Freedom.

She'd been trapped. Kept like a bird in a cage with her wings clipped until her magic was as useless as every reason she'd given Molkan to set her free.

She'd known everyone had thought her dead.

With the exception of explaining how Molkan had managed to steal her upon our return to the manor, she hadn't told me much. She hadn't seemed to want to. Not yet. Perhaps not ever.

The shapeshifting faerie who'd died wearing the skin of my sister had been dumped upon the drive of the manor after Lilitha was stolen by Molkan.

*He wanted to ensure he had me secured first*, Lilitha had written upon a scrap of parchment. *That his plan would work.*

She'd then gone on to write that he'd taken her after a desperate plea to meet him on his father's boat at the river. He'd heard the rumor spreading throughout the realms. That her betrothal to Fume to keep her away from him was imminent.

All she remembered was his anger. Then she woke in a lavish cell—and never left.

I hadn't pressed her to write more.

The quill had been set down with a clank upon my desk that, coupled with the wary glance she'd cast around my study, conveyed her desire to leave the small room.

Olin had just about fainted, stumbling down the stairs when we'd entered the hall.

After his tears had waned, and he'd kissed Lilitha's wet cheeks half a dozen times, he'd shocked me by scrutinizing the otherwise empty foyer. "Where is she?" he'd asked.

I hadn't wished to explain. I hadn't wanted to admit that maybe I'd hurt Tullia just as much as discovering that stupid kiss had hurt me.

I was a grown male. A king.

Yet my queen could reduce me to a surly beast with far too much fucking ease.

Pushing my anxiety and wounded pride aside, especially when Lilitha had turned to gaze curiously at me, I'd cleared my throat. "Tullia has some important matters to tend to," I'd said in a tone that warned there'd be no more talk of my idiocy. "Of course."

"Of course," Olin had said, far too knowing as I'd followed Lilitha outside.

It wouldn't be until the sun began to set that Lilitha finally found the courage to visit her rooms.

She set the brush down with a stroke so longing over the old strands of hair that I wondered if she'd been pondering the female she'd once been.

A completely different one to the sibling I'd brought home.

I couldn't bear to think of all she'd endured while held beneath Molkan's palace to tend to his every sick and twisted need. He hadn't just used her. He hadn't just taken her tongue and twenty years of her life.

He'd taken her soul.

But as she crouched to a low shelf to retrieve a dusty piece of parchment, she looked up at me with a familiar glimmer in her eyes. She gestured writing on the parchment, then pointed at the dried inkpot atop the shelf.

I left her rooms so fast, I swore I heard a sound of stunted laughter behind me.

When I returned with an inkpot stolen from Olin's rooms, Lilitha was staring through one of the windows lining the far side of her bedchamber. Her dark hair reached her rear, seldom trimmed, I surmised.

But the curls shined, as did the blue gown she still wore.

Molkan had ruined her, but he'd bathed her in opulence while doing so.

It failed to make me feel any better. In fact, it only made me wish to see his head removed repeatedly. I hoped I saw it whenever I fell asleep to help satiate that need. His demise hadn't quelled the anger.

Just as he'd known it wouldn't.

Lilitha turned away from the window and took the inkpot, the parchment still pinched between her lithe fingers.

Molkan's use of my sister to distract and nearly kill me had worked. If it had failed, then victory was his regardless. All along, he'd known he would win either way. That just by looking upon her, I would be haunted by what he'd done to her for years and years to come.

Lilitha blew and swiped dust from the stool at her dressing table before lowering to it.

My teeth and hands clenched, I waited to see what she might write. I waited, though it physically hurt to watch her hand move over that parchment while I wondered what she would reveal.

Surprise tore my teeth apart with a rush from my lungs when she beckoned me closer.

Standing behind her, I looked over her shoulder.

*He didn't want to kill all of those warriors.*

I knew she was not referring to Molkan. Which could only mean . . . "Avrin?"

*Yes*, she wrote. *You mustn't seek retribution.*

I would seek retribution for more than that, but I didn't say so. My desire to see the street thief bleed far more than he already had for placing his mouth on my wife would need to wait.

Curious that Lilitha wished to protect him, I asked curtly, "Why?"

Undeterred by my tone, Lilitha wrote again. *He was forced to do it.* She paused, then added, *He was forced to do a great deal of things he did not want to do.*

"And how would you know this?" I asked, unable to keep my tone from further frosting as I recalled the look on Avrin's face when he'd removed Molkan's head.

Rage.

Blistering and all-consuming rage.

Something within Molkan's shit-talking about my sister had caused the warrior turned royal puppet's control to snap.

But Lilitha simply wrote, *He's my friend.*

"Your friend," I said, and clipped enough to suggest I did not believe her.

She looked up at me, her brows gathered and a glare brightening her vivid eyes. I glared back, but even after all this time, she knew how to wait me out.

Just as another creature had learned to do.

*He's done some terrible things, but he is not those things. He did them to survive because he was told to and because he was being tested constantly.* Another pause, then, *He didn't want to kiss your mate, Florian.*

My teeth met, and the question pushed through them. "He told you about that, did he?"

*He told me everything.* She spun my anger into white-hot fury by adding, *And he also didn't want to invade Tullia's privacy in the springs.*

"The *springs*?" I growled at a volume that might have made every member of our staff gasp. "If you're trying to save your *friend*, you are so very far from succeeding." I cared not that the damned springs were communal and only that Avrin had intentionally been in the presence of my naked wife.

A sheepish look was quickly tossed at me before Lilitha wrote, *Avrin only discovered me a few years ago. Molkan trusted him. More than that, he needed him for matters he did not wish to leave the palace to tend to. Molkan relied on him too much to punish him, but he still forbade him to visit me unless he'd been sent.*

Seeing as Molkan had removed the tongues of his servants to ensure his secret was kept, he must have indeed trusted this adviser more than he ever should have.

Years of surveillance on Molkan and those close to him—the numbers slim after he'd killed his wife, Corina—had given me some knowledge on of the male my sister wanted to protect.

Avrin had been plucked from the streets after stealing from the wrong royal guard. Too young for execution, he was taken to the palace for punishment, where Molkan had seen something of interest in him.

Likely his magic. The ability to decompose.

Shortly after Molkan had trapped Avrin behind his palace walls, his older brother joined the Wild Hunt. But even after he'd fulfilled his punishment, Avrin remained loyal to Molkan. So much so, he'd stayed to train as a member of his military. Molkan used that loyalty for his own gain. Rumor implied he did so by dangling the promise of inheriting a kingdom in return for his service.

A kingdom he would have inherited, too, had it not been for the return of my wife.

So I failed to believe he would do as he'd stated before I'd left Baneberry Palace with Lilitha, my threat chilling the air between us—that he'd personally see that no harm would befall Tullia.

Though something now told me inheriting Baneberry was the last thing on Avrin's mind when he'd cleaved that steel through his king's neck.

Regardless, I was glad I'd made other arrangements for Tullia's safety.

*You look very mad.*

I huffed, but I didn't deny it. "I'm merely . . ." I pursed my lips before saying carefully, "Intensely bothered."

That earned me a blinding smile.

I couldn't keep from brushing my fingers over the color in her cheek. Relief bruised when she allowed it. Her eyes closed. Her skin was warm. Real.

Alive.

I swallowed thickly. "If I'd thought for one minute that I hadn't buried you and it was someone else . . ."

Lilitha's hand smoothed over mine. She brought it to her mouth to kiss, then squeezed it at her chest and shook her head.

"It's not okay," I said. "None of this is fucking okay, Lil."

She released me with a tremulous exhale, then began to write again. *I'm here now, just as Avrin vowed. He promised that one day, I would be free. He kept it, and now I'm home.*

"Vowed?" I repeated, disbelieving. "How beneath the skies could he promise you any such thing?" The direction all of this had clearly taken was beginning to settle irrefutably, and it fucking grated. "And *why* would he?"

That Avrin would risk years of service that would see him inherit a kingdom did not make sense.

334

Lilitha gave me another glare. I ignored it.

Then she wrote, *He is my friend, that's why. He brought me books from his visits with his brother and the hunt, and these lovely hair pins . . .* She stopped, seeming to realize she was merely cementing my beliefs.

The curtain of her hair couldn't hide the pink tinge to her cheeks.

*He didn't know how he would manage it, of course. Neither of us did. All we could do was bide our time. Await the opportunity. But we both believed. Even on Molkan's worst days, we always believed the opportunity would come.*

She'd just confirmed it for me.

Avrin was in love with my sister.

I didn't dare say so out loud. Lilitha was exceedingly clever. She knew.

I almost laughed. Perhaps she'd even made him fall in love with her to better her chances of escape. She'd shaken his unflinching loyalty to his king and taken it for herself.

Turning away, I rubbed at my chin while I paced. Of course.

Of fucking course. The explosion of rage that'd compelled Avrin to end Molkan's life was all the confirmation I'd needed, really. Now, I was torn in deciding what to do with this male who'd crossed so many lines, yet had ultimately risked everything to save my sister.

He'd surrendered a crown for Lilitha's freedom. A kingdom.

Power unlike any other on this rotting continent.

A tap on the wooden dressing table halted my feet.

Lilitha handed me a look of such impatience, I could've wept at the glimpse of the mischievous creature I'd lost twenty years ago.

I did as she wished and returned to read what else she'd written.

*Is your mate coming back?*

Every word pressed the blade I hadn't shaken deeper into my chest. "Of course, she is."

Another glacial look, then the scratch of the quill over the parchment. *When?*

I couldn't answer when I didn't know. All I knew was that I'd give Tullia time to acclimate to everything that had transpired.

But I wouldn't give her long.

I would bring her home, and she could finish being resistant toward me right here where she belonged.

Lilitha tapped the end of the quill on the table again, waiting.

I was rescued by a rough bout of cussing.

Olin's outrage echoed up the stairs to Lilitha's rooms. "I do not adhere to demands from rude generals, and take those filthy boots outside."

"Where the fuck is she?" Fume repeated, each word a threatening growl.

I looked at my sister, who stared at her open door with unmistakable anxiety. "It would seem you have a visitor." Too much, I knew, and so I said, "I'll deal with it." I closed the door behind me, being careful to leave it ajar so she didn't feel trapped.

Fume was already climbing the stairs.

Blood still stained his face and uniform. He'd stayed in Bellebon to assist with the fallen and wounded. Rumor of Lilitha's existence had now evidently reached him.

I stopped before him on the landing as he sneered. "You didn't think to tell me?"

As he made to shoulder past me, I clasped his soiled tunic and shoved him. "Downstairs."

He merely laughed, the rough sound void of humor, as he rounded me.

Snarling, I stood nose to nose with the asshole. "Go ahead, disobey me one more fucking time." Rarely had I needed to use my position to get what I needed from him. He was my friend. More than that, he was like a brother.

But he'd repeatedly proven that brothers could be just as hard to keep in line as sisters.

Lilitha made her presence known with a knock on the floor-to-ceiling glass beside the landing.

Fume and I both looked upon her gentle smile.

I saw right through it. For although she'd longed for my friend to show her attention when she'd been maturing, her feelings had dried into an affectionate husk after she'd met Molkan.

Fume's had only awakened.

It had irritated me endlessly. Not merely because she was my sister but because Fume had begun to crave what he could not have—which led me to believe he hadn't cared until someone else had. Not enough, anyway.

Regardless, Lilitha's touch on my arm told me to stand down.

I studied her, and when she nodded once, I glared at my friend with ice-sharp warning. Before I reluctantly left them, I whispered to him, "He stole more than her tongue, so take fucking heed."

Fume's ire fell away like ash upon the wind.

He tried and failed to mask the same horror I'd felt and would likely carry with me for eternity as he slowly looked back upon Lilitha.

Though I had no remorse for the way I'd informed him, I had no desire to see her expression.

I descended the stairs before I ordered him to leave. Before I ordered Olin to seal every entry to the manor and send for a witch to create wards to keep everyone the fuck out. The only thing that stopped me was Lilitha.

Even if she could withstand it, after years spent in a pretty cage under Molkan's heavily fortified palace, I did not wish for her to.

Olin stood beneath the stairs, shock still brightening his lavender gaze as he watched my sister leave with the general for her rooms.

I stopped in the foyer, my eyes glued to the portrait of the female she'd once been.

The steward didn't dare say a word as he came to stand beside me. But the clap of his hand on my shoulder did the job just fine.

An instant flood of relief and insurmountable guilt and regret burned through my chest and reached my eyes.

I materialized to the woods.

# 36

**Tullia**

I'd found where I was born.

And I'd known even before I'd left this palace naked and bleeding that it was not where I belonged.

A mere three days had passed since Florian's departure. His absence hadn't made me feel any differently. There was nothing to be found without his presence stealing all of my attention.

But I'd needed to stay all the same.

I needed to hold this kingdom close. Not only to know that Molkan was truly gone, but to feel it seep beneath my skin to the flayed heart beneath. He and this home that had discarded me could no longer rob any of my soul from me.

For despite what some of the guards murmured to one another, this kingdom was mine.

We had seized its cruelty.

All of it was now at my mercy.

Never more than during those hours spent watching the spring-touched land surrounding me had I understood my husband so well. But I'd found so much more than retribution.

And so much more than the truth I'd spent years longing to know.

A sparrow landed upon the stone ledge of the window, a piece of rolled parchment tied to her foot. The bird poked at the string with her beak until I gently freed the message. I stroked her head, willing her to wait.

The bird chirped, bopping along the ledge as I left my bedchamber and went in search of an inkpot and quill.

I knew who the sender was before I read the simple command in the drawing room, his voice velvet talons within my mind.

*Midnight, two days from now.*

I stared at his handwriting, running my finger over the thickened curves of each letter. Then I wrote him back.

*I'm busy.*

Returning to my bedchamber, I tied the torn parchment to the bird's foot and watched as she flew toward the sunset. Only when the darkened dot against the glow disappeared did I see to the contracts I'd drafted and the never-ending reports I'd requested regarding the servants.

Many had been taken from the streets, just as Avrin had been. Just like him, many hadn't a family to return to. No one who would have missed them. This palace, the staff quarters upon the grounds, was their home. Regardless, they'd served a monarch who'd tormented them enough.

Should they decide to stay, they and others subjected to unjust and horrific treatment from Molkan would at least be paid for their commitment to a royal house who did not deserve as such.

Another sparrow visited the following evening.

Avrin delivered the message when he arrived at dinner, setting the tiny piece of parchment beside my plate.

He'd been a quiet and stoic comfort in the days since Florian and Lilitha had left. He was one of the reasons I dared to close my eyes each night. He'd told me, and perhaps even Florian, that I'd be safe from the vitriol of Molkan's staunch supporters.

That whatever I chose to do, he would see to that.

Yet Florian had conveniently forgotten to send fifty warriors home. They patrolled the grounds and halls among those they'd just battled. Another comfort I hadn't known I needed until I'd discovered they weren't leaving.

I still barricaded the door and kept two blades in the same singular room I'd slept in all those weeks ago.

340

My hair failed to hide my smirk as I stared down at the message. Avrin huffed. Ignoring him, I continued to read the three simple words over and over.

*I'll be waiting.*

The chambers were not as grand as I'd expected.

One of the wooden posts of the large bed was cracked and bent at an angle that repeatedly caught my eye during my exploration of the space in which my murdered mother had sought refuge. Perhaps the post had been damaged then, I thought sorrowfully.

The nightstands were tall and rickety, the cane and wood worn from time and evident abuse. Both splintered in places and swelled in others. A drawer in one was missing. Nothing hid inside them.

Just like Florian's chambers had once been, Molkan's rooms were curiously bare.

A drawer in the dresser was stuck halfway open. Only Molkan's clothing resided inside, and also within the dressing chamber. Through a door in the shadowed room, my father's scent a ghost at my back, I entered a small bathing chamber.

There was no bathing pool or tub. There was only a privy and washstand, a woven basket collecting cobwebs between.

A creak sent me back to the bedchamber.

Avrin stood by the armchair in the far corner.

He faced the balcony and wore the same fitted brown tunic and olive britches—as if his future had not irrevocably changed. This room was possibly the only one in the palace with a glass window, arching beyond the bed. Panes in the shape of flowers climbed the two wooden doors Avrin had opened.

He'd known I was here. It was why he'd visited Molkan's chambers.

We'd stepped around this conversation long enough.

So I said, "Molkan didn't let me live to save his soul from damnation." I averted my gaze to the pressed and patterned green linen of the bed. "Not when he kept Lilitha here all these years . . ." I didn't dare put voice to what exactly might have happened during those years.

Avrin knew. He knew better than anyone that his king had done more than feed from his captive.

"Molkan never quite knew what to do with you after hearing that you'd survived his abandonment," he said, a hint of amusement in his tone. "I believe, although it was certainly fleeting, that he enjoyed the idea of having an heir he'd thought to be lost. Alas, you were not only a complication, but a reminder of what he'd done."

"Of my mother," I whispered.

He hummed. "After finding out you were wed, he indeed wanted you dead, yet he suspected it would incite more of Florian's wrath," Avrin said, still staring through the doors. "The type of wrath that would see Lilitha discovered and taken from him when your husband inevitably took Baneberry."

My husband.

It had never felt more real, and perhaps more right, than during his absence. As if there was no absence at all. I felt him within each heartbeat, in the gentle caress of sleep unmarred by darkness, and in the embrace of each decision I'd made.

"Molkan was determined to wait him out, but Florian just grew more bloodthirsty. He kept trying to swat him away like one would a pest." Avrin huffed and rubbed his short black hair. "He never had the power."

"Until the fog." I asked a moment later, "Where are the ingredients kept, Avrin?"

His chuckle was dry. "I cannot give you every advantage I have, Princess." Perhaps sensing how that troubled me, he added, "I've no intention to use it. It's cowardly and an insult to my abilities."

"But you will keep it."

"It's safest with me." Hard words that dripped with conviction and left no room for argument. He would never surrender such a weapon.

But I understood what he hadn't said. "You never wished to use it."

He didn't answer. He didn't need to.

We'd discussed little that did not pertain to Baneberry's future. Though we had agreed that, for now, it was best not to make it known who had killed Molkan.

It was best to let the people of this kingdom assume it had been Florian.

Avrin's guarded and contemplative state had been unnerving at first, yet understandable. As each day passed, I began to see it. Feel it. A tinge of sorrow permeated his energy—the longing looks he'd cast to the sky whenever he saw it.

The morning prior, I'd tracked his scent beneath the palace to the opulent cage Molkan had kept Lilitha in for two decades. Avrin had been seated upon the silk and knitted bedding of her giant bed, head low as he'd stared down at a book held between his spread knees.

Though he'd sensed I was there, I hadn't interrupted him to have the conversation we were now having. I'd quietly left, the bookshelves and the overflowing rack of beautiful gowns staining my mind and tightening my chest.

Avrin seldom spoke of Florian for the same reason I'd seldom touched on Lilitha. But looking at him now, feeling that longing as if it were my own, I couldn't keep from saying, "You miss her."

Ever so slightly, he stiffened. "It's time we discuss the coronation," he said.

I didn't press further. I gave him a knowing smile when he turned, his hands clasped before him and his bristled chin raised. He would not speak of her. I surmised it was not because he did not trust me with what he'd say but because he lacked proper words for what he felt.

His gold eyes narrowed when my smile spread.

I tipped a shoulder, as if to say *fair enough* and rounded the bed. "You know I'm not keeping this, Avrin."

He didn't respond for a long moment.

When he did, it was clipped. "Keeping it?" He shook his head with an incredulous exhale of laughter. "It's not a pet, Tullia. It is a kingdom."

"Pet," I said, images of Florian and the heat cascading through my mind like a kiss of boiled water over cold stone. "I know exactly what it is." My finger traced the damaged bedpost. "And it's not mine. I am a traitor, Avrin."

"You were forced to wear the brand." At my silence, his tone hardened. "You were born here." His composure broke. His hands flung wide, then smacked at his sides. "In this very room. All of it is yours."

It was no more mine than it was his.

Except Avrin actually cared about this kingdom that'd dubbed me a traitorous wife of the enemy. Far more than I could ever grow to care for it. This place, this palace, had saved him. Ruined him. Made him. Protected him.

Just as another place had done for me.

"Show me the contract."

His head tilted, sunlight sharpening the edges of his bruised features. But the scratches healing upon his face didn't move. He remained impassive as he asked, "Contract?"

He knew I was well aware that Molkan would have kept such a promise to the orphan turned warrior turned royal right-hand— especially after they'd discovered I was married to their enemy.

Molkan had a contingency plan. One I was counting on.

So I stepped back to lean against the doorframe and blinked slowly, waiting.

Avrin studied me until a smirk finally fractured his facade. "Queen indeed." At my scowl, he raised his hands and chuckled. Then he bent into a mocking bow. "Right away, *Majesty*."

The title nicked at my chest.

He returned some minutes later, but before relinquishing the wax-sealed scroll, he said, "What will you do with it?"

I met his gaze and grinned. "Burn it right before your eyes."

He gave me a bland look.

I tugged the parchment from his hand and unrolled it, skimming the words Molkan had written quickly so as not to let them touch me more than necessary. "An illegitimate heir." My eyes rose. "Did my half-brother kiss me?"

Avrin laughed, real and raw and somehow comforting in the face of Molkan's continued torment. "Wouldn't that be a tale to tell." He sobered. "It's merely what I was to inform people so that the Baneberry line would continue."

A lie that would be exposed when his heirs lacked the power my father's bloodline possessed. Though Avrin's own magic had proven to be powerful enough that most might not care to even notice.

Powerful enough that his presence would feed this land, and in kind, the land would feed his strength.

I rolled the parchment, then offered it back. "You had to kiss me," I stated more than asked. I didn't wait for a response. "You were ordered to get close to me."

The gold eyes fixed upon mine seemed to glow brighter as his fingers curled around the parchment. "I will say this and this only, my queen." The contract slid from my fingers when he tugged and stepped close to whisper near my ear, "Everything I did, I did for her."

As he stepped back, I held his resolute stare without saying a word. None were necessary.

Avrin might have been loyal to Molkan, but over time, that loyalty had transferred to Lilitha.

I clasped his face. He tensed, then relaxed when I smiled. "He will likely never say it, so I will . . ." Brushing the harsh rise of his cheek with my thumb, I murmured, "Thank you."

For I had a feeling whatever life still lingered within Florian's beloved sister remained solely because of Avrin.

Then I left him to begin my final preparations.

# 37

**Tullia**

Fiddles fought against the rising volume of voices steadily flooding the throne room.

No royals or nobility from other kingdoms would be in attendance. I'd intentionally made my arrangements last minute to ensure it. Only every creature of importance from Baneberry who'd witnessed my humiliation would bear witness to this moment.

None of them dared to approach me. None of them so much as whispered about me. But their judgment was a thickening and itching cloak at my back.

I let it enfold me with a small smile. Not much longer, and my work here would be done.

The servants and groundskeepers were now staff with contractual agreements, and Oleander's queens would have something returned to them.

Aura had arrived two days after Florian's departure. As it turned out, the incentive to assist in Molkan's downfall was a morsel of land along the border of Oleander and Baneberry. Aura's mother had sold it to Molkan's grandfather—a bribe to keep one of the late queen's many affairs a secret from her hostile husband.

"A kindness, believe it or not, as it was expected he take something in return for keeping such troublesome news to himself." Aura had said the words with a familiar look. One that reminded me what she'd once said.

*We are not human.*

347

Wishbone, a small community surrounded by lush forest and sandy waterways, was where Aura and Mercury had met after Aura's mother had dragged her there to visit her favored lover. Mercury had spent her whole life in Wishbone before moving inland soon after meeting her future wife.

I'd sold it back to Oleander for a singular gold coin. Although I knew the land meant something to the queens, it was still an unexpectedly small payment in return for their aid against Molkan.

Noticing my bewilderment, Aura had said with velvet resonance, "A queen always rises for another, darling. And if they're wise, only ever a queen."

I'd been thankful she'd materialized from the drawing room before my eyes had overflowed with gratitude.

Aura had retaken Wishbone for the same reason my great-grandfather had taken it from her family in the first place—it was expected. Trust was fostered with ulterior motives.

Now, I couldn't say I was any different from the rest of my kind. And I no longer cared to be.

Avrin found me in the corner of the room, tucked between the musicians and the darkness. "Been hunting for you."

I didn't acknowledge that. Instead, I asked, "How do you feel about it?" I wasn't sure why I bothered. It didn't much matter. That, and I'd deduced plenty from watching him over the past six days. "Remaining adviser."

Avrin took his time responding. I noted the way he shifted, as if worried those in attendance would overhear us.

I prodded. "If you can't speak honestly, then don't." I studied the framed female before me further, fearing I'd missed even the most minuscule qualities that made the entirety of her beauty.

I might have had my father's eyes, but their large and alluring shape was hers. The rest of me was all Corina.

Avrin pressed close until his arm brushed the sleeve of my dark blue gown.

A choice that had not gone unnoticed by the guards wearing dress uniforms and the guests in the throne room. The latter seemed to have chosen not to don anything close to Hellebore's signature color of blue. I would wager not many wore crimson, either. Another color favored by the north.

"I don't yet know what I wish to do."

Intrigue almost tore my eyes from the portrait. "With me?"

"With myself," Avrin said, and with a grit that conveyed he didn't like it—admitting it and feeling torn between the power he'd earned despite the odds and his longing for the princess he'd grown too attached to.

"A good thing I've decided for you, then." I turned away from the portrait of my mother and my confused adviser. "It's time to take your contract and my family name and put them to good use, Avrin *Baneberry*."

I felt no guilt.

Forcing this kingdom upon his broad shoulders did not mean he couldn't one day earn Lilitha, too. Even if he evidently had no idea how to accomplish that quite yet.

Avrin trailed me to the awaiting priestess and throne, its golden leaves now bent and scraped. "Tullia," he growled low. Through his teeth, his whisper hissed at my back. "What are you playing at?" Beside the dais, he seized my arm, his grip gentle but firm until he had my attention. "Everyone is here to witness *your* coronation."

Just as I'd intended. Only, I had no intention to place the crown my father had worn upon my own head.

Vengeance was divine, but I needed only a taste.

"This coronation won't be for me," I declared, and loud enough that silence began to crawl across the throne room in a steady wave.

I stepped onto the dais and plucked the crown from the cushioned gold seat of the throne. I waited until I had the unbroken attention of every creature in the room.

Then I dropped the crown at Avrin's feet.

"I don't want your kingdom." The gold clinked over the stone, and as many flinched and gasped, I began to materialize. I smiled as darkness embraced. "I already have one."

Another ball was taking place.

Jovial voices and even merrier violins filled the halls of the manor. A small group of inebriated warriors stumbled up the stairs to the landing, grinning when they glimpsed me standing in the foyer. Liquor splashed as they all bowed and hollered a chorus of greetings.

I nodded and smiled, warmth enfolding my heart.

Nirra appeared at the railing of the second floor. "He was last seen in the gardens." She rolled her eyes. "Brooding the night away."

All of them laughed on their way to the ballroom, shouts of, "The queen returns," echoing down the stairs.

"Queen." Nirra returned to the railing before I rounded the staircase, her question slurred. "Wine?"

"You keep it."

"You need it, though," she said, taking a sip from the decanter. It flopped over the railing with her arm as she whispered loudly, "I told you he's moody, yes?"

I smiled. "You did indeed."

The general cursed when she realized wine spilled from the decanter and hugged it to her chest. "I'll wait right here in case you need rescuing."

I nodded, knowing she meant it even though she would likely soon forget. "As a good friend should."

Her hazel eyes widened comically. "Might cry now." I laughed as she hollered to my back when I walked on. "I'll be the best damned friend you ever had, changeling."

My fingers trailed over the wall, my smile remaining. My lips curled higher when I passed the doors to the drawing room.

Snow didn't fall, but the air carried a chill foretelling that, despite Lilitha's return, it was imminent.

The courtyard was empty, save for one creature standing in the dark of the arched entry to the rear gardens.

He'd sensed my arrival long before I stopped mere feet behind him. Perhaps he'd even heard it shouted from inside the manor.

Yet he didn't move. His back remained facing me, the harsh breeze rustling his silken shirt and unbound hair.

His rough voice quaked my knees. "You're late."

Those words, the first words he'd ever spoken to me in that private room of the pleasure house, feathered through my heart.

Breath fled in a shaken exhale. I played along, though his stiff stance and the energy flaring from him warned he hadn't spoken them in jest. "I am?"

Glass exploded over the stone when he tossed his whiskey and whirled upon me.

I held up my hand.

He ignored it.

My palm met his hard chest—absorbed the violent thud of his heart. His eyes sparked a brightening blue as they soaked me in, and then I was lifted. He crushed me against him, his arms chains I'd happily never leave again.

He stuffed his nose into my neck, and I did the same. As I inhaled his scent, I felt the final lock of my fated cage click into place.

My captor. My unexpected freedom.

My home.

"You owe me a wedding, husband."

He laughed, my hair scrunched in his fingers as he clutched me tighter.

# *Epilogue*

## Tullia

*One year later . . .*

My gown felt like snow, a cold silk hugging every curve.

It squeezed my thighs and widened below my knees into a small trail of silk and lace. The sleeves gently flared at my wrists. Lace snowflakes twined around each arm like vines and met at the edging over my chest.

The same lace pattern lined the deep dip at my lower back—outlining the exposed traitor brand I wore on full display.

The witch priestess murmured incantations in the old language that made little sense to me.

But I didn't need them to.

A soft kiss was given to my palm before Florian brought my hand to his mouth. Beneath dark lashes, his blue eyes lightened as they met mine, and he licked the sensitive skin of my inner wrist.

Our ceremony was private, as per Hellebore tradition, but even if it hadn't been, I would have forgotten more than the priestess. The stone temple open to the autumn elements dripped away in drops of night until all that remained was the heat of his mouth, the brightening glow of his eyes, and the dual pounding of our heartbeats.

Those beats slowed to a crawl of anticipation when my king finished preparing my skin for his teeth. The warmth erasing the sting of his canines spiraled up my arm to slither through every part of me.

A taste of one another's blood would seal our union.

Of course, Florian was never satisfied with just a taste.

His eyes remained fastened to mine as he lazily drew my willing essence into his mouth. Need flared and coiled tight within my body. His high collar couldn't hide the slow dip of his throat as he swallowed.

My knees wobbled at the sight.

The priestess cleared her throat, reminding us of her presence.

My husband teased me with a final dragging lick of my wrist, but he didn't release me. As per custom, he pressed his thumb over the punctures while I took his other hand and waited for the priestess to finish her mutterings.

Then I dealt him the same torment he'd given me. His jaw became ticking granite, his hold on my wrist firming, as I finished serving my revenge with a flick of my tongue over the pinpricks I'd left upon his inner wrist.

As she circled us, the priestess waved a cloying smoke carrying the scent of blood and earth, and we inched so close our chests nearly touched.

To my ear, Florian translated the witch's chant. "Soil below, stars above, Mythayla witness this pledge of love." I shivered, and he splayed his hand over my bare back. "Through rising seas and setting suns, this bond will endure, two souls linked as one."

My eyes closed over the arrival of unexpected tears.

For years, I'd dreamed of finding my way home. I'd dreamed of making a life for myself in a place where I was wanted. A place in which I belonged—among those I belonged with. I'd dreamed of peace, of love, and of freedom.

But none of my wildest imaginings could compare to the fruition of this moment.

I'd thought my demand for a wedding would be brushed off as yet another poor attempt to tell this king that I loved him. Instead,

353

Florian had talked with Olin the day after my return to Hellebore, and the preparations soon followed.

I would have been happy without it. Florian knew that, too.

Yet as we walked through the decaying stone of the towering mountainside temple toward the starlit night, our union now blessed, I acknowledged what I'd missed during the months spent preparing for this evening.

That Florian wanted this—perhaps needed it—just as much as I did.

Turning to him at the cracked steps, I swept my hands over the dark blue waistcoat and matching shirt covering his overabundant form and rose to my toes. As my mouth grazed his, he clutched me close. "Ready?"

"Ready," I whispered.

But he didn't move.

He simply stared, our noses touching and his eyes far too bright.

The harsh wind rustled my gown but failed to disturb the bound hair beneath his crown. The near-black strands, now even longer, had been tied with a charcoal ribbon at his nape. My own hair was wild and free, save for two braided pieces pinned beneath my crown and snowy curls.

I pressed closer against the hardness in his pants. "Are *you* ready, Majesty?"

"To peel that gown from you?" He groaned, soft and low. "Beyond ready." He kissed me hard when I laughed and wrapped my arms around his shoulders.

The night split, then melded into deeper darkness as we materialized to the manor's ballroom.

Snow escaped the twins and barreled down the walkway made by our parting guests.

Florian crouched to reassure the wolf with a caress of her head. He rose as she sniffed us, and he tucked my arm in the crook of his. His other hand clasped mine over his forearm, thumb rubbing my fingers as we smiled and nodded our greetings.

Olin, feigning exasperation, plucked a handkerchief from the breast pocket of his glittering sky-blue waistcoat.

Kreed accepted it without removing his wet eyes from us, his large shoulders shaking.

The steward and cook had been arguing over preparations regarding this celebration for months. Lilitha and I had quietly poked fun at them, all the while tending to everything they'd overlooked due to barely seeing anything but one another.

Snow trailed us, on guard and curious, though there were no threats. The crowd consisted mostly of crimson and blue. There were exceptions, of course.

Such as the two queens of Oleander.

Aura wore fitted gold trousers that matched her jacket and caught the light from fireflies in the glass orbs of the chandeliers. Her wife was resplendent in silver, the gown form-fitting yet overflowing at her thighs in crimped ripples to the floor.

The two females came forward as our guests resumed mingling, and flutes and violins took flight from the podium before the balcony.

I kissed each of their cheeks, as did Florian, and laughed as Aura said, "Do try to linger long enough to give the pretense of patience."

Mercury took her hand. "Don't listen to her. She lasted all of an hour."

Aura scowled, but it was gentle—green eyes agleam with the promise of retribution as she turned to her wife. "Oh, that was me, was it?"

Mercury soothed her teasing with a flutter of her lashes and a press of her pink-painted lips to her mate's hand. Aura raised a brow, but her smile was sincere as she gazed upon us. Stepping close, she cupped my cheek. "You wear it beautifully, darling."

I didn't need to ask what she was referring to. The traitor brand likely drew many eyes to my exposed back, but I didn't mind. If anything, I hoped they looked. I hoped they knew that I was no longer afraid or ashamed.

That I wore it with pride.

Mercury nodded her agreement, her eyes glistening. Aura patted her hand as they retreated, and Florian's palm smoothed over my bare lower back. He guided me toward a willowy figure wearing a patient smile.

Peony stood alone with a glass of wine in hand. Her amber eyes held a sheen, her arms spreading when I reached her. She smelled like lavender and barley, her short golden curls a touch of evening spring air.

All of her was a comfort I'd nearly been too scared to claim— until Florian insisted I give her the courtesy of one visit.

"Breathtaking," she whispered, fingers brushing my hair as she released me from her tight embrace. Taking my hand, she continued to smile while searching my eyes. "Every inch of you, just like her."

My mother.

I was grateful for the return of Florian's reassuring touch on my back when her teary eyes overflowed as she gave us her heartfelt blessings.

Peony was a lone wolf with hundreds of stories to share and a fierce love but little skill for aromatherapy. At first, Florian had accompanied me to visit my only relative, and although Peony had been shocked to find the king outside of her home, she hadn't balked.

We'd both been welcomed with stern gentleness into her cottage.

It had since become one of my favorite places to be, so I made sure to visit at least once a month.

Books lined every wall, in stacks and within shelves. Among them, herbs, dried flowers, and a myriad of other odd and wonderful gatherings for her creations. After the second visit, Florian deemed her no threat and gave us the privacy to discuss tender subjects, such as my mother. But he'd joined us again last month when Peony finally came to the manor.

I squeezed her hand before releasing it. "Have you changed your mind yet?"

Peony clucked her tongue disapprovingly. "I've already told you . . ." She sipped her wine, eyeing a passing warrior who grinned at her. "I have no need of it."

The sweeping estate by the sea that once belonged to my mother now belonged to Peony. Unsure what to do with it, I'd placed it in her name before leaving the kingdom of Baneberry with Avrin.

"Your rodent infestation certainly does."

Peony smacked Florian's chest playfully. "Cats are not rodents, King."

"If you say so," he drawled.

Snow found us again. The wolf sniffed my aunt before accepting a pat upon the head, tail swishing. "You should take it, Tullia."

I blinked, then frowned. "But I don't want it." She knew that. Otherwise, I wouldn't be trying to get rid of it.

My hard tone lured Peony's gaze. "Baneberry is not your enemy." Stepping closer, she glossed her knuckles across the crest of my cheek. Her whisper was just as gentle as her touch. "The true enemy is attachment to unpleasant memories." She kissed my cheek before retreating, a taunting smile curling her nude lips. "So make new ones, my sweet soul."

We certainly had been, yet as I watched my aunt float toward the warrior who'd caught her eye, her loose emerald gown floating behind her, more of that addictive warmth invaded my chest.

Hope.

"The Elixir Sea is quite a sight first thing in the morning," Florian murmured.

"And you would know this from waking half intoxicated upon a beach, I presume?"

"Upon a cliff edge, actually." Laughter crinkled my wide eyes when he mused, "I never did overindulge near any great heights again." His fingers pressed into my back as he added heatedly to my ear, "There's also plenty of low-lying caves along the coastline."

Snow left us for the twins.

"Tempting." I withheld a shiver as the memory of where we'd sealed our mating bond infiltrated, and he guided me toward the shadows cast by the orbs illuminating the musicians.

My heart froze at the sight of the goblin tucked away in the corner and glancing warily around the grand room. It then melted when his almond eyes landed upon me.

Without words, I looked at Florian. That icy exterior remained in place, but I'd learned to see beneath it. I'd learned to read his eyes, that tic of his jaw, and to listen to the melody within his chest.

Grateful, I kissed his chin and hurried forward.

Gane's eyes widened upon me, then the king behind me. He bowed deeply, tugging at his plaid vest when he straightened. "I've not seen a creature quite so lovely, Flea."

I lowered and pulled him to me.

He grunted, stiff until he exhaled and finally hugged me back. He smiled as I stood. The rare sight nearly frightened, his tiny sharp teeth revealed. "Happy," he whispered. "You look truly happy."

"I am," I said, taking his gnarled hands in mine. "How is the library?"

"Far too quiet." A glance was given to the king behind me. "I've been considering relocating."

Unsure what that would mean, I frowned. That library was

more than a form of employment. It was his home, his place of refuge and healing after he'd lost his wife.

"The city librarian has been requesting experienced assistance for some years now," Florian informed. "Pestering, really."

I turned to him as he accepted a glass of wine from a bowing server bearing a silver tray.

He sniffed, then tasted it. Though we were no longer at war with anyone, he would never let his guard lower too far. Satisfied, he handed it to me before taking another glass for himself. "So I offered the position to Gane."

I looked back at Gane, who shrugged. "More space and less mildew are rather appealing."

My brow rose. "You hate space."

We'd even offered him Rolina's apartment after I'd told Florian I was aware he'd been paying the rent to Madam Morin each month. The goblin had declined with vehement horror, and although Florian said I should, I never returned for my old books before Morin leased it to someone else.

A week after the conversation, I'd discovered my worn and favorite titles in the manor library.

Gane scratched at the white tufts of hair beside his ears. "The food is truly far superior here."

"Your diet consists of cheese, nuts, and tea."

"Fine." He pushed his spectacles farther up his nose and lifted it indignantly. "I miss my friend."

Victorious, I smiled, then seized his face to kiss his cheek. "I miss you, too."

"I didn't say it was you," he grumbled, yet he failed to hide his smile.

I laughed. The sound deepened when I found Florian scowling at the goblin. I placed a hand upon his arm. "That's just one of his many ways of saying he cares for me."

"It had better be," he said, staring glacially down at Gane.

The shrinking goblin was saved by an invading silence crawling steadily beneath the music.

A portion of the Oleander warriors who'd aided us against Baneberry were dots of bronze and gold among the merry fray, all in dress uniform. As were our own attending warriors, who'd welcomed them as if they were as such. Many of them looked toward one of the two entrances.

A large figure wearing a familiar brown cloak had entered the ballroom.

Shole appeared beside me and whistled low. "It would seem this evening's entertainment has arrived."

I didn't need to look to know Florian glowered at his friend.

Gently, I knocked Shole's ribs with my elbow.

He chuckled, but it died when Lilitha stepped away from Aura and Mercury. She tucked her small pad of parchment and the quill spelled to continuously spout ink into the hidden pocket of her skintight cerulean gown.

Avrin's eyes had locked upon the princess before her own could find him between the bodies of our murmuring guests.

Lilitha had known he would likely be attending. We'd invited him.

To say Florian had been unimpressed was putting it mildly. Alas, he'd learned that fighting Lilitha's wishes was a battle he would lose, so he'd reluctantly agreed that I should write to Avrin to formally invite him.

Lilitha's obsidian hair had been trimmed numerous times since her return home, yet it still graced her hips in gentle curls. Often, I'd thought she resembled the merfolk I'd obsessively read about while growing up in the middle lands. Never more than this evening—with her gown hugging her breasts, rear, and legs until it widened beneath her knees into a gradual darkening blue.

She was frozen.

I couldn't see them, yet I still knew tears filled her eyes.

During the months after my return to Hellebore, I'd gotten to know the lost princess while she'd gotten to know who she was after being nothing but Molkan's trapped secret for half of her life. During that time, she'd shared pieces of herself with me as a means to have me do the same.

The returning spark of mischief matching that of the female in the portrait lining the foyer had been enough reason for me to play along.

It didn't take her long to realize that I was aware of what she was doing.

Nor did it take me long to realize that even though she'd manipulated me to a certain degree, it was because she cared. Not only for her brother, of whom she adored far more than spending time with the horses and traipsing aimlessly within the woods, but she also cared for me.

At first, it was with a heaping dose of reluctance.

I was her brother's mate. His wife. The reason his soul had lightened until autumn graced these lands after decades of unbreakable cold.

But I was also a near replica of my mother—Molkan's late wife—of whom Lilitha's mate and captor had killed to better keep her as a pet.

When she'd finally confided in me without the expectation of return, freely and in ways that made me wish to see my father burning within the pits of Nowhere, I'd learned she'd grown to trust me and to think of me as a friend.

For no matter how grim the retellings, not once had I shared them with Florian.

He'd never pushed me to. I suspected he'd rather not know, and that winter might ravage the kingdom before our people were ready if he did.

As voices and laughter began to rise in a volume that matched the violins and flutes, I slid my hand over Florian's and linked our fingers. I squeezed them as we crossed the room to greet the king who stood alone, watching the revelry though his attention had been stolen by one creature.

Avrin met my gaze when we neared. His brown tunic and fitted pants were out of place, for both the setting and that of a king. But it was his stiff posture that told me he still wasn't entirely comfortable with his new life as a monarch.

That he was perhaps still adjusting to holding such power and learning what to do with it.

"Congratulations," he said, dipping his head to me with a small smile that faded when he did the same to my husband.

Florian stood unmoving beside me, the only exception the clenching of his hand around mine. I squeezed his again in warning. He sighed through his nose and nodded once. "I hear the precious wall has been repaired." The word precious was said as if he'd meant cowardly.

I almost rolled my eyes. Of course, he'd choose to break the tense silence with that.

Avrin just smirked, gold eyes agleam on me before he said to Florian, "Indeed, though we will not deter visitors as we have done in the past."

I nearly choked on my sip of wine.

Reading the unsaid meaning to Avrin's words, Florian practically growled, "Generous, though I cannot say when we will have time for a tea party, on account of being freshly wed."

The king of Baneberry grinned, seeming unperturbed although he'd clearly not been hinting at a visit from us. "But of course." He looked upon me with another incline of his head. "Yolond sends his warmest regards. He has recently put in a request to visit with his brother, Delen."

The servant whom had tended to me during my first stay at Baneberry Palace.

I nodded, my throat tight as I thought of him reuniting with

Delen, the beautician who had helped prepare me for tonight. "And will you grant him permission?"

Avrin's raised brow accompanied a look that said, *don't ask stupid questions*.

I laughed, even as Florian's energy flared and emanated his growing displeasure.

He lowered his mouth to my ear. "Butterfly, I need you to check on Lilitha." In other words, leave them be so that Florian could dig for the reason Avrin had accepted our invite.

Knowing what I did and witnessing what I had from Avrin in the days after Molkan's death, I'd never doubted his attendance. I didn't think Florian had doubted it either. He likely merely wished to show this young king how much sharper his frosty claws were.

Smirking, I narrowed my eyes on my husband. Then I lifted to my toes to kiss his cheek. "Play fair."

"Always," he purred, his dark gaze on Avrin.

I gave them both a small smile, and went in search of Lilitha.

Halfway across the room, Fume gently seized my arm. "What is *he* doing here?"

I glared at his hand.

He removed it with a mumbled apology. "He shouldn't be anywhere near her."

"Why thank you, Fume, for your genuine well wishes and heartfelt congratulations," I remarked a tad snidely before leaving him to seethe on his own.

The general cursed and trailed me as I continued my search for Lilitha. I smiled at the warriors who dipped and raised their glasses to me.

"Tullia," Fume said. "Please."

The roughened plea halted my feet. Slowly, I spun to face him, my gown dragging over the stone floor behind me. "I invited him, General."

Betrayal and confusion scrunched his smoothly hewn features.

"I gave him my crown. My kingdom. It would behoove us to make sure that was a wise decision by keeping things friendly." I loathed that I even had to say what he already knew but was just too furious to understand.

"I know, but he was there." He stepped close, his sky-bright eyes searching mine. "For years, he could have saved her, Tullia, and he didn't."

"He didn't?" I pressed, though not unkindly.

His brows still flattened.

Taking pity on him, for the general was far too enamored with a female who seemed to want little more than friendship from him, I explained, "Avrin is not our enemy, and he is certainly not Lilitha's." I looked beyond his shoulder to where the princess stood between the open doors of the balcony. "He is perhaps the sole reason she survived, and you know it."

His jaw clenched.

"You hate him for reasons that cannot be changed, but you cannot hate him for that truth. We will not create tensions with him because of that and more." I placed my hand over his arm in farewell. "We must keep the peace, Fume."

The general was watching the two kings when I reached Lilitha.

She'd already written her request on her pad of parchment. *I need you to distract him.*

"Fume?"

She shook her head.

Florian, then.

Her blue eyes, two shades lighter than her brother's but fringed in the same dark lashes, met mine. Her smile was secretive, also a touch tremulous as she gazed back at the crowd hindering her view of Avrin.

"You would get me into trouble on my wedding night?"

Lilitha gave me a look that said she held not one ounce of concern for me.

I laughed, as she was right not to. Countless times I'd poked at my husband to make his temper flare into a hunger that delivered hours of toe-curling punishment.

"Oh, fine," I said with feigned hardship.

She made a noise similar to a laugh, barely audible above the music before us. Then she wrote something else upon her small pad. *You look too beautiful for words.*

I rolled my eyes. "I've already said I'll help you."

She nudged my shoulder and underlined the words to say she'd meant them. I knew she did. Still, I smirked and nudged her back. "As do you, trouble."

Lilitha startled at hearing the name. A name a certain adviser turned king had given her during the time she'd spent hidden beneath Molkan's palace of lies.

I squinted, toying with her some more. "Are you blushing, Princess?"

She scowled. It fell with her smile and near-laugh when I withstood that scowl with a growing smile of my own.

Florian was now making his way to us, and I whispered between unmoving lips, "Go."

Lilitha wasted no time, hurrying through the crowd toward the first entrance of the ballroom where Avrin remained. His plan was foiled if he'd intended to leave after making his presence known.

Florian halted his advance upon spying the rush of blue and black darting between our guests.

I gave my wine to a passing server as I walked over to him. My hands swept up his chest, and I lifted to my toes to place my mouth softly upon his. As my arms wrapped around his shoulders, I watched Lilitha throw herself at Avrin.

He seemed as stunned as everyone nearby, golden eyes widening as he caught her. They closed as he held her to him. His head

365

turned, and he seemed to whisper something to her—seemed to inhale her—while holding the princess far longer than what most would deem appropriate.

They didn't care. Perhaps after everything, they were beyond caring.

The two of them left the ballroom. Lilitha led the way, dragging Avrin behind her as though he were not a king but a male who would always do her bidding.

I had a feeling—one that warmed more than it alarmed—that regardless of whatever stood between them, he forever would. And that despite using Avrin's affections to whatever advantage she could while kept in her gilded cage, Lilitha had yearned for more than open skies since leaving Baneberry.

Nirra's gaze caught mine over Florian's shoulder. Grinning wide, she raised two glasses of wine into the air and swung her hips.

I muffled my laughter against Florian's waistcoat.

His hands ran down my sides, fingers teasingly brushing my ass. "Hungry, butterfly?"

"Eternally, apparently," I taunted at his ear, heating more with each breath as his lethally soft chuckle raised gooseflesh beneath his roaming touch at my back. "The dress itches." I kissed his neck, my confession turning him to stone. "Likely because I'm wearing nothing beneath."

I'd barely finished speaking before I was also taken from the ballroom.

## Florian

I was being distracted.

And I was far beyond giving a fuck.

My wife grinned as ice crusted the doors. Her heart jumped, beating erratically before I'd even set her down upon her lovely feet. Her lip was stolen by her teeth, her eyes murky with anticipation and need.

I could have stared at her forever, and I would.

Right now, I needed my cock tucked within the warmth of her pulsating cunt. I tore open my waistcoat, buttons clacking on the floor. "Hands against the wall, wife."

Tullia obeyed, the gown that'd been sending me to the edge of insanity an issue I couldn't wait to deal with. Plucking the crown from atop her winter-touched hair, she set it on the drawers beside her, and her hand back against the dark stone.

I tossed mine across the room. It clanked somewhere by the fireplace. "You think I don't know what you're playing at."

"You know I'm well aware that you know." Her huskier voice was akin to feeling her nails running down my back. Her eyes flashed at me over her shoulder. "Yet we'd both rather be here anyway."

My mouth curved against my will.

I dropped the coat, then stepped in behind her. Slowly, I dragged the silk and lace from the floor, fingers grazing as they gathered it over her thighs and hips, and listened as each inhale grew thinner.

There was indeed nothing beneath.

"Daring creature," I murmured, struck still by the sight of all that beautiful flesh. "Bend over for me."

She did, and I groaned, crouching to inspect just how much she needed me. A lot, I determined, parting her with a lone finger. Her legs shifted for her thighs to open wider. Her hips jerked, an exhale carrying sound blessing my ears when I circled her swelling clit.

I dunked that finger inside her soft heat.

We both groaned.

I sucked it as I rose, then released my cock from my pants. Her back arched, the gown falling forward over her hips and tangling under her heeled slippers. I placed my hand at her stomach, guiding her onto me as I pushed into her.

She welcomed me with a clench that caused my teeth to grit.

Cool warmth spread from the base of my spine. It climbed toward my neck, flaring muscle and igniting the instinct to take, claim, feed, and devour until nothing but blood and seed permeated the air barely touched by the fire.

Rolling my neck, I cursed and blinked heavily.

My vision was hazed, and my tone nearly unrecognizable. "Pull your arms through the sleeves." She did, moaning when I bucked against her. "Good. Now peel it down over your tits."

The sound that left me was beastly.

I didn't care. The glimpse of those heavy globes caused another jolt of my hips, which earned me another beautiful moan. I reached around her and seized one, holding her nipple tight between my fingers.

Her head turned, lips seeking mine. I gave them to her but only briefly.

She nearly whined when I drew back, my cock leaving her desperate body. I smacked her ass when she scowled, then slipped my hands inside the dress gathered at her waist to pull it down her legs.

It ripped, a loud scream that made my wife tense and glower. "Monster."

My fingers skimmed her calves and thighs. "Yet"—I bit her ass hard until she squirmed—"you love me."

She'd never said it. Not really. Not since that first time in these rooms after we'd spent days catering to the demands of the heat.

Though I wanted her to—would give just about anything to hear it—I didn't need her to say it.

It was there. Every time she looked at me. Every time she woke relieved to find me or an ice sculpture upon the nightstand. Every single time she touched me. Tormented me with teasing games and treasured me with quiet wonder.

All that mattered was that I knew.

My lips traversed her back as I slowly rose, my hands squeezing her hips while my tongue traced the tattooed snake.

Her response was breathy. "Deeply, Majesty."

I moved her hair aside and kissed the nape of her neck. Then I took her from the pool of lace and silk and tossed her onto our bed. I leaped atop her, her laughter fading as her thighs spread, and I pushed my cock back inside her body.

A sharp thrust accompanied my taunt. "How deep?"

"So deep it aches."

"Then be a good wife"—I kissed her jaw, then dragged my lips over it—"and show me." Faster thrusts followed the command.

Immeasurable satisfaction boiled my blood and brought forth my own release when a croaked moan later, my endless obsession came apart. Her slippers fell from her twitching feet, her rapture prolonging mine.

A slew of curses left me to heat her neck. She trembled, squashed beneath me, her fingers untucking my shirt to reach my skin.

"Is it rude to spend the rest of the evening just like this?"

"Sweet creature . . ." I turned my head to lick her fluttering pulse. "Let's not pretend to care." As she shook with laughter, I pushed up to stare down at her goddess-blessed beauty. Her skin was flushed, those big adoring eyes and that bright smile weapons I would never escape.

Her smile slipped as she watched me study her. Her fingers met my cheek, traced my jaw, then my mouth. I nipped them, and her smile returned. But those dark eyes were damp.

I searched them, alarm thundering through my chest. "What is it?"

Hesitation pursed her lips.

I scowled.

Again, she laughed, fingertips dancing over my jaw to my chin. Clasping it, she forced my mouth to hers as she whispered, "Thank you."

I knew she wasn't merely referring to the wedding. I would drain our coffers to give her one every year if it would make her happy. I waited, my heart a frosted rock sitting in my throat.

Her mouth brushed mine, eyes aglow with the peace that had brightened her soul in the months after we'd returned from Baneberry. Her lashes fluttered. "For all of it."

I glared. Not only because I couldn't seem to fucking breathe, but because I'd done some horrid shit to get her where she now was—forever bound to me in every way and filled with my seed beneath me upon our bed.

The taunting question snuck between her pillow-soft lips with a rough exhale. "All of it, butterfly?"

Tullia grinned and captured my cheeks in both hands. She bumped my nose with hers and kissed me once. "I would do it again." Another kiss. "And again and again and again."

I swallowed thickly, then smirked. "I love you, too." My hardening cock pressed deep, and I lowered on my forearms to devour her mouth.

My bride tore free of my bruising kiss, breathing in a rush, "Florian, I love you."

My eyes widened, then immediately burned.

"I love you," she said again, a tremble to her lips that joined forces with her admission to annihilate me.

My forehead dropped to hers.

She easily pushed me to my back as she murmured those three murderous words. "I love you."

Tullia tore at my shirt until her palms could climb my skin to lay over the violence taking place in my chest. Slowly, she impaled herself on my cock as she kissed me. "I'm so wretchedly in love with you."

Wholly at her mercy, and with my rotting pants still sitting beneath my ass, I could only lay there in pieces while she rode me into further oblivion.

Before she found release, I sat up. Doing so pushed me so deep, she gasped, her head falling back and her throat calling to me. I trailed my lips and tongue up her neck, straight to her chin. I bit it, tilting her head down until our mouths touched.

Vulnerability and desire swam within her eyes, even as she teased me. "Have you no words, Majesty?"

"Oh, plenty," I rasped. "But right now . . ." My hands smoothed up her back, one curling over her shoulder while the other tangled in her hair. "I've a wife to punish."

My not-so-sweet creature laughed, the melodious sound uninhibited and free.

# Acknowledgements

I stopped writing these because I began to feel like a broken record. However, it's been a while, and this is the first time I'm doing it for a traditionally published book (just writing that is wild).

My husband, you may never read this or my books (more than okay with that), but your support is still the strongest embrace I've ever felt. Thank you for the countless cups of coffee, eggs on toast, the best dinners, and for being my best friend.

My two children, you're certainly not as little as you were when I last wrote one of these, but you're still the reasons I open the laptop on the dark days.

My in-laws, your support means more than I can express without crying. Laura, you are the second mother every daughter-in-law dreams of having—thank you for the swag, the chats, and the excitement. For everything.

Michelle, Allie, and Annette, thank you for the many wonderful things you do for me. Most of all, thank you for the magical friendship.

Tash, "maybe one day" is what I've always thought when I've walked into a bookstore. Thank you for making that one day come true. Your belief in my work is empowering. I'll forever be so grateful.

The team at Hodderscape, thank you, thank you, thank you for also making "maybe one day" a reality.

Meire and Flavia, you are tireless dream chasers. Thank you for all that you do for me, and for believing things are possible when I don't.

My beloved readers, new and old, you have reshaped my life in ways I'll always be so immensely thankful for. Thank you for reading and for your love.

# About the Author

USA Today and international bestselling author Ella Fields resides in Australia with her husband, two children, and furry critters. A lover of chocolate, magic, and words – she enjoys exploring the sharper sides of love in varying genres of romance.

Instagram – @ellafieldsauthor
Facebook – authorellafields/
Website – ellafields.net

# WANT
# MORE?

If you enjoyed this
and would like to
find out about similar
books we publish,
we'd love you to
join our online Sci-Fi,
Fantasy and Horror
community, Hodderscape.

Visit hodderscape.co.uk for
exclusive content from our authors, news, competitions
and general musings, and feel free to comment, contribute
or just keep an eye on what we are up to.

See you there!

## HODDERSCAPE

NEVER AFRAID TO BE OUT OF THIS WORLD

🐦⊚📷@HODDERSCAPE     HODDERSCAPE.CO.UK